Traci Harding lives on the Hawkesbury River, with her husband David and their two beautiful children, Sarah and John.

Traci has written two best-selling trilogies — The Ancient Future Trilogy and The Celestial Triad — as well as three stand alone novels, *The Alchemist's Key*, *Ghostwriting*, and *The Book of Dreams*. Traci is currently working on the third book of the Mystique trilogy, to be released in 2008.

Thanks to the web team at HarperCollins, Traci has a very lively website and she visits the message board in the community section daily to discuss the greater mysteries with her readers. At the website there are glossaries of the terms used in Traci's books and there are author notes for those interested in delving deeper into different esoteric and historic aspects of her work.

Visit Traci Harding's website
and message board at:

www.voyageronline.com.au/traciharding

Books by Traci Harding

The Ancient Future Trilogy
The Ancient Future: the Dark Age (1)
An Echo in Time: Atlantis (2)
Masters of Reality: the Gathering (3)

The Alchemist's Key

The Celestial Triad
Chronicle of Ages (1)
Tablet of Destinies (2)
The Cosmic Logos (3)

Ghostwriting

The Book of Dreams

The Mystique Trilogy
Gene of Isis (1)
The Dragon Queens (2)

THE DRAGON QUEENS

BOOK TWO
THE MYSTIQUE TRILOGY

TRACI HARDING

Voyager
An imprint of HarperCollins*Publishers*

Voyager
An imprint of HarperCollins*Publishers*, Australia

First published in Australia in 2007
by HarperCollins*Publishers* Australia Pty Limited
ABN 36 009 913 517
www.harpercollins.com.au

HarperCollins*Publishers*
25 Ryde Road, Pymble, Sydney NSW 2073, Australia
31 View Road, Glenfield, Auckland 10, New Zealand
77–85 Fulham Palace Road, London W6 8JB, United Kingdom
2 Bloor Street East, 20th floor, Toronto, Ontario, M4W 1A8, Canada
10 East 53rd Street, New York NY 10022, United States of America

National Library of Australia Cataloguing-in-Publication data:

Harding, Traci.
  The dragon queens.
  ISBN 13: 978 0 7322 8111 3.
  ISBN 10: 0 7322 8111 3.
  I. Title. (Series: Harding, Traci. The Dragon Queens; bk. 2).
823.3

Cover design by Jenny Grigg
Cover and author photograph by Montalbetti+Campbell
Hair and makeup by Zenga Butler
Photographed at Baltronic Studios, Artarmon, Australia
Typeset in Goudy 11/15pt by Helen Beard, ECJ Australia Pty Limited
Printed and bound in Australia by Griffin Press on 70gsm Ivory

5 4 3 2 1   07 08 09 10

To all the wonderful women in my life.
You are all Dragon Queens to me.

ACKNOWLEDGEMENTS

First on my list of people to thank for this book are my readers. Due to illness, the release of this book was delayed a year. I hope *The Dragon Queens* will prove worth the wait, and thanks so much for your patience.

My family, friends and work associates put in a lot of overtime to help me complete this book. I cannot thank everyone enough for their support and understanding — and that goes for all my message board posters and Trazling citizens too: I couldn't have done this without you all.

A special thanks to Ann-Marie for helping me with the Amenti research, and to Chez for reading this manuscript so many times and giving me good, honest feedback every time.

My deepest gratitude to Sue for aiding me through the longest and most arduous edit I have ever undergone!

All my love and hugs to Sarah, John and David, who endured all alongside me and brought me back to health and happiness.

CONTENTS

LIST OF CHARACTERS

19th Century

Lady Suffolk, Lady Ashlee Granville-Devere

Lord Suffolk, Lord Earnest Devere

Levi Granville-Devere, *Ashlee's eldest son and heir of Suffolk*

Rebecca Granville-Devere, *Ashlee's eldest daughter*

Charlotte Granville-Devere, *Ashlee's youngest daughter*

Thomas Granville-Devere, *Ashlee's youngest son*

Lord Malory, *Grand Master of the Sangreal Knighthood*

Lord Eric Cavandish, *Earl of Derby*

Cingar Choron, *Gypsy captain*

Albray Devere, *Knight of the Ringstone*

Chiara, *Witch of the Ringstone*

Mr J. E. Taylor, *Site manager at Ur*

Miss Ajalae Koriche, *Site linguist*

Nasr ed-Din, *Shah of Persia*

Kazem, *Shah's official*

Raineath Saray, *Cingar's student*

Cienna, *Harem girl*

Thoth (co-joined with Levi); Mathu, *The Great Scribe*

Zalman, *Guardian of Signet Station Ten*

Denera, *Mistress of the Desert*

Cardinal Guarino Antonazzi, *Representative of the Holy See*

Pintar, *Head of the Dracon*

Taejax, *Draconian warrior*

Constable Fletcher, *London-based investigator*

Captain/Prince Henry Sinclair, *Guardian of Signet Station Nine*

Lugh Lamhfada, *Leader of the Anu*

A NOTE
FROM THE AUTHOR,
MIA MONTROSE

I cannot claim to be truly the author of this book, even though it is the second I have been commissioned to write in this trilogy. For the most part, I am the compiler and editor of information obtained from the journals of my foremothers, who in turn inspired me to continue the family tradition of chronicling — an obsession that I have passed to my daughter, Tamar, whose first hand-written journal has also contributed greatly to this work.

I have disguised these interconnected autobiographies as fantasy fiction for the lives of the members of my family line are the source of all the human legends and earthly mysteries that underpin this genre.

At the time I began chronicling my personal exploration into the bloodline of the Grail, it was not with the intent to be published. Yet as so many fascinating insights have been revealed to me since that time, I have been compelled to try to get this information out to the general public for consideration. Even in the guise of a fantasy novel, some of this information will offer insight to others who might have had similar experiences, for I feel sure that I am not the only one who has seen a ghost, realised my own psychic potential or found a few supernatural skeletons hidden in the family closet.

During the course of the account to follow, you may wonder why, as a mother, I was not more concerned about my daughter's role in these affairs. The truth is that before my little girl was even born I was forewarned of certain life-altering events that would come to pass once she reached womanhood. I had thought the prophecy concerning my daughter rather exaggerated at the time, but I see now that the predictions regarding her destiny were no understatement. As a mother is usually the last to know when some major occurrence is taking place in the life of her teenage daughter, on my daughter's thirteenth birthday I presented her with her first hardcover, lock-up journal — something she was very excited about as paper and pen are so rare and expensive these days. I hoped that if she did not tell me of the extraordinary events unfolding in her life, she might at least confide in her journal, and thankfully I was not proven wrong. It is true that when my daughter began her account, she hoped to see some of it published, but by the time she handed her journal over to me, it was not her personal ego that was her motivation for sharing. She felt that the revelations she had stumbled upon would be food for thought for my readers. Like myself, she has no desire to attract fame and attention at this time, for she is preoccupied in far more mysterious work; by the time this book comes to publication, that work will be completed.

It was her reading of the journal of her foremother, Lady Ashlee Granville-Devere, that led my daughter to the realisation of her destiny, just as I suspected it would. The journal of inspiration was Lady Ashlee's account of her explorations in Persia and Egypt beginning in the year 1856, many, many years after her Sinai adventure as documented in the first book of this trilogy. I have read to my daughter from many of the journals of our foremothers, but this particular volume I purposely set aside, knowing that the discoveries contained therein pertaining to the Staff of Amenti and the Dragon Queens of ancient myth would awaken dormant memories and powers in my child, and my young, innocent, bright-eyed daughter would be gone forever.

PROLOGUE

Finally I have you, the journal that will become the basis of my first family chronicle. Yet the moment of your bestowment was not at all as I imagined it would be, as my perfect parents were having their first full-blown argument in living memory.

Why did Dad's little surprise for my mother have to be let out of the bag on the morning of my thirteenth birthday? Although it wasn't really his fault that it wasn't as well received as expected. Still, I had envisioned being doted upon all day by my adoring parents and being showered with gifts and other surprises. As it was, I only had the opportunity to open my first present (this lock-up journal) when the phone rang and threw my special day into complete chaos!

If I'd had to choose only one gift to receive today, however, this journal would have been my pick. I have been waiting for it since I was old enough to comprehend the purpose of a journal. I have kept diaries in the past in preparation for this moment — mainly electronic palm journals — however, the typed word has proved less durable than the good old-fashioned written word. Convenient little electronic pocket devices have a way of getting lost or stolen, and they tend to stop working once they've been left in a pocket and put through the wash cycle. And, as the intention behind the penning of this journal is to pass information on to my descendants, I am aware that an electronic device will never stand the test of time. Technology moves so fast, parts fail, and one can never rely on finding the right-sized battery in the

3

next decade, let alone a century or a millennium from now! Paper is so expensive in this year of 2017 that a penned manuscript is something altogether rare and precious, much as it was long ago.

The women of my family have been chronicling their life and times for centuries now. In our home library cum study, we have journals dating back as far as the twelfth century. Admittedly, there is a large gap in the family history until early in the nineteenth century, when my great foremother, the Baroness Lady Ashlee Granville-Devere, began recording the events of her lifetime. No ordinary Victorian woman, Lady Ashlee was a famed psychic who had links with many secret societies and was involved in some covert investigations carried out during this pious age of Church rule — investigations concerning the bloodline that was the basis of Grail and Fairy Lore. My mother has not allowed me to read the journals of Lady Granville-Devere, myself, but she has read to me from them. I suspect they contain sexual references that Mum feels she must censor — as if I don't know what sex entails!

What I like most about Lady Ashlee's tales is that they feature the ghost of a Crusader knight named Albray Devere. This is my father's name and, as he is also brave, dark and handsome, I have always imagined him to be the knight in the tales. My parents have never discouraged this belief; in fact, they perpetuate my little fantasy! Mum often refers to Dad as her knight, and my father unashamedly claims that he was brought back to life by the mystical Ladies of the Elohim because of his love for my mother. I used to believe their romantic fairytales as a child, and even though I am now a teenager, I still enjoy my parents' yarns.

The reason my father is so good at playing the role of a twelfth-century Crusader knight is due to the fact that he lectures on the Crusades, having earned degrees in early European and Eastern History, and he has written numerous books on the period. Mum's doctorate is in ancient languages, and during the course of her work on several archaeological explorations she's also developed an interest in the scientific know-how of the ancients — as hinted at in many of the ancient texts she has deciphered and the investigations of Lady Ashlee, her peers and family. Thanks to these rare sources and insights, Mother realised that she was being awarded a unique

4

opportunity to do what none of our foremothers was capable of: to seek an explanation of the ancient mysteries through the lens of the modern scientific microscope. Consequently, my mother has spent the last twelve years researching and chronicling information pertaining to the ancient enigmas surrounding our family's bloodline.

Recently, taking a page from Lady Ashlee's book, my mother merged her research and family histories with the fairytale romance she and Dad have been spinning me all these years to create a rather fantastic piece of fiction. For Mum, this sideline endeavour was never meant to be anything more than a hobby. The purpose of the text in her eyes was to make her own contribution to our family's chronicles, every one of which mingles an element of fantasy with history to create a thought-provoking read. This style of writing follows the tradition of the folklore and legends that sprang up to preserve the old culture of my bloodline after the church rose to power in the eighth century — stories of valiant princes turned into frogs and princesses put to sleep for a hundred years, trapped in towers or turned into swans. Yet interwoven within these fairytales are allegories and symbology pertaining to the pre-Christian world order. Due to the mix of fiction and fact in our family chronicles, one never really knows where the facts stop and the fantasy starts, leaving it to the reader to discover how much of the text is true. Personally, I cannot wait to have a crack at writing such a tale about my life!

One part of the family chronicles that is absolutely true is the hereditary birthmark of those who belong to the Grail bloodline. It takes the form of a small cross — known as the mark of Cain — and my mother has it between her breasts, as does my father, whereas mine is on my back, between my shoulder blades.

But to get back to why my parents were arguing on the morning of my thirteenth birthday ...

My father, after reading Mum's recently completed manuscript, took it upon himself to secretly run a copy by his publisher for an opinion. This morning the publisher rang Mum to tell her how enraptured she was by the tale and how extremely eager she was to buy it for publication. Most people would be thrilled to get such a call — I know I would! But not my mother.

'I thought you'd be excited to learn that your work has merit.' Dad was reasoning with Mum in the kitchen, and although they were keeping their voices low, my hearing is very acute. 'This woman reads manuscripts all the time and she claims she hasn't been so excited by a first novel in ages!'

'That's because she can see how controversial it is!' Mum didn't sound very excited, more like petrified! 'It's not the theories it contains, but the questions they raise, Albray. We've been through this.'

'The truth is a good thing.'

'Not for us!' Mum said.

'Well, you don't have to name names,' Dad pointed out. 'And as far as anyone knows, it is a *fantasy* novel.'

'That's worse than if I'd written a textbook!' Mum retorted. 'I don't want any of my professional associates finding out that I've written a fairytale! I'll lose all credibility, and I don't want my field work to suffer because of my hobby!'

'Then we'll tell them no, that you're not interested in being published,' Dad said firmly, trying to end the dispute.

'But part of me *does* want to be published.'

Ah, Mum's ego kicked in.

'It's a great story,' Dad said encouragingly.

'You would think so, you're the hero,' Mum snapped.

'That's not the reason I want to see it published,' replied Dad in his 'you should know better' tone. 'The publication of these tales was predicted. Or have you forgotten why you started writing them?'

'This could backfire on us badly.' Mum's voice dropped to a whisper.

'Or it could be a saving grace,' suggested Dad.

All went quiet. I imagined they were probably kissing — my parents smooch a lot! Either that or they'd dropped their voices so that I couldn't eavesdrop.

'Come on, it's our daughter's thirteenth birthday, we can discuss this later.'

Good old Dad, finally someone remembered I'm alive!

'You're right.' Mum forced a laugh. 'All her presents are still sitting on the table, poor kid.'

'Except her new journal,' Dad observed. 'I'll warrant that's what's keeping her so quiet in there.'

'What do you think she's writing about?'

As I figured it wouldn't take Mum long to work out the answer to that question, I quickly ended my first entry and locked up my journal.

I was having such a great time that I didn't have the opportunity to get back to my new journal for two days! Needless to say, my birthday turned out to be better than expected. Still, I shan't bore my descendants with the details of how I spent it. I feel you would all much rather know what my mother has decided to do about the publication offer on her book.

Mia — that's my mum — is warming to the idea of being a published author. She's always aspired to publish, only she imagined that her first published work would be about the Semitic language or her startling translation of some ancient text. But Mum has been unfortunate in that the finds worth writing about have been too controversial, or, as she's often in the employ of someone else, much of her best work has been attributed to the discoverer and not the translator.

The one thing she has decided is that if she does publish, she'll do so under an assumed name — no big surprise there. She hasn't decided what her alias will be; actually, the manuscript itself doesn't even have a title yet! I suggested 'Mystique' and both Mum and Dad seemed well disposed towards it, although they may have just been humouring me on my birthday.

Now my father has taken my mother out for dinner and I've been left alone to choose which of our ancient foremothers' texts I would like to read first. How awesome is that!

As a teenager I am officially entering womanhood and so my mother's decided that I'm old enough to read the journals for myself. Before my parents left for dinner, Mum gave me the key to the steel-reinforced cabinet that houses the ancient books and told me to take my pick.

So that's where I am now, in the study. I'm eyeing the journals on the shelf and I recognise those that Mother has read in part to me.

Lady Ashlee's journeys in the Sinai was my favourite, and I've also heard excerpts from the Sinai journals of Lady Susan Devere, and Douglas and Clarissa Hamilton, who were acquaintances of Lady Ashlee. I've passed over the journals written by Ashlee's children for the moment, and I don't dare touch the twelfth-century scroll written by the Cathar priestess Lillet du Lac. But now I've just found another huge volume written by Lady Ashlee regarding a journey she took to Persia to visit the site of the great Ziggurat of Ur.

As I can't recall Mother ever reading to me from this journal, I feel it to be the best selection. I shall go back and fill in the blanks of Lady Ashlee's other tales at a later date. The thought of reading an adventure of Ashlee's that I know nothing at all about is way too appealing.

I wonder if the Crusader ghost will feature in this tale too? I hope so, as, unlike most girls my age, I still think my dad is the greatest guy on the planet!

Anyway, here I go, back to the year 1856 as seen through the eyes of Lady Ashlee Granville-Devere ...

PART 1

THE SEARCH FOR UR

REVELATION 1

GENESIS

FROM THE JOURNAL OF LADY ASHLEE GRANVILLE-DEVERE

Hawah conceived and bore a son named Qayin and she said, 'I have gotten a man from the Lord, Sama-El.' Next she gave birth to Qayin's brother, Hevel, son of Atabba.

Hevel was a keeper of sheep, whilst Qayin was elevated above Hevel and acquired dominion of the Earth. Hevel made offerings to the Lord from the firstlings of his flocks, and these were acceptable to the Lord, who approved of Hevel. From Qayin no such offering was needed, for he was of the Lord's own Royal seed. And the Lord said, 'If anyone should slay Qayin, vengeance shall be taken upon him sevenfold!' And the Lord set his mark of Kingship upon Qayin — a cross of red — and thereafter Qayin dwelt in the land of Nodh (in restless uncertainty).

Qayin's wife was called Luluwa, the daughter of Lilith, who was the daughter of Nergal and consort to the Serpent of the Night, Sama-El.

'This reads suspiciously like Genesis.' I was astonished by the translation Lord Malory had summoned me to his private library in London to read.

Richly adorned with art, treasures and furnishings from all over the known world, Malory's apartment was located above one of the ultra-fashionable men's clubs on Pall Mall, which was owned and run by the secret brotherhood to which he subscribed. I must say that I felt a certain feminine superiority every time I was invited to a meeting there, even though, as a woman, I was escorted in and out

11

via Lord Malory's private entrance. It just wouldn't do to have the brothers know that a sister was doing most of their top-secret work for them.

I turned to Lord Malory, intrigued. 'This implies that Cain was not the son of Adam, but the son of one of the gods, and contradicts the Old Testament's claim that the line of kingship descended from Seth, Eve's third son.'

'Yes, it does, doesn't it?' The stately old man grinned at me, well pleased by my first observations. 'If it proves to be authentic and the translation correct, then this text will validate the beginning of the Grail bloodline, from which we are both descended.'

'Where on Earth did you acquire this?'

'My dear Lady Suffolk, I am not at liberty to disclose my source,' Lord Malory teased. 'I present this text to you in the hope that, with your psychic expertise, you may be able to comment on whether you perceive it to be authentic.'

I shook my head; he was asking the impossible. 'Obviously, this is an English translation of the original, which must be Egyptian? Or Babylonian, perhaps?'

'The original text is Sumerian,' Malory finally admitted. 'And this version of events is consistent with that of early Jewish Midrash text, as taught by the Qabalistic masters. We believe this earlier text could even be the source of the later doctrine, before it was corrupted in the Old Testament.' Malory stood and approached a set of shelves filled with books and old parchments.

'Sumerian text?' I gasped in excitement, as Lord Malory selected a rolled-up parchment and passed it to me. 'How fascinating!'

I unrolled the parchment as the lord poured the tea. The rubbing it held took my breath away. I knew several ancient languages, and although these picture symbols were completely baffling to me, that did not lessen my awe at laying eyes upon some of the oldest script known to mankind.

'What does your instinct tell you now?' Malory prompted expectantly.

I ran my fingers lightly over the text and received flashes of a desert landscape. 'A woman did this rubbing,' I said. 'She is very excited by this find and believes it to be authentic.'

'But what of the original scribe? Do you perceive anything in that regard?'

I focused intently for some time upon the parchment, but eventually had to concede failure with a shake of my head. 'No, nothing. I would have to lay my hands upon the column from which this rubbing was taken.'

Lord Malory appeared disappointed but not surprised.

'I feared that would be the case. Ah well,'. he returned to his seat, 'all things come to those who wait.' He took a few sips from his teacup whilst he contemplated his predicament and then added, 'That parchment represents only a small portion of the texts that are currently being unearthed.'

I realised that the lord was trying to arouse my curiosity further. 'Really?'

He nodded. 'Obviously, we are eager to verify and document the scripts before the church gets wind of our discoveries.'

'And buries them in the Vatican archive along with every other text ever unearthed that doesn't agree with the church's account of history.' I smiled as I considered the church's reaction to the entire Old Testament being contradicted by a text that predated anything from which their doctrine had been derived. 'Would you not consider sending me to this site to verify and document the finds of the excavation?' I offered.

Malory's disappointment abruptly vanished. 'You would consider undertaking such a journey? All expenses paid, naturally ... and you would be handsomely rewarded for lending your expertise to our cause.'

I shrugged, indifferent to the money, but enchanted by the notion of the adventure. 'It would not be the first such journey I have embarked upon.'

'But your husband? Your family?' He raised what he considered to be my obstacles.

'My family are fully capable of functioning without me for a time,' I assured — my youngest child was now aged ten, the oldest, twenty. 'But perhaps you might consider revealing my destination before I agree to this assignment? Or does the brotherhood dictate that you would then have to kill me?' The Sangreal adhered to a strict code of secrecy.

Malory was amused by my jest and his oversight. 'The excavation is taking place in Persia, on the site of what it is believed might be the ancient city of Ur.'

'Sounds intriguing!' I sipped my tea, trying to contain my excitement. I had not travelled abroad in twenty years and at the age of thirty-nine I felt ripe for another adventure. Victorian England was a repressive, boring place for one with my unusual interests; a trip to the Near East would be a welcome change of scenery. 'I shall require a little time to ponder the proposal,' I added.

'Of course.' Malory seemed delighted that I was even contemplating the quest. 'You do your mentor proud, I feel.'

My governess, Lady Charlotte Cavandish, had been the only woman ever inducted into the Sangreal Knighthood. I had refused Lord Malory's many kind offers to become the second female member of the secret brotherhood, but I had been happy to consult on many an otherworldly issue over the past twenty years of our association.

I finished my tea and rose to take my leave. 'We shall speak again soon.'

'Before you go, Lady Suffolk, I have something for you.' The old gentleman pulled from his pocket an envelope sealed with red wax. 'I was going through some of our archives the other week and I found this.'

I understood this to mean the archives of the Sangreal Knighthood and my curiosity was piqued. 'A gift, my Lord Malory?'

'It is a gift, in so far as you may never have known of its existence had I not dug it up. You see, I was cataloguing some new additions to our collection when I came across an entry that stated that this envelope contains a piece penned by your mother, thirty-one years ago.' He passed the envelope to me, the outside of which was marked only with a number.

I was eight years old, I thought as I accepted the gift with awe and also with loathing, for 1825 was the year I had been committed to a mental institution. My mother had become ill and withdrawn during the episode, but that was all I knew of her state of mind during that darkest time of my young life. Perhaps this piece would shed some light on her thoughts.

'But why should something my mother wrote have been confiscated by your order?' I asked.

'As I was not Grand Master at the time, I am afraid I cannot tell you.' Lord Malory sounded sincerely sorry about that. 'What I do know is that it was your father who brought the document to light after Lady Suffolk's death.'

My father, Lord Suffolk, now also passed on, had once confessed to me that he had been involved with the Sangreal Knighthood around the time he married my mother. However, he claimed to have cut all ties with them after being subjected to a secret rite on his wedding night, during which he believed he had been drugged.

'How odd,' I said, then frowned as I observed that the wax seal on the back of the envelope had not been tampered with — but whether the document had been sealed after submission or before, Lord Malory could not advise.

I could scarcely believe that the Grand Master would pass on an uncensored document to a non-member of the order, and a female at that!

'For whatever reason this document has come into the hands of your chapter, surely it must contain information worthy of your code of secrecy?'

'Most likely,' Lord Malory agreed. 'But I trust that if it contains anything I should know about, you will let me know.'

'But as Grand Master you could have read this.' I was puzzled by his restraint.

'If it were a document meant for reference, then it would not have been sealed,' Malory said. 'My feeling is that this document is personal in nature, and I do not wish to pry into the private affairs of my very dear friends.'

I appreciated that Lord Malory considered me a dear friend and yet I had to mock him. 'I was under the impression that no one born into my bloodline had any private affairs that your order did not get wind of.'

Lord Malory was amused and did not refute my statement. 'Then you may feel all the more honoured by my gift, Lady Suffolk.'

THE NAME OF THE FATHER? THE NAME OF THE SON

'*The name Levi is derived from the Latin word meaning "light", as are the words "levitate" and "levitation". The name has a more ancient association with the Priests of Levi — the designated guardians of the Ark of the Covenant. According to written descriptions, the Ark weighed over a ton and, as it was reportedly lifted on two wooden shafts by only four men, it is suspected that levitational powers were employed.*'

This was the insight that Lord Malory had awarded me some seventeen years ago, when my eldest son, barely three years of age at the time, had informed my husband and myself that his name was not Thomas — as he'd been named after my father. Our son insisted that his name was Levi.

The moment Lord Malory informed me of the history of my three-year-old son's unusual choice of name for himself, I had immediately realised why it was so appropriate.

My journey to Sinai had been motivated by the dying wish of my dear Lord Hereford, the man I almost married. The day before his unexpected death, he entrusted me with a vial filled with a remarkable gravity-defying substance known to the ancients as *Thummim-Schethiya*, the Highward Fire-Stone, the Star. Hereford's dying wish was that the vial be returned to its place of origin, a mount named Serabit in Sinai, where he had once led an archaeological dig in his younger days. During the journey I discovered that the smallest dose of the vial's contents temporarily boosted my psychic powers considerably, enabling me to accomplish impossible feats. I'd taken several doses of the Star substance before I discovered that I was pregnant with Levi. The Star vial had also proven to be one of two keys that unlocked one of the two Arks that had been fashioned on Mount Serabit.

With so many subtle connections to the East and the Ark, it was plain to me that Levi's choice of name was far more apt than he could possibly have realised as an infant.

Levi was on my mind during the carriage ride between Malory's city abode in London's West End and our own. I knew that the moment my eldest child found out that I was considering another epic voyage to the East, he would do all within his power to ensure that he accompanied me. And Levi *would* find out.

I suspected that my son was more psychically nimble than I, and I am considered to be the foremost psychic in the country by those in the know who value such insight as I can provide. However, I taught Levi from a young age not to divulge the extent of his talents to anyone, including his father and myself.

Levi had always had a strong fascination for the Holy Land and Egypt. Although a fellowship at Cambridge in ancient languages had postponed his dream of travelling there, our son was more familiar with the languages, history, myths and geography of the Holy Lands than he was with their English equivalent. I was fairly sure that although my husband would protest me taking up this quest, he would never forbid me to go. Whether my dear Lord Devere was going to allow our son to toss away his fellowship in order to go adventuring with me was quite another matter.

We were in London for the Easter holiday and I expected Levi's arrival at our London residence in St James some time tomorrow afternoon. That gave me a day to broach the subject of my journey with my husband, before Levi began complicating the issue. Upon my arrival home I was gratified to find myself at liberty. Our butler, Tibbs, informed me that my two daughters were out visiting their cousins in Hyde Park, and that my youngest son had accompanied his father into town. I requested tea in the library and there I sat, holding Lord Malory's gift in my hand. One half of me was excited by the prospect of reading something my mother had penned, as we had never been very close. The other half of me recoiled at the thought of revisiting that dark time in my life, for although I had dealt with many of the emotional aspects and horrid memories of that episode, it was still prone to upset me.

'Well, better to be upset now, in private, than to waste my energy wondering about the contents of this envelope.' I broke the seal and opened the document, which was a few pages in length.

The account began solemnly.

I am dying of anguish and guilt. History will applaud my crime against my family as an integral part of human evolution and thus I shall be blameless and deemed a saint. I feel that I can sympathise with how Our Lady Mary must have felt as she witnessed her child's crucifixion, for her life and mine have many parallels.

My daughter has been committed to a mental asylum and there is naught I can do to save her, unless I confess my infidelity to my husband. In retrospect, I am so ashamed of my seduction at the hands of an angel on the night I wed my Lord Suffolk that I cannot bring myself to speak of it. Thus I shall confess all on this paper, that I might give it to my lord and convince him that our daughter is not to blame for her psychic attributes. I am to blame.

My certainty stems from knowing that ancient blood runs through my family line, which has flowed down from the Dragon Queens of the Ancient East and through the ages to me via my Pictish foremothers. The Dragon Queens are said to have been the consorts of angels, whose offspring ensured human bodies fit for an angel to inhabit. Even with the strictest intermarriage laws, the bloodline has become diluted through the aeons, and so every now and then a female of the Dragon bloodline mates, on a spiritual level, with one of these angelic beings. The issue from this union reintroduces the angelic genetic material into the human genetic code, whereby angels can continue to reincarnate into human form and instigate the ground work for the evolution of our species.

18

As Ashlee is the issue of such an event, she may well be an angel incarnate, as will be many who descend from her. This explains her superhuman abilities and her diverse interests.

I am not insane. I would prefer insanity, for the condition would mean that I had not lied to my husband for all these years and my daughter would be as carefree as other girls her age. My judgement was swayed by the extensive greatness of the plan for humanity ... I felt small and insignificant and submitted to it. The older members of my family, whom I respected and trusted implicitly, were the masterminds of my indiscretion. What would have become of me had I rejected their design? Not that I had warning of the event, any more than my dear husband did; I learned what I know of our family secret during and after the rite.

My wedding began as most marriages of privilege do: with a church ceremony and a lavish breakfast with family and friends. This took place at the Granville estate in Suffolk. The match of Lord Suffolk and myself was greatly welcomed by our peers, and at the time I knew not the full reason why. I suspect now that my Lord Suffolk had been inducted into the secret knighthood to which my male relatives belong; in which case, my husband-to-be would have been offered some insight into the mysteries of the bloodline we share — his family line more distantly than my own.

After the celebrations, when most newlyweds would head off on their honeymoon, Lord Suffolk and I were encouraged to delay our departure until the morrow. Come evening, many of our more honoured guests were yet to depart and so my husband indulged his male associates with drinks, whilst I was led away to prepare for my wedding night, which my mother and her remaining female guests insisted on overseeing.

I had expected that my female companions would leave me to await my husband. Instead, I was stripped naked, shrouded in a hooded robe of deep red and led out into the woodland to a clearing where a huge old oak tree stood. Here I was instructed to await my lord, and all but my mother returned to the house.

'Mama?' I asked her for an explanation, as it was coming on to nightfall and the strange choice of location for my first union with my husband made me feel exposed and anxious.

'You are safe here,' Mama assured me. 'Your lord will join you presently.'

I watched her depart through the encroaching night shadows of the wood, and when I turned back to move further into the clearing I noticed a light coming from within the huge hollow of the oak tree — the entrance of which was high enough for a full grown man to enter standing upright. At first the source appeared to be a large ball of pure light, which, although brilliant, did not hurt my eyes. I stood paralysed in awe as the ball unfolded into the form of an extremely tall and beautiful man, whom I could see straight through. The figure was completely white, thus it was impossible to discern nationality or colouring.

A ghost! My conclusion struck terror into my heart, but before I had time to consider a retreat, the handsome apparition looked to me and I was immediately calmed and enchanted by his gaze.

'Who are you?' I asked, timidly taking a few steps nearer to get a closer look at him. His features were rather elongated, his eyes very large, his hair long, and his ears came to a point at the top — like a pixie's.

The figure smiled and all my cares departed for a beautiful, fleeting second.

'My Lady Suffolk?'

I heard my husband call to me from beyond the entrance into the large tree hollow. My panic returned and I ran to him.

'My lady, praise God!' my husband exclaimed when he saw me coming towards him in the moonlight. 'I think I have been drugged!' He stumbled as he spoke.

I put out my arms to support him. 'Why do you think so?'

'All my senses are extremely acute.' He frowned as he endeavoured to explain. 'And I can see in the dark! There's brilliant colour in everything!' He waved an arm about, motioning to the woodland around us, and then looked back to me. 'You ...' He staggered backwards, amazed by what he beheld. 'You look like an angel.'

I was amused and flattered by his observation, until I realised it was not me he was pointing at but the figure that now stood alongside us.

'An angel ...' My lord's eyes rolled into the back of his head and his body began to collapse towards the ground. As he fell, the spirit dispersed into light-matter, which rushed into my husband's body. Inches from the *ground, his descent stopped and his body righted itself to a standing position.*

My lord's eyes remained closed, so I brushed a hand against his cheek to wake him. His lids raised to reveal eyes that glowed intensely. The shock of seeing the angel's presence inside my husband caused me to withdraw, but he clutched my hands to gently delay me. His touch was magnetic and altogether calming. His lips gently enfolded my own and I allowed my lord to pull my body closer. It felt as if my entire self was being injected with wave after wave of euphoria. At some level I knew the physical act of sexual intercourse was taking place, yet the subtle energy transfer was so overwhelming and intense that I remember little of losing my virginity. I recall my consciousness shooting through the universe in a blissfully hyper-aware state for a time, yet I was compelled to rejoin my body as I reached a point of sexual climax.

So now you see how guilty I am.

Ashlee, however, is a unique being who is too integral to humanity to spend her life imprisoned. There must be another solution to be found, where her talents may be nurtured, understood and put to good use. Why else is she here? On threat of banishment from my home and family, I pray that my lord can forgive my deceit long enough to consider this plea for mercy.

I was more shocked by the claims in this document than those I had read in the ancient translation in Malory's library earlier that afternoon. I considered that if Malory had not read this account, then his gift to me was a startling coincidence when one considered the similarities between the two texts.

Obviously Mama had never given this letter to Papa, as he had been persuaded by my late mentor, Lady Charlotte, to release me from the asylum — which must have come as a great relief to Mama. Papa must have found this confession after Mama had passed away, and perhaps he had taken it to the Grand Master of the secret knighthood — which he'd abandoned shortly after his wedding night — to confront him with the contents. I could really only speculate as to how the document had ended up in the archives of the Sangreal Knighthood; of more concern to me was the esoteric implication of Mama's confession.

Father had complained of feeling drugged the night of his wedding, and I knew that for my father's psychic senses to have been heightened enough to see my mother's aura and an angelic being, he must have been fed Star-Fire. But where would the brotherhood have acquired the otherworldly substance? Legend had it that the otherworldly race the Nefilim were the master producers of Star-Fire, which seemed to imply that the Sangreal brotherhood was still acquainted with the Nefilim and was supplied by them. Or perhaps the knights had acquired the knowledge to produce their own Star-Fire. Of greater interest to me was my mother's claim that I was of the bloodline of the Dragon Queens, about whom I knew nothing.

A knock on the library door startled me. I folded the document and hid it inside the nearest book. 'Enter.'

Part of me was delighted when Levi joined me in the library, for my mother's account was disturbing and I was pleased for the distraction. On the other hand, Levi's early arrival was a nuisance in so far as my travel plans were concerned.

'I thought I might find you in here,' he said with a large smile on his face.

I suspected that my son already knew about my pending journey. Unlike me, Levi did not need to be in a person's close vicinity to know their thoughts; he had a knack of plucking any information he desired from the stratosphere, as easily as others selected flowers from a garden. I wondered why his arrival had not been announced.

'I did not expect you until tomorrow.' I moved to greet my tall, handsome lad — as blond as his father but with not even the hint of my waves or my Lord Devere's curls.

'Indeed ... but I managed to get away early.' Levi took hold of both my hands and kissed my cheek. 'And I came here directly, so that we might have more time to talk.'

'Was there something in particular you wanted to discuss?'

If my son's early arrival was due to the cause I suspected, that meant he had known the outcome of my meeting with Malory this afternoon before it had even taken place.

Levi returned my loving smile, his blue eyes twinkling with mischief.

22

It was always a happy and lively occasion when our family came together over dinner. Levi was something of a harmonising force in our lives; he brought out the best in everyone. Since he had been away studying, the mood of all in our house had been rather subdued.

Our eldest daughter, Rebecca, was a feisty sixteen-year-old redhead who rarely stopped talking and so missed exchanging lively banter with her older brother. Daughter number two, Charlotte, was fourteen and exactly the opposite of Rebecca, as she rarely said a word. Unlike her older sister, who was psychically void of talent, Charlotte, like Levi and myself, had the gift of clairvoyance and was particularly interested in the natural world. Hence Charlotte and Levi had a psychic bond and understanding, which Charlotte did not have with her other siblings. The youngest of our children, Thomas — who did not object to being named after my father — was a typical ten-year-old boy who missed having his brother around as he resented being left in a house with so much female company. I think my Lord Devere missed Levi for the same reason. Myself, I missed Levi's constant little psychic challenges — like the current one concerning whether or not I would break the news to my husband of Levi's intent to accompany me to Persia.

My suspicion concerning the reason Levi had wanted to speak with me had proved correct, and I had insisted that I intended to tell my lord of my plans only. If Levi wanted to throw away his fellowship to accompany me, then that was a matter for him to take up with his father. I had no intention of championing his cause, despite the fact that Levi predicted quite the opposite — and his predictions were seldom wrong.

Upon the conclusion of the main course, Tibbs entered to announce that there was a strange man at the front door, who refused to leave a calling card and was requesting an immediate audience with myself.

'How do you mean "strange", Tibbs?' Lord Devere inquired.

'The gentleman appears to be a gypsy, my lord,' Tibbs said with disdain.

'A gypsy?' The announcement sent my heart soaring into my throat and I looked to my husband in disbelief. 'Could it be . . .?'

The dulcet sound of a violin wafted from the entrance hall through to the dining room. My husband and I both smiled broadly. 'It is!' we cried in accord.

'Show the gentleman in,' Lord Devere decreed. 'And have another place set at our table.'

Tibbs seemed rather puzzled by our resolve. 'Very good, my lord.'

In France, I had once saved the man at our door from imprisonment, after duelling with the finest swordsman of the duke who held him captive. He had composed the tune now being played in our foyer in honour of my success. It sounded as if the gypsy captain was still able to enchant the heart of any woman with his music — which was what had landed him in the duke's prison in the first place, having briefly enchanted the Duchess de Guise.

As my old gypsy friend entered the dining room, I stood and moved to greet him. 'Cingar Choron.'

The years of outdoor living had aged my old travelling companion — streaks of grey now tinged his long dark curls, moustache and beard, and his skin was more leathered and tanned — yet he was as handsome as ever. Cingar was still long and lean, but his stride seemed to have lost a little of its bounce. It seemed to me that he had experienced a tragedy recently — which was confirmed when I clearly perceived the deep muddy patch that encompassed the heart centre of his auric body.

'Welcome to our home, captain.' I embraced him tightly. 'After twenty years what could possibly have brought you to our door?'

Cingar's clan usually travelled through southern France and Italy, although Cingar had also travelled in the East, in search of exotic wares to peddle on the continent. Never had he ventured so far north as to visit us in England, however.

'Chiara sent me,' the gypsy replied. 'She said you were embarking on a journey and would require my assistance.' He looked concerned when my husband appeared confused, and I was stumped as to how to react.

'But what of your wife, Jessenia?' I asked, hoping to change the subject. 'And how will your clan manage without their captain?'

The look on Cingar's face said it all.

'Jessenia has passed,' I surmised.

'Last winter,' was all the explanation he could bring himself to give. 'As for my people, my son, not much younger than your own boy,' he motioned to Levi, 'has taken charge of our band to get a feel for his future responsibilities ... leaving me free to serve you once again.' He bowed.

I took Cingar by the arm and leapt into the formalities, to prevent my husband enquiring after our gypsy friend's purpose. 'Allow me to introduce you to our children,' I said, and led him around the table to meet them one by one.

My Lord Devere waited patiently as our children had their say, then proved he was not to be distracted from the matter at hand. 'Lady Devere and I have no knowledge of an imminent journey,' he informed Cingar. 'Do we, darling?' He turned to me.

I have always refused to tell my love a barefaced lie, so what choice did I have but to confess ... or at least refrain from responding for a moment or two?

'Do we?' my husband fished, beginning to suspect that I had some explaining to do.

I raised both brows and forced a smile, which more than adequately answered his query.

'Oh no.' Cingar looked to me apologetically. 'Is my arrival a trifle premature?'

'That's the price you pay for associating with spirits,' I said, dismissing the inconvenience. 'With such a scarce awareness of time, they are bound to get it wrong on occasion.'

'It seems we need to talk,' my husband suggested amicably, motioning towards the door.

As my Lord Devere excused himself, I looked back to the table to find Levi smiling broadly. He made a small punching motion with his fist to spur me on to my confession.

'I think an adventure is a splendid idea!' My husband surprised me with his response once I had confessed all. 'How soon do we leave?'

We! I was doubly floored by this premise. 'But what about your parliamentary duties?'

Devere waved me to silence. 'A complete bore ... I trust my brother shall get word to me if my presence is necessary. To get anything through parliament seems to require a lifetime of argument, so I'm quite sure we shall return long before I am urgently needed.'

'Are you sure? I will be fine on my own,' I said, subtly trying to discourage him. I didn't know why I wanted to go on this journey without him; maybe I just needed to escape being Lady Granville-Devere, wife and mother, for a time and recall what it was like to be Ashlee.

'Ahh ... you don't want me to come.' My husband saw through my intent in a second — he was quite the psychic himself these days. 'You think I am prepared to let you go running off with Cingar, Levi and that ghost of yours without me?'

'I do not intend to take *that ghost of mine*.' Then his words registered fully. 'You are aware that Levi wishes to accompany me?'

'As such a journey is our son's life ambition, naturally he will want to go,' my husband replied. 'Levi never wanted the fellowship anyway, nor has he the slightest interest in politics, his inheritance, running an estate, or even *England* for that matter.'

'Much like his parents,' I commented, pleased that my husband was considering our son's wishes. My Devere was not like most men in this day and age; he knew his family well and I loved him for it. 'Of course I want you to come with me, if that is what you wish.' I approached my husband and wrapped my arms around his neck. 'But what shall we do about Levi?' I had sworn not to take up my son's battle and here I was doing just that, proving his prediction right.

'He's a grown man, free to choose his own path,' Devere said wisely, his brilliant blue eyes alive with thought. 'You do know why Levi wants to go to the Holy Lands so desperately?'

I had always assumed it was because he had been conceived during my Sinai trip, but something suddenly told me this was not the case.

'Levi believes that he's going to meet a woman there,' my husband went on, 'someone integral to his destiny.'

'He told you that?' I was delighted that our son would disclose such intimate insights to his father.

My husband nodded and grinned. 'He was twelve years old at the time, but I believe that the premonition is still a large part of his passion for knowledge about the region.'

I didn't know quite how to react to this news, but it certainly explained Levi's lack of interest in the marriage market in London. 'So in the end it all boils down to a woman?' I said.

My husband thought my comment ironic. 'Always, my dear.' He bowed gallantly.

THE FERTILE CRESCENT

'In 10,000 BC a moon-shaped expanse of land, ideal for cultivation, encompassed much of Mesopotamia, Canaan and Egypt. This area was the cradle of civilisation that became known as the Fertile Crescent.

'Although we know of the city of Ur from Biblical accounts, its exact location has remained a mystery. Still, the Bible hinted at its whereabouts, stating that Abram — Abraham — came from Ur of the Chaldees, which is believed to refer to the Tigris–Euphrates region of what was once southern Mesopotamia. This would place Ur at the extreme south-eastern tip of the Fertile Crescent.'

Levi, Lord Devere, Cingar and myself were standing at the rail of our vessel, the *Sea Rose*, gazing out over the Persian Gulf, while Levi gave us a brief overview of the legendary city of Ur.

'So what you are saying is that this excavation we are travelling to may have unearthed the birthplace of Abraham?' Lord Devere said.

'It is a distinct possibility,' Levi confirmed.

It had taken four months to get here. From London we had sailed all the way to Alexandria, then travelled overland to the Red Sea, where this vessel had been waiting to take us via the Arabian Sea and the Gulf of Oman into the Persian Gulf. Three years previous, the British had signed a maritime truce with all the *scheikhs* on the coast of Oman prohibiting the building of big ships and fortifications along the Trucial Coast. As a result, the British East India Company ruled the Gulf and hence our vessel had sailed the once-infamous 'pirate coast', without incident.

As the land we sought to explore drew close, Levi was finding it increasingly difficult to repress his anticipation. He'd endured the camel ride through the desert from Cairo to Suez like one of the Bedouin, when the rest of our party had been affected by the heat. A few hours in the company of real Bedouin and Levi was chatting to them in their dialect and making friends rapidly. He was so interested in the culture and history of the region that he found plenty to talk about with everyone we met, and his knowledge of their civilisation greatly impressed the locals.

'What is the political climate in Persia at present?' I asked, focusing on the more practical aspects of our journey.

Levi cleared his throat, eager to impress us with his knowledge and prove his worth as a member of this expedition. 'The King of Persia is Shah Nasr ed-Din of the Qajar Dynasty. In him are vested the threefold functions of government: legislative, executive and judicial.' He counted them off on his fingers, as if giving a lecture. 'His word is law. The Shah appoints and dismisses all ministers, officers, officials and judges. He has the power of life and death over his own family and the civil or military functionaries in his employ, without being answerable to a tribunal. He holds the rights to the exploitation of any of the resources of the country, and all requests for the making of public works, the working of mines or archaeological excavations must be approved by him.'

'So the Sangreal brotherhood is paying off the King of Persia,' I said. 'I imagine that must be costing a pretty penny.'

'They would never *pay him off*,' Cingar corrected sarcastically. 'They would present the Shah with *gifts*.'

I found the gypsy's interpretation amusing. 'What a polite way of putting it.'

'Mother misunderstands you,' Levi said. He turned to me. 'It is the custom in Persia — from the Shah downwards, there is hardly an official who is not open to gifts, nor a post that cannot be acquired or an income that has not been amassed by the receipt of gifts. This has been the way of government in Persia for centuries and the system poses a solid barrier against reform. The practice of gift-giving is known as *madakhil*. This word has no exact English translation, but may be roughly rendered as "commission", "perquisite" or "profit". It represents the sum total of personal advantage one has in any transaction.' Levi noted my frown and decided that a simpler explanation was in order. 'You see, upon the receipt of a gift, not only must you make a return gift of equivalent cost to the donor, you must also liberally compensate him in a ratio proportionate to his gift's monetary value.'

'Making for a lot of very rich officials in Persia,' Cingar finished.

'Indeed,' Levi said. 'There is scarcely a province, district, city or town in Persia that is not governed by one of the previous Shah's princelings. All of whom prey upon the country like a swarm of locusts, in order to maintain their own court and a large harem.'

'In Persia, camels, fleas and princes exist everywhere!' Cingar cited an old saying.

'So the Shah has a big family?' I asked.

'Oh yes.' Levi raised an eyebrow. 'The Shah's wives and concubines number in the hundreds. Needless to say, his offspring are bountiful.'

'Poor man,' muttered Lord Devere; he was finding one wife and four children more than enough to handle.

A crewman interrupted us, advising us that the captain wished to speak with Lord Suffolk. My husband departed to answer the summons, and Cingar followed him to the bridge.

'By sunset tomorrow we shall be on Persian soil,' Levi said as he and I turned back to admire the coastline, now bathed in a late-afternoon glow. 'I can hardly wait to see the excavation.'

I felt sure it was not just our quest that had my son so excited. 'Your zest for knowledge is most inspiring,' I said. 'One would almost suspect you are expecting to find something in particular there.'

'Whatever do you mean, Mother?' Then Levi observed the grin on my face. 'Father told you,' he said, sucking in his cheeks to hide his embarrassment.

'Whatever do you mean?' I imitated his innocent tone.

Levi turned away from me, letting me know that he found the subject unworthy of further discussion. 'I am sure my prediction does not mean what you imagine it to mean.'

'Your father dreamt of me long before we met,' I said, regaining his full attention.

'Did you dream of him?' he asked. I knew that his real question was: Has she dreamt of me?

'Only after we met,' I said. 'But at that time I had my heart set on marrying the much older and well-travelled Lord Hereford.'

'Your dreams of Father proved prophetic then?' Levi assumed.

'In a way.' I recalled the vision as if it had occurred only yesterday. 'In my dream I was off on a wild adventure and your father kept showing up to save me right when I needed him ... which proved true enough.' A smile warmed my face as I remembered all that my husband had endured to protect me, regain my trust and secure my heart. 'I remember waking with a feeling of great intimacy and attraction to your father.'

This comment brought a grin to my son's face, until I added, 'Which lasted all of seconds before my conscious reasoning stuffed it into my mind's closet and ignored it.'

'But in the end Father was victorious.'

'Oh yes.' My voice broke over the words, for I loved my husband with all my being. 'No other man has ever come close to rivalling my affection for him.'

'I am very touched to hear that.' Levi and I turned to find that Lord Devere had snuck up behind us. 'However, your mother's testimony is not entirely truthful.'

Levi was a little disturbed by his father's claim and I was rather puzzled myself.

'Albray?' Lord Devere suggested, to jog my memory.

'Who is Albray?' Levi asked.

I laughed. 'Albray is not a man.'

'He is not a dog,' my lord countered.

'Who or what is he then?' Levi was intrigued.

'Albray is a ghost,' I informed him. 'The ghost of a Crusader knight that I have had nothing to do with for twenty years.'

'Is that right?' my husband challenged.

'Yes,' I insisted. 'And I have no intention of ever contacting him again.'

'Interesting to hear you say that.' My lord frowned, appearing most perplexed. 'Then one wonders why you would pack the sword and accompanying attire that was given to you by the Duke de Guise. We both know you can barely lift the sword without Albray's aid, let alone wield it.'

During the challenge in which I had bested the duke's finest swordsman, with Albray's assistance, I had near lost the upper hand when I had tripped over my cumbersome skirt. Afterwards, when I had secured my victory, the duke had made me a gift of a green velvet suit of clothes that consisted of pantaloons, a thigh-length coat and a long green hooded mantle that made the masculine guise more modest, and which could be used to conceal my gender altogether. I had also been given long riding boots that folded down at the knee and a leather belt for my weapons.

'The weapons belt of that outfit also holsters a *pistol*, which I can wield perfectly well alone,' I justified. 'As Levi has just been telling us, there is a certain element of lawlessness in the district where we are bound; we enter at our own risk.'

'I see.' Lord Devere humoured me with a smile that conveyed he was not entirely convinced. 'Did you bring the stone?'

'What stone?' As a psychic, Levi prided himself on knowing everything about everyone, but clearly he'd never heard of this mysterious ghost we were arguing over. Indeed, Lord Devere and I had gone out of our way to bury the issue.

I faltered; I could not lie to my husband.

'Ah!' Lord Devere knew he had caught me out. 'So you did bring it.'

'Chiara is also attached to my treasure stone,' I reminded him. 'I might need her counsel, so *yes*, I brought the stone.'

Chiara was the ghost of a gypsy witch; Albray had introduced me to her when I had needed to consult with someone proficient in spell-casting and potion-brewing. She was also the great-grandmother of Cingar, and it was at her request that I went to rescue Cingar from the prison of the Duke de Guise. When I succeeded in saving her great-grandson, Chiara had pledged me her services for life and now her spirit was attached to my ringstone.

'Are you wearing it now?' my husband asked with a hint of hurt.

'Yes.' I had no idea why I felt guilty to admit this, when I had done no more than think of Albray over the past twenty years.

'Not over your heart?' Devere pleaded.

'No.' I peeled the glove off my left hand to expose the chain around my wrist and the ring-shaped stone that hung from it.

My lord, reasonably appeased, took hold of my other hand and urged me closer to him. 'I don't know if I like the idea of you holding another man's spirit in the palm of your hand.'

I gazed into my husband's eyes to reassure him. 'There is no other man for me, Mr Devere.'

'Oh please, not in public,' Levi cried. Our open affection for each other had always served as an embarrassment for our children.

'How on Earth did we ever raise such a family of prudes?' my husband commented.

'It defies the imagination,' I replied, looking to our boy who had distanced himself from us in disgust. 'You'd think Levi would be encouraged to know that it is possible to find true love.'

'I am not here to fall in love!' Levi was vexed, but when he saw that his protest had not swayed our belief, he had to struggle to keep from smiling. 'I mean it.'

Once our son had disappeared below deck, Lord Devere and I had a wee chuckle at his expense. 'We shouldn't tease,' my husband said, hugging me from behind and kissing the top of my head.

'Nonsense! What else are children good for?'

This comment was in jest, for I'd had quite a time bringing myself to leave my other three children for a year. My only solace was in knowing that I had left them in the very best of care. Mrs Beatrice Winston had been my nanny and more of a mother to me than mine ever was. She was now head of all our female staff and yet she would not give up her position as nanny to our children. Nanny Beat went everywhere with us, or should I say she went everywhere with the children, who adored her just as much as I had. I was proud to say that, unlike my parents, whom I'd barely known, I was close to my children; still, after twenty years of dedicated motherhood it was time for me to again pursue my own vocation. But, oddly, I found that I could not enjoy the same sense of liberation during this journey as I had during the last, as my mind was constantly distracted by thoughts of home and how my three youngsters were faring.

'Enjoy the moment,' my husband whispered in my ear. 'We shall be bound again by the conformity and responsibilities of England soon enough.'

He was right. After all, we did not every day get the chance to explore a previously undiscovered ancient city, especially one that the Catholic Church had yet to censor.

Yes, we were heading into hostile territory, but I expected the desert bandits would be the very least of our problems.

The excavation site was located roughly halfway between Baghdad and the Persian Gulf, some ten miles west of the Euphrates. Along the great river little villages of mud huts were sparsely scattered in clumps, but westward extended a vast desert. Out of this wasteland rose the hill the Arabs called Tall al-Muqayyar, the Mound of Pitch, which Malory and his team suspected had once been the grand city of Ur.

As our camels approached the summit of the great mound, heatwaves shimmered across the wasteland surrounding us, mocking us with mirages of placid waters. From the higher ground we were able to distinguish the palm gardens lining the riverbank along the eastern skyline, from where we had departed earlier in the day. North, west and south there was little to distract the eye from the vast sandy desert, but to the south-west the horizon was broken by the tall grey pinnacle that marked the ruins of the staged tower of Eridu, the sacred city which the Sumerians believed to be the oldest upon the Earth.

The project sponsors had spared no expense. Rather than the camp of tents I had imagined, the excavation base was a large house surrounded by a recently erected village. Our camel train came to a halt in front of it and a man came out to greet us.

'Welcome to the site house,' he said, clearly an Englishman. 'Mr Taylor, British Museum and Consul at Basra, at your service.'

'But you are not in Basra now, old friend.' Lord Devere jumped from his camel to greet Mr Taylor, with whom he was obviously on familiar terms.

Another member of the Sangreal Knighthood, no doubt, I surmised.

'I am on a research sabbatical,' our host explained. 'I feel far more useful in the field than behind a desk.'

Taylor was a slender figure of a man and, like many archaeologically inclined persons, red-skinned from years in the sun. His dress was a casual mix of well-weathered English attire and Persian desert robes. His dark hair hung straight, clearly in need of a trim as it took considerable effort to keep it from falling over his eyes. His slight moustache and beard were very neat, however, giving him the overall appearance of a rather dashing and handsome man. Despite being around Lord Devere's age, he had yet to marry. Still, if he were part of Malory's boys' club it was not uncommon for members to remain unattached, due to their pursuit of secret interests. Unless, like my own Lord Devere, who had been initiated into the ranks of the Sangreal Knighthood when he was still a boy, they were encouraged to marry a daughter of the blood for reasons of strengthening the ancient, holy line. My husband had distanced himself from the secret order after our marriage.

A large smile crossed Taylor's face as he shook my husband's hand. 'The prodigal son returns!'

'As a temporary observer only,' my lord assured.

'Quite. And where is the famous Lady Suffolk I have heard so much about?'

I was not surprised that Mr Taylor had yet to spot me. I was wearing the hooded white cloak of an Arab male, with a pair of summer trousers underneath and a white shirt that I'd borrowed from my youngest son before leaving London, as he was just my size. The ensemble was completed by the riding boots that the Duc de Guise had given me twenty years before, and they served me just as well on this journey as they had on my last. Victorian female attire had no place in the East, and especially not on an excavation site.

Taylor gave a laugh as my husband gestured in my direction.

I slid off my camel to approach, Cingar at my side.

'You are just as I imagined you.' Our host took my hand, but before he could kiss it, I changed our grip and shook his hand firmly.

'How do you do, Mr Taylor.' I let go of his hand and motioned to my associate. 'This is a dear friend of mine, Mr Choron.'

Taylor shook the gypsy's hand. 'And what is the purpose of your visit to our excavation?'

Cingar didn't like the suspicious inflection of Taylor's voice. 'I'm not here to loot if that is what you mean.'

I intervened before the situation turned ugly. Gypsies had a reputation for being nothing but a dirty bunch of thieves; an assumption that, in my experience, was completely unfounded. 'Cingar's purpose is personal. Lord Malory has sanctioned Mr Choron's presence here, as they are friends of old.'

'Well, any friend of Lord Malory's is a friend indeed.' Taylor made an effort to disperse the sudden chill in the atmosphere. 'I assure you, I meant no offence by my enquiry, Mr Choron. The Fertile Crescent is a long way to come without an objective; I just wondered —'

'Oh, I have an objective,' Cingar said. It was true that neither he nor I knew what his purpose was, but if Chiara deemed that I would need her great-grandson's aid on this journey, then it would be so.

'All shall be made clear in time,' I told Taylor, smiling broadly and changing the subject. 'I gather that Lord Malory informed you that our eldest son would be accompanying us on this journey? Let me introduce you to him.'

'So this is the youngest man ever to be awarded a fellowship at Cambridge, only to resign it in favour of a stint in the Near East.' Taylor shook Levi's hand firmly, impressed by the lad's decision.

'I would rather study the facts than the theory,' Levi explained. 'And I am confident that my decision will prove most rewarding.'

'And so it shall,' Mr Taylor agreed. 'I believe that we may be unearthing the great Ziggurat of Ur.' He pointed to the craggy peak of the Mound of Pitch, where fifty or so diggers were hard at work. 'Come, let me show you.'

As we negotiated the scattered dig sites of the outer excavation, Levi noticed a young woman climb out of a hole in the ground and hold a rubbing up to the sun to inspect it. She was a local woman judging by her attire; between her long, simple dress and the scarf wrapped about her head and shoulders, only her face and her hands were exposed.

'What is down that hole?' Levi inquired of Taylor, pointing to where the young woman stood engrossed by her work.

'It is a small burnt-brick building from a later period, and of no real significance.' Taylor pointed to the mats that covered the large hole in the ground. 'The walls are so high that the workmen have roofed it and use it as a shelter.'

'So what is that young woman's interest in the dwelling?' Levi wondered.

'I have no idea. She is my linguist ... come, I'll introduce you. Miss Koriche!' he called ahead to the young woman.

She looked up, and was startled to find she had a rather large audience. She rolled up the rubbing, obviously to avoid showing it to us. 'Mr Taylor.' She nodded to acknowledge him, although judging from her tone he was not one of her favourite people. 'Your new translators have arrived, I see.'

Taylor appeared exasperated by her comment. 'These people are not here to replace you. I thought I had made that clear.'

'I am Lady Suffolk, Miss Koriche.' I stepped forward to introduce myself, holding out a hand to shake hers. The moment I touched her, I recognised her energy. 'It was your translation I read in Lord Malory's library — the account was very impressive,' I said. 'I am not a translator,' I went on. 'My son, Mr Levi Granville-Devere, is the expert on languages.'

I referred her to Levi, only to realise, when I noted how fondly he observed her, that this was the woman he had foreseen meeting here.

'I am still a learner,' Levi said, bowing to Miss Koriche. 'I was hoping I might pick up a pointer or two while I am here.'

Miss Koriche appeared a little overwhelmed and embarrassed, so I continued with the introductions. 'This is my husband, Lord Suffolk.'

My husband tipped his hat to her. 'A mere spectator.'

'And my dear friend Mr Choron.' I directed her to Cingar, who held high two fingers and gave a wave.

'Mysterious guest,' he said, to vex Taylor.

'Is that a rubbing you have there?' Levi dispensed with the formalities, unable to contain his curiosity any longer.

'A small one.' Miss Koriche downplayed her find.

'I would dearly love to see a rubbing of an actual Sumerian text,' Levi persisted, despite the linguist's obvious reluctance to share.

'We can go one better than that.' Taylor pointed to the hole in the ground. 'Come down and take a look at the original engraving.'

'That would be splendid.'

Levi and Taylor both climbed down the ladder.

I noted Miss Koriche suppress an urge to protest; she was trying to hide something, which explained my son's interest in this particular hole in the ground. I threw Miss Koriche a smile of consolation as I too climbed down into the dwelling.

It was a two-roomed ruin made of burnt brick with two arched doorways. Levi was inspecting the brickwork, which, unusually, was set in bitumen mortar, when he noticed something and moved in very close.

'What is it?' I asked.

'These bricks have been stamped with an inscription.' He turned to Mr Taylor. 'Have you had this translated?'

'I believe we have had it looked at.' Taylor referred to Miss Koriche, who had followed us down into the pit.

'As there are several eras of history all deposited on top of one another here, it is difficult to pin this dwelling to a specific period,' Miss Koriche advised.

Her words faded as I wandered through one of the arched doorways and into the next room, where I found a quiet corner to place my hands upon the ancient brickwork.

One of my most developed psychic talents was psychometry, meaning that I could read the psychic imprints off inanimate objects. Levi had inherited this talent, which was how I knew he was lying about not being able to shed any light on the inscription that had him so intrigued.

As I focused on the atomic structure of the brick, the first thing I perceived was the cool darkness of being buried. As the memory worked backwards, the dirt receded and the dwelling reconstructed itself into the two-roomed dwelling Taylor had claimed it to be. It was not the abode of simple folk, however; it was a temple shrine dedicated to a god-king that I did not recognise. The symbol featured on the walls was that of an ibis sitting on a perch; I made a mental note of it to reference later. Sunlight penetrated the dwelling and, looking to the light, I spotted an arched doorway that led outside. I directed my consciousness to move in that direction … a brick pavement led straight ahead between two tall walls to a wide-open space. I was awestruck as I found myself standing on a high level platform of the great ziggurat, overlooking the huge paved inner courtyard. I turned to look in the direction of the Mound of Pitch: there stood the grand uppermost level of the ziggurat, but another huge shrine was located there.

'Are you coming, my dear?' My husband's voice startled me back to the present.

'Yes,' I called back to him in the other room. 'Just a moment.'

My eyes scanned the earthen floor; my psychic perception clearly defined that there was more to this structure, directly beneath us, even though I didn't recall any stairs in my vision of the little shrine. I noticed the earthen floor dipped considerably near the far wall, where someone had been digging. The brickwork differed there; a closer inspection confirmed the bricks were stamped with an entirely different inscription.

'Must be from an earlier period,' I muttered to myself. Sensing someone behind me, I turned to confront my husband.

'Find something interesting?' he asked.

'Not really,' I replied, taking his arm to leave. I would return later to investigate these older bricks.

Lord Devere leaned close to whisper in my ear, 'Liar.'

'Later,' I returned, just as quietly, and, satisfied he had the truth out of me, he let the matter rest.

As we climbed the ladder out of the pit, Levi was still discussing the finer points of Sumerian text with Miss Koriche. 'Go on without me,' he told us. 'I shall catch up.'

Both Lord Devere and I had to struggle to repress a smug grin.

'It was a pleasure meeting you, Miss Koriche,' I said.

'We shall see you again,' Lord Devere concluded.

THE GREAT ZIGGURAT

'The ziggurat is a peculiar feature of Sumerian architecture,' Taylor explained. 'The people who settled the Euphrates Valley came down from the hilly country in the east and, finding themselves on vast level plains, set about building a "high place" where they could worship their gods and keep watch for their enemies.

'The ruins at Ur are, in the main, the remains of the great ziggurat built by Ur-Nammu of the Third Dynasty. However, his was only the last of many such structures to have been built on the site since a much earlier dynastic period.'

Taylor's lecture was fascinating, but quite frankly I was surprised that anything had been dug out of the ground here in one piece.

Taylor's main objective was to find sacred relics and texts to enrich the shelves of the British Museum (and the secret brotherhood's library, no doubt) and in his haste to do so, little consideration was being paid to the excavation itself. A lack of experienced excavators meant that the ruins were being butchered by the local workmen's picks, and Taylor complained that more often than not the small precious finds that were exposed in the course of the digging were pocketed by the workmen and sold privately. He had ordered security checks of personnel at the end of each shift, which at first had exposed some of the thieves, but it had failed to be an effective long-term solution, and even spot checks had failed to catch any further looters. It seemed the men had found another means to smuggle out their little treasures.

Over dinner I inquired if anyone could remind me which ancient god was depicted by the glyph of an ibis sitting on a perch. Levi informed me that the ibis was the symbol of Thoth, the scribe of the gods.

I waited until the dishes from the main course were being cleared away to bring up the subject of the two-roomed ruin, to avoid this topic being connected with my question about the symbol.

'Mr Taylor, I have a bone to pick with you,' I began.

'Already, Lady Suffolk?' Taylor replied in good humour.

'I am afraid so.' I kept my tone light but professional. 'It is in regard to the two-roomed dwelling we inspected today.'

'What of it?'

'Unlike you, Mr Taylor, I believe that no archaeological find is insignificant and I really do not think that you should be allowing the discovery to be used as a shelter. On behalf of the authority vested in me by Lord Malory, I would like to ask that you have the area vacated pending further investigation.'

'But there was nothing found there of any value whatsoever, bar the inscriptions on a few bricks.' Taylor couldn't understand my concern.

'However, as Miss Koriche mentioned earlier, there are many layers of history compacted together in these ruins.' I looked to the linguist, who forced a smile in acknowledgement of my credit. Despite this, I sensed she was concerned by my interest in the dwelling. 'Thus, why run the risk of damaging the find further? Huts are for shelter, Mr Taylor; an excavation site is for excavating. Even if you have no interest in such a find, please consider the archaeologists who will follow you here and leave the structures as intact as possible for their reference.'

Obviously Taylor felt a little perturbed by my lecture. 'As Lord Malory has claimed many times, you give wise counsel indeed, my lady.'

'So you will have the dwelling vacated?' I pressed.

'First thing tomorrow,' he assured me, holding up his glass to decree that the matter was settled.

'But what of the men who have made the dwelling their temporary home?' Miss Koriche protested on behalf of the locals.

I was surprised by her stance and took the opportunity to expose something of her little secret.

'I am sure Mr Taylor will see them suitably relocated,' I said. 'As a scholar, Miss Koriche, I had rather expected that you would be eager to see the site properly preserved.'

'Of course.' She realised her error in speaking up. She placed her napkin on the table and stood. 'Could you all please excuse me? I have just remembered something that I must attend to.'

Everyone at the table stood to bid her a good night.

From her light-body I could tell that Miss Koriche was a good person and yet I knew that she could not be trusted. She had a hidden agenda, and something told me that her quest and ours were about to cause a very disagreeable collision.

First thing after breakfast the next day I headed over to the two-roomed dwelling that Taylor assured me had been vacated and was now off limits to the general site staff until further notice. Lord Devere, who had extracted all my psychic observations from me in the privacy of our room the previous night, accompanied me on my investigation.

Down in the pit's second room, I was not surprised to find that more of the older brickwork had been exposed since I had been there yesterday. The labour had not yet found the floor of the lower dwelling, however, and, considering the height of the walls around us, there might still be quite a dig ahead.

'A last attempt by the workmen to find a little treasure in here?' My husband suggested a reason for the fresh effort.

'Or a last attempt by a linguist expecting to find something in particular?'

'You do not trust Miss Koriche,' he observed.

'And she does not trust us,' I retorted.

'No, Mother, it is Mr Taylor that Miss Koriche does not trust.' Levi stood in the archway between the two rooms, covered in dirt.

'You did this?' I referred to the freshly dug soil.

'I did,' he grinned, 'with some help from the men we evicted. I paid them, naturally.'

'And what inspired this sudden burst of energy?' I asked, keen to know how much he had already discovered.

'The dwelling we stand in is not of a later period, as Taylor suspects, but dates back to around the fourteenth century BC, to the time of the Kassite king Kuri-gulzu,' Levi began.

'It was his name stamped on the bricks?' I interrupted, and my son nodded. 'Miss Koriche told you this?'

Levi could tell that I was still wary of the woman he was so taken with. 'I can read the glyphs, as you know,' he said, 'but Miss Koriche has been deciphering a king list inscribed on an ancient clay column, and from this we were able to deduce a rough time line. The older bricks date back much further, to the time of the Larsa king Ishme-dagan. The rubbing that Miss Koriche took from the wall in the other room yesterday confirms that Kuri-gulzu restored the ancient house, which, from days of old, had been decayed. He rebuilt the four sides and restored the E-dublal-makh to its glory, by making good its foundation.'

'In other words, he built over the top of the old ziggurat,' I said.

Levi nodded. 'However, he did not follow its design exactly. The original ziggurat was smaller, with many temples outlying and, I suspect, underlying too. See for yourself.' He motioned to the bricks I had taken an interest in the previous day.

Without further ado I placed both palms flush against the brickwork, then turned my focus inward to perceive the history of the wall before me.

The two-roomed dwelling I stood in crumbled to the ground and vanished. Above me, night and day, dark and light, flashed by in a heartbeat over and over, creating a rapid pulsing effect. Beneath my feet there was a pounding sensation, and in a great explosion of fire a building erected itself underneath me. I floated down to stand on the uppermost level of a far grander ziggurat than the first, for even though it was not of the same huge proportions, the detailing on the architecture was far more intricate and beautiful. Indeed, the whole design of the building was a masterpiece. In the entire structure there was not one straight line; every wall and every walkway was a carefully calculated curve, creating the same optical illusion that the builders of the Greek Parthenon were to achieve many centuries later. To my right, the platform on which I stood dropped to an amazing garden courtyard, so lush with vegetation that it could have been in Europe. In fact, there were hanging gardens adorning every level and corner of the structure. To my left was a sheer drop off the side of the ziggurat and a view of the city below, which was also reminiscent of Ancient Greece. Some of the grand dwellings appeared well aged already and had probably been built in an earlier period. I was amazed to see man-made waterways running through every level of the great ziggurat and also through the city below. Surely, if one were able to stand and admire the ancient city of Atlantis from such a viewpoint, it would appear very much like this.

Look behind you.

I perceived Levi's instruction and swung my consciousness around to see stairs leading downward into the ziggurat.

I followed the brick staircase down to a long corridor that was lined with twelve huge golden statues, six goddesses and six gods, placed in a male-female pattern. In the centre of the six sentinels, a huge golden orb was set in the wall. In the centre of this orb was the all-seeing eye and inside the pupil was a lotus, the flower of life. On the outer wall, long, thin slitted windows allowed the rising sun's rays to warm the statues. One end of the long corridor curved around a corner. The other end — that closest to me — led to a large arched doorway adorned with jewels and painted gold. Inside was a shrine bearing the same ibis glyph that I had seen in the site that would later be built above it. A large stone altar stood in the centre, on which to place offerings. This centrepiece was covered with glyphs that I could not read.

'It *is a discourse about the god to whom this shrine is dedicated,* Levi told me. '*It begins:*

The venerable Ibis, heart of the Sun and the Moon shining in the Heavens, who brings the knowledge that was faraway that giveth Life to men. The Universal Benefactor, splendid in speech, astute in his plans, the Orderer of Fate, the Gracious One who can avert this evil. Lord of Eternity, Magic and Script. The Reckoner of Time for Gods and Men. The Lord of the Amulet and Scribe of the Divine Book that gives breath to the weary of heart. The Golden Youth who came forth from the Lotus Flower will be thrice born. The Guardian of the Island of Blue Flame, who tests the hearts of men in the Hall of Life, beneath the Ray of Force, awaits the next aspirant . . .

My curiosity pulled me from my trance and back into the present. 'So what is the shrine of Thoth, an ancient Egyptian god, doing in a Sumerian structure?' I asked.

'Nowhere in the discourse did the scribe name the god in question,' Levi said. 'It is only from our modern understanding that we recognise the god spoken of as having the attributes of the Egyptian god Thoth, or the Greeks' Hermes. In Mesopotamia he was the youngest son of Enki, Ningizzida, Lord of the Tree of Truth. In Roman myth he was known as Mercury, son of Zeus and so on. I thought the choice of stone for the altar rather curious,' Levi went on. 'Very hard to come by in this neck of the woods at the time. That altar was built to last.'

'Yes, everything else was built of mud brick,' I said. 'And judging by the size, it wasn't to be moved either!' A thought came to me. 'You're not going to try and dig down to the altar, are you?'

'Hardly,' Levi said. 'That would be more like tunnelling and it would take an age. I wish to dig to the next level of flooring, as, according to the impression I perceived from these walls, the staircase that descends to the level of the old shrine was enclosed to accommodate the rebuilding of the newer, higher ziggurat.'

'*The Guardian of the Island of Blue Flame . . .*' I thought back over the inscription. 'Could this refer to the plane of Sharon and the Fire-Stone that grants entry to that realm?'

'In ancient Egyptian cosmology, there is a place known as Amenti,' Levi said, 'which has been mistakenly construed as an abode of the dead. Unlike the Egyptian underworld, however, where the souls of the deceased are judged by Osiris and punished or rewarded for their deeds, I understand Amenti is more correctly translated to mean "the hidden place", where dwell the souls of the eternally living who guard a blue flame that is said to hold the blueprint of human evolution on this planet. Hathor was considered to be the Lady of Amenti and Thoth was the scribe. Among the outer chambers of Amenti is the Hall of Records, reputed to hold the writings of the scribe Thoth and the ancient doctrines of Atlantis. In some esoteric circles, Amenti was believed to be located beneath the sunken city of Atlantis; others claimed it was beneath Giza. It does not exist on the physical plane, however; on that point everyone agrees.'

Footsteps on the ladder alerted us to company.

I gave myself a quiet scolding — I should not have been discussing the Fire-Stone in the open where we could be easily overheard; it was better that that ancient mystery remain buried.

'Miss Koriche.' Levi greeted our intruder warmly.

She had a smile for him too.

'The workmen are wondering if you wish to employ their services in this part of the dig today?' she queried, almost playfully. Then, noting the presence of Lord Devere and myself, she quickly concealed her openness towards Levi with a more professional countenance.

'You can tell the workmen that I would very much like to employ them today,' Levi said. 'Let us see if our hunch about finding some of the old structure underneath this one proves correct.'

Miss Koriche's smile returned. 'I fear Mr Taylor is not going to welcome your interest in this area. I have suggested many times that this ruin is worthy of further investigation, but he will not listen.'

'Well, I am listening,' Levi assured her, 'and as Mother and I both agree with you —'

Do we? I thought at him, although outwardly I served him a supportive smile.

'— Mr Taylor will just have to grin and bear it,' Levi finished.

Miss Koriche climbed back up the ladder, presumably to recruit a small work force. 'Your presence here is proving far more fortuitous than I expected,' she told Levi.

'I am comforted to hear you say so,' Levi called after her.

Then, looking back to us and seeing the odd look on our faces, he said, 'What?'

'I am not here to fall in love.' I repeated the claim he had made just before landing in Persia.

'Let us not get ahead of ourselves,' he said, but his smile confirmed his attraction to Miss Koriche, and he didn't bother refuting my inference.

'Well, we psychics have a tendency to do that,' I bantered,

knowing I did not have to impress upon him my distrust of the young woman.

'I believe your instincts will prove wrong in this case,' he challenged.

'I hope they do.'

I really did not wish to play devil's advocate with my son's relationship choices, but there was something about Miss Koriche that was not sitting right with me. I hoped it was just a mother's jealousy of her son's first real love interest.

Nearly a week later and, twenty feet of earth beneath where we had started our private excavation, Levi's dig team hit mud bricks akin to those found on the lower-level walls of the dwelling that were close to four thousand years old.

'Now what?' Levi consulted Mr Taylor, who had come to view the discovery.

'Keep going, of course!' Taylor encouraged, rubbing his hands together at the prospect of perhaps finding more ancient treasure than he could hope to exhume from the top of the ziggurat in the near future. 'Picks will make light work of disposing of those bricks.'

'You cannot use picks for such an operation,' I protested. 'These bricks are ancient and must be extracted and catalogued one by one. We could be desecrating a structure that is perfectly intact; I see no reason to destroy this site further.'

'Well, Lady Devere, you might want to think again, as it seems that time may now be very much of the essence,' Taylor retorted, obviously exasperated by my persistent conservation demands. 'I have heard a whisper that the independent rulers of Herat are looking to the Shah to aid against their reabsorption into the Afghan kingdom.'

'But Herat is a British protectorate. If Persian troops were to occupy the city, then the British would declare war on Persia,' Lord Devere said, alarmed by the possibility.

'The British have already issued a warning to the Shah against considering occupation,' Taylor said.

I wondered at Mr Taylor's resources. 'For a man stuck in the middle of nowhere, you seem very well informed,' I said.

Taylor sensed my curiosity and sidestepped it. 'It is my job to keep informed — but I must confess that the information I have received could be weeks old, thus our need for haste.'

'What will happen to us if war is declared?' My husband was naturally more concerned about our safety than our quest.

'The Shah will seize everything and we shall be sent packing,' Taylor said. 'Of course, that is the best-case scenario.'

As my husband fell silent and began mentally weighing up the risks of us staying at Ur, Mr Taylor turned his sights my way.

'So I put it to you, Lady Devere, shall we spend what time we have remaining cataloguing bricks, or shall we discover what is beneath them?'

Selfish though it was, I allowed my concerns to be silenced, and it took no time at all for the workmen to smash to pieces a floor that had remained unscathed for most of recorded history. I could not watch, and climbed the ladder into the mid-afternoon heat to get some air.

'The destruction disturbs you.'

I finished drinking down my hourly ration of water before I responded to Miss Koriche's observation.

'I really cannot say who is worse: the Catholic Church or the millionaire boys' club here.'

This actually got a smile out of the linguist, who had warmed to Levi but had done her best to steer clear of the rest of us.

'May I ask how it is that a woman comes to have so much influence within such a club?' she said.

It was a fair question, but I got the distinct feeling that I was being interrogated. 'I am in insurance,' I told her, knowing that she was still curious about my area of expertise.

'You are an assessor?'

'You could say that,' I concurred. 'And speaking of assessing, I need to take a look at the cylinder clay columns you've been deciphering. It would not do to come all the way here and not complete the one request that Lord Malory made of me.'

I had been shown over the finds in the restoration rooms of the site house, along with the rest of my party, but had put off trying to probe any of the pieces for psychic imprints until a quieter, more appropriate time. I already knew from the bricks in the dig area, that had kept us all so engrossed this last week, that the text found on this mount predated all religious chronicles.

'What the inscriptions have taught us already is priceless.' Miss Koriche did not like the idea that a price might be placed on the ancient script she'd found so insightful.

'I am sure that I agree with you. Still, I am unable to report as much until I can authenticate the said items.'

Miss Koriche was intrigued. 'How do you plan to do that, my lady?'

'I have a well-trained eye,' I said, and I wasn't lying: my inner eye was very developed. 'Hence my influence with men of power — I have a gift they respect and need.'

'Of course.' She realised that she was being overly protective and pulled out her set of keys. 'Come and I shall let you in.'

'I am much obliged.'

On the way back to the site house we walked in silence; Miss Koriche was not one for idle chitchat — not with me in any case. I was so very tempted to psychically probe her thoughts. I wanted to know why she was wary of my party; was it just because we were foreigners? Miss Koriche was not a native of Persia herself, but was born into a wealthy Moroccan family and educated in Cairo. My other concern was her interest in my son. I could see Levi's attraction, as not only did the linguist share his interests, but she was beautiful and astute as well. She was a good five years older than Levi and would have to have been deaf, dumb and blind not to notice the crush he had on her. They had been spending a good deal of time together this last week, and Levi maintained that he as learning a lot from Miss Koriche — a claim I was not entirely sure how to interpret. Miss Koriche was not your typical subservient Eastern woman, and even more unusual was the fact that she was a scholar who claimed to subscribe to no particular religion. The archaeological evidence that she had deciphered seemed to indicate that no doctrine was able to expose the entire truth behind the origin of life on Earth — on that point we were in total agreement.

Despite my curiosity regarding the young woman, I resisted violating her mind. I had learned through experience that more harm than good came from spying on the private thoughts of others, as one seldom perceived any train of thought in its entirety and thus it was easy to draw the wrong conclusion.

Inside the adjoining rooms in the site house that served as a storage area for the treasures recovered during the excavation — kept tightly locked by Miss Koriche — I cast my eyes over the relics laid out on tables and the large clay tablets and columns placed around the walls to see if anything in particular drew my attention. I bypassed the clay pottery and seals in favour of a woman's hair comb made of ivory. It was engraved with the symbol of a gold serpent coiled in a circle and consuming its own tail. My fingers reached for the item, but Miss Koriche took up the piece instead.

'You have a fine eye indeed,' she conceded. 'I believe this may be the oldest of the artefacts that we have found so far.'

'May I?' I held out my hand for the piece.

Miss Koriche knew that she had no authority to deny me, although I could clearly discern that given a choice she would have. Was she concerned about the artefact being damaged, or had she found out I was a psychometrist? I doubted very much that Levi would have disclosed as much to her, when I had drummed into him how important it was to keep his own talents hidden.

Miss Koriche reluctantly placed the ancient hair accessory into the palm of my hand and observed me closely.

'Do not let me keep you from your work, Miss Koriche. I will seek you out if I have any questions.' I smiled and waited for her to depart.

'I shall be in the next room,' she said, leaving me to my business.

I turned to face the opposite direction to the room where Miss Koriche had gone and held the comb up to the light to make a good show of assessing it — for I had a sneaking suspicion that I was still being observed. Then, holding the item in my left palm, I ran my right-hand fingers over the smooth ivory and within seconds of focusing my inner eye upon it, my sight, inner and outer, was engulfed by a vision.

I was in a single-file procession of young women dressed in long, flowing red robes. The dark hair of the woman directly in front of me was wound in an intricate knot that was held in place with a serpent comb — all the scarlet women wore the same comb, including myself. But this was no ceremonial procession; it was an evacuation! I felt the sensation of panic and a great urgency to scale the stone stairs beneath my feet. When I reached the top of the stairway, I entered the shrine of the great Ibis via an opening in the floor where the huge stone altar should have been. The huge, heavy block was floating directly overhead. Four older women, also dressed in scarlet, were focused intently upon the boulder and it was they who held it aloft. The last woman in the procession was not far behind me and in our wake the great stone altar was lowered to the ground to conceal the temple entrance.

Without the sacred food the altar cannot be moved ... the Key to Amenti is safe. I was deeply comforted by this knowledge.

No sooner was the great altar in place than a horde of warriors came screaming down the corridor of the Ennead towards us — to my great horror, they were not human! Their eyes glowed yellow and their skin was scaled and green, like demon-lizards. Several of the invaders grabbed hold of me and forced me to the ground. The serpent comb was ripped from my hair by one of my attackers, to be kept as a memento of the day's conquest.

At the sound of ripping fabric, I swiftly placed the comb back on the table, to escape witnessing the rape and murder of the priestesses of Ur by the sub-human creatures. Was it a nightmare I had perceived from the comb, I wondered. I couldn't comprehend how the woman's account could have been real. Still, if it was a true account of events, then there was a temple passage beneath the corridor of statues. And Levi's dig team had just broken through the bricks that had once lined the floor of that same corridor. The fact sent waves of excitement surging through my body.

I pondered the last thoughts of the young priestess: *The Key to Amenti is safe.* She had referred to the 'sacred food' required to levitate the altar; this 'food' was the Highward Fire-Stone. What, then, was the 'key' she was so concerned about protecting? And was it still buried beneath the ruined ziggurat?

I looked up and caught Miss Koriche observing me from the other room.

'Forgive my curiosity,' she said, venturing back into the room I was occupying, 'but what is your opinion on the comb?'

I suspected that she was testing my ability to assess the piece. 'I think this find could predate even the Larsa period. Was that your assessment, Miss Koriche?'

'The symbol of the serpent eating its own tail was synonymous with the Dragon Court,' Miss Koriche said. 'In Egypt, the Dragon Court was established as a Pharaonic institution by Queen Sobeknefru of the Twelfth Dynasty in about 1785 BC, which is roughly where I estimate the Larsa period would fall.'

'The Dragon Court?' I asked curiously.

'The Dragon Courts were academies dedicated to the teachings of Thoth, which existed from the time of King Raneb of the Second Dynasty, who is estimated to have reigned about 2800 BC. So, in reality, this hairpiece could have been fashioned anywhere in between.' Miss Koriche confirmed my assessment.

'The Dragon Court being an institution of the Dragon Queens?' I hazarded a guess, my heart thumping in my chest as I made the connection.

'Of course.' Miss Koriche seemed stunned by the query.

'Are you surprised by my knowledge or my interest?' I smiled, hoping to set her at ease, as she obviously knew more about the Dragon Queens than I did.

'Both!'

'So who were the Dragon Queens?' I put her on the spot with the question.

Her reluctance to answer seemed to confirm she was hiding something. 'I do not know very much about them,' she stalled. 'There are various theories . . .'

'Such as?'

'Well, the most popular theory is that the Dragon Queens were the female descendants of Cain, and, according to my translation of the text you read, the first of the Dragon Queens was —'

'Luluwa,' I said.

'No,' Miss Koriche corrected, 'the royal line of Serpent Princes descended from Qayin, or Cain, and Luluwa, and the first of these princes was Enoch. However, the line of the Dragon Queens is said to have descended from Lilith, being the first woman who claimed to be a spiritual daughter of Sama-El. In fact, it is said that Sama-El fathered all of the Dragon Queens, of which ancient texts claim there are six plus one.'

Through the ages, Sama-El had been reinvented as the devil that had shown humanity the way to the tree of knowledge. *Fathered by the devil* — I amused myself with the premise, as there were many people over the years who might have agreed. The idea would have worried me too, had I not known that Sama-El was also called Enki, the most ancient god of the waters. And recently I'd discovered that I may be his daughter. I was beginning to suspect that my mother as well as my father had been drugged on their wedding night.

I changed the subject, as I was now as uncomfortable with it as Miss Koriche. 'Which of these clay columns did the Genesis account come from?'

'It is here.' Miss Koriche motioned to the far wall of the room she had been working in, and so I followed her back inside. 'This column obviously dates from the last rebuild of the ziggurat, perhaps 3400 years old. But this Genesis account may be older still, as the story itself could have been preserved from an earlier period.'

I moved closer to the column and placed a hand upon it.

I felt warmed immediately, for I found myself as a young man hard at work under the hot afternoon sun of ancient Sumer. Before me, protected by the shade of a wall, was a smooth and still-damp clay column that I had begun to inscribe with the aid of a sharpened reed. Beside me were pieces of a clay tablet that had been smashed and then reassembled like a jigsaw puzzle. I was relaying the contents of the ruined item onto the fresh column and, from all appearances, the text on the old clay tablet seemed complete.

'We need to talk.' The note of alarm in my husband's voice catapulted me back to the present.

I opened my eyes and looked in my lord's direction to find Mr Taylor and Levi were with him. 'What has happened?'

'Talk some sense into Father,' Levi pleaded, most out of sorts.

'We have been given our marching orders,' Taylor informed me. 'Some of the Shah's officials have just paid us a visit. We have a week to get out of Persia.'

'But I have only been here a week!' I protested. 'And it took me months to get here.'

'Regrettable,' my husband agreed. 'However, we *are* leaving.'

'No! We can't leave now — ' I cut myself short of confessing what I'd learned from the serpent comb and quickly covered my error. 'We are right in the middle of something.'

'That's exactly what I said!' Levi threw up his hands in exasperation. Still, I knew that the dig was not the only reason Levi was so keen to stay.

'It doesn't matter what you *say*,' Lord Devere spelled out the problem to our son, 'because in this case, we are going to be *arrested* if we do not comply.'

'We must be able to appeal the Shah's decision?' I looked to Mr Taylor hopefully.

'You would appeal to the local kad-khuda, or headman, who is the administrator of the Common Law,' Taylor advised me.

I smiled, pleased to have a route to manifesting my will.

'But it was his officials who served us our eviction notice,' Taylor went on, dashing my hopes. 'And there is no point appealing to him, as his orders came directly from the Shah. A kad-khuda will never overrule the word of his sovereign.'

'Then I shall appeal directly to the Shah,' I said.

Levi gave a cheer of encouragement.

'And say what?' My husband appealed for me to be reasonable. 'Understand that this man is the law here. He could have your head severed from your shoulders for one misconstrued word!'

'Actually, the Persians haven't beheaded women for thousands of years,' Levi assured his father, who looked suspiciously at him, sure that he wasn't getting the whole story. 'I do believe they hang them these days,' our son confessed at last.

'And much worse,' Miss Koriche added. 'In recent times, condemned criminals have been crucified, blown from guns, buried alive, impaled, converted into human torches, and torn asunder by being bound to the tops of two trees which are bent together and then allowed to spring back into position.'

Lord Devere glared at me. 'I do my best to support you in most things, Mrs Devere, but I draw the line at a suicide mission.'

'I shall present the Shah with a gift,' I said, avoiding my husband's protest and looking at Mr Taylor. 'Then it would be considered rude to have me executed, would it not?'

'It would have to be a rare gift indeed,' Taylor cautioned. 'And I would certainly find a dress to wear in the Shah's presence.' He gestured to the male attire I donned for excavation work.

'What gift could we possibly come up with that would be considered rare to the King of Persia?' Lord Devere was exasperated. 'And even if we could think of such a gift, we don't have it.'

'But we do,' I said.

My husband served me a look of caution, sure that I was referring to my psychic abilities.

'It's not what you think,' I said. 'However, I do believe that I now understand why it was so important that Cingar accompany us on this quest.'

'No. We shall not endanger his life too,' my lord said firmly.

'But do you not see that it was fated?' I argued.

'I was under the impression that you did not believe in fate.'

My lord had caught me out, for indeed I do not believe in fate. To do so is to believe that one is at the mercy of external forces, whereas I am quite aware that I create my own reality.

'I should have said it was predestined, by myself,' I granted. 'I need something to offer the Shah, and the universe provided it long before I even knew I needed it.'

'It is not right for you to take advantage of Cingar's devotion to you.' My husband refused even to consider my plan.

'Let us put it to Cingar,' I suggested, which only angered my husband more.

'He owes you his life and will refuse you nothing!' he snapped. 'Even if it costs him his own life in payment.'

'Do you not see that pledge is only an excuse?' I said gently. 'The real reason that Cingar has come back into my life is not wholly to do me service. He has come looking for a new purpose.'

Lord Devere calmed a degree as he considered this new idea that Cingar was using our voyage to escape the loss of his wife. 'Very well,' he said, 'we shall let our friend decide for himself. But I shall pose the question to him, so that he may feel less obliged.'

I agreed.

When my husband put the idea to Cingar, his response was: 'Of course I shall play for the Shah if it will be of service to you and your quest. I feel sure this must be why Chiara sent me to your aid.'

Clearly Lord Devere was outnumbered. The rest of our party were keen to at least attempt an appeal, and thus, as usual, I got my way. Still, the hard look my husband gave me indicated that I should not expect him to be happy about the decision, or my defiance of his wishes.

On the morning that we were preparing to leave for Baghdad, Levi sought out his father and me to tell us that Miss Koriche had disappeared.

'She is probably on site somewhere —' I began.

'No, she isn't,' Levi cut in. 'I have had the entire site searched.'

'Perhaps she had to go and pick up supplies or —'

'She would have mentioned it,' Levi insisted, becoming more desperate by the second.

'What makes you think that Miss Koriche would inform you of her every move?' Lord Devere probed curiously.

Levi appeared stunned by his father's question. His reaction was answer enough.

'Where did you last see Miss Koriche?' my lord persisted.

Levi appeared suddenly discomfited. 'In my room.'

'You saw her leave?'

'No.' Levi blushed, his expression still solemn as he shrugged. 'I fell asleep.'

'I see.' My lord attempted to suppress his masculine pride in his son's conquest. 'Well, perhaps Miss Koriche is having second thoughts about her association with you, and that is the reason she has made herself absent?'

This was obviously an explanation Levi had not considered, and my heart broke as I witnessed the pain it caused him.

'If that is the case, I had not an inkling of it,' he said.

'If it makes you feel any better, the same thing happened to me, several times,' Lord Devere sympathised.

I had to chuckle.

'But he always found me right when I needed him,' I said, then added, 'Is there any reason for you to suspect foul play?'

'No.'

'Was Miss Koriche concerned about anything or anyone?' I went on.

'Not that I know of.' Levi frowned. 'Only Taylor.'

'Mr Taylor may be an exploiter of ancient relics and desecrator of ancient structures,' I said, 'but an abductor?' The idea was a little far-fetched. 'I feel sure Miss Koriche will return of her own accord before too long.'

Levi reached into his coat and pulled from it a scarf. 'She left this behind. I was hoping that you might . . .'

'Oh no.' I flatly refused to read the psychic imprint. 'If you want to pry, then you do it.'

'The truth is, I am afraid that perhaps I am the reason Ajalae has vanished,' Levi said softly. 'But what if she is in some sort of trouble?'

'Then that would be her affair, perhaps yours, but definitely not mine.'

'I see.' He was clearly disappointed but did not push the issue. 'Have a good trip,' he said, and left before I could respond.

'I could possibly have handled that better,' I commented.

'It seems that you are destined to aggravate every man in your life this week.' Lord Devere forced a smile as he locked down his trunk.

I thought it best to sidestep my husband's disapproval, just as I had been doing ever since I'd decided to appeal our banishment from Persia. 'Hopefully I shall fare better with the Shah.'

'We can but hope.'

REVELATION 5

THE KING OF PERSIA

As Consul at Basra, Mr Taylor was able to contact the consul in
Baghdad, who secured us an appointment with the Shah and an
extension to our one-week departure deadline in order to allow us time
to make the trip to Baghdad for our audience. Now, on the day of our
appointment, Mr Taylor was giving us some advice regarding the Shah
over afternoon tea at the English consulate.

'To the people of Persia, the Shah is the Shahinshah or the King of
Kings. He is the Shadow of God and the Centre of the Universe —
hence, there is no written check upon the royal prerogative. That
which is approved by the king becomes a virtue, and to seek opposite
counsel is to sign your own death warrant. Such is the Shah's divinity
that he never attends state dinners or eats with his subjects. The
attitude of even his most senior ministers is one of complete homage
and adulation. "May I be your sacrifice, Asylum of the Universe" is the
common address adopted by all the Shah's subjects. There is no one to
tell him the truth or to give him unbiased counsel. Foreign ministers
are probably the only source from which he learns facts as they are, or
receives unvarnished advice. Shah Nasr ed-Din is also fond of cats and
practical jokes.' Taylor completed his assessment of the man we were
about to meet.

'Wonderful!' said Lord Devere. 'King and court jester.'

'In the most majestic fashion, of course,' Taylor replied.

'And how should I address the Shah?' I queried. 'Will he speak with
a woman?'

'Oh yes,' Taylor assured me. 'I made the request for an audience in your name. As a foreigner, you may address the Shah as you would our own queen: your Majesty, your Highness and so forth.'

I was feeling a little nervous about the audience now, but not as much as Cingar seemed to be. Clearly he was not comfortable in the moderately lavish surroundings of the consulate, so how on Earth was he going to cope with the court of the King of Persia?

In truth, when we arrived, we were all humbled by the extravagance of the Persian court. And this was not even the main palace of Persia; the Shah's chief abode was in the far northern city of Tehran. Fortunately for us, his Majesty was currently visiting Baghdad on business, no doubt meeting with foreign officials regarding the current dispute in Herat.

There were guards at every gate and doorway, armed to the hilt. I could see that another of the Shah's names, 'Monarch of armies numerous as the stars', was no understatement, although I was aware that Persia had no sea fleet to speak of.

An official met us outside the Shah's room of court, where we were told that the Shah was expecting us and if we would just wait where we were, we would be led through for our audience after we had been announced.

'No going back now.' My husband looked to me and I could tell that he had finally relinquished his grudge against my scheme. 'Be great, Mrs Devere.'

I smiled, grateful for his show of support. 'Always.'

Cingar, behind us, whispered, 'I think I need to pee.'

'I fear you shall just have to wait,' I said, and nodded towards the Shah's official, who had returned to fetch us.

'This way, please.' He led us into the room of court.

There were many officials and court advisers in the Shah's audience chamber, and I sensed that the presence of a woman, not to mention my flaming red hair and the huge hooped skirt of my dress, was the cause of the hushed whispers of amusement all around us as we were brought before his Highness.

The Shah was not at all as I had expected. I had imagined a fat, aging man dressed in lavish silk robes and wearing a turban. But Shah Nasr ed-Din was a young, trim and impeccably stylish fellow. His dark hair was very short and his beard was slight and neatly trimmed, thus making his thick moustache all the more prominent, although it too was immaculately groomed. He wore a finely tailored Western-style suit with a short waisted jacket, which fitted his slim form very well indeed. No turban, just a small black brimless hat. He sat in a large, comfortable throne with his legs crossed, a position that showed off his brilliant white socks and fine black leather shoes.

We bowed to the Shah and he nodded in return.

'Lord and Lady Suffolk, Mr Taylor and ... friend ...' The Shah eyed Cingar, curious as to why the gypsy was with our party. 'I am informed that you come bearing a rare gift for me, in exchange for the continuation of your excavation permit.'

'That is correct, your Majesty.' I motioned to Cingar, but was not given a chance to say more as his Highness fell into stitches.

'This is a joke, surely?' he chuckled, looking about at his advisers, trying to figure out which of them had planned it.

'No, your Majesty,' I said politely.

'My dear Lady Suffolk,' he wiped a tear from his eye, 'you have brought me a gypsy. Do you not know that my kingdom is already overrun with them?'

'Not just any gypsy, your Majesty.' I had to speak up, as the members of the court had dared to share in their monarch's amusement. 'I have brought you the finest violinist in Europe, Cingar Choron.'

His Majesty stopped laughing abruptly and so did all in his court. 'Not the infamous Cingar Choron!' he exclaimed. 'The man who was nearly executed by the Duc de Guise for enchanting the Duchess de Guise with his performance?'

'The very one.' I was delighted, and Cingar appeared flattered that his reputation had spread so far.

'The same Cingar Choron who was rescued from his fate by a mysterious lady swordsman, who bested the duke's finest in a duel?' the Shah went on.

Cingar, caught up in the excitement of the moment, pointed to me and announced, 'Your Majesty is doubly blessed, for before you stands my saviour.' Then, seeing how I cringed, he figured that the information might have been better left unsaid. 'Sorry,' he squeaked.

'You are the woman that de Guise called the Lady du Luc?' The Shah looked most impressed.

'I am she,' I admitted shyly. 'Where on Earth did your Majesty hear of that tale?'

'Why, from de Guise himself,' he enlightened me. 'I have travelled extensively through Europe and was a guest of the duke for a time. Indeed,' he clapped his hands together, delighted, 'I recall thinking that the duke was telling tall tales, but here you both are! To meet real legends in their lifetime is a rare treat. You must demonstrate your skill for us.'

'It will be my honour.' Cingar bowed proudly, but the Shah frowned.

'I was referring to the Lady du Lac.'

My heart jumped into my throat. 'My skill, your Majesty?'

'With a sword,' he prompted.

Oh no, I thought and glanced at my husband for suggestions. I had no sword skill without Albray. I still wore his stone beneath my glove, but I would not dare summon the knight without my husband's consent. Lord Devere ever so slightly shook his head.

'Your Majesty, I could not possibly oblige you in this clothing.' I offered up the first and most obvious objection I could think of — Victorian attire was even worse than the dress that had nearly cost me the duel against de Guise's man twenty years ago.

'I feel sure that we can find you something suitable to wear,' the Shah offered kindly. 'And a few hours to limber up.'

'Your Highness, please.' My husband appealed on my behalf, as I was getting nowhere with discouraging the Shah. 'That was twenty years ago; my wife no longer has the form for such a challenge.'

I placed my hands on my hips, insulted. 'Oh really?' My reaction scored a laugh from the royal audience; if it was a show the Shah wanted in return for our permit, I thought, then a show I would give him. 'I have survived childbirth four times over and you think that I am not up to *this* challenge?'

'Dear woman, be reasonable.' My lord turned to appease me, realising his objection might have been hurtful to me. Yet when he saw how amused all in the court were by our little dispute, he guessed what I was doing.

The essence of the daring young woman who had risked all for her venture twenty years ago suddenly filled me with fresh nerve. 'I shall be happy to oblige his Majesty,' I said, and bowed to the Shah, who looked very pleased. Then I turned back to my husband. 'And I shall be *great*.'

My husband's well wishes came back to haunt him. 'And I shall be jealous,' he said quietly, knowing that in this situation he really had no option but to tolerate what must be done.

'Arrange it,' the Shah decreed and his subjects snapped to it.

'Follow me, please.' Our appointed official returned to escort me to my change of clothes and a practice area.

In comparison with the women of the Persian court that I had seen so far, including the Shah's mother and sister, the males were, in the main, remarkably slender, and so my suit of men's clothes fitted me very well. Quite frankly, I looked frightfully smart in the dark trousers, fitted vest and long white shirt, which I left hanging loose to my mid-thigh for modesty's sake. I slung my sword belt over the top; sitting on my hips, it kept the body of the shirt in check. The black boots that had been supplied for me were shorter than those the Duc de Guise had given me, coming to below the knee, but their soft leather made me feel as if I had been wearing them for the last ten years.

As I had been left alone to change, I thought this the perfect opportunity to summon Albray. I clutched his ringstone in the bare palm of my left hand and said his name out loud three times over.

Lady Suffolk, he said in greeting as he materialised, his appearance unaltered by the years we had been out of contact.

I had missed the company and counsel of my dear Albray, and his growing smile told me he knew it too — we were psychically linked whenever I was wearing the ringstone next to my bare skin.

'I am sorry to drag you back into my world, dear friend, but I seem to have got myself into a spot of bother.'

Yes indeed, Albray agreed. I knew he would have been following everything that had transpired in my life since I had started wearing the ringstone again. *Still, I am not sure whether we are in deeper trouble with the Shah's swordsman or your husband.*

I laughed at his summation of the situation. Albray was still the dashing, dark, mischievous knight I had known as a young woman, and his smile was as warm and friendly as my memory served. 'I am hoping that neither will cause us too much bother.'

Very wishful thinking, he said. *But I am certainly game for the contest, if you are.*

'If you are confident of besting the Shah's man despite my aging body, then I can assure you that I will appease Lord Devere.' I gave my old friend a confident wink.

He was wrong, you know, Albray said in all seriousness, *about you not having the form you did twenty years ago. Lady Devere, let me assure you that you are still in great shape!*

I was flattered, but I also recognised this little game that Albray was fond of playing — using the knowledge he obtained via his telepathic link with me to make my husband look bad. 'A little focus, sir, if you please,' I said, sounding discouraging but unable to wipe the smile from my face. I was so glad to have my knight back, if only for this brief reunion.

To the arena! he exclaimed boldly.

'You are aware that we have been awarded some time to practise beforehand?' I pulled on a set of black leather gloves.

I do not see the need myself, he said, cocky as always.

'The practice is for my benefit.'

I can assure you, my lady, that your body is safe with me.

He was flirting again and I pretended not to notice, although I knew he knew that I found his game amusing. He also knew that to me it was only a game. I loved Devere and none would ever rival him in my heart. 'Humour me?' I asked.

Albray bowed deeply. *I am at your service, O Daughter of Isis.*

He was teasing, as he knew I hated being addressed thus.

'Do not start with that Grail Princess homage rubbish, or I shall start calling you the Shining One, or do you prefer the Great Over Light, Albe-Ra?'

I had discovered a lot about my knight in the wake of our last adventure. He had always been reluctant to talk about his Crusading life with me, but from my dear sister-in-law's journal of that time, I had learned that he had been something of a double agent, operating within the Sion knighthood on behalf of another secret order operating within the Holy Lands, known as the Melchi. More than just knights, the Melchi were also priests of a holy order. To this day the Melchi operated still in the Near East, protecting the ancient mysteries of the gods and the places and treasures left on Earth by them. Even now, six hundred years after Albray's demise, every member of this warrior priesthood could recite for you the legend of Albe-Ra.

So now you know, he conceded, his smile losing some of its cheer, for his short but eventful life had caused him eternal grief. He had pledged his soul to the service of the Ladies of the Elohim in order to save a woman he loved.

'What I know is that you know a lot more than you have been willing to disclose in the past,' I replied, and he appeared wary of where this conversation was heading. 'Tell me about the Dragon Queens, Albray.'

He seemed amused by my predictability.

The Dragon Queen, Elf Queen, Fairy Queen and so on is the female of the Grail line who is strongest in the blood at any given period of history.

'I have learned that Sama-El was supposed to have fathered all the Dragon Queens.'

I honestly know nothing of that, but it is said that the Grail bloodline has been reintroduced into our line and strengthened through the ages. My knight raised both brows and put on a cheeky expression. *Which would seem to indicate that at least one of the ancient gods is still taking an interest in the daughters of men, and would also explain many of those immaculate conception tales.*

'And what does it mean to be one of the Dragon Queens, I wonder?' I looked to Albray, seeking an insight, but he only shook his head.

'That is a secret sacred to your gender, and thus I could not say.'

As it seemed I had extracted all the information I was going to get out of Albray on the topic, I rang the bell to let my appointed guide know that I was ready for my practice session.

64

'Your gentlemen friends await you in the armoury hall,' my guide informed me. 'If you will follow me.'

The walls of the huge armoury chamber were a veritable smorgasbord of weaponry, and in the centre of the huge space two marble steps descended to a large circular practice area.

Very inspiring, Albray commented as we beheld the selection of killing utensils.

'The Shah has asked after your sword preference for this afternoon, my lady. What should I tell him?' the official inquired.

I looked to Albray as I had not a clue.

The Shah's choice, Albray said with indifferent confidence.

I relayed the response to the Shah's official, and he bowed. 'Very good.' He left us to report to the Shah.

'You are full of surprises, Lady Suffolk,' Taylor commented, clearly thinking I was tempting fate with my resolve — as I probably was.

'Oh yes,' my husband agreed, his gaze planted firmly upon the ghost at my side. 'I do not know what possesses her at times.'

I gave a weak smile to acknowledge my lord's attempt at humour.

Lord Devere, Albray greeted his old rival with exaggerated warmth, *what a joy it is to see you again.*

My lord acknowledged the ghost with a slight nod, knowing it was best that nobody become aware of my secret.

On our last adventure, Cingar had witnessed Albray possess the body of my sister-in-law in order that she may fight her way into the favour of a formidable foe. However, the gypsy could not see the phantom knight. Cingar did not have any psychic talent, despite the long line of female clairvoyants from which he had sprung; his talents were all physical in nature. Whether or not Cingar suspected that Albe-Ra was the force behind my own skill with a sword, he never said.

'I am thrilled that I shall get to witness your victory this time around,' Cingar said cheerily. My husband and Mr Taylor gave him a stern look of disdain. 'Well, last time I was rotting in prison!' he said defensively.

I gather you do not mind if I borrow your wife's body for the afternoon? Albray could not resist pushing his luck with my lord.

Do I have a choice? my husband responded, his jaw clenching. *That is, if I still want my wife alive this evening?*

I had to admit I was savouring seeing my husband so jealous; it had been a long time since he'd had any cause to be.

At your leave, my lady. After a deep breath I nodded and the spirit of the knight stepped into my physical form.

I tried to hide how pleasurable it was to be suddenly filled with masculine strength and valour, but felt sure that my own final expression probably betrayed my delight. Yet, it was rather perturbing to lose control of my body. The second Albray seized control of me, he made for the wall of weapons and selected two identical Saracen swords, whose huge curved blades he began to whirl around my body with death-defying speed and precision.

'And you thought she wasn't up to the task!' Cingar nudged Lord Devere, but was shamed to silence by the look he received in return.

'You are good with a sword, Devere,' Albray challenged my husband via my vessel. 'Or should I call you Danior Terkari?'

'Hah!' Cingar gave a laugh. 'I'd forgotten all about that charade.'

'I saw you fight off several bandits at once that night,' Albray recalled.

'My wedding celebration,' Cingar said, having some recollection of the events of which Albray spoke. 'That was one hell of a night, was it not?'

But Albray had his sights locked on Lord Devere, awaiting a response. 'Pick a weapon, my lord,' he baited.

Must you pick a fight with my husband? I demanded.

I warrant that he is the best swordsman here, but if it will make you feel better, I won't be so obvious about it, Albray thought back to me.

'All of you, pick a weapon.' Albray extended his challenge to the other two men present.

'I could never fight my lady,' Cingar said and took a seat.

'What about you, Mr Taylor?' Albray put it to him directly.

'Far be it from me to beat up on another man's wife,' Taylor said, and stepped backwards to take a seat on the stair alongside Cingar.

Albray looked to my husband.

'I guess that leaves me to put you through your paces,' Lord Devere said, glaring at Albray through my eyes.

'Shall we dance?' Albray split my mouth into a grin of invitation as he crossed the two sword blades at my chest.

'An engagement that is long overdue.' Lord Devere snatched up two medium-sized broadswords and advanced to engage the knight. In a great clash of metal my workout began.

'What an interesting relationship these two have,' Taylor commented to Cingar as they watched the fight. 'If I did not know better, I would honestly think they were trying to kill each other.'

''Tis a bit more vigorous than expected, I must say.' Cingar cringed with every resounding clang of metal on metal. 'Best not slay her before she gets to the Shah's competition,' he suggested to Lord Devere.

'Nonsense, I have not even broken a sweat yet,' Albray assured the gypsy on my behalf, abruptly breaking a deadlock of swords by thrusting Lord Devere backwards. 'Come on, Devere, put your back into it.'

Stop baiting him, I said; it was unnerving being on the receiving end of my husband's aggression.

After half an hour of sparring, Albray finished toying with my husband. Disarming him of both swords in one swift motion, he called, 'Next!'

Frankly I did not think my husband cared about his defeat; he was absolutely exhausted. Once Albray had been my lover's older rival; now the ghost was younger in valour than my lord.

'Mighty fine show!' Taylor gave us a standing ovation, as did Cingar, and Albray bowed graciously to accept the applause. 'You must be proud?' The diplomat placed a hand on my lord's shoulder.

'Every man's dream,' my husband replied sarcastically as he took a seat to catch his breath. After a moment he looked to Albray and I had never seen his expression so dark. *I want you out of her body the second this duel is done*, he ordered.

The doors to the armoury opened and the Shah's official, accompanied by several armed guards, announced, 'It is time.'

'The Shah need have no fear of me forfeiting this duel, thus there is really no need for such a large escort,' I said, replacing the swords on the wall. 'On the contrary, I am quite looking forward to it.'

I could not help but notice how concerned the Shah's man appeared about my enthusiasm as I approached to accompany him to the field of combat. But all he said was, 'The Shah is also greatly looking forward to it,' and led me through the doors of the armoury.

The guards waited for my associates to follow me into the corridor before falling in behind our party.

The Shah had chosen a large paved courtyard in which to stage the display, as it corresponded with the location that de Guise had chosen for my duel. As it was mid-afternoon, a good part of the open area was shaded.

Along the walls of all four of the courtyard's lower-level pillared walkways stood armed guards. The Shah was seated, with his minions, on a shaded balcony on the second level of the palace that overlooked the courtyard. A stairway led from within one of the lower pillared walkways to the balcony, where, we were informed, his Majesty had provided seats for my associates.

My husband looked my way as he was led from the field. *Deliver her safe and sound, Albray.*

Have I ever failed to do so? the knight responded.

Lord Devere forced a smile as he considered Albray's boast; the fact was that the knight had saved both our lives on more than one occasion.

The design of the courtyard floor was not unlike that in the armoury — several steps led down to a central circular platform, in the middle of which I positioned myself. I bowed to the Shah and awaited the appearance of my challenger.

Once my associates were seated, the Shah waved his hand and six warriors, all but their eyes masked in black, filed into the courtyard and took up position around me in a circle.

Assassins, Albray observed for my benefit.

To the best of my understanding, the assassins were affiliated with the Melchi who had raised and trained Albray. *Should I be worried?*

Heavens, no, Albray replied. *They are all sporting my weapon of choice.*

Predictably the Shah had chosen the local weapon, and I was

presented with two Saracen swords akin to those I had just been wielding in the armoury.

I heard my husband's voice raised in concern. 'Is this one of the Shah's famous practical jokes? At the court of de Guise, my lady was required to best only one swordsman!'

'Come, come, my Lord Suffolk, this is only a friendly demonstration, not a duel to the death,' the Shah emphasised.

Clearly, something in his tone was not very reassuring to my lord.

'I was not aware that assassins gave friendly demonstrations,' he retorted.

The Shah served my husband with a look that implied he was being overly dramatic. 'Your wife is not complaining,' he pointed out, as he observed me getting a feel for my weapons. 'These men do not make errors, Lord Suffolk; your wife is far safer sparring with them than a novice, and they are under my specific instructions to engage the lady one at a time.'

As my husband opened his mouth again, no doubt to issue a sharp rejoinder, Taylor discreetly nudged him; a reminder that it was not wise to debate the Shah's motives. 'I never doubted your Majesty's good intentions, of course,' my lord said.

The Shah forced a smile and allowed the incident to pass. He gave a nod in his crier's direction and the servant shouted, 'Begin!'

The onslaught was immediate. I could feel Albray's utter delight; he was truly in his element with a blade in his hands. Still, if I could have closed my eyes until the frenzied assault was over, I would have happily done so. As it was, I felt as if I was riding a thoroughbred stallion over which I had no control; all I could do was hold on for dear life and hope that I was still alive when the creature came to a standstill. Nevertheless, after the first ten minutes had elapsed, I began to feel a little more confident and actually started enjoying the ride and appreciating the fact that Albray was making me look truly accomplished. Some of the locals even started barracking for my cause, including the Shah himself, who had tears of delight flowing down his cheeks. Now he too had a story to add to the legend of the Lady du Lac and the gypsy rogue, which he would take great delight in telling de Guise upon their next meeting.

'Play me my gift, minstrel,' the Shah requested of Cingar without looking at him.

'Right now, your Majesty?' Cingar had trouble dragging his attention from the spectacle I was embroiled in.

'What better time than the present to capture the mood of this moment for posterity?' his Highness confirmed.

Although the challenge made Cingar boggle a moment, he quickly retrieved his instrument from its case and, looking to the event in progress, began to compose.

At first the tune was one of suspense and peril, but as the gypsy observed how well I was faring against the assassins, the theme became bolder and filled with admiration. As the frenzied music began to build, Albray was fuelled anew and all present were stunned when I started adding a few punches and kicks to my repertoire.

'And I thought my wives were a handful,' the Shah said, laughing at my husband's bemused face.

Lord Devere saw the humour in the situation and allowed a smile to melt his stern expression. 'Life is never boring,' he conceded, and the Shah laughed even harder.

Fortunately, Cingar soon realised he was setting the pace of the duel and mellowed his passion a tad. I was a fairly fit woman for thirty-nine years of age, but I had not done anything so physically strenuous in a long time; I was really going to hurt come the morrow.

The Shah gave the nod and his crier yelled, 'Enough!' The assassins immediately ceased their attack and Cingar wound up his composition with one long, inspired stroke of his bow.

The Shah applauded the display and, to the shock of all present, gave me a standing ovation. The court scrambled hurriedly to follow suit. 'You must stay in the palace as my guests tonight,' he told my associates. 'And we shall discuss your permit.'

I'd best be going then, Albray said, complying with my husband's demand to make himself absent from my person as soon as the match was over. Suddenly I felt the full weight of the swords I was holding aloft; the blades dropped to the ground so hard my arms were near wrenched from their sockets. Every muscle in my body began screaming at once and, unable to cope with the onslaught of pain, turned to jelly. I fell to the floor in a faint.

The first sensation I felt on regaining consciousness was that of being buried to the neck. My immediate thought was that I had done something to offend the Shah and he had dreamt up some horrid death for me. A moan escaped my lips as soon as I attempted to move myself, then my eyes parted to behold my husband's smiling face. 'I am not dying?' I assumed, seeing he was at liberty and in good spirits.

'No,' he confirmed, 'but you have seen better days.'

When I laughed all my muscles seized and then I was moaning again. 'I should have listened to you,' I cried. 'It feels as if my entire body is bruised!'

Sorry about that. Albray waved at me from behind my lord. *But we did achieve our goal — the Shah has asked you to dinner.*

'I was under the impression that the Shah never ate with anyone?' I directed the question to Lord Devere, who appeared a little irked by Albray's presence. I had hoped to dismiss my knight after the demonstration and avoid any more unpleasantness, but as I had not been given the opportunity, I sensed that my protector and my husband had had a clash while I was unconscious.

'His Majesty will not eat with us, but,' my husband's smile grew broad once more, 'we have been granted a private audience with the Shah as he wishes to discuss the terms of renewing our permit.'

'Honestly?' The news was such a painkiller that I sat bolt upright and hugged my husband. 'Then what is a little pain?'

As the shock of my victory wore off, my aching limbs squeezed another moan out of me and Lord Devere aided me to resume a horizontal position.

'I am going to tell the Shah that you will not be attending the meeting,' he said. 'Taylor can negotiate the terms of the excavation.'

'No, please,' I said. 'I just need a hot bath.'

'Can that be arranged?' Lord Devere looked to the palace official attending us.

'Without question,' he advised, and departed to see to the request.

'Oh, my lord,' I whispered, upon finally noting how lavish my recovery room was.

'Yes, it seems nothing is too good for a living legend.' I could tell by the look on my husband's face that he was very proud of me.

'Albray is the legend,' I said, looking to my knight and thanking him dearly for his aid. 'I shall try to keep the Lady du Lac in the closet from now on.'

I assure you it was my pleasure entirely, Albray replied. *It is good to keep my skills honed*, he added, so that his prior comment might not be taken the wrong way by my husband. *But if you have no further need of me, I should bid you farewell.*

I did so want to waffle on with thanks and praise of my knight's talents, and tell him how I would miss him and how wonderful it had been catching up, but with my husband right beside me, I knew it would only fuel the rivalry between them. 'Fare thee well, Albray, you have been a dear friend to us both.'

I placed my hand upon my lord's to reassure him as I dismissed the ghost. My reasoning was that if Lord Devere pulled his hand away, then his resentment of Albray ran deep. His hand remained with mine, but I could see he was not sad to see the back of the knight.

'Alone at last,' he sighed, tossing his hat aside to award me a lover's kiss — long, soft and involved.

The Shah's official was heard to clear his throat; upon gaining our full attention he announced, 'My lady's bath is ready.'

'That was quick,' I commented, as my husband aided me to my feet. Placing an arm around me, he walked me over to the official.

'I am sorry,' the official said, 'but my Lord Suffolk should wait here.'

'Please —' I went to address our official by his name and realised that I had yet to learn it.

'You may call me Kazem,' he said, awarding me the use of his first name even though he was obviously an official of some importance, perhaps ranked more highly than I was as a baroness.

'Kazem.' I nodded my head to him respectfully. 'As I am still feeling unwell, I would like my husband to stay with me while I bathe. Could you not make an exception in this case?'

'The Shah instructed that I should grant your every wish,' Kazem said with an obliging smile. 'So if you will both follow me . . .'

Kazem gave us a running commentary on the palace and its treasures on the way to our destination, which was in one of the palace's adjoining buildings, where the living quarters were located. The walk actually did me some good, as I got to stretch my aching muscles.

At a huge set of double doors built in an arched doorframe, Kazem bowed to us. 'I trust that you will find everything you need therein.'

'Thank you, Kazem.' Both Lord Devere and I bowed in return.

Kazem advised that he would return within the hour to show us to dinner, then he departed in the direction of the court.

'Good heavens,' I gasped upon beholding the huge pool of steaming water. It was surrounded by a dozen huge marble pillars that held up a roof that was open to the sky over the huge expanse of water. The floor around the pool was black slate, but the pool itself was lined with white mosaic tiles inset with smaller tiles of black and jade to create beautiful patterns around the rim and on the floor.

'Well, it might be a bit of a tight squeeze, but I think we should both fit,' Lord Devere said cheerfully.

We often bathed together at home; indeed, the bathroom was the only place where we could find the peace to sort out our affairs, both private and professional.

'I had heard that the Persians are very particular about cleanliness, but *wow*,' was all I could say as I began stripping off my layers. There was a heavenly scent coming off the water and I could hardly wait to immerse myself in it.

The sensation of the warm water streaming over my body as I plunged into the depths of the pool was so revitalising that I surfaced to let loose a great sigh of delight. 'I *love* Persia,' I decided in that moment. 'I think we should move here.'

Lord Devere was taking his time undressing and seemed to be finding my frolicking frightfully engrossing. 'Or we could simply build an indoor pool at Suffolk,' he said.

'Splendid idea!' I rolled onto my back to gaze up at the evening sky and my body rose to float on the surface of the pool.

A few seconds later came the splash of my husband joining me in the water.

'Is there any need for this right now?' He had noticed that I was still wearing the gold chain bracelet that held Albray's ringstone.

'Right you are.' I removed it from my wrist and placed it on the side of the pool. 'Now we are truly alone.'

It was not the first time we had made love in a bath, and it would not be the last, but together with the evening we'd spent in Alexandria on our honeymoon, this encounter was among the most blissful and erotic of my life experiences.

'We should think about dressing before Kazem returns,' Lord Devere commented, and although I knew he was right, I felt we would be hard-pressed to move from where we had settled into a reclining position together on the steps leading out of the water.

It was one of those moments when I wanted to freeze time and just stay put for a couple of days, but my little glimpse of Nirvana was brought to an abrupt end when the giggles of many women were heard close by.

Lord Devere got the fright of his life when he spotted the large gathering of women who had entered via a door at the opposite end of the bathing room to where we had been shown in. He slid further into the pool and hugged me tighter to cover himself.

After several confusing moments of conversation in several different languages, I finally hit on Italian, which one of the younger women present understood. She advised me that we were in the bathing quarters of the Shah's harem.

'Wonderful.' Lord Devere smiled graciously as one of the women passed him a robe, her gaze averted. 'Caught swimming naked in the Shah's harem — that ought to go down well with his Highness.'

'No wonder Kazem didn't want to sanction your presence here. I understand the Shah does not allow any men to enter his harem — still intact, that is.' I laughed at my husband's predicament.

A young woman handed me a robe also and explained, 'We were sent to aid my lady to dress.'

'Well then, I should really depart and leave you to it.' Lord Devere pulled on his trousers under his wet robe, then removed the dripping

74

item to a mixed reaction from the female audience; the older women gasped in horror whilst the younger ones giggled and cheered. Feeling halfway decent, Lord Devere gathered together the rest of his clothes and made a hasty departure, aided by Kazem, who had arrived just in time.

'A thousand apologies, Lord Devere,' the official said, suppressing his amusement. 'I meant to be here before his Excellency's ladies arrived.'

'Better late than never, Kazem.' Lord Devere moved quickly to join the official, as several of the older women of the harem were shouting and shaking their fists at him. Kazeem spoke to them sharply, presumably informing them that my lord was there with the Shah's permission, for they fell silent and allowed the men to leave the room peacefully.

For my part, I could not stop giggling. I was feeling very relaxed after my swim and other recreational activities, not to mention utterly elated by the knowledge that I was well on my way to achieving my goal. Now there was a chance my son would speak to me upon my return to the excavation site. I wondered if he had been reunited with his Miss Koriche yet.

As I pondered these questions, I was pushed and prodded into my attire. Although my clothes were very different from the local fashion, it was clear that the women of the harem knew what they were doing. As they delighted in styling and playing with my long auburn locks, I noted that some of them were having a good giggle about something. I asked Cienna — the young woman who spoke Italian — what the joke was.

'They are saying that it must be very exhausting having to attend to a husband all by yourself,' she explained. 'But they consider that your husband is rather beautiful and must be a pleasure to indulge.'

I smiled. 'That he is,' I said proudly. 'I could not bear to share him with another woman.'

Cienna conveyed my thoughts to the women tending me, and they responded perplexedly. 'But how do you ever manage to get any time to yourself to study or learn a language, create great art, or perfect your skill with a musical instrument?'

In that moment I suddenly realised what was so attractive about harem life — it was the best place for a woman in Persia to receive an education, without the distraction of accommodating a husband and with few or no children to worry about.

'I read a lot,' I informed them, 'and I have travelled a good deal.'

A sigh slipped from Cienna's mouth. 'I travelled too when I was young, I do miss that. But I am safe within these walls and I have much to learn here. I would not wish to be at liberty again.'

I knew instinctively that she'd been abused in the past and thus was happy to be hidden away beyond the clutches of all men; indeed, her aura confirmed my suspicion for she had residual muddy patches over her root and heart chakras. The other light centres of her subtle body were very beautiful, however, and I felt that Cienna would soon completely heal herself of past injury.

The light-bodies of many of the other women here were much worse; one in particular did not appear at all happy with her isolated life. She stood in the doorway apart from everyone else, reading a book. Her light-body showed large muddy patches engulfing just about all of her light centres; she was truly suffering.

Cienna saw my curiosity. 'That is my older sister, Raineath,' she explained. 'We were brought to the Shah's harem at the same time. She claims she would rather be dead than give herself to the Shah, and has shamed herself badly for telling our Supreme Sovereign so, right to his face. Thankfully his Merciful Highness showed her compassion and spared her life.'

Raineath overheard her sister's comment and spat on the floor. 'He took away the only thing I love! I watched my reason for being crushed before my eyes!'

My first horrid guess was that Raineath was referring to a lover or a child.

'She is talking about her instrument,' Cienna said.

'How am I expected to exist without a means to express myself?' Raineath asked me.

'You brought it on yourself, Raineath,' Cienna said. 'You should not have offended our Lord and Master.'

One of the older women demanded silence from both the girls, and instructed Cienna to tell me that they had finished with my hair. I was ready to attend my dinner engagement with the Shah.

Kazem led me to the huge double doors of the court dining room, where two male attendants, dressed in silken finery, bowed to me.

'The guest of honour, Baroness of Suffolk, Lady Granville-Devere,' the Shah's crier announced and the entire court was upstanding as I entered.

I stood in the doorway a second, absolutely speechless.

'No, you are not dreaming.'

A hand slipped into mine and I turned to see Lord Devere. I squeezed his hand tightly to let him know that I was glad of his presence.

'My lady.' He raised my hand to his lips and kissed it. 'I am here to lead you to our private function,' he whispered in my ear, so that I might hear him over the blessings that the court were verbally bestowing upon us. 'It seems we are not eating with the court.'

'Are we not?' I smiled and nodded to the courtiers as we walked down the red Persian carpet in the centre of the room towards another set of double doors that were smaller and more elaborate than the first.

This room was far more lavish and intimate. The Shah was seated at the head of a low-lying table, around which were placed many large cushions for lounging on. There was food aplenty laid out on the table and many attendants standing around the periphery of the room, waiting to fill a glass or remove an empty plate. The Shah was speaking with Mr Taylor and Cingar, who were seated alongside each other on one side of the table. Both men rose as I entered, but the Shah, being a living god, remained seated. Lord Devere and I bowed to his Majesty, who motioned us to rise and approach.

'Please, sit by me, Lady Suffolk,' he said graciously. 'I believe you are a fascinating person.'

'I am honoured, your Highness.'

With some awkwardness, thanks to the huge hooped skirt of my dress, I seated myself next to the Shah in a great puff of fabric. Oh how I wished to be wearing my male attire, or at least one of the slimmer-cut dresses of my youth — I felt that current fashions were a frightful bore for the females of Europe.

The Shah kept the conversation light until his guests had finished eating. He talked about his country and about his various schemes to modernise the cities. He spoke to Taylor about several other excavations taking place in his country at present. He remarked on this afternoon's display and asked after my wellbeing.

'The bath was extremely rejuvenating, thank you, your Majesty. I felt very spoilt by the opulent surroundings.' In my mind's eye I was dwelling on the afternoon's intimacy with my lord. 'I cannot imagine I shall ever have a bath so splendid as that I enjoyed today.'

The Shah was pleased by my praise of his hospitality and he looked to my husband. 'I hear that you are a very good swimmer, Lord Suffolk?'

The query nearly made my husband choke on his wine. 'I indulge whenever I can, your Majesty,' he granted, without confirming or denying what the Shah had obviously been told.

His Highness found the comeback amusing. 'As do I,' he said, chuckling. Then his manner shifted, indicating that the social niceties were coming to an end and it was time for business. 'So,' he said, 'as I am very pleased with your gift of the minstrel, I am willing to extend your permit until such time as a war between our two countries is an actuality.'

'Hopefully, that shall never be the case,' Taylor commented.

I felt he was probing the Shah for his thoughts on the issue, for this was the first time he'd even broached the subject of Herat. The Shah, however, made no further comment that hinted at his intention in that regard.

I had other concerns. The way his Majesty had phrased his proposal, it sounded as though he had mistaken our intent entirely.

'I am pleased that your Majesty was impressed by Mr Choron's performance,' I said. 'Perhaps he could play again for you before we leave.'

Now the Shah looked perplexed. 'You are taking your gift home with you?'

'The gift was the performance, not the performer, your Highness. I thought I had made that clear. Mr Choron is my dear friend; I cannot give what I do not possess.'

'But what point is there to a gift of a musical composition if there is no minstrel at my court to play it?' The Shah was very reasonable about the misunderstanding. 'I was hoping to stage a complete re-enactment for de Guise next time he visits.'

'I could teach one of your musicians the piece,' Cingar suggested. 'I could stay with your Majesty for as long as my friends remain at the excavation site.'

'There is no one accomplished enough on the violin whom you could instruct,' the Shah stated.

My mind flew to Raineath. 'Is there not a woman in your harem who plays an instrument?' I queried.

The Shah appeared most displeased by the suggestion. '*That woman* is not a possibility. She will never lay a hand on a violin again so long as I live; that is her punishment for insulting her king.'

I looked to Cingar, who was immediately empathetic towards the woman in question. 'Why not just kill her?' he said. Obviously the gypsy felt death would be preferable to a life without music.

'She wants to die,' the Shah explained.

It was clear Cingar was about to say something we were all going to regret, but thankfully Lord Devere jumped in. 'If you do not mind me saying so, your Highness, as a husband and father myself, it seems a frightful waste to be paying for the maintenance of a woman who serves no purpose to your Highness whatsoever.'

I sensed that my husband was praying he had not caused greater insult than Cingar might have, but the Shah's face melted to a smile once more.

'You make a good argument, Lord Suffolk.' The Shah paused, seeming to be seeing things in a new light. 'Perhaps if I show great mercy and award this woman the opportunity to better herself, her attitude might improve.'

I felt the Shah had a secret soft spot for Raineath, for when he spoke of her the lower light centres of his subtle body flared. It was not love, however, for his heart centre remained unaffected.

'The way I see it, your Majesty, better she is a useful addition to your court than a useless overhead.' Lord Devere was reasoning like a local now.

'And Raineath is very pleasing on the eye, your Highness,' I added. 'I feel sure the Duc de Guise would be envious of your musician, whereas I greatly doubt he would be pleased to see Cingar again.'

'Ah yes, Mr Choron's infamous enchantment of women.' The Shah had forgotten about that little detail. 'Perhaps it is not wise to let such a man anywhere near my harem.'

Cingar spoke up in his own defence. 'That was twenty years ago, before a very happy marriage, your Highness. That legend died the day I wed my wife.'

'But I understand your wife is now deceased?' the Shah queried.

'Not to me, your Majesty,' Cingar replied, with such heartfelt sincerity that it caused his voice to tremble.

'Perhaps your Highness could have the tuition sessions supervised?' I suggested.

'Oh, I shall.' The Shah smiled to let me know we had reached an arrangement. 'Mr Choron will be treated as my guest until such time as circumstances bring our arrangement to a close. At which time I will see him safely returned to you, for the journey home.'

CURSE OF THE RINGSTONE

'In the Gospel of Witches, it is said that to find a stone with a hole in it is a special sign of the favour of Diana. A round stone, be it great or small, is a good sign, but it should never be given away, because the receiver will then get the good luck and some disaster will befall the giver.'

I was explaining the legend to my husband because, due to my own absent-mindedness, I had lost my own precious ringstone and my connection to Albray and to Cingar's great-grandmother, Chiara. I had realised my grave oversight as Lord Devere and myself were being escorted to our private rooms after dinner. I immediately informed Kazem about the missing item and he kindly accompanied us back to the bathing area to look for my missing treasure, but my ringstone was no longer where I had left it.

I had tried laying my hand on the spot by the pool where I had left the stone, to see if I could perceive who had picked it up, but the bath saw a lot of traffic every day and I could not pinpoint the claimant in the sea of faces that I descried.

'The piece would look like a mere river pebble to anyone else, but for me it holds great sentimental value,' I told Kazem, who said he would make enquiries to see if anyone had found my keepsake.

'But the Gospel of Witches does not state whether bad luck will befall a person who loses such a stone, as opposed to someone who makes a gift of the item,' my husband said in the privacy of our room, trying to reason with me. He could see I was fretting terribly.

'I feel that as long as the ring changes hands, the curse will apply.'

'I thought that you created your own reality, Mrs Devere? It is not like you to give power to some ancient superstition.'

'To accept and believe in the magic, one must also believe in the curse,' I said. 'Polarity demands it.'

'But you cannot be cursed with bad luck,' he told me confidently. 'You just negotiated a dream deal with the Shah of Persia.'

'That was before I was aware that the stone had gone missing!'

'So it is all downhill from here then,' he mocked gently.

'You fell victim to the curse yourself the day we met and I dropped the stone. Remember? You picked it up for me, although I insisted it would bring you bad luck, and then look at the hell I dragged you through after that!'

My lord frowned, seeing my reasoning, but still disagreeing. 'What you put me through was my own damned fault for lying to you; it had nothing to do with any curse!'

'But you might have got away with the deception had your luck been better,' I countered.

Lord Devere was becoming rather exasperated by my argument, and my concern for the loss of the ring was arousing his jealous streak. 'It is not as though you have lost all your psychic talent,' he said. 'You have only lost Albray's services, and if you intend to keep the Lady du Lac in the closet then I do not see what the problem is.'

'You're happy about this, aren't you? I should never have taken it off.' For a moment, in my frustrated state, I even suspected my lord might have arranged for the stone to go missing.

'I know what you are implying,' Lord Devere cautioned. 'And although it is true that I would not be sad to see the back of your ghostly friend, I would never purposely destroy your peace of mind in this fashion. If I knew where the stone was right now, believe me, I would tell you.'

My lord did hate it when we were at odds. I reined in my frustration and explained what my real concern was.

'If Albray's curse is ever to be lifted by one of my descendants as predicted, I need to find that stone. For without it, how will one of our great-great-granddaughters ever be able to contact Albray? Let alone help him!'

'Can you not summon him to another stone?' Lord Devere suggested.

'I do not know,' I admitted. 'I would have to find such a stone again ... it was only by the luck of the Goddess that I found the first one!' I began to pace, hating myself for jeopardising Albray's one hope of future happiness, after all he had done for me. 'I should have left it in its box at home. If I had, it would be safe now. And what if whoever found the stone recognises it for the tool it really is?' This was the most horrifying prospect of all. 'Anyone versed in the Craft would immediately suspect its value.'

Lord Devere had heard enough. 'Now you are getting carried away — witchcraft is hardly all the rage here in the heart of Islam. I feel sure Kazem will find the stone and return it to you in the morning.'

My husband stripped off his boots and collapsed onto the bed.

'I wish I shared your optimism,' I said, and continued my aimless wandering back and forth, albeit at a slower pace. As much as I wished Lord Devere to be right in this case, my psychic premonition told me that the recovery of my treasure was not going to be so simple.

I barely slept that night, or for several nights after. I was not the kind of woman to pine, but the thought of Albray lost forever in the Netherworld, his quest unrealised, his soul unable to reincarnate, kept causing my eyes to well with tears.

It was with a heavy heart that I travelled back down the Euphrates towards the Mound of Pitch. Kazem had ordered the palace searched from top to bottom and anyone questioned who might have come in contact with my lost stone, but no one had seen it.

'I do hate to see you so depressed.' Lord Devere offered me a cup of water. 'Especially over another man.'

My sights were transfixed on the far bank of the river, where some children were frolicking in the water. I was thinking about my own children and how much I adored them. Albray had never had children or known the bliss of married life, and in all likelihood now he never would.

'Mrs Devere?' My husband nudged my shoulder with his.

I looked to him. 'Sorry, did you say something?'

He rolled his eyes and placed the cup of water in my hand. 'This is so unlike you. Can you not trust that your charm was lost for a good reason? I mean, you have always had the luck of the Goddess with you, why should now prove any different? Perhaps there is someone else out there who needs Albray's help more than you do? Or perhaps this is the cosmos's way of telling you that you should be utilising your own skills and not relying on outside forces to solve your problems for you?'

'Is that what you think?' I took offence, although part of me knew this was only to resist accepting that my lord might be right. 'I would not have lasted two seconds against those swordsmen without Albray's aid.'

'I know that.' Lord Devere was being very patient with me. 'What I am saying is that if you did not have the Albray option, you would have figured out a way to sweet-talk the Shah and get what you wanted, in the same manner you have succeeded for the past twenty years without any help from your ghosts.'

'Well, I do not have the choice any more.' I breathed a huge sigh to prevent my tears welling anew. 'And I have failed a dear friend.' That was what really hurt.

'You cannot say that for sure.' My husband placed a hand on mine. 'You may still be able to re-establish contact with the knight via another stone. Why be defeated before you have exhausted every avenue?'

Now he really was right and I hung my head, ashamed of my pessimistic attitude. 'I am just so remorseful,' I confessed. My heart was so heavy that it felt as if it had dropped into oblivion and left a gaping hole in my chest.

'I know you are,' he sympathised. 'And I was the one who asked you to take off the charm, so how do you think I feel?' I knew he was not mocking me. Although Albray was not his favourite soul, I could tell Lord Devere truly felt bad about what had happened. 'Yet you only feel remorse because you choose to react that way to this situation,' he continued, quoting my own philosophy back to me. 'You could just as easily choose to know that somehow everything will turn out for the best, and that, even if there is a curse, it will only have as much power over you as you choose to give it.'

'You are right,' I conceded, sniffling back my emotion and breathing another great sigh to release the lump of guilt that had been squatting in my chest for days. 'Anything is possible if I will just allow it to be.'

'That's the spirit! No pun intended.' He tapped my water cup, urging me to drink before I got dehydrated.

I took a sip and continued with the attempt to turn around my negative state of mind. 'I have been up against worse than a curse in the past. I will find Albray again, one way or another,' I said, feeling decidedly more optimistic.

'I so look forward to that,' my lord replied.

I gave him a look that implied I was well aware he was being sarcastic.

'No, truly,' he insisted. 'Then I might be able to get you to think of something else.'

'I am sorry.' I decided it was high time I changed the subject. 'I wonder how much progress Levi has made in our absence.'

'You refer to the dig site, I gather?' My husband wore a cheeky smile, unable to hide his pride that his son was so attractive to women.

'I have been wondering about his progress with Miss Koriche too,' I admitted. 'I hope it is not her intention to break his heart.'

'I think it rather impressive that Levi could seduce such a woman at all,' my husband said. 'Eastern women are far more chaste than the women of Europe —'

Lord Devere bit his tongue as he noticed the expression on my face. 'Is that right?' I said, pretending to find the comment insulting.

'What I meant to say was ...' He had a think about it and realised there was no fixing the statement. 'Miss Koriche is just so closed to most people, and yet with Levi ...' he said, and shrugged.

'Yes, it is a little odd,' I agreed. Why was this the case? Because he was younger than the rest of us and more easily trusted?

'Not to worry,' Lord Devere said. 'In a few days, we shall hear all the news right from the horse's mouth.'

'I hope the horse is not still mad at me,' I said. I regretted that I had not made my peace with Levi before leaving — that was how disputes festered.

'Levi can never stay angry with you for long, you know that.'

'But I have never come between Levi and his lady love before,' I added.

'Well, if we are going into "but ifs"...' my lord grinned. 'But if the situation has righted itself in our absence, all shall be forgiven, especially as you have managed to get our permit extended. I think that is a much more positive scenario to meditate upon.'

He actually drew a laugh out of me. 'You are in fine mental form today, my lord. You put me to shame.'

My husband was pleased to see me laugh, and it felt good to let my worries go for the moment.

We arrived at the Mound of Pitch to find the site completely deserted. Far from my troubles being over, I feared they were just beginning. The only movement we could see was that of an eerie wind scattering sand about the excavation and its little village.

'Oh my ... what has happened?' My first thought was that bandits or the local law enforcement agents had raided the site.

'There does not seem to be any sign of a struggle,' Taylor said, having had a quick look around the village. 'Nor does there appear to be anyone here. I am guessing that we have been shut down.'

'Against the Shah's orders?' I thought that unlikely. 'The kad-khuda has surely received the royal decree by now?'

My husband exited the site house, where he had been conducting a thorough search. I had not seen his expression so grave in a long time. 'Levi is not here either,' he said, 'and all the household servants are gone.'

'Maybe Levi is down in the dig?' I suggested.

We all made haste towards the pit. As much as I did not want to concede that the curse of losing my ringstone might have something to do with this strange twist of fate, it seemed a rather bizarre coincidence.

In the second room of the ancient dwelling we had been excavating, the hole in the floor had dropped to new depths and the walls had been reinforced with timbers. A rope and pulley were rigged up to an overhead beam, providing the means for an individual to lower himself down. We could not see the bottom of the hole, it just dropped into darkness.

'Well, someone has been very busy.' Taylor was obviously impressed by our son's progress.

'Levi!' I called down into the dark depths, but there was no reply.

'I believe a torch might be in order,' Lord Devere suggested.

Mr Taylor retrieved the said item from the site house and, setting it alight, we dropped the flaming brand into the shaft. It landed about thirty feet below us and then clattered off out of sight.

'Stairs,' Mr Taylor deduced. 'I am all for going down.'

'I shall go.' Lord Devere removed his jacket. 'It is my son that is missing.'

'He is my son too,' I said, not about to be left out.

'You can be right behind me for all I care, Mrs Devere,' my husband said, taking hold of the rope. 'But *I* am going first.'

Mr Taylor lowered Lord Devere down, then aided me to descend after him. Fortunately I was attired suitably from the camel ride back to the site. Once I was safely down, Taylor threw us several unlit torches, which we could ignite from the first torch, which was still flaming a little further down the stairs. Lord Devere then helped lower Mr Taylor down to join us.

'These stairs are stone,' I commented, noting the rarity of the material. Immediately I remembered the priestess who had owned the serpent comb, and her dash up these very stairs before they were buried and forgotten for aeons.

'The walls are also stone.' Taylor could hardly believe what he was seeing. 'Such extravagance for a mere stairway.' He looked excited at the prospect of finding great treasure.

'That could explain why this structure is not filled with earth like the rest of the ziggurat,' Lord Devere speculated. 'The walls are resilient enough to have held back sand and flood.'

'Until now,' I said. 'Or rather, until Levi unearthed this passage.' My anxiety for my son's welfare was paining my chest more with every passing second.

'Let us see where our unusual stairway leads, shall we?' Taylor said. 'With any luck we will find our missing crew.'

The stairs, constructed from huge stone blocks, led deep underground; where they plateaued stood a large arched entrance. Expertly chiselled into the stone were ancient glyphs that I could not read. However, by tracing my finger over the inscription, I was able to discern the psychic imprint of the scribe who had originally recorded the message in the stone. I spoke the translation aloud: 'Let no man enter this Court who has not prepared himself to appease the great scribe and his mistress, she who holds the divine key. In the Halls of Amenti, the righteous will earn the blessing to bask in the sweet vitality of the sacred flower. The unrighteous will never leave this Court.'

'You have many hidden talents, Lady Devere,' Mr Taylor commented, surprised that I seemed to share my son's aptitude for deciphering ancient languages.

I sidestepped his curiosity. 'Oh, I have picked up a thing or two in my travels.'

'This warning does not sound very promising for the likes of me,' Taylor joked. 'You two may fare better.'

'The question is, how did Levi fare?' Lord Devere raised his torch and moved on through the archway.

The immensity of the next chamber took my breath away — the light of three flaming torches did nothing to fill the huge edifice. The stone walls tapered upwards to a central flattened ceiling that was the same width and length as the walkway ahead of us. Six massive stone columns on each side of the thoroughfare supported the great stone blocks of the ceiling.

'How the hell did they erect this?' Taylor shook his head, stumped, just as scholars had been doing for ages regarding just about every ancient structure known to man.

'Perhaps levitation was big in ancient Mesopotamia?' I suggested.

Mr Taylor assumed I was joking and gave a laugh; Lord Devere knew I was quite serious.

On the inside of the huge columns, facing the walkway, were carved images of six goddesses. On the opposing side of the columns, facing the outer stone walls, were carved the likenesses of the corresponding six gods.

'The goddesses facing inward would seem to indicate that this shrine was tended and watched over by females,' I noted out loud. 'I am guessing that this was a Court of the Dragon Queens — the Princesses and Priestesses of Ur who studied the teachings that the scribe, Thoth, allegedly inscribed on fifteen emerald tablets. The scribe was the servant of the great mother, known as Ninharsag or Hathor, and she in turn protected Thoth and guided him towards enlightenment.'

'Okay.' Mr Taylor raised both brows, open to run with my theory as he obviously had little knowledge of the treasures and texts he was digging from the ground.

I could not see what was at the end of the walkway, but to the side of the pillars, along the outer walls that the gods faced, we discovered a wide stone canal that appeared to have been bricked up on both sides, and most likely at the far ends as well.

'I imagine they were water canals once,' Taylor commented.

'It is said that the ancient city of Ur was entirely surrounded by a huge moat, which fed canals that ran through the great ziggurat and its splendid outlying city,' I said. 'So your theory is highly likely.'

We made our way cautiously along the walkway towards the darkness at the far end. Beyond the pillars arose a huge statue of stone — a sculpture of a woman's torso, with the head of a bull, and between the great arced horns on her head was a sun disk.

Taylor smiled as we admired the massive centrepiece that encompassed nearly the entire end wall of the structure. 'Even I recognise which goddess this sculpture personifies.' He looked to me, impressed by my earlier commentary. 'I now see why Lord Malory sent you here, my lady.'

Suddenly a light appeared ahead and we all stopped in our tracks.

'Levi?' I called.

The open flame, which appeared to be a torch, began waving back and forth. I sensed movement behind me and turned to see Lord Devere waving his torch about.

'A reflection,' I realised.

Taylor peered at the reflection, which was still some way off. 'The flame in the mirror seems somewhat richer in colour,' he said. He approached the mirrored surface expectantly, and when his torch illuminated its material we all gasped. 'Gold,' Mr Taylor said, stunned. The gold formed two doors on the massive statue of Hathor, where the goddess's womb was located. Before Mr Taylor could reach out to touch them, the doors retracted into the walls. Flabbergasted, he stopped dead in his tracks. 'Impossible!'

'Not impossible,' Lord Devere corrected. 'There are reports of such doors in a temple in ancient Alexandria. The deception was based on a trigger under the floor that set a counterweight into motion, causing the doors to part.'

My husband walked over to where Taylor stood and pointed to the floor. 'What did I tell you?'

In his hurry to get to the golden doors, Taylor had inadvertently stepped onto a long timber strip of flooring that continued beyond the entry to the next chamber.

'Once you step off the trigger, the doors will close behind you.' Lord Devere moved forward again. 'You scare far too easily, my friend.'

As we passed through the arched doorway into the womb of Hathor, the chamber within lit up around us, the walls comprised of what appeared to be solid gold tablets. These huge rectangular blocks varied in width and were positioned to form semicircles on both sides of the circular room.

Out of curiosity I counted the tablets. 'Fifteen,' I said.

'They are not emerald, though,' Lord Devere stated the obvious, 'so they are clearly not the Emerald Tablets of Thoth.'

'But they could be very lovely copies,' I suggested. 'Thoth did travel extensively and probably recorded his insights wherever he went.'

In the centre of the room was a raised round pool of liquid. When ignited, it lit the entire chamber. The strange thing was, at the moment of illumination I heard a sound like that of a large group of people drawing a long, well-needed breath.

'Oh my Goddess!' Taylor's eyes watered with joy at the sight of all the gold tablets, each one meticulously engraved with blocks of ancient text. 'This is beyond all —'

'Shh!' Both Lord Devere and myself ordered him to silence.

'You hear it?' my lord asked me.

'I do.' I looked to each of the tablets in turn.

'Hear what?' Taylor whispered.

'Either these tablets have a telepathic projection capability, or there is some sort of conscious intelligence connected with each.'

Lord Devere moved forward to address each tablet in turn.

'Do you mean to tell me that the tablets are speaking?' Mr Taylor clearly wanted to scoff, but was too polite. 'What are they saying?'

'They are reciting the text engraved on them,' I explained. I gestured to the tablet nearest me. 'This one is called the Key of Wisdom, and this one,' I pointed to the one alongside it, 'is a discourse on the Space Born.'

'This is the Key of Time,' Lord Devere advised of the tablet he was currently concentrating upon.

It seemed that the simple awarding of one's attention was the key to activating the discourse of each tablet, although, as Mr Taylor was incapable of hearing anything, it was clear that one needed a certain amount of psychic aptitude to make the telepathic connection. I discovered that if I skimmed my attention further down the tablet, the discourse would skip forward and resume its tutorial from wherever had captured my interest. Even more astounding was that the discourse was in English, but if I willed it to be Latin or Italian or any of the other languages I was familiar with, then the tutorial adjusted to suit that desire. This suggested the tablets had some sort of intellect, but whether it was human or artificial I could not say without further investigation.

'What an incredible feat of psychic ingenuity,' I uttered, in awe of the creator. Did I dare to touch one of the tablets and discover who that creator was?

'Wait!' Mr Taylor frowned as he listened harder. 'I do hear something. It sounds like . . . a woman, moaning.'

I stopped short of touching the tablet and dragged my attention from the text — sure enough, I heard the moaning too.

'It is coming from over there.' Taylor pointed to an archway that led further into the ruin. Reluctantly, Lord Devere and I turned away from the tablets; there would be plenty of time to study them later.

Through the archway was another huge chamber. Lord Devere paused at the arch to note a cavity within the framework that was filled with gold. 'Another set of doors,' he guessed, 'which were opened by an advance party.'

'Levi?' I voiced what we were both wondering.

'Just look at this!' Mr Taylor was turning circles as he walked further into the chamber, which was also round. The shape of the shrine seemed to indicate that this temple had never been part of the ziggurat above, but had originally been structured as a secret subterranean dwelling. Huge pillars supported the ceiling, which featured an enormous downward-facing lotus flower crafted entirely from gold. The flower's petals opened high above a raised central platform in the centre of the temple. Atop the platform stairs stood a circular altar block, crafted from silver. 'This find is unprecedented!' Taylor cried.

I noted that the floor beneath my feet did not sound like stone or timber and crouched to view the shiny, smooth surface. 'Red-gold,' I said to my husband.

We had both seen this rare metal before, in the Sinai, and it meant only one thing: those who had built this temple knew the ancient alchemic art of Star-Fire production.

Star-Fire, besides its use for accelerating the spiritual enlightenment of those who carried the Gene of Isis, was also used to reinforce precious metals with extraordinary strength and weight, once the metal had returned to a cool and hardened state. But when these resilient metals were heated to extreme temperatures, their superconductivity caused them to levitate and sometimes even dissipate altogether.

'Good luck trying to strip this temple bare of its treasures,' my husband muttered to me.

Mr Taylor had not noted our observations; he was still turning circles, admiring the gold ceiling feature.

I noticed something on the silver altar and pushed past Taylor.

His torchlight illuminated the silver stone and I could see that some dark liquid had tarnished the sides and run all the way down the steps.

'It is blood,' I said upon touching it and raising my fingers to the light. 'And it is still moist.'

I clambered up the steep stairs expecting to find our son, but it was the body of a woman lying on the great silver block of offering and both her wrists were cut. I brushed the hair from her face. 'Miss Koriche!'

My fingers searched her neck for a pulse. 'She is still alive,' I called to the others. It was a miracle considering the amount of blood she had shed, and I began ripping my head scarf into strips to bandage her wounds.

'My God!' Taylor was shocked to find his linguist in such a state. Then, noting the seductive, sheer white silk dress Miss Koriche was wearing, he added, 'It is always the quiet ones that surprise you.'

'No ...' Miss Koriche, semiconscious now, made a weak protest against my first aid. 'I am not worthy ...'

'What has happened here?' I shook her a little to see if I could bring her to full consciousness. 'Where is everyone? Where is Levi?'

'Gone ...' she muttered.

'Gone where?' I urged, raising her body to rest against me.

'They came for him ...'

'Who did?' I stroked her face in the hope of keeping her with us, but her form became a dead weight in my arms.

'Let us get her back to the surface,' Lord Devere suggested, as calmly as his anxiety would allow. 'And pray that she lives.'

He bundled the girl up in his arms and we made haste back towards the staircase.

'Are you coming, Mr Taylor?' I asked, noticing that our host seemed unable to drag himself away from assessing the potential profit of this find, despite his dying colleague.

'Right behind you,' he said, his gaze lingering on the huge golden lotus overhead.

Miss Koriche was in a very bad way: pale, cold and still unconscious.

'All you have to do is touch her and we could know what happened,' my husband tempted me. Mr Taylor had left us alone with the patient, claiming he had to take care of some urgent correspondence.

It was a real moral dilemma; I detested invading the private thoughts of others, although in this case I did have good cause.

'If she dies, her knowledge will die with her,' Lord Devere pushed. It was unlike him to encourage the abuse of my talents.

'Her ghost may choose to converse with me,' I said, knowing it was a weak argument.

'And it may not.' He politely demolished my protest. 'What makes you think that Miss Koriche would trust you any more in death than she did in life? For that matter, even if she wakes, she may not choose to tell us anything.'

I caved in. 'All right, I shall do it ... for Levi's sake.'

'You do not have to justify this course of action to me,' Lord Devere pointed out, smiling. I knew he was grateful for my decision.

I placed a hand upon Miss Koriche's and focused my inner eye to connect with her subconscious. I posed the question: *Do you know what has happened to Levi?*

A string of images and sounds flashed before me in reverse, then came to a standstill. I was — or rather Miss Koriche was — in the two-roomed dwelling that stood above our discovery, speaking with Levi. It appeared to be the first day of our arrival at the Mound of Pitch, as the serious excavation of the second room had yet to begin ...

Levi had remained with Miss Koriche after our party had left to inspect the rest of the excavation. He said he wanted to discuss the finer points of the ancient Sumerian language with her.

Miss Koriche was explaining the symbols on her rubbing when Levi interrupted her.

'You can stop pretending now that we are alone,' he said.

'I am not entirely sure what you mean, Mr Granville-Devere.' I felt her smile, sparked by curiosity.

Levi returned her smile with a very charming one of his own. 'I mean that I was expecting to meet you here in Persia. Were you expecting me? I thought I detected a hint of recognition when we were introduced — was I wrong about that?'

Miss Koriche was so impressed by his frank confidence that she was torn between telling the truth and maintaining her cover. Perhaps she could do both?

'It was foreseen that you would be coming into my life,' she admitted, to Levi's great delight.

'Foreseen by you?'

'Perhaps,' she teased, and Levi's grin turned wary.

'Are you just humouring me?' he asked.

Miss Koriche shook her head and began to unbutton her dress from the neck. Levi was pleasantly shocked to see the familiar birthmark between her breasts. 'Do you believe me now?' she said.

Levi melted into a smile, for her birthmark was identical to his own, located on his back between his shoulder blades — as was mine. 'Your argument is most convincing,' he assured her.

Miss Koriche refastened her dress, then pulled an item from her pocket. It was wrapped in a scarf — the same scarf that Levi had wanted me to psychically assess the day I had left for Baghdad. 'In fact, I have a gift for you,' she said, approaching my son and gently placing her offering in his hands.

'It is rather weighty,' Levi commented, and was surprised when he opened the scarf to find a long, fine gold chain upon which hung an elongated gold pendant embossed with ancient hieroglyphs. 'He awaits under the lotus.' Levi read the inscription aloud, puzzled as to why Miss Koriche should give this object to him.

'It is a message from the Ladies of the Elohim,' she said. 'I was informed that it will make sense to you in time and serve your purpose here in the East.'

'I was under the impression that my purpose here was to meet you,' Levi said.

'I am but a messenger,' Miss Koriche replied, but I knew she had a greater involvement in Levi's quest than she was prepared to admit at their first meeting.

'That is not what I foresaw,' Levi ventured, flashing her a cheeky grin.

Miss Koriche gave him a shy smile in response. 'Allow me.' She lifted the pendant from the scarf and placed it around Levi's neck.

As he took hold of the long medallion to admire it, he immediately closed his eyes and became entranced by his inward perceptions. After some time, his eyes parted and he announced, 'I know what this means.'

'I was sure that you would,' Miss Koriche told him, her heart filling with admiration.

'I need to get some workmen in here,' Levi informed her, full of zeal for his project.

'Yes.' Miss Koriche was clearly caught up in his excitement, for she actually laughed. 'You are just how I was led to believe you would be.'

'Led to believe by whom?' Levi queried.

'A higher power,' was all she would say. 'Those who tell do not know; those who know ... do not tell.'

Levi was amused by her response.

'I can help you find a crew.' Miss Koriche changed the subject. 'When do you want them to start?'

'Tonight,' he informed her.

Miss Koriche was taken aback by his eagerness to assist her with her own secret quest, however unwittingly. Levi Granville-Devere was truly the godsend she had been promised.

'I shall see what I can arrange,' she said.

My perception was swept forward in time and I glimpsed only small snippets of the private hours Miss Koriche had been spending with my son. Their shared interest in the dig brought them very close, very quickly, although Miss Koriche was careful never to disclose her particular interest in the excavation. I felt that Levi had the impression that Miss Koriche was there merely to aid his quest, which he had not openly discussed with her. Either Levi assumed she knew what his aim was, or he was purposely keeping to himself what the necklace had disclosed.

Then Miss Koriche's recollection skipped to the night before Lord Devere and I had left for Baghdad, the night she had vanished from my son's bed. From the little I perceived of the evening, I could tell she was genuinely falling in love with Levi and had given herself to him freely, and yet she fled his bed weeping in the middle of the night, leaving my son to sleep on, unaware of her departure. She felt she had done something horribly wrong in giving herself to Levi so soon, and yet to seduce him had been her intent all along.

'I cannot go on.' I let go of Miss Koriche's hand. 'This is too personal, and too strange. I do not like being a voyeur of our son's love life.'

'Did you find out what happened to Levi?' Lord Devere demanded.

'No. I did not get that far.'

'Then what was the point of breaching your moral code at all?' My husband grew frustrated with our lack of progress.

'There is another way,' I realised, as I recounted what I had learned already. 'We can give Miss Koriche a blood transfusion, and when she recovers she can tell us what we want to know … All we need is a syringe.'

'Are you mad? Did you not read Dr Blundell's findings on the subject — in only fifty per cent of his cases was blood transfusion successful, and they do not know why. We could kill her!'

'She is dying anyway, my lord.' I could sense the yearning of her weary spirit to withdraw from its weak earthly vessel. 'Is finding our son more important than this girl's life?'

Lord Devere was silent as he mulled that question over.

'I am fairly confident that my blood will revive her,' I added.

'What makes you so sure?' My lord was running short on patience.

I pulled down the blanket and the plunging neckline of Miss Koriche's silken dress and exposed the birthmark that Lord Devere and myself both bore.

'She is of the blood,' he gasped. Then his eyes narrowed with suspicion. 'Why do I suddenly get the feeling that this quest of ours actually has very little to do with gathering information for the brothers? What if it is really —'

'— all about Levi?' I was having the same thought. 'Getting him right where the brotherhood want him!' I was immediately infuriated. 'I hope I am wrong, for Malory's sake. If we are proved right, I will kill him!'

My surge of fury sent out a shockwave from my being that near knocked my husband off his feet.

'Easy, my love,' Lord Devere urged upon righting himself. 'Nothing is certain yet.'

Only twice in my life had the full velocity of my psychokinetic power been unleashed; both times I had been in mortal danger, and both times there had been fatalities. This energy had only ever been activated by fear and anger and thus was beyond my control, which was why I feared calling upon it by choice.

Mr Taylor appeared, looking a little shaken as he stumbled through the door. 'Did you feel that tremor just now? It nearly knocked me over!'

It took all of my will not to lash out at our host. With a mere thought I could pin him to the wall and squeeze what he knew out of him. Still, that would expose my full potential to my possible enemy — better that he did not know what I was truly capable of.

'Is there a medical supplies cabinet around here somewhere, which might hold a syringe and a scalpel?' My lord distracted Mr Taylor with the query, turning him around and heading back towards the door.

'Of course.' Mr Taylor looked perplexed by the request.

'Would you be so kind as to show me?'

My husband closed the door behind them, leaving me alone to calm myself and reassess the situation.

Was Miss Koriche friend or foe? And if she proved to be the latter, did that make my reading her thoughts any less reprehensible? What if I was wrong about the blood transfusion? What if my husband was right and Miss Koriche took what had happened to Levi to the grave with her? If one of these secret brotherhoods had him and did not want him found, it would prove near impossible to track him down — even for me. Miss Koriche was my very best chance.

Worry for my son overcame my morals. I seated myself beside the dying woman and again took up her hand.

What happened after you left my son that night?

Miss Koriche had taken a camel and fled the site for the nearest village, where she had hidden herself away for a week to prevent herself from exposing what she knew to Levi. Love was the last thing she'd been expecting to come from their meeting; why had none of the elders foreseen this? Or had they? She knew this was a test, but her heart was too confused to decide what the right course of action was. What would become of her Western mate? She had never thought to care. But now that she had got to know Levi, she had no desire to betray him; to carry his child would be every bit as honourable as carrying the child of a god! Miss Koriche knew that her superiors would not agree, however.

I must go back, she had decided in the end. *And complete the task that I was created for.*

Levi clearly had mixed feelings about seeing Miss Koriche again when she showed up on site a few days before our return. 'Why did you leave without a word?' he said. 'I have been beside myself with worry.' He refrained from embracing her until he had received an answer.

She held a hand to his cheek affectionately. 'It was not my intent to worry you,' she said. 'A situation arose suddenly, of divine import, which required my immediate attention. I had no time to inform anyone. Please believe that I would have told you if I had been permitted to.' She spoke the truth, which hid her deceit all the better.

Levi was appeased by her caress and took hold of her waist with both hands to pull her closer. 'You are a very mysterious woman, Miss Koriche.'

'And you are a very mysterious man.' She kissed him, without a thought for who might see, but when they parted at last she realised there was not a soul within eyeshot. 'Where are the workmen?'

'I gave them all a week's paid holiday — the house staff too,' he informed her, leading her towards the excavation pit.

'Why would you do that?' She was concerned that this would delay the discovery of the Dragon Court.

'We broke through to a staircase of stone, Ajalae.' Levi's voice was filled with excitement.

'What?' She was delighted and mortified all at once.

'Come, let me show you.'

He urged her to take his hand and she did so, trying desperately not to reconsider her decision to hold true to her quest and tell Levi nothing of the pending danger to his being.

Down in the tablet chamber, the golden doors leading to the temple were yet to be opened. Embossed into the doors was a question, written in the same ancient script with telepathic translation capability:

In the Old Land an enchanted Word was created
To define a demon of the shadows from a man who walks in light.
Utter the word only man can pronounce
Or return to your realm of eternal night.

Levi conveyed the meaning of the inscription to Miss Koriche, who was overwhelmed. 'Even I cannot read this,' she said. She looked to Levi, amazed by him yet again, just as she had been over and over since they had met. She had been warned that Mr Granville-Devere was suspected of harnessing great psychic potential, but he never flaunted the fact and had certainly never spoken of it beyond that he had dreamt of her. 'Do you know the word the inscription refers to?' she asked.

'Not yet,' Levi admitted, although he did not sound deterred by the fact.

Miss Koriche breathed an inward sigh of relief.

'But I am certain the answer lies in one of these tablets.' Levi motioned to the fifteen golden tablets of text that formed the walls of the round chamber. 'I have been studying and committing them to memory. It will not be long before I find the answer to the riddle.'

Miss Koriche sucked back all the awe that the incredible discovery inspired in her. Perhaps if she could delay Levi's quest for knowledge, some circumstance might arise that would spare him from his fate.

'Did you miss me?' she asked seductively, but Levi was focused on the tablet before him.

'Here, in the Key of Mysteries, it refers to Atlantis and the coming of the Children of Shadows that were called from the great deep —' Levi was surprised by a kiss.

'All work and no play is very bad for a man's soul.' Miss Koriche took Levi by the hands and led him out of the tablet chamber.

My son did not need much coaxing to set aside his task for a while. 'I have been down here for days, so I guess I am just about due for a rest,' he said.

Miss Koriche smiled. 'I would not be planning on too much rest if I were you.'

THE BETRAYING WORD
OF SHADOWS

'Before the sinking of the Old Land, beings of a lower cosmic cycle were summoned through an interdimensional gateway by men who lusted for material power. Only by the will of man and the extracting of spirit from blood could they take form. They moved only through angles and never through curves. With their glamour, the shadow ones could assume the appearance of any man. The Seven Cosmic Lords, mighty in magic, had crafted a secret word, which man alone could pronounce and the word was ...' Levi read aloud from a tablet. 'Kininigen!'

Miss Koriche entered the tablet chamber in time to hear Levi speak the ancient word. She had managed to detain Levi from his study for a day and a half, but her vigil had eventually been overwhelmed by the need for sleep, allowing Levi to slip away from their bed unnoticed. To her great horror the golden doors that had barred the entrance to the temple opened in response to Levi's utterance.

'Yes!' Levi cheered his own success as he headed towards the doorway.

'No, Levi, you must not enter the temple.' Miss Koriche went after him and grabbed his arm.

'What are you so afraid of, Ajalae?' he asked tenderly.

'I am afraid of losing you,' she confessed, although it meant that her life would not be worth living.

'That is silly,' Levi said, his voice full of comfort, 'when you have lied to me with every word and gesture that has ever passed between us.'

Miss Koriche's heart jumped into her throat. 'You know?' She shrank away from him, ashamed and bewildered.

Levi appeared saddened by her response. 'I do now.'

Miss Koriche was doubly shocked to find that Levi had just called her bluff.

'I feel a memory of vast proportions awaking inside me,' he went on. 'It is calling on me to relinquish this physical form for some time, and I could not bring myself to answer that summons if it meant breaking the heart of someone I care about so deeply.'

Miss Koriche gasped with emotion. She so wanted to reassure Levi of her love, but he held high a finger to silence her until he was done with his own confession.

'I hear the voice behind the word projections of the tablets. It spoke to me directly this morning, of my true purpose and destiny in this life. It also spoke of how I might confirm all that I have been told. When the scribe told me that my love believed she was leading me into a well-baited trap, I contested his foul claim profusely. Then the scribe explained that you are not in love with me, but are here to serve *his* desires once I have relinquished control of this earthly vessel to him.'

His words cut deep into Miss Koriche's heart, for she could see Levi was hurting from a fatal blow that she had dealt him. 'Please do not do this to spite me,' she begged, tears openly streaming down her face now. 'I do love you, Levi, or I would not be here to prevent you from doing this.'

'You still believe this is a trap,' he said, taking her reply as confirmation of her guilt. To hide his tears and hurt, Levi retrieved his torch from a wall mount and passed under the temple entrance.

'I have agonised over telling you the truth!' Miss Koriche cried, but her rapidly deteriorating emotional state did nothing to sway Levi from his course. 'I came back to betray all that I have known and learned, in order to save your life.'

'Whether that is the case or not, my true purpose is now confirmed,' Levi said. 'You should go now and prepare for the destiny you chose, for a lifetime of preparation should not be wasted. I see you for the test you are, Ajalae. Clearly, the physical world has nothing to offer someone like me at this time.'

Miss Koriche gasped, hurt by the comment.

Levi stopped to look back at her. 'Do not be offended, for my destiny was not of your choosing and none of what has happened is your fault. You have done me a great service ... really.' He appeared unfazed and at peace. 'For you were meant to lead me to this epiphany. If anyone should feel guilt it is I, for not realising the truth about us sooner and preventing any issue between us. We were never meant to be together, you and I.'

'Don't say that, please —'

Miss Koriche made a move towards Levi only to find herself airborne and rocketing backwards. She screamed as she passed through the entrance chamber, up the stone stairs, out through the roof of the two-roomed dwelling, across the excavation area and into the site house, where she was cast down upon her own bed.

Once the initial shock had passed, the young woman was left shaking and in tears. If this was what Levi the man was capable of, it frightened her to think of his potential as a god. The only way she was going to get anywhere near Levi again was to prepare herself as he had instructed. She sniffed back her tears, and from a secret compartment in her trunk quickly pulled out the attire of a vestal virgin. It seemed rather hypocritical for her to don such a costume, but in all actuality the man and the god would be one and the same now, only the consciousness would differ.

By the time Miss Koriche returned to the temple shrine, Levi was lying motionless on the altar block. The huge round chamber was lit by his single torch, mounted beside the raised stone of offering beneath the lotus flower.

She wasted no time in scaling the altar and pulling herself up beside her lover. 'Levi?' She ventured to brush a hand against his cheek. 'Can you hear me?' Her tears began welling anew when there was no response. Then, rather abruptly, Levi's eyelids parted and he stared at her. 'Hello,' she said at last, to break the long silence.

'Hello,' he replied, sitting up to look around him. 'Why are you here?'

She frowned, suspicious. His countenance was strange and unfamiliar, and an unearthly glow had permeated the whites of his eyes. Their gaze was mesmerising. 'Levi?' she ventured.

'No,' he replied. 'He may not be back for some time.'

Miss Koriche gasped in horror, both at the loss of Levi and the fact that she was addressing the great Ibis. 'My *lord*.' She bowed down to the ground beside him. 'Please forgive my familiarity.'

He smiled, amused by her veneration and fear. 'I understand that you knew my vessel very well, so your concern is understandable.' He raised himself to standing without using a muscle, merely levitating into an upright position.

Miss Koriche did not dare question the entity about Levi's whereabouts. If the soul that she loved was now banished from this world, there seemed little point in clinging to the hope that she might be able to lead a normal married life with him one day. This was the fantasy that had prompted her to be truthful with Levi, but now there seemed only one course of action left to take — her predestined one.

'My lord,' Miss Koriche found it hard not to stammer as she spoke, 'I am here to satisfy any earthly desire you may have upon waking from your long sleep. As a Daughter of Isis, I pray that I am worthy to receive your seed.'

He laughed heartily at the offer. 'I have no desire for earthly pleasure, and the needs of this body have been well and truly fulfilled in the past few days.' He looked around, appearing to have other concerns. 'Where are my priests, I wonder?'

He floated down from the raised platform and strode towards the tablet room, where a group of hooded men had appeared and awaited his word.

Miss Koriche was shattered; a lifetime of preparation, study and service wasted because she had given away the prize too soon. Had she resisted Levi's charms and led him on as she had been instructed to, perhaps the lord would have been keener to satisfy his vessel's physical needs. There was little point in returning to her sisters now; her shame was twofold and she could not bring herself to confess her gross miscarriage of duty.

Perhaps in death I shall find my love and live my dream . . .
She drew the blade that was concealed in the sole of her shoe.

My perception of events faded, and I was about to open my eyes when I detected an additional life-force that was attached to Miss Koriche. Looking beyond her physical being to the fading light centres of her subtle body, I spied one tiny bright spark of cosmic light, buried deep within her womb. It was the humble beginnings of a whole new light-body.

My heart nearly stopped beating as I realised that Miss Koriche was carrying my first grandchild.

I raced to the door to find out what was keeping my husband. 'Hurry!' I yelled down the corridor in a most unladylike fashion, and rolled up my sleeve to prepare my arm for bleeding. If this girl thought she was going to die while carrying one of my descendants, she had another think coming! Not the will of the gods, secret societies, brotherhoods, sisterhoods or any damn curse was going to deprive this child of its right to live.

By the time the transfusion was complete and Miss Koriche lay breathing easily with colour in her cheeks, I was covered in blood, both hers and my own.

'Luck appears to be with us,' Lord Devere commented, as he checked the vital signs of our patient.

My husband could see as clearly as I that this woman was now kindred, although he kept his observation to himself until Mr Taylor departed to get on with his pressing business — which, I imagined, was selling off our find to the highest bidder.

'Grandparents.' Lord Devere both smiled and winced at the thought. 'But what of Levi? Did you find out anything?'

I thought he had rather a hide to assume that I had betrayed my morals at the first given opportunity. But the fact was, I had. 'I do not know where our son is at present, but I can tell you that his body and his spirit are in two entirely different places . . . one easier to find than the other.'

Lord Devere was understandably concerned by my claim. 'Tell me everything,' he said, taking a seat beside me.

I conveyed what I had learned, then attempted to answer my lord's queries until my throat was hoarse and my eyes were threatening to roll into the back of my head.

'When he referred to his priests, who do you think he meant?' Lord Devere pondered.

'I am not entirely sure; the Melchi perhaps?' I yawned.

'Ah yes, the order of Melchizedek.' We had briefly met some of these warrior priests during our last stint in the Near East. 'Were they not the brotherhood to whom Albray held true?'

I nodded. I was not going to be the one to say it.

Lord Devere put me out of my misery. 'Damn it! We need Albray.'

'I believe he would know where some of the priesthood may be found,' I offered, thankful that we were both thinking along the same lines.

'Curses!' Lord Devere looked as if he wanted to hit something.

'I will simply have to return to Baghdad and look for the stone again,' I said calmly.

'That will delay the search for Levi for weeks!' Lord Devere stood and began to pace.

'I suspect that where Levi has gone, time is not really an issue. And besides, that will give you a chance to scour the tablet room for information before Taylor has it sold, boxed and shipped off.'

'You do not seriously think that he is planning to strip the site? That would attract far more attention than Malory would like, not to mention what the Shah will have to say about it.'

'Only God knows what Taylor has in mind. What I do know is that Levi studied those tablets to find the answers he needed, so if we are lucky they will tell us something of what has happened to our boy.'

'And who shall travel to Baghdad with you?' my husband asked.

'I have travelled by myself before.' Only as I said this did I realise what the grave difference would be this trip.

'You had Albray's talents with a sword to rely on then,' my lord pointed out.

'Then I shall just have to rely on my own talent with a pistol this time around,' I resolved, raising my hand to smother another yawn.

'After all, my lord did suggest that I should start utilising my own talents instead of relying on outside forces to protect me.'

My husband smiled at me and bundled me up into his arms. 'Time to find you a bed, Mrs Devere.'

The next morning I was up and packed early. I wanted to be on my way before my lord managed to talk himself out of letting me go.

'So there is to be no more discussion,' he said, as he rolled over in bed to find me strapping up my trunk.

'You are the one who does not wish to waste any time.' I walked over and placed a new journal in his hand. 'This is for you, to record your observations. I want to know everything of interest and import contained within those tablets . . . And keep an eye on Mr Tay—'

There was an urgent knocking on the door.

'Enter,' we both called.

Taylor stuck his head around the door. 'Come quickly, she's opened her vein again.'

I made it to Miss Koriche's room ahead of both the men and spied her huddled in a corner, fresh blood on her already bloodstained dress, dagger in hand, ready to strike at any who came near her.

'Out.' I pushed Mr Taylor into my husband and ushered them both out of the room. 'I shall handle this.' I closed the door.

'Stay away from me,' Miss Koriche advised. 'I want to die.'

'I am sorry but I cannot allow that to happen.' I strode towards her, and no sooner had I willed the knife in her hand into my grasp than I clutched the item.

Miss Koriche gasped, and for a moment there was horror in her eyes.

I had actually surprised myself; I had not realised my psychokinetic ability could be wielded without inflicting mortal damage. 'Do not fear,' I said, 'I have not been possessed by an ancient god, I am just a daughter of the blood, like you.' I tossed the knife across the room and crouched down to rebandage her wrist.

'Why should you care if I live or die?' she implored, too weary to resist my help. 'Do you know what I have done to your son?'

'I know everything,' I said, without confessing how, 'and I feel very sure that anything that may have happened to Levi was of his own choosing, so never you mind about assuming responsibility for his actions. You have other concerns now.'

'I will be sacrificed for my failure.' Miss Koriche clearly considered that my efforts to keep her alive were pointless.

'Over my dead body,' I told her resolutely.

Miss Koriche thought she had figured out why I should be so protective of her wellbeing. 'You need me alive for information.'

'No, I need you to take good care of yourself, so that my first grandchild can be born healthy and strong.'

I finished off her dressing and looked up to find the girl too stunned to breathe.

Finally she gasped, and tears welled as she fathomed the fact that she was with child.

'You are sure?' she queried, before daring to smile.

'Never surer. So will you please keep what blood you have left *in* your body, as I can ill afford to give you any more.'

'I have *your* blood in *my* veins!' Considering what she had just seen of my talents, I wasn't surprised Miss Koriche was shocked.

'In more ways than one.'

'I am astounded that you would give me such a precious gift.'

'As it happened, I had some to spare.' I shrugged it off as a minor inconvenience. 'I know that you love my son, despite what has happened. I also know that he loves you, despite your deception, and that he would be very proud indeed to know that you are carrying his child.'

Miss Koriche forced a smile, as she obviously considered that I was being too kind. 'He is the most beautiful man I have ever met.' Her tears welled again. 'You must be so proud.'

'Not proud that he would leave you as he did in order to prove a point.' I considered a scolding was in order when I found Levi, although I was not really in a position to preach about the abuse of cosmic power just now.

'I should not have lied to him.' Miss Koriche insisted on taking the blame.

'A lie is not a sin when you believe it is serving a higher cause,' I said, trying to let her off the hook.

'But to lie is not divine,' she replied, the realisation coming to her in retrospect, 'and thus can never really serve the divine way.'

'Bravo,' I said softly, admiring her eagerness to claim responsibility for her mistakes. 'We live on and we learn.'

Miss Koriche nodded. 'I shall do my best.'

'When I get back from Baghdad —' I began.

'You are returning to Baghdad? Why?' She sounded concerned.

'Because I have a friend there who may be able to help us find Levi ... his body anyway,' I clarified.

'I wish I could tell you where his body has been taken, but I do not know.'

'I know that,' I told her.

'Not even my superiors know,' she added.

'I know,' I assured her again. If she did know, the information would have been forthcoming when I was probing her mind. 'I have a plan, so there's no need to worry.'

I moved to stand but Miss Koriche grabbed my arm to keep me with her.

'Do you really think you can bring your son back from the Halls of Amenti?' She sounded as if she thought the notion was hopeless.

'Is that where you think his consciousness is right now?'

'Not yet, but soon,' she replied. 'Now that he has joined with the great Ibis, Mr Granville-Devere has the Key to Amenti, but I do not know where the door may be found.'

'The God himself is the Key.' I suddenly understood what the last thoughts of the ancient priestess had meant.

'And once the lord takes Levi's physical body through the gateway to Amenti, he may not return for a hundred years or more.'

'What?' I was stupefied, then startled by a knock on the door.

'Is everything all right in there?' It was Lord Devere.

'All is well,' I called back, and looked to Miss Koriche, who managed a genuine smile and a nod. 'You may come in.'

Lord Devere entered, and helped me get Miss Koriche back to bed.

'Lord Devere is staying here to study the tablets, so he shall watch over you until I return,' I advised our patient, as we tucked her in.

'I certainly will,' my husband concurred, happy that the dramatics had been sorted out before his arrival. 'I may need your aid with my task,' he told Miss Koriche.

'I will be glad to help,' she assured him.

'Once you're feeling better.'

'And that may not be for some time,' I said, having survived four pregnancies myself. 'Now make sure she eats well —'

'Yes, I know the drill.' My husband reminded me that he had also survived four pregnancies.

'Listen to my lord,' I told Miss Koriche, 'he is quite experienced in such matters.'

'If my child grows up to be half as fine as your son, then I shall be blessed,' Miss Koriche said, implying that she would be well disposed towards any advice we could give her. 'I never knew my mother, nor any other family to speak of.'

'Well,' I said, taking her hand, 'you have family now. And we shall not allow any harm to befall you or this child.'

'That we promise,' my lord seconded.

We both left the room followed by Miss Koriche's beaming smile. In the hallway, my husband gently squeezed my shoulder to convey his admiration for my way with people. 'That is your greatest gift,' he said. 'No wonder I am bound to do whatever you tell me I must.'

'So there shall be no more argument about my leaving for Baghdad today?' I queried, holding myself back from his kiss until I heard his agreement. But my lord merely shook his head and had his way for a change.

PART 2

THE SEARCH FOR LEVI

THE ADULTERESS

I arrived in Baghdad to find Cingar distraught by recent events in the Shah's palace. The musical tuition he had promised Raineath had gone horribly wrong, and although it was not Cingar who had been thrown in prison this time, the gypsy felt responsible for the incarceration of his student.

Cingar told me how the women in the Shah's harem were kept apart from the rest of the palace.

'The seclusion of women in the Islamic household has its origin in the laws of the Koran,' he explained. 'A man may have as many wives and concubines as he can support, and each of these women is his exclusive property. These women are slaves in the main, and must veil their faces to all men except their father, brother and husband. Any violation of this rule is regarded as the gravest offence and grants the husband the absolute right to mutilate or kill the offending wife or concubine.'

The Shah had arranged for Cingar's tuition of Raineath to be chaperoned by a couple of his white eunuchs that guarded the outer harem, and for the first few weeks all was well. A curtain separated Raineath and Cingar during the sessions, and Raineath wore the required veil, despite the fact that it made playing the violin difficult. Then, one day, there was a disturbance outside their music chamber, which drew their chaperones from the room. Raineath had seized the opportunity to speak to Cingar in her own tongue.

Cingar was astonished to find that she was Romani.

However, Raineath was more interested in discussing the famous Cingar Choron. 'I have aspired to meet you since I heard your story over fifteen years ago, when I was just a little girl,' she said. 'You are the reason that I first picked up my instrument.'

Cingar was flattered by her confession, saddened by her plight, and then horrified as he saw her hand take hold of the curtain dividing them.

'I would give my life to be able to perform for you,' she said, and drew the curtain back to view him.

Her eyes opened wide upon seeing her idol.

'You are even more handsome than your legend foretold,' she said, paying no heed to his panic.

'I am an old man whose cavorting days are long done,' he said, knowing her praise came from isolation and frustration. 'Please, draw the curtain.'

Instead, Raineath began to lift her veil.

'Will you not watch me play? Just this once?' she requested. 'It would be a dream come true for me.'

I knew that a goodly part of learning to perform like Cingar Choron came from mastering not only the music played on the instrument, but the perfection of the body movement that enhanced the allure of the performance.

Cingar hated to deny the girl her one dream in the nightmare that was her life, but if she was caught displaying herself to him they would both be dead, or worse. 'I can only listen, as I have been doing,' he said. 'Please, do not endanger your life on my account.'

'My life is worth little compared with this opportunity that, against all odds, the Great Mother has granted me,' Raineath appealed. 'Will you not do me the honour?'

She began to play, hoping that Cingar might be inspired to turn and watch her. Although it broke Cingar's heart to do so, he did not turn. At that moment, the eunuchs returned. Seeing Raineath unveiled and exposed, they immediately covered their eyes and made haste to correct her crime.

The woman's performance ended abruptly as she was brutally slapped to the ground, her instrument sent flying across the floor.

Cingar did not say it as he related his sad tale to me, but I knew the real reason that had prevented him from granting Raineath's wish. It must have seemed to the woman as if her idol had refused her to save his own skin, but in fact Cingar would not risk placing my mission in jeopardy.

'But surely the Shah is not so offended as you fear?' I proffered. 'After all, he was happy to speak with me when I was not veiled.'

'His Majesty is well travelled and understands and respects the customs of his Western neighbours,' Cingar explained. 'But when it comes to the running of his own household, he is not so liberal in his thinking. The Shah intends to cut off Raineath's hands and have her eyes put out!' Cingar was near hysterical. 'I have appealed to his officials already, explaining that it was my legend that compelled her to reveal herself, but the Shah refuses to speak with me.' The gypsy knelt before me. 'I hate to ask, my lady ...'

'Oh, Cingar.' I knelt beside him. 'I couldn't possibly fight another duel, the last one near killed me from the effort.' I put forward the only excuse I could come up with. If I had not lost my ringstone, he would not have had to ask at all.

He stood, ashamed of himself. 'Of course, forgive me.' He began to pace and curse. 'Damn my legend! If I had known the trouble it would cause, I would never have picked up a violin!'

The violin had been Cingar's whole life, and now he was cursing his talent because of Raineath ... because of me. 'I hate to hear you talk so,' I said, 'your music has brought so much joy to many, many people. Do you hold feelings for this woman, Cingar?'

'No, nothing like that,' he said, looking perturbed at the question. 'But I cannot allow a girl to be mutilated because she has a crush on the man I was twenty years ago!'

I sat down on a chair in the palace courtyard and supported my aching head with both my hands. 'What a mess ... First Levi goes missing and now this!' I was beginning to think I should never have returned to the Near East, for it seemed I created havoc with every visit.

'Your son has gone missing! And here am I burdening you with my problems!' Cingar looked as if he wanted to hit himself.

'Do not concern yourself, my friend. I know where he is ... more or less.' I frowned as I considered what to do next.

'I did not even ask what brought you back to Baghdad,' Cingar realised. 'Has your visit got something to do with Levi?'

'You could say that I am looking for someone ... Do not ask me who,' I added, making my quest sound very mysterious, when in fact I was just ignorant. There followed a moment of silence in which I found the opportunity to formulate a plan of action.

'The first thing we should do is appeal to the Shah on Raineath's behalf,' I said. 'If she is a slave then perhaps we can buy her?'

'Under normal circumstances perhaps, if Raineath had committed no crime. But as it is ...'

I gripped Cingar's hand in encouragement, although in truth I held as little hope for the girl as he did. 'Well ... we shall not know unless we try.'

'I shall pay any amount required,' Cingar assured me.

I knew the gypsy had limited means. 'No need,' I replied. 'I feel quite sure Lord Malory will be happy to reimburse me for my pains on his behalf. After all, it was I who suggested you teach Raineath, so ultimately her plight is my responsibility —'

'No,' Cingar insisted. 'You could not have known what would happen.'

'Oh yes I could,' I said, inwardly scolding myself. I had not listened to my psychic voice anywhere near as much as I should have. When Cingar leapt to the unknown woman's defence at dinner with the Shah that night, I had seen that some sort of spark would be ignited between them. I was familiar with the basics of harem law and yet I had allowed the dangerous situation to unfold anyway.

In that moment I realised it was no coincidence that so much disaster had befallen me of late. I had cursed myself with my own carelessness and psychic complacency. I may have a chance of handling the Shah without my ringstone, but finding the Melchi would be quite another matter. I had to find that stone!

It was nowhere near as easy to gain an audience with the Shah this visit; I had to wait several days. I would have been concerned for Raineath's welfare had Cingar not informed me that her punishment would not be carried out until the week's end; apparently, the Shah was delaying her sentence so that she would have time to sit in isolation and fret about her inevitable mutilation.

Kazem met us in the palace foyer. As he led us towards the Shah's audience chamber, he informed me that there had been no further progress made in the search for my missing trinket. This news was most disheartening indeed, although Kazem promised that the search would continue and I thanked him for his efforts.

As we approached the large arched double doors of the Persian court, they parted and a party of officials exited the room. In the midst of the guards, priests and deacons strode a cardinal from the Church of Rome; I could tell by his attire. The holy entourage did not pass by us, but were led off in another direction. I quietly wondered after their purpose here in Persia — perhaps they were pleading the English cause in Herat?

The court was nowhere near as crowded today, with only a few advisors alongside the Shah and the usual guards.

'Lady Suffolk.' The Shah's acknowledgement gave me leave to speak, but he ignored Cingar. 'How fortunate that you have returned to grace my court, for I am afraid that I must inform you that our agreement is at an end. You may take your minstrel as promised and return home.'

My heart leapt into my throat at his decree; did this mean the British had declared war on Persia? Or was the change in his Majesty's tune due to the Cingar–Raineath incident? My hope of searching for Levi was fading fast.

'Your Majesty has been most gracious in his hospitality,' I replied, 'but several incidents have arisen that bring me to plead an extension of my time here in Persia.'

'Such as?' the Shah prompted.

'My eldest son has gone missing, your Majesty, thus I have returned to Baghdad to beseech your patience whilst we attempt to unravel what has become of him.'

I waited with bated breath as the Shah pressed the fingertips of both his hands together, his index fingers resting against his lips as if to prevent himself from speaking before he had thought through my request.

117

'You implied you had more than one reason for this audience, Lady Suffolk?'

I could tell his Majesty was prompting the Raineath discussion in order to have good cause to reject my request to extend my visa. Cingar knew it too. I looked to my friend, who ever so slightly shook his head to advise against mentioning the slave girl now; Levi's welfare was more important. I ignored him and began my appeal.

'Yes, your Majesty. I understand that the woman I suggested as the recipient of Cingar's composition has offended your Highness?'

'That is correct,' he said evenly.

The response of his light-body was not so even, however. As soon as I raised the subject of Raineath, a dark patch over the Shah's lower centres began to churn — it seemed Raineath vexed his Majesty rather severely. I knew I was pushing my luck to continue with my proposal but I had little choice.

'As I feel responsible for this sad turn of events, I was hoping that I might be able to compensate your Majesty for the trouble this woman has found herself in due to my bad judgement and ignorance.'

The Shah motioned to some of his guards, who brought forth a veiled woman. All I could see of her was her eyes, one of which was badly swollen and bruised.

'My dear Lady Suffolk, I fear you assume too much responsibility in this case, for your intentions were honourable,' the Shah granted. 'It was this treacherous creature who chose to abuse our good intentions, and now she must pay the price for her insubordination.'

One guard forced Raineath to her knees, whilst another held her bound hands out in front of her. A third guard drew his sword to carry out his Majesty's decree.

'Would your Highness not consider allowing me to purchase the accused?' I proffered in a final desperate attempt to keep this woman whole. 'Name any price,' I implored him.

'Once her punishment has been carried out, perhaps we can negotiate something,' his Highness considered. 'Unless ... my Lady du Lac would care to fight on behalf of this creature's limbs?'

I had a dreadful feeling that this was where the Shah's patience had been leading the negotiation all along — he wanted a legend all of his own. My husband had warned me that my reliance on Albray would cost me one day; it seemed this was that day.

'Your Majesty, I —'

'I can protect my own limbs!' Raineath declared.

She pulled forward the guard that was holding her hands, using the rope that bound her, and knocked him out with a vicious head butt. As he fell to the floor, she grasped his sword from its sheath, jumped to her feet and turned to the guard behind her to crack him in the forehead with the hilt of the weapon. He was sent staggering backwards, blinded by the strike. As the third guard brought his blade down upon her, Raineath spun to face him and stepped back, holding out her hands before her. His blade cut only her bonds. Raineath thanked her attacker for the service then punched him in the throat, leaving him gasping for air.

Albray! My heart leapt to see his spirit form within the body of Raineath — it was she who had found my stone! As one of the Rom, Raineath must have been familiar with the old Craft and recognised my stone for the charm it was. No wonder she had dared to be so bold with Cingar, for if she had been in contact with Albray, the knight would surely have counselled her to pursue her heart's desire — as Albray never had, and had not lived to regret it.

In the blink of an eye, Raineath held her sword to the Shah's throat. 'Good enough show for you, your Majesty? Or must I kill you in order to secure my liberty?'

'Now we are in real trouble,' Cingar whispered to me, as guards closed in on us.

'This is a stalemate, Raineath,' I warned, urging Albray to back off before we were all incarcerated.

'Yes, you would not want us to have to murder your idol right before your eyes,' the Shah said, remaining very cool in the face of death.

'That is not what I envisage unfolding,' Albray advised the Shah through Raineath, 'because your Majesty is going to order your guards to back away from my defenders. In fact, let us have this room cleared altogether.'

The Shah stared Raineath right in the eyes, stalling to discern whether she was bluffing.

'This blade is very sharp, your Majesty,' Albray said. 'Do not force me to prove myself by scarring your holy person.'

I had stopped breathing at this point. I could not believe the nerve of the knight, and I could not imagine how he thought we could escape this situation. Still, whatever his plan, I was with him all the way.

The Shah gave a nod and his guards backed away from us and filed out of the room. As Cingar and I moved cautiously towards Raineath, I noticed one of the Shah's officials reaching for a pistol. Instinctively, I pulled my own pistol from the deep pocket of my skirt, and aimed it at the Shah, ordering the man to cast aside his weapon. The official complied and Cingar retrieved the discarded gun.

After some delay, the court's doors were closed and the Shah was left alone with us.

'Well, this is an interesting turn of events,' commented his Highness, who still appeared as cool as a cucumber.

'It is rather.' I looked at the Shah down the barrel of my weapon. 'It seems as if your Majesty has become an intimate part of the legend after all.'

'So it would seem.' His Highness was not amused, but by the same token he was not perturbed either. 'I fear the ending of this chapter will not be so victorious for you, Lady Suffolk.'

'We shall see,' commented Raineath, who moved quickly to bolt the doors. She returned to our midst and pulled a small vial from her robes, which she held out to the Shah. 'Drink this.'

Naturally his Majesty refused. 'I would rather die by the sword than poison.'

'And you probably shall,' Raineath said, shoving the vial into the Shah's hand, 'for this will do naught but put you to sleep. Or I could use more brutal means, if you would prefer?'

I felt sure the brew being offered was one of Chiara's, which I had used myself on more than one occasion.

His Majesty still refused. 'There is no way out of this chamber, so you may as well give yourselves up to my mercy.'

'To lie is not very divine, your Highness.' The knight that had control of Raineath lost his patience. 'Drink!' The sword blade lashed out in warning and the Shah flinched as his hat was knocked from his head.

Without further hesitation his Majesty drank down the potion and then cast the vial aside. 'None of you will leave Persia alive,' he swore as his eyelids began to lower. Within minutes he was sleeping peacefully.

'That was magnificent!' Cingar told Raineath. 'Here we were, thinking we were coming to save you, and you end up saving all our skins.'

'Our skins are not safe yet,' I pointed out, and addressed myself to Albray. 'How on Earth do you plan to get us out of here when we are besieged?'

'The same way his Majesty would be spirited away from here, should this kind of situation arise.' Albray, still inhabiting Raineath's body, moved around behind the Shah's throne and, with a mighty push, slid the seat forward to reveal stairs to a secret passageway beneath the palace. 'Quickly,' the woman urged Cingar and myself, as we both stared in amazement at the hole in the floor. 'Let us be gone before anyone realises our intent and sends guards to meet us at the other end.'

Cingar was the first to descend. 'I cannot see a thing down here,' he complained. 'We could walk right into a pit and drop to our deaths . . . and I think I hear rats.'

'Must you be such a girl?' Albray queried via Raineath, then looked to me. 'No offence to us, of course.'

I just shook my head; the comment sounded ridiculous coming via Raineath's mouth.

'I was only thinking of you ladies,' Cingar explained, sounding a little hurt by Raineath's comment as he aided me down the stairs — I really was not dressed for negotiating underground tunnels.

'We shall live,' I assured him.

Raineath was the last to descend, and when she turned to push the throne block back into place Cingar was quick to aid her. When they had succeeded, we were left in total darkness.

Raineath moved past me to lead the way. 'Just follow my voice,' she instructed and began to hum the tune that Cingar had taught her.

*   *   *

I turned the page of the Persian journal to find a clump of loose pages shoved securely into the spine of the huge volume, and the handwriting was entirely different to that of Lady Ashlee. However, she had made a note at the top of the inserted text, attributing the additional material to her husband, Lord Suffolk, Earnest Granville-Devere.

'Bonus,' I decided, having never read anything penned by the lord himself. These must have been the notes that Ashlee asked Devere to pen in her absence.

Still, as I had been reading for a while now, I decided to get some refreshment from the kitchen before continuing with the tale.

I was perusing the snack cupboard for a suitable treat, when the phone rang. I guessed the call was my parents checking up on me, and so I answered it. I pressed the receive button, expecting to see the faces of my parents illumed on the screen, but to my great surprise the screen remained dark — whoever was calling, was doing so from an old audio phone — an item that I thought had been extinct for over a decade.

'Hello, Devere residence,' I said politely.

'Is that Tamar Devere?' It was a man's voice that I did not recognise, and as I could not see the face of the inquirer and I was home alone, I was wary to answer.

'Who wants to know?'

'An old friend,' was the reply.

'And your name?' I insisted.

'My name is not important.'

'I don't think that any old friend of mine would hesitate to tell me their name,' I scoffed, and then covered my mouth too late to prevent giving my identity away.

'So you *are* Tamar,' my caller assumed and I was angered and frightened at once.

'Goodbye.' I reached for the disconnect button.

'No! Please don't hang up.' His plea was rather desperate, and so I refrained. 'I believe you are in grave danger.'

'Yeah, right,' I scoffed. 'Who the hell would be interested in me?'

'Many, many powerful people.' He appealed for me to take him seriously. 'You, and your family, are being observed.'

I was a little spooked by the claim, so I turned around to check that all the blinds were drawn, and they were. 'What am I doing now?' I held up my middle finger and raised the offensive gesture high as I turned around three hundred and eighty degrees.

'It is your enemies who are watching, not I,' he calmly advised.

'I don't have any enemies,' I said rather bluntly, as this caller was giving me the creeps. Time to terminate this conversation.

'But you *do*, key-holder,' he added. 'You need to avoid the bright lights —'

I pressed the disconnect button. 'Loser!' I barked at the phone, feeling the caller was some uni student who was bored, pissed, or both — but I sure as hell was not going to let him get his kicks by scaring me witless.

The phone rang again and startled me, so I answered, disconnected and disengaged the receiver. 'Cop that. You'll just have to find someone else to annoy.'

I returned to my reading, but not before I checked that all the windows and doors were locked. I briefly considered calling Mum to tell her about the prank call, but I knew I'd spoil her evening with Dad and I was not going to give my anonymous coward of a caller the satisfaction.

Besides, I was eager to hear what Lord Granville-Devere had to say for himself, thus I lifted his inserted pages from the journal and read on.

THE TABLETS OF THOTH

FROM THE JOURNAL OF LORD GRANVILLE-DEVERE

Although I have passed into the Halls of Amenti, I leave the Secret of Secrets hidden in these Tablets to light the way for the adept seeker. Through the aeons my spirit will watch from the hidden land and wait for the worthy few who have passed the trials of the outer. Summon me, the Key, and I shall come forth from the Halls of the Gods in Amenti to receive the initiate. I know where the gates to the Isle of Fire may be found and I will disclose the words of power to lift the initiate to the heavens to receive the wisdom of the ages.

I found this passage on the tablet that identified itself as one of two supplementary tablets to the initial thirteen, so I shall number this tablet fourteen for the sake of clarity, as it has no other name. The last of the tablets, which I have numbered fifteen, identifies itself as 'the Secret of Secrets' and promises to be most interesting, but as I am greatly in need of sustenance, I shall get started on it immediately after a very late lunch.

It seems that my study of the last tablet is to be delayed. Our work force have all returned from the holiday Levi granted them and thus Taylor has put them to work and is attempting to transport one of the tablets to the surface. He will not disclose to me what he plans to do with the tablet once he achieves his goal, but I dare say he has an interested party coming to view it. I admit that I am impressed that the men have managed to get the huge golden slab as far as the staircase; they are currently attempting to rig up a pulley system that is strong enough to hoist the tablet to the surface.

A new day dawns to see a huge golden sentinel standing gloriously atop the sandy plateau of the excavation, glistening in all its splendour beneath the warming rays of the early-morning sun. Taylor is a very determined man.

The good news is that after this mammoth effort, which lasted well into the night, the entire work force here at the Mound of Pitch are still sleeping, thus the site is deserted this morning. I intend to take full advantage: let us now discover what this great Secret of Secrets is ...

This tablet speaks of the unveiled mysteries. It tells us how darkness (disorder) and light (order), although seemingly different, are of one nature, for they both arose from the source of all there is — referred to here as the Sovereign Integral, which we know as God. The tablet also speaks of Guardians, twelve plus two in number, who, as channels of the Sovereign Integral, shall direct the unfoldment of being. It states that humankind's purpose in being is the transmutation of darkness to light. Man is bonded to the Earth, which is encircled by a wave of vibration. Here follows a detailed instruction, along with key words, for bypassing this vibration barrier so that one might explore beyond in an astral form. Next, the tablet instructs on the very subject we seek information about — how to enter the Halls of Amenti. There is a detailed meditation, which I shall copy presently.

Again my study of the tablets was interrupted. I was summoned to the surface by one of the staff to find our dear Mr Taylor, this time having a complete fit!

Surprise of surprises, his huge golden tablet, which took tens of men to move, has simply vanished into thin air. Of course Taylor's first conclusion is that it has been stolen.

'You cannot seriously believe that,' I said. 'And where on Earth do you think the locals are hiding it?'

'Then you explain it,' Taylor barked in frustration.

'I shall,' I promised, 'this evening.'

'Why not now?' Taylor asked warily, noting how amused I was by his panic.

'I have my reasons,' I replied calmly. 'But I assure you, you have nothing to worry about, as your tablet will return of its own accord.'

'This evening?' Taylor sounded rather sceptical and perplexed by the suggestion.

'Trust me,' I said, keen to retreat back into the cool of the tablet room and out of the midday sun.

Taylor grabbed my arm. 'And what if I cannot wait until this evening for answers?'

There was a hint of desperation about his appeal that I found disturbing. 'What is the urgency?'

His gaze drifted towards the horizon in the direction of the Euphrates, where I beheld a large party headed towards us, flying the banners of the Church of Rome.

'You idiot!' I grabbed hold of him with the intent to knock him senseless, but then realised I did not have the time or energy to waste — I had to get back to the tablet room to record the key words and meditations we needed to find Levi. I released Taylor and made for the ladder.

'The brothers did not map out for me a road to great fortune and happiness, as they did for you, Devere.' Taylor's voice stopped me in my tracks.

I glanced back to see him pointing a pistol in my direction.

'I have had to make my own arrangements,' he concluded. 'Now . . . you will tell me what has happened to my gold tablet.'

'I do not explain secret doctrine to traitors,' I said, inviting him to shoot if that was what he intended.

'You were as psychically deficient as me before Malory married you off to that superwoman of yours! I guess all that nonsense the knighthood rammed down our throats about honouring the Goddess has proved relevant after all.' When I made no comment, he tried another way to vex me. 'Ashlee is still a very fine-looking woman,' he taunted. 'Tell me, do you think Malory will consider breeding her again once you are dead and buried?'

You would have been proud of me, Mrs Devere, for I suppressed my first urge — to beat the man senseless — which would surely have resulted in me being shot. I was still formulating a plan B when a rock hit the back of Taylor's head and he fell to the ground, unconscious.

Miss Koriche rushed towards me. 'Are you all right?'

'Yes ... thanks to your deadly aim.'

'Deadly? We should be so lucky!' Miss Koriche said, and crouched briefly to check Taylor's pulse. 'He is only unconscious, I am sad to say.'

I got the impression that Taylor might have tried to impose himself upon Miss Koriche during the time they'd been sharing the site house before our arrival; however, I did not pry.

'Many thanks for coming to my rescue,' I said, 'but I cannot imagine that we shall get around the representatives of the Holy See quite so easily.' I could see Taylor's guests approaching as I moved to the ladder to descend back into the tablet room.

When she too caught sight of the entourage, Miss Koriche gasped, panicked. 'We must leave.'

'I could not agree more. Arrange to have our belongings loaded on camels, whilst I make a few last-minute notes down here.'

'What about him?' She pointed to Taylor, spread-eagled in the midday sun.

I told her I would toss up some rope for her to bind him, and then she should get a few of the workmen to take him to the site house and lock him in the restoration room.

Miss Koriche urged me to be swift about my research. 'The church burns women like me,' she said.

'I took an oath to prevent any such thing occurring,' I assured her.

'A knight's vow,' she assumed, and looked to Taylor, unimpressed.

'A husband's vow,' I corrected, 'a father's vow and ...' although I hated to admit it, 'a grandfather's vow.'

Miss Koriche ventured a smile. 'I shall have us ready to leave within the hour,' she said.

'I shall be ready.' I dropped to the ground, and tossed up a spare length of rope. 'One moment, and I shall give you a hand.'

'No need,' she called back. 'Just do what you must and meet me back at the site house.'

When I entered the tablet room I was painfully aware of the missing tablet; all that remained was the metal plate it had been seated upon.

The plate appeared to be made of common steel, and yet it gave off a very faint eerie glow, so subtle it could be excused as a trick of the light — indeed, Taylor had dismissed it as such. The fact that this steel must have been in existence many thousands of years before steel was ever discovered was irrelevant to Taylor; all he could see was the possible monetary value, and thus he had attempted to have the plate removed from the floor. All the picks, spades and brute force could not even scratch the surface, however, quite literally; but we did discover that the plate was highly magnetised, as every time the men approached with their digging utensils, the tools adhered to the steel and had to be pried away by several men.

I was tempted to investigate the strange material further, but was too pressed for time. Instead, I sat myself before the final tablet and recorded the ancient rites and key words in the back of this journal.

By the time I had finished chronicling this information, I felt sure that I had used up the better part of the hour that Miss Koriche had given me. With one last long, mournful look at the magnificent ancient room of learning, I departed to meet Miss Koriche at the site house.

My apprehension was aroused when I found the area in front of the site house to be completely deserted — no camels, no servants loading belongings for our imminent departure.

Silently I cursed that in my hurry to record the information we needed from the tablets, I had failed to dispose of Taylor's weapon. Furthermore, I should have seen him bound and locked up myself.

There was little point in trying to surprise my adversary; he was no doubt watching me and awaiting my presence, with Miss Koriche as hostage.

I entered the drawing room to find Taylor seated on a lounge with Miss Koriche standing alongside him, motionless. Our charming host had one arm about the thigh of his hostage and in his other hand he held his pistol, the barrel of which was aimed point-blank at the woman's womb.

'Devere ... it is about time you honoured us with your presence.' Taylor caressed Miss Koriche's thigh; she was clearly repulsed by his touch. 'Now, unless you wish to lose the next generation of super-beings, I suggest you tell me what has become of my gold tablet.'

'Nothing has become of it,' I informed him, exasperated, for I was unable to provide a full explanation now that Taylor had proved himself a traitor. 'The tablet is still where you left it; I suspect that it has just levitated to a frequency of resonance where we can no longer perceive it.'

'Rubbish,' decided Taylor after a moment, and he dug the barrel of the pistol deeper into Miss Koriche's form.

I tried to disclose what I could without mentioning my personal experience with Star-Fire. 'According to what I have read, the ancient manna was mixed with metals and precious metals to produce a product that, when exposed to great heat, will levitate. And, once it reaches a certain temperature, will vanish from this plane of existence altogether. So, if you must blame someone for the theft, I am afraid your culprit is the sun.'

Taylor still appeared sceptical.

'If I am lying, then my deception will be plain enough this evening when the temperature drops,' I said. 'If I am correct, then you are really in luck, for no trace of the legendary substance has ever been unearthed.'

'To the restoration room then?' Taylor suggested, relieving Miss Koriche of her keys before he stood and shoved her in my direction. 'It appears you get to live for a few more hours. I feel very sure the representatives of his Holiness will wish to speak with you both.'

Miss Koriche appeared genuinely fearful of that prospect, and I didn't blame her. The Church had little enough respect for any woman, let alone one who was Eastern and not of the faith.

By the time I had finished chronicling the above, the sun hung low in the sky and the temperature was dropping rapidly. I expected the tablet's reappearance any time now.

Miss Koriche had fretted herself into a state of exhaustion and fallen asleep. I had not the heart to wake her to advise that the party of the Holy See had arrived several hours ago, despite her request to be alerted if there were any new developments.

Still, she was awake in a flash when Taylor burst through the door at sunset, accompanied by several men of the holy guard.

'It would seem your theory was wrong,' he said angrily.

Miss Koriche and I were taken to the crime scene, where the holy entourage awaited us.

'This is where I left the tablet,' Taylor said, skipping the introductions to get right to the point. 'It is evening now, so where is it?'

'Have you checked the tablet room?' I suggested.

'You said it would return to where I left it,' Taylor countered. 'So why would I check the tablet room?'

'You know as well as I do that the plate on which the tablet was seated is magnetised.' I left it to Taylor to draw his own conclusions.

He begged the patience of his guests while he descended into the dig to investigate the possibility himself. An uncomfortable silence prevailed as we awaited his return. No member of the holy party would even look at us, let alone speak with us. They appeared frightfully unamused about their little foray into the Persian wilderness.

Taylor re-emerged looking overjoyed. 'Devere was right,' he announced, sounding rather amazed. 'The tablet has returned to its rightful place.' He let out a laugh. 'Extraordinary.'

'Indeed,' replied the only cardinal amid the holy throng, who, by contrast, sounded not surprised in the slightest. 'Have the arch at the bottom of the staircase bricked up,' his Holiness instructed the head of his guard. 'And then have the entire hole filled with dirt.'

'What?' Taylor exclaimed in panic.

'I do not want a single trace of evidence left to suggest that this piece of dirt was ever disturbed.' The cardinal then leaned close to whisper in his guard's ear a moment, before he turned to retire to the site house. 'We shall depart as soon as you are done,' he concluded.

Taylor chased after his vanishing audience. 'What about our agreement?'

The cardinal held high a finger, as if he had suddenly realised that he had overlooked something. He turned to me. 'Mr Taylor informs me that you have a notebook in which you have recorded information you obtained from the tablets. May I have it, please.'

Miss Koriche glanced at me, her concern plain in her expression; I sensed she was as desperate to find Levi as you and I, Mrs Devere. I forced a half-smile of surrender for the benefit of the cardinal, which was clearly of no consolation to the young woman, and reached into my pocket for the notebook.

'It will prove of little interest to you,' I told his Holiness. 'I am sure you have a hundred texts just like it hidden away at home.'

'But none with your unique interpretation, Lord Suffolk.' The cardinal indicated I should hand over the item to one of his underlings, as he would not waste his divine energy by holding out his own hand.

'I am flattered by your interest,' I said.

The notebook was snatched from my hand by one of the guards and quickly passed to the cardinal.

'Oh, no need for such modesty, Devere, the church has been interested in you for some time,' his Holiness assured. '*No truth higher than the truth*,' he recalled our family motto. 'Perhaps, *no truth without proof* might be more appropriate.' The cardinal tucked my notebook deep into a pocket of his robe and turned to depart.

'The Church has never needed proof, so why should I?' I should have bitten my tongue, but I knew my dear wife would have chosen to speak out.

'Because when a man is gone, his words live on.' The cardinal turned back briefly to have the last say. 'Only I get to decide who sees those words.'

He smiled, which seemed an unnatural strain for him, then turned and left our vicinity, accompanied by every other man of the cloth in his party. The holy soldiers seized Miss Koriche, myself and Taylor.

'What are you grabbing me for?' Mr Taylor objected.

His query was ignored. The guard who had received the cardinal's whispered orders instructed his men to take us to the ruins we had uncovered — the same ruins they meant to brick up for all eternity.

'We are under the protection of the Shah, Nasr ed-Din.' I took a final stab at saving our skins as the men jostled us along.

'We have already been to see the Shah,' the guard said, and laughed. 'It would seem your gypsy friend has caused his Majesty some offence. I believe you will find that you no longer hold the favour of his Highness.'

My first concern was for you, my love. If this was true, I hated to imagine how your audience with the Shah had concluded.

Taylor and I were cast roughly into the pit, forced to bypass the descent ladder. By some miracle I had only the wind knocked out of me. Taylor was not so lucky; he landed on his arm, breaking it, and seemed to have fractured several ribs as well. Thankfully, Miss Koriche was allowed to descend the ladder. She came to my aid the instant she reached the ground, leaving Taylor to his own devices.

'I have already called you an idiot, have I not?' I said to Taylor, and received a very dark look in response. 'I just wanted to be sure we had established the fact.'

But there was little time for recrimination. 'Let us get inside the temple before we are cast into the stairwell,' I suggested to Miss Koriche, and we made haste to make use of the pulley and hoist.

Our landing on the steps was rather more abrupt than usual, but at least we were both still in one piece.

'Go and shut yourself in the tablet room,' I instructed the young woman, fearful that the soldiers may get bored during their labouring and use Miss Koriche for amusement. 'The word that opened the doors to the temple on the other side will also close them, if you must. When it is safe I shall come for you.'

'But how shall we escape once they have bricked up the entrance and filled the pit with dirt!' she panicked, her arms wrapped around her still-slender belly. 'And what is the point when we no longer have the codes we need to find your son?'

I produced the pages I had ripped from the back of the journal whilst she had been sleeping and handed them to her for safekeeping. 'One calamity at a time, Ajalae,' I said, and winked. 'I have been trapped inside an ancient dwelling before, so this is nothing new for me, I assure you.'

As she made haste for the tablet room, Taylor came crashing down the stairs to land at my feet, moaning and groaning.

'Are you still alive, old boy?' I asked.

He attempted a response but only a moan was forthcoming.

'Damn shame,' I said, then walked away to take a seat against a pillar and concoct a strategy for getting us out of this ruin alive.

It was only a matter of hours before the guards had the last brick in place and the ruin fell into complete darkness.

'*The Unworthy will never leave this dwelling.*' Taylor recited the warning engraved on the archway that now imprisoned us, just to let me know he was still alive. 'I knew I was tempting fate by entering this place.'

I was actually amused; Taylor might be a scoundrel but he certainly had charisma. I just could not bring myself to dislike him. I did not flatter him with a response, however.

I slid up the pillar at my back and, in the pitch dark, shuffled a short distance to where I judged the mid-point of the stone platform to be. I turned to face the opposite direction to the bricked-up archway and steadily made my way towards the doors to the tablet room. I expected Miss Koriche would be waiting inside, as the guards had not been distracted from their task.

When my foot hit the wooden strip in the floor, the doors to the tablet room parted and I was bathed in golden light. For the first time I was viewing the learning chamber in its full splendour, for the tablets emitted their own light, a phenomenon that was only apparent in complete darkness.

Miss Koriche walked forth from the chamber with tears of joy and wonder streaming down her face.

'Is it not magnificent!' She near choked on her awe as she glanced around at the glowing chamber. 'They spoke to me. I could not hear them before, but for some reason now I —' She cut herself short, her hands coming to rest upon her womb as she suddenly realised what had changed since her last visit to the chamber. Miss Koriche's psychic ability had finally been stimulated and she appeared truly humbled by the gift.

'Love opens all doors,' I told her.

'I believe I understand why your son has chosen to pursue the path he has,' she said calmly.

'Levi did not know he had a child when he made that decision,' I pointed out, my instinct telling me that her selfless resolve came from fear; for how was she to compete with the chance of achieving cosmic consciousness? 'I guarantee you that, had Levi known, he would certainly have chosen differently.' At least I sincerely hoped so; I liked to think we had instilled such morals in our son that he would not willingly leave the mother of his child to fend for herself.

'So, what is the plan?' I could tell Miss Koriche was very much hoping that I had one.

'Yes, what *is* the plan?' Taylor hobbled towards us.

Miss Koriche looked at me, perturbed. 'I thought nothing could destroy my current euphoria … I was mistaken.' She crouched and produced a dagger from the tip of her shoe and held it towards Taylor. 'If I were to finish him off, no one would ever know, or care.'

I sensed she was only toying with Taylor and it was delightful to see him squirm. He drew back from her, disabled, weaponless and vulnerable.

'Fair go!' he cried.

The sound of crumbling rock brought the confrontation to a halt.

The disturbance seemed to be coming from the canal-like area ahead of us. I stepped off the trigger, the tablet room doors closed and darkness fell in the entrance chamber once more — but only momentarily.

'Lord Suffolk?' came a cry.

'I am he,' I called back, not recognising the voice but hearing enough of its tone to realise it was probably one of the local workmen.

'We have come to get you out.'

I moved towards the voice. Aware that I was approaching the edge of the platform, I began to feel for the canal ledge with my foot. 'A dangerous resolve on your behalf,' I replied, finding the rim and lowering myself down into the canal. 'To what do I owe this great favour?'

'We feel obliged to your son to see you to safety, Lord Suffolk,' the man explained as he widened the gap in the rock wall with his hands. 'None of us has ever had a *paid* holiday before.'

I should have known — Levi made staunch friends and allies everywhere he went, a result of his ability to read and grant the secret needs of others.

'Are you injured, my lord?'

'I am not,' I relayed. 'However, Mr Taylor is not in the best of health.'

There followed much hushed debate in the local dialect, before the voice in the darkness was again heard. 'We would prefer that Mr Taylor remain here.'

I saw the light of a torch flickering beyond a small breach near the top of the rock wall that blocked the canal. I began clearing rocks from our side.

'I am sure we all would, my good fellow,' I said. 'But I know I have no desire to answer to God for the demise of such a pitiable soul.'

I peered through the opening to see four local men bearing torches; they were able to stand tall in the tunnel beyond. The fellow who spoke English was twice the age of the other three, who, he explained, were his sons.

'And might I know the name of my saviour?' I asked.

'Mohammed,' he replied.

I was not sure if the fellow had misinterpreted my question, but as just about every second man in the Near East was named Mohammed, I figured probably not. 'I am very pleased to meet you, Mohammed. *Very pleased.*' I reached through the gap to shake his hand.

As Miss Koriche approached, I noted that she had returned her blade to its hiding place. 'I have been schooled in the premise of crafting reality through thought, but only now do I fathom the full scope of the concept,' she said. 'It seems your willpower is phenomenal, Lord Suffolk.'

'How do you know that our rescue was not of your design?' I posed.

Miss Koriche rolled her eyes, feeling I was flattering her, and yet she smiled broadly, for we would live to see the light of day again.

'It could have been my design,' Taylor quipped as he attempted to lower himself down into the canal and fell to land on his back once more.

We chose to ignore him.

The opening in the rocks was now big enough to accommodate our escape. Miss Koriche was pulled through first, and set down on her feet by Mohammed and his eldest son.

'How did you find us?' she asked.

'There are many tunnels beneath the Mound of Pitch that have been used to rob graves over the centuries,' Mohammed explained as he and his sons pulled me through. 'Very few people know about them, and those that do consider them too dangerous to use. Hence we would prefer that their existence remain a secret.'

The man looked to Taylor, who was holding his one good arm out through the gap. Mohammed seemed very reluctant to take hold.

'Do you mean to say that you have known about the Dragon temple and its treasures for some time and have never attempted to remove them?' Miss Koriche was impressed.

'Remove them!' Mohammed laughed heartily at the folly of the idea, as did his sons. 'Of course not. This place is cursed to all but a handful of souls.'

'And I now realise that I am not one of them.' Taylor's hand waved about, beckoning aid. 'I promise I won't disclose your secret to anyone.'

'Hah! I feel sure that once you are away from here and recovered, you will never give a second thought to that huge golden lotus in the roof of the temple and how you might extract it,' Miss Koriche chided. 'And I might grow wings and fly away!'

'I always said you were an angel,' Taylor flirted, in a desperate attempt to save his skin.

'Leave him,' Miss Koriche said.

Mohammed's sons agreed with Miss Koriche, and the man in charge looked to me for the final word.

'We can blindfold him,' I resolved. 'And I give you my personal assurance that Mr Taylor shall leave Persia with me and never return.'

Mohammed finally took hold of Taylor's arm and, with the aid of one of his sons, hoisted our associate through the hole and dumped him on the ground. The action drew much moaning from Taylor as his injuries were agitated.

'You had better keep up,' Mohammed grumbled, as he and his sons led us up the tunnel.

'Sometimes you are too good a man, I fear,' Miss Koriche commented to me as she set off after our guides.

I crouched beside Taylor and, taking hold of him under the arms, hoisted him to his feet. 'Only God knows why I would bother having you spared,' I said. 'I regret it already.'

Once he was upright, Taylor appeared rather more humbled by his little ordeal than I had expected. 'I would have seen you killed,' he stated and I knew he spoke the truth.

'You may still,' I assured, in case he was disappointed about that. 'Are both your legs working?'

Taylor nodded, then caught my arm to delay my departure. 'I will not forget this, Devere. You are a true friend.'

'I would not take that for granted if I were you,' I advised. 'Just because I had your life spared does not mean I am prepared to forgive your treachery.'

'Your forgiveness seems a minor detail when you would give me my life.'

'Do try to be more constructive, that is all I ask.' I gave him a chug on the shoulder, for I had never seen the man appear so chastened. 'We are not out of Persia yet.'

I got us moving, before the light of the torches escaped us.

Further down, the tunnel split into three canals that branched off in different directions.

'Which way do we go?' Miss Koriche asked, as our guides had come to a standstill.

A rope dropped from above; we looked up to discover a hole in the ceiling and another two local lads waving down at us.

'How many sons do you have?' I asked Mohammed, assuming these boys were his too.

'Thirteen.' He grinned proudly. 'To different wives.'

'Thirteen!' I echoed and shook his hand again. 'It is a miracle that you are still alive.'

'My sons keep me alive,' Mohammed assured me.

'You are lucky,' I retorted, 'my eldest just nearly got me killed.'

'Your son is a very good man,' Mohammed impressed upon me. 'He has great light within him.'

I was not too sure what Mohammed meant by this and did not have time to pursue it, as Miss Koriche had already been hoisted up safely and I was next.

'Where do we go from here?' Taylor looked concerned, but Mohammed thought him prying.

'As if I would tell you.'

'Are there more tunnels, smaller than this?' Taylor appeared to have the shakes.

I allowed one of the lads to ascend before me and stayed behind to deal with our reluctant companion. 'Is there a problem?'

'I cannot abide small enclosed spaces,' he informed me rather bitterly.

'I feel sure you could make an exception to save your life.' I attempted to gloss over the drama.

'No, you do not understand,' Taylor said, frustrated. 'I panic!'

Mohammed gave an exasperated sigh and Taylor exploded.

'I do not like it any more than you! Do you think I enjoyed being locked in a tiny, cramped space as a child? Wondering through all the long starving hours whether my father was going to leave me to rot!'

'Taylor!' I restrained him from lashing out at Mohammed with his good arm. 'I *will* get you out of here. I am not leaving you behind.'

My assurance broke the back of his fear and his anger ebbed. But then the fear returned. 'There must be another way back to the surface.'

'The Romans are filling it with dirt as we speak. This is the only way out now.' Mohammed moved to the rope. 'I will wait for you above, take your time.'

Our guide seemed a little more kindly disposed towards Taylor following his outburst; adoring his sons as he did, I guessed Mohammed found it tragic that any man would abuse the privilege of fatherhood.

We watched our guide shin up the rope to join his sons and Miss Koriche and I looked to Taylor who was crumbling to pieces before my eyes. I had never once, in all the time we had studied together, suspected that he had been so deeply scarred as a child.

'This is your opportunity to seize back your own power,' I told him.

'I cannot,' he insisted, barely resisting the urge to drop to the ground and curl up in a ball. If this was what the thought of the passage did to him, I hated to think how he would handle the actual event.

'No, Taylor, in this case you *will not*, as there is a *huge* difference.' I walked over and took hold of the rope. 'Unlike when you were a child, this time you have a choice and you *can* choose not to be a victim any more.'

Taylor was shaking his head and yet I could almost see his will battling to escape that dark place buried deep inside him.

'Surely it is not your choice to stay and rot?' I said. There was no point trying to avoid the issue now; Taylor had little choice but to face his fears or perish.

'No! I want to be outside. I need air!' He ripped open the collar of his shirt, seemingly on the verge of hyperventilating.

'Taylor, listen to me. Your physical, mental and emotional freedom lie this way,' I persuaded. 'Take one last journey into the darkness and you will never have to revisit it again.'

He had to think about it a moment, but he finally nodded to concede he understood my reasoning. 'What if I have a panic fit in one of the tunnels?'

'Well, having a fit in a tunnel is preferable to rotting in a tomb,' I said. 'Would you not agree?'

He was amused by this and I saw a glimmer of the Taylor I knew. 'When you put it that way.'

He shrugged off his horror outwardly, but required a few deep breaths to actually approach the rope.

'I shall be with you all the way,' I reassured him as I tied the rope around his waist.

'I have never had company in the darkness before.' He sounded rather touched by the concept.

'Let us hope it makes all the difference.' I motioned to Mohammed to hoist him up.

*   *   *

In the tunnel above, the ceiling was tall enough to kneel upright comfortably. At this point I tied a rope around my waist and had Taylor attach the other end securely around his waist. 'If worst comes to worst and you panic, I shall drag you out of here,' I said. The comment was made partly in jest, but Taylor seemed to appreciate my intent. 'Are you ready?'

He appeared as if he might be sick at any moment, but he nodded reluctantly.

We set off, half-walking in a crouched position and half-crawling. We kept only one torch alight and that was in the hand of Mohammed's son who was at the head of our convoy. Taylor and I had nominated to go last, as he was in disfavour, so we were moving in near total darkness. I had not heard anything from my attachment for some time, but I knew he was still moving along behind me as I could hear him breathing and the rope between us remained slack.

As the roof of the tunnel lowered and we were forced onto all fours, I attempted to get Taylor's mind at least into the wide-open spaces.

'You know what I would like to be doing right now, Taylor?'

'Do tell, Devere.' Taylor was breathing deeply to control his panic, but was managing to keep it in check.

'A nice game of cricket.'

'A splendid thought.' He was grateful for the distraction. 'Drinks at the club afterwards?'

'*Absolutely*. Malory's shout.' I considered that our fee for this little stint in Persia had just gone up.

Taylor laughed, but it quickly degenerated into nervousness and then panic. 'How much further?'

I relayed the question to Mohammed ahead of me.

'Five minutes,' he called back. 'Not far.'

'Does the ceiling get much lower?' I pre-empted Taylor's next query, for I was starting to feel somewhat claustrophobic myself.

'We will have to crawl on our bellies for a small way and then we will be back to standing.'

The rope around my waist jolted me to a halt. 'Taylor?'

'I cannot breathe,' he said faintly. 'I feel dizzy!'

'No! Passing out is just another way of avoiding your fear. You have to relax your breathing, you hear me?' I heard him weeping. 'Answer me, Taylor! There is no point having a voice in the darkness if you refuse to communicate with it.'

I felt him squirming behind me, battling his demons.

'Damn you, Devere! All right!'

'Good man.' I resumed crawling. 'We shall get this over with as quickly as possible.'

I felt a great deal of empathy with Taylor, for the tight squeeze and the lack of air seemed to make this stretch of passage last an age. The torch had been extinguished as it was no longer safe to carry, thus a heavy darkness enveloped us.

Taylor finally cracked. 'Get me out!' he yelled.

As his body gave a violent convulsion, he disturbed the old wooden support planks above and alongside us and we were all coated in a shower of dust, which got in our mouths, noses, throats and eyes. This only compounded Taylor's panic and he continued to kick violently. The shower of dirt increased and I wrapped my arms around my head to endure my imminent burial. Next thing I knew, I was being dragged into the open. As Taylor landed with a thud behind me, I perceived an image of a young boy kicking open the lid of the trunk in which he'd been encased so long; the feeling of exhilaration was all-consuming.

Much coughing, spluttering and spitting ensued, but as soon as I had regained my senses I moved to congratulate Taylor, who was still shaking like a leaf. 'You did it, old boy, you are free!'

Taylor looked around in a daze as the realisation dawned. 'We got out.'

The cave in which we had landed was a huge space by comparison with the tunnel, and Taylor breathed easy once more. Tears streamed silently down his face as he emerged from his dark past and came back to the present. 'I feel amazing,' he said. He sounded surprised, although I could tell he was embarrassed to have fallen apart in front of so many people. 'I apologise for creating a scene and for any grief I have caused, for I am greatly indebted to you all.'

Miss Koriche crouched beside Taylor and handed him a scarf to wipe his face. 'At least I understand your need to play power games now, and always to look out for number one,' she said.

'I believe this is the first time that I have understood it,' he confessed.

There was such sincerity and hurt in his voice that Miss Koriche was compelled to embrace the man who only an hour before she had threatened to kill. Taylor buried his head in her shoulder and cried until his heart was content.

Mohammed walked with me to the cave's mouth. It opened onto the desert, which was lit brightly beneath a waxing moon. I could see the silhouettes of a herd of camels that awaited close by, tended by two more of Mohammed's male offspring.

'If we travel overnight, we should be able to get you to the river before the Romans finish filling in their hole,' our saviour explained.

'If Miss Koriche feels herself capable of departing at once, then I shall be happy to do so.' I thanked Mohammed again for his aid. 'Is there something I can do for you in return ... some payment or *gift*.' That was the term I was looking for.

The man shook his head. 'Please, your son has already been too generous,' he assured. 'This deed is my remuneration to him.'

I was surprised to hear that one could be too generous here in Persia. But then I realised that if I made Mohammed a gift, he would feel obliged to recompense me. In the circumstances, a simple 'thank you' was far less complicated.

FROM THE JOURNAL OF TAMAR DEVERE

Lord Devere's notes ended here, whereupon I shoved them securely back into the inner spine of the journal, and moved straight to Lady Ashlee's Persian tale.

REVELATION 10

LIGHT

FROM THE JOURNAL OF LADY ASHLEE GRANVILLE-DEVERE
We emerged from the secret passage leading out of the Shah's court into a tiny room within a squalid residence in Baghdad. Awaiting us was a guide, Zalman, who claimed that he had been instructed to lead us to safety — by my son presumably. It was impossible to find out as Zalman was a man of few words. Eager to escape the city, we placed our trust in this tall stranger and now found ourselves walking into a vast desert without any sign of transportation.

Despite our lack of knowledge about our guide, Albray — still inhabiting the body of Raineath — seemed well disposed towards him, as was I, for his subtle body was the most brillant I'd ever seen. Cingar, however, was more wary, feeling that there was something not quite right about our new travelling companion.

It was only as we crossed the flat desert wasteland, our shadows stretching long beside us on the parched earth, that Cingar and I finally realised what was amiss with Zalman — the man had no shadow. I gasped aloud, and turned to Albray for an explanation.

'Every light casts a shadow when it encounters physical matter, but once a physical body generates its own light, then it no longer casts a shadow upon its surroundings,' the knight told us.

It was strange to hear these wise words coming from Raineath's mouth, but Albray knew that as soon as he departed the young woman's form, she would black out and become a burden to our escape. At least if he maintained wilful control of Raineath, he could carry her to safety.

'Are you suggesting that our friend is some sort of spiritual master?' Cingar asked, stunned. This had obviously been the furthest conclusion from his mind.

'There is only one kind of spiritual master,' Albray clarified.

'One of your Melchi?' I guessed, for Albray had once belonged to the underground order of warrior priests.

'Perhaps one of the very high initiates.'

My knight sounded as if he were guessing. 'You are unsure?' I asked. I found this curious, as Albray had been something of a legend in the brotherhood himself.

'A masterful warrior is something quite different from a spiritual warrior, I assure you,' he told me. 'If I were one of the latter, I would certainly not be in my current state of limbo.'

Cingar was frowning, having lost track of the conversation, especially as, to his eyes, it was Raineath volunteering this information. 'I have seen Melchi warriors, and they have shadows just like the rest of us,' he said.

I found his view amusing and it prompted me to observe my own shadow. I was rather surprised to note that it was not so prominent as the shadows of the two people in my company. I might have dismissed it as a trick of the light, but we were all standing under the same huge light source, so why should my shadow appear different? Was it possible that one's shadow denoted the extent to which the atomic structure of one's body was absorbing and transmitting cosmic light?

I changed the subject to one that would interest Cingar. 'So where do you think our friend might be leading us?'

'Nowhere you will find on any map,' was Albray's guess.

Just as the last rays of daylight were leaving the sky and a chill swept over the desert, I spotted a large dwelling on the horizon.

'Praise the universe,' I muttered, when it became clear that Zalman was leading us toward it. Rest and water were imminent.

By the time we arrived at the large, lush homestead, it was lit by a waxing moon.

'Do you know the residents?' I asked Zalman.

He smiled at me broadly.

'Oh yes,' he said. 'Your blissful rest this night is assured.'

I was very grateful to hear it.

The entranceway to the two-storey house was lit by flaming torches, which were very welcoming in the cool darkness.

'The grounds are so lush and beautiful.' Cingar was greatly impressed by the oasis. 'There must be an underground water source.'

I knew I must look a terrible fright after our long journey and felt almost ashamed to present myself at the front door of so grand a dwelling.

A stunningly beautiful Eastern woman opened the door. What struck me immediately about her was that she wore no burka to cover herself from the sight of our male company. 'Welcome,' she greeted us warmly and opened the door wide. 'We have been expecting you. I am Denera, mistress of this house.'

'I am —' I began.

Denera held up a hand politely, to save me the trouble. 'No need for introductions, we know who you are. If my Lady Suffolk and Miss Saray would like to follow me, Zalman will show Mr Choron to the men's quarters, where he can freshen himself.'

Interesting, I thought, that Denera should know Raineath's second name, when I did not know it myself.

Although Cingar was clearly concerned about being separated from us, he did not argue with the request as it had been delivered by one so beautiful. Indeed, the gypsy had trouble dragging his gaze from Denera as he was led away by Zalman.

'Please, this way.' Denera escorted Raineath and I in the opposite direction.

I could not have imagined a more congenial chamber. The room was as grand as that the Shah had supplied, but not so huge and impersonal. There were two beds, a large sunken bath filled with warm scented water, and a table spread with fresh food, water and wine. A multitude of candle clusters stood about the chamber — this was a wealthy household indeed that could afford the extravagance of so many candles burning at once.

'I shall return when you have had time to recuperate,' Denera advised. 'Please make yourselves at home.'

I thanked our hostess most sincerely as she exited and closed the doors behind her.

'If there is a bath within a hundred miles, you will always find it by nightfall,' Albray said, pleased to finally be at leisure to speak openly with me.

'There is a goddess watching over me, to be sure,' I agreed, and watched my knight as he collapsed Raineath's form onto the bed. 'So, if you could take your leave some time soon, that would be most appreciated.'

'Even if I depart this body, I shall not be able to leave until Raineath awakes and dismisses me,' he pointed out.

He was right. And as I was not the current holder of the stone, I could not so easily perceive my ghostly knight's comings and goings. I realised that Raineath was still wearing her head cover.

'Why are you still wearing that?' I asked. 'Raineath does not willingly subscribe to the faith, you realise?'

'I would not have walked all day in this by choice,' Albray replied. 'Raineath is not ready to remove it.'

'Because of her injuries?' I took a step towards the woman. 'Shall I assess —'

'No.' Albray held out a hand to keep me at bay. 'Swear you will not look.'

It was clear Albray was relaying the message directly from Raineath. I respected her wish and backed away. 'I swear.'

Albray removed the bracelet that held his stone from the woman's wrist and held it out to me. 'Raineath is sorry that she lied about finding our stone, and would like me to return it,' he said.

'I cannot allow her to give the stone back, for that will invoke a curse upon her,' I explained. I wondered how we were going to get around that little sub-clause.

'All you have to do is make a gift to Raineath in exchange; something that may serve her as well as I,' Albray challenged. I could tell he would judge my offering as a reflection of how much he meant to me personally.

'Well, although I do not possess anything that could match your worth, my friend, I do have something that will aid Raineath to make a new start for herself.'

I reached down inside my cleavage and began rooting around in my corset. Although I could not see Albray's face, I could sense his amusement. Indeed, this was no ordinary corset — Nanny Beat had made it specially for me, to store my emergency currency when travelling. Eventually I produced a large diamond to exchange for my lost ringstone.

'Raineath is satisfied — sorry, no,' Albray corrected himself, 'she is overwhelmed by your generosity and forgiveness.'

He took the diamond from me, handed back my treasure stone and then waved me goodbye. Raineath's body collapsed back onto the bed, her hand clutching to her heart the jewel that would ensure her future prosperity and freedom.

'The poor girl must be exhausted after her ordeal,' I said, gazing down at her. Then I sensed my ghostly knight standing at my side once more, and turned to find him staring at me fondly.

'Yes, but she handled herself very well,' he said.

I felt that he was paying me the compliment. 'You could not begin to conceive how I have missed you, old friend.'

Albray's smile conveyed that he had missed me too. 'So I may stay while you bathe?' he teased.

I savoured his cheeky grin a moment, then said, 'I hardly think so. Dismissed, dismissed . . .'

'Ah,' he appealed, disappointed. 'The harem was much more fun.'

'Dismissed,' I said a third time, and the knight vanished from my presence.

Alone at last, I turned my attention to the scented bath and shed my clothes with haste.

I do believe that this was the longest bath I'd ever had on my own. I just couldn't seem to drag my aching body from its warm, watery repose. Only when my belly ached for sustenance and my skin was as shrivelled as a prune could I bring myself to emerge.

I slipped on the cotton shift that had been supplied by my hostess and took a seat at the table to satisfy my hunger.

Soon afterwards, Denera returned.

'You appear much refreshed,' she commented as she breezed in quietly, carrying a bowl of liquid that she placed beside Raineath's bed.

There was something very familiar about this woman; I felt I knew her, although we had never met before today.

'Thank you,' I said, 'I feel infinitely better.'

I was about to broach the subject of her seeming so familiar to me, when she reached down to lift the veil from Raineath's face.

'Raineath does not wish for anyone to see her injuries,' I warned.

'I understand,' said Denera, 'but this salve will aid the healing process.' She drew aside the veil and gave a heavy sigh. 'She will heal on the outside, but on the inside ...' Denera shook her head '... I am not so sure.'

I had averted my eyes, wishing to keep the vow I had made to Raineath. 'I fear that her suffering has been long-term, but she has survived,' I said. 'Perhaps the freedom she has fought so hard to secure will also help to heal her.'

'Indeed,' Denerea agreed. 'It is a momentous achievement.'

As Denera treated Raineath's wounds, I wondered about our hostess. It was unusual for the mistress of the house to tend to her guests personally, or to answer the door for that matter. I was about to make a polite query regarding all this when Denera began to hum a tune that was completely mesmerising. I found myself nodding off in my chair and, not wanting to waste a perfectly good bed, managed to raise my weary form. I crawled onto the bed's soft silky surface and was asleep before my head hit the pillow.

When I awoke it was still night, or perhaps I had slept through until the following evening? One thing was certain: I felt like a new woman, having enjoyed the best slumber of my life.

Raineath was awake and seated at the table, still wearing her head cover, conveying food to her mouth beneath it.

'How are you?' I inquired, trying not to sound as chipper as I felt, for I knew Raineath would still be ailing.

'Much better, thank you.'

But her hunched form and her reluctance to unveil, or even look at me, told me different.

'Have you inspected your wounds?' I asked.

She shook her head. 'I left my face in that prison cell,' she replied. 'It will be the veil for me from now on.'

'You will need air and light to heal, so the process will be much faster without the veil,' I said, trying the sensible approach. 'And as you are among friends, surely it would be wiser —'

'I do not want him to see me like this.' Raineath finally looked at me.

'Cingar?' I assumed, and she gave a nod and lowered her eyes once more.

'I understand that Cingar admires you greatly. He will not care —'

'Yes, he will! All men do!' Raineath retorted with a spite that was not really aimed at me. 'I was so beautiful ... he will never really see me now.'

Her words made it clear that what she felt for Cingar was more than just a crush on the legend that he'd once been. I wondered if Raineath was aware that her love was in vain.

'Do you know that Cingar recently lost his wife of twenty years?' I asked her.

'No.' She looked to me, sounding hopeful, and I held up my hands to stop her from jumping to the wrong conclusion.

'My friend believes he will never love again, and so you see, even as beautiful as you were, Cingar would not have seen you — at least, not the way you desire him to.'

Raineath gave a heavy sigh. 'He sees you.' She sounded envious. 'His saviour from the dungeons of the Duc de Guise.'

'And now you know how I managed that legendary feat.' I held up my hand to show her the ringstone dangling on its wrist-chain once more.

'Does Captain Choron know about Albray?'

I shook my head. 'I am sure he suspects something, but I believe Cingar likes the legend the way it is.'

'I will not tell,' she assured me. 'I owe you so much —'

'Nonsense! All I did was lend you my stone for a while.' I approached the table to pick at the food.

'That is not true. I stole it. Although I fully intended to find you and return it,' Raineath said. 'I could hardly believe that you had raised my case with the Shah.'

'I did so upon Cingar's request,' I explained. 'Although, as it was my suggestion that the Shah consider you for Cingar's tuition, I did feel partly responsible for your plight.'

'I just so needed to be seen ... and when the legend I had idolised all my life was brought to me despite my isolation, I thought that surely our meeting was fated by the Goddess.' She burst into tears. 'I did not consider how he would be affected by my actions, or you! I was wasting away ... my talent, beauty and identity fading. I know it was selfish, but I just had to do something!'

I wrapped my arms around the young woman and allowed her to sob out her hurt, fear and guilt.

'I would have done the same thing in your place,' I assured her when her outburst had subsided. Then I stepped back to look her in the eye. 'But once I was free, I would not hide myself away for anyone else's benefit. You have earned the right to be seen.'

'But now I am an offence on the eye,' she said.

'You, my friend, are a warrior, and any scars you may have are testimony to victory.'

With a sniffle, Raineath nodded at my alternative view. 'Battle scars ... I think I can live with that.'

She lifted the veil from her head.

To my great shock, Raineath looked exactly as she had when I first met her.

'Is it very bad?' she asked, fearful from my reaction.

'No ... not at all.'

I recalled seeing a mirror by my bed and I ran to fetch it.

Meanwhile, Raineath found the courage to touch her face; feeling her smooth, unscathed skin she hesitated to smile. 'Am I dreaming?' She urged me to hurry with the mirror, which I held up before her. Upon sighting herself reborn, Raineath's tears welled anew, this time with joy. 'How could this be possible?'

'Denera.' I could only think of one explanation. 'She bathed you with some healing salve last night. Though I cannot imagine what was in it for it to have worked so swiftly!'

Not entirely true, as there was one substance I had encountered that would heal like this, but it seemed unlikely that Denera, or anyone in this day and age, would have access to Star-Fire — bar the Melchi who guarded the last known vial of it.

Raineath was a little disconcerted. 'You promised you would not lift my veil,' she said.

'I did not lift it … nor did I look when Denera did,' I assured her with a smile, and Raineath smiled also as she looked back to her reflection and admired it.

'Now he will see me,' she fancied.

Yes, Cingar would see her, I thought, but whether he was ready for love again was quite another matter. Although, as Raineath had pointed out several times, Cingar had yet to lay eyes on her and I had to confess that the young woman was not unlike his beloved Jessenia in many regards.

A knock on the door heralded Denera's entrance.

'Greetings again, ladies. Zalman has asked me to advise that he and Mr Choron await you in the foyer. As soon as you join them, your journey will resume.'

'We will be travelling by night?' I queried.

'It is near dawn.' Denera placed a bundle of clothes on each of our beds. 'Is there anything else you require?'

I looked to Raineath, who moved swiftly towards our hostess. 'Thank you,' she said, and took hold of our hostess's hands and kissed them.

Derena lifted the young woman's face to look her in the eye, and stroked her smooth dark hair. 'No need to thank me, little one …healing is my vocation.' Denera leaned forward and kissed Raineath on the forehead.

I had been too weary to observe the light-body of our hostess when first I met her, but now I saw that here was another soul with a perfectly clear subtle body. As she held Raineath in her arms, I perceived Denera's light-body expanding to envelop the other woman. Her energy reinforced her patient's light-body with great surges of cosmic light, which rushed through Raineath's seven light centres, dispersing the cloudy blockages that had built up in the course of her traumatic past.

'You are very accomplished in your chosen field, my lady,' Raineath granted as she was released from the long embrace. 'I have never felt so well or elated.'

'And you have every reason to feel so,' Denera told her with a sincere smile. 'You have a very promising future ahead.'

The lady of the house made for the door. 'Now I must leave you to prepare.'

We thanked our hostess and, as I partook of some breakfast, Raineath moved to dress herself. She sorted through the fresh attire Denera had left and exposed a beautiful polished wooden box hidden beneath the clothes. When Raineath opened the case to find a violin inside, I was moved to tears.

Raineath gasped as she took the instrument in hand. The young woman was so overwhelmed with happiness all she could do was weep. 'I must be dead, for I have passed into the Land of Bliss,' she said.

I shook my head to reassure her. 'We are not dead. And even if we were, I would still beg the honour of hearing you play.'

Raineath collected herself and, tossing her long, dark, straight hair behind her slender shoulders, she raised the instrument to her chin. 'The honour will be all mine, my Lady du Lac.'

She played the composition Cingar had taught her, and performed it skilfully, with all the seduction, passion and precision of the legendary master himself.

When the last note sounded, I applauded her most sincerely. 'Denera is absolutely right — you have a very bright future ahead.'

The beaming smile on Raineath's face conveyed that she was daring to believe that prediction.

I felt considerably more prepared for a desert trek wearing the long white cotton robes and sensible walking boots that Denera had supplied, and I believed Raineath was happy to have shed her harem attire too.

It was a lovely moment when Cingar and Raineath finally met face to face in the foyer. 'Could this be my young student?' the gypsy asked, surprised that she appeared unscathed from her ordeal.

I took it upon myself to do the formal honours and ease the

awkwardness of the moment. 'Cingar Choron, allow me to present to you Miss Raineath Saray.'

Raineath curtsied as Cingar took her hand, and was hard pressed to smother her delight when her idol kissed it.

'It is my greatest pleasure to make your acquaintance at last,' he said. 'You are a woman equalled in bravery and heart only by my own lady patron.'

'That is a compliment indeed,' Raineath said, smiling shyly.

I believed it was so long since she'd flirted with a man that she had forgotten how. Or perhaps Raineath was wiser in the game of love than I gave her credit for, and had decided to conceal her feelings for the man until she had figured out how best to win his heart.

Underlying Cingar's friendly address, I sensed much guilt that he desperately needed to purge himself of. He began to speak, but was interrupted by Zalman.

'I am sorry, but we must get moving before sunrise. There will be ample time to talk on the way.'

Aware of Cingar's need to speak with Raineath alone, I decided to keep pace with Zalman, who had walked on ahead. It was wonderful striding across the open desert towards the sunrise, with just a breath of warm wind caressing my face. Respectful of Zalman's love of silence, I refrained from asking any of the many questions I had about our journey. For in truth I already knew that there was only one answer to all of my queries: wait and see.

I had many questions about our brief stopover too, and now that the sun had cast its light over the landscape, I turned back to view the oasis — to find nothing behind us but the same bare, flat horizon that lay in front. I stopped in my tracks, dumbfounded.

'I did not think we had walked so far,' I said.

Cingar and Raineath also looked back. 'We have not,' Cingar agreed, looking to Zalman, who had stopped and turned back to face us. 'What is going on, Zalman? Where are you taking us?'

'You will know by sunset,' Zalman replied.

'Sunset!' Cingar looked concerned.

Zalman walked on. 'I know where we can find water and shade. Trust me one more day.'

'I do not like this,' Cingar said, but we had no choice but to follow our mysterious guide.

I noted the wind getting stronger as we walked, but Zalman did not break his stride, even though he was leading us towards a great wall of dust that stretched across the horizon, seemingly without end.

'Are you mad?' Cingar yelled to him.

'We cannot go around it,' our guide pointed out, without looking back.

I turned a full circle and, seeing no shelter anywhere, had to agree that there was no choice but to push on.

'We could try and make it back to Denera's house,' Cingar suggested.

'If we knew where it was, you mean? No, we should stick together.' I waved the gypsies forth, and together we headed off in pursuit of Zalman.

It wasn't long before the windstorm was upon us. The dirt in my eyes made vision impossible, but with little fear of encountering any obstacles I just kept my head down and kept putting one foot in front of the other. I felt that I was weathering the situation rather well, when someone unexpectedly collided with me and I was sent off-balance and onto all fours.

'I am so very sorry.' The English gentleman aided me back to my feet.

His face was wrapped against the weather as mine was and yet I knew him at once.

'My Lord Suffolk, fancy meeting you here.'

As his beautiful blue eyes opened wide with surprise and delight, the storm seemed to ebb a little and I heard him utter my name. He embraced me and I him, the relief washing the dirt from our sights.

'Thank God. When I heard we'd lost the Shah's favour, I feared the worst,' he said.

'Never.' I held my wrist high to expose the ringstone and my husband rolled his eyes.

'I should have known.' He held me tight under one of his arms as we pushed on forward. 'You two make quite a team.'

'Not as good a team as we do.' I hugged him tighter. 'You would not

154

have landed us in so much trouble with the Shah in the first place, I fear.'

Lord Devere nodded, amused. 'The Shah is probably the least of our problems just now,' he went on. 'A representative of the Holy See just ordered Taylor, Miss Koriche and myself buried alive in our dig site.'

'What!' I recalled the party I had seen exiting the Shah's court before my own audience. 'So that is what they were discussing with the Shah.'

'My murder?' jested my husband.

'Burying the find,' I clarified, knowing he understood my meaning well enough.

'When did you encounter the cardinal's party?'

'I saw them yesterday. And you?'

My husband was perplexed. 'It was only a few days ago that I had the displeasure of meeting them at the site, so they cannot have been in Baghdad yesterday.'

I agreed that it seemed very unlikely there would be two such parties in Persia at once.

My husband's confusion doubled. 'And I would have expected you to have seen the Shah over a week ago. Were you delayed somewhere?'

'No,' I answered, until I considered last night's blissful slumber — it had felt like I had slept for a week. 'No, that is impossible,' I mused. 'I would be dead.'

'What is not possible?' My lord had lost my train of thought.

'What is the date today?'

Lord Devere's reply shocked me; by his reckoning I had indeed lost a week somewhere. 'You are sure?'

'Positive,' my husband confirmed, 'for I have been counting the days until your return.'

All these years of marriage and he could still make my heart flutter. His kiss made me forget my curiosity, and when we came back to reality the storm had completely died away.

'If you are quite finished, Devere,' Taylor yelled back at us, 'we are losing our guide.' He pointed towards Zalman, who was leagues ahead.

Had I heard Taylor wrong? 'Zalman is your guide?'

'Yes, he showed up yesterday claiming that he had been sent to lead me to safety,' my husband explained, and then wondered at my mystified expression. 'What did I say?'

'Pardon me, folks.' Cingar directed us to Zalman once more. 'Is it just my eyes or is our friend disappearing?'

We all looked ahead to see Zalman sinking into the horizon.

'There must be an incline ahead,' I deduced.

'We should catch up.' Lord Devere clutched my hand tight as we ran to see if I was right.

'Oh my Goddess!' Cingar yelled, supporting his head with both hands as he beheld what lay over the rise, for he and Raineath had won the dash. Lord Devere and I passed the limping Mr Taylor and our pregnant daughter-in-law to come to a halt on the rim of a huge maze of deep chasms recessed into the ground before us.

'Where on Earth are we?' Lord Devere said.

'There is no such place in Persia, I assure you.' Taylor was an authority on the geography of the country where he had been posted for some years now.

'*Nowhere you will find on any map,*' I said, repeating Albray's prediction.

'I told you not to trust Zalman,' Cingar said. 'How are we to find our way through this precarious labyrinth without a guide?'

'I can see plainly that Zalman is an enlightened being,' I explained but Cingar was still not convinced.

'It does not seem very enlightened to leave us stranded in the middle of a desert,' he grumbled.

'I would say he has taken his leave to avoid any more questions before sundown,' I offered, spotting the steep path of descent into the canyon close by.

'Like where we are?' Taylor was bemused; he'd never been lost in the East before.

'I think I know where we are.'

We all looked to Miss Koriche.

'Set Amentet,' she announced, admiring the vast canyon.

'I was under the impression that Set Amentet was a cemetery in the mountains on the west bank of the Nile,' Taylor said.

'Set Amentet actually refers to the mountain of the underworld,' Miss Koriche enlightened him, 'which was located where the sun set.'

I looked up at the sun's path, to discover that it would set directly over the canyon ahead.

'Mountain of the otherworld?' Taylor queried, looking into the huge crevice.

'The mountain of the *underworld*,' Miss Koriche emphasised, pointing downward. 'The abodes of the gods are always subterranean.'

'And do you know why?' Cingar added. 'Because it is so bloody hot up here on the surface!' He wiped away the sweat that had soaked through the bandana under his hat and was now rolling down his forehead.

'Let us head down into the canyon,' Lord Devere suggested, 'there is at least shade to be found down there.'

It took several hours to reach the canyon floor and the shade only seemed to intensify the hot stillness of the day.

'I need to sit,' Miss Koriche appealed, sweating enough for the entire party. None of us objected to the pause in the proceedings, and only Cingar still had the energy to get annoyed at our plight.

'This is not right!' Cingar yelled, and his voice echoed through the chasms. 'Damn you, Zalman, where is the water you promised?'

As Cingar's plea echoed away into silence, I lowered my head, sorry to have led my friends into this. I was beginning to doubt my eagerness to trust Zalman when I heard a bubbling sound. I raised my eyes to discover I was not the only one who had heard it.

'This way.' My husband found his second wind and ran to investigate. I was close behind him.

The canyon curved around and ran straight into a huge deposit of crystal-clear spring water. My husband did not hesitate to strip to his shirt and trousers and launch himself headlong into the waterhole. Some palms and other plant life had taken root in the dirt and sand deposited around the bank and they offered some shade from the heat.

My husband surfaced in a great splash of water. 'It is cool down deep,' he sighed with relief and did a little backstroke before swimming back to shore. 'There must be an underground stream feeding it.'

'Is it fresh?' I bent down to wash my face.

'Better than any water I have ever tasted.'

My lord splashed a quantity of it in my direction, managing to completely drench me in one attempt.

I gasped only a moment, for the water came as a great relief to my person, and with a shrug I fell into the pool. I swam down deep, where liberation from the heat and fatigue came over me in cool waves. Before I could reach the breach in the rocks that allowed the fresh cool water to bubble forth, I was forced to surface for air.

Moments later the rest of our party joined us.

'Shelter *and* water,' I pointed out to Cingar as he waded into the pool.

'Zalman never said anything about food though.' Cingar held his rumbling belly and smiled as he sank into the cool water.

'Ouch!' The gypsy began jumping about. 'My foot!' He raised the offending appendage out of the water to find a large mud crab attached to his toe.

'Ask and thou shalt receive,' I said, chuckling at his predicament as I attempted to detach our lunch from his person.

A few hours later, I finished my husband's redraft of his account of what had unfolded at the Mound of Pitch in my absence. 'Poor Taylor,' I commented after reading of his ordeal to escape the temple tomb.

'Poor Taylor?' Lord Devere was surprised by my view. 'Poor me!'

'You did very well, I am proud of you.' I had a little chuckle, however, as I considered another part of the tale I had just read.

'What is so funny?'

'The tablet disappearing in the sun.' I suppressed my amusement. 'I would have loved to have seen the look on Taylor's face.'

My husband looked to Cingar, who was seated by Raineath, instructing her on the violin, then to the darkening sky above the high canyon walls. 'It will be dark soon,' he said.

I lifted the journal to fan my face and some loose pages slipped from the back of the book. 'What are these?'

'Directions to Amenti,' he advised with a smile.

I hugged him, relieved.

'I can always rely on you.' I kissed his cheek and looked back to the pages. 'How cryptic are they?'

'I am afraid there is a fair bit of groundwork involved, not all of which I comprehend. I also made notes regarding the preparation required, but as they are now the property of the Holy See, we shall have to rely on my memory.'

'Wonderful! Now we are all going to freeze to death!' I looked over at the sound of Cingar's voice. The temperature in the canyon was now dropping rapidly. Surely Zalman would return to us soon? He had promised that we would know where we were going by nightfall.

Miss Koriché was distracted from the encroaching cold, staring at the water's surface.

'That is a little odd,' she commented.

Cingar went over to observe the water too, although he was careful not to step too close.

'What could be doing that?' he wondered.

My Lord Devere and I rose to see what had them so intrigued.

Where the bubbles rose up from the underground spring and churned the surface of the pool, the water appeared to be compressed flat, as if a sheet of glass had just been placed over the surface.

I focused my inner eye on the pool and beheld a modest round structure in the shape of a tall hat, the brim sitting flush with the water and a cylindrical structure rising from the centre. It was a dwelling of some sort, constructed entirely of light, and there was a pathway from the shore over the water to the outer rim of the mysterious structure. It had no windows or detailing, only a door that was so intrinsic to the structure that one could barely discern it. There was no handle or keyhole, not even a knocker.

'Are my eyes playing tricks on me?' Taylor asked. 'Or is there a structure materialising on the water?'

All present were stunned to admit that they could see the formation too. As it solidified, the manifestation began to glow with a rich intensity.

'Gold,' Taylor said, overawed by the grand scale of the treasure before our eyes.

'And not just any gold,' Lord Devere added. 'This is light-reinforced gold, like the tablets.' He smiled as he considered how brilliant the use of the super-metal was in this instance. 'A fortress that rises to a different dimension during the day and can only be entered at night. Now I ask you, is that not a brilliant defence strategy?'

We all stood motionless, enchanted by the glowing dwelling with water churning all around it — all except Raineath, who took her violin case in hand and set out on the golden path.

'Wait! We should exercise some caution.' Cingar moved swiftly to prevent her getting too far ahead of us.

'We are in a canyon that does not exist, approaching a dimension-shifting dwelling of the underworld.' She emphasised the absurdity of the situation with a shrug. 'If there is another way out of here, please point it out.'

'Are you still in such a hurry to die?' Cingar demanded crossly.

'On the contrary, I have a life to be catching up on, and whatever path gets me there fastest is my preferred route.'

The door to the dwelling flared with light and vanished, an event that made us all stop and gasp.

My Lord Devere recovered the fastest. 'A simple matter of heating the super-metal rapidly, I expect,' he rationalised, setting us all at ease.

'Nobody has seen a trace of this material for aeons,' Taylor said, regaining his sense of humour. 'And we find two examples of the mythical metal within a week!'

'Aren't we the lucky ones?' Lord Devere sounded less than honoured, but, being the fearless man I loved and adored, he moved to lead us into the unknown. I kept pace with him as he strode towards the entrance. Beyond it we could perceive only darkness — very odd indeed when the outer walls of the structure were emitting so much light.

'I would have thought Zalman would have been here to meet us,' Cingar commented as he brought up the rear. 'A little reassurance that this was his intended destination for us would not go astray right now.'

'How many habitations do you think lie within this canyon?' Raineath said sarcastically.

The gypsy relaxed a little, granting that his young friend had a point. 'I have never been very comfortable with the supernatural,' he explained. 'I feel more comfortable knowing the capabilities of what and whom I am dealing with.'

'You and me both, my friend,' Lord Devere commented, his pace slowing slightly as we neared the darkened doorway.

He took hold of my hand. 'Stay together and we shall all be fine,' he suggested.

We entered the unnatural darkness of the celestial dwelling and the door reconstituted closed behind us.

REVELATION 11

TA-SHE-RA EL AMUN

'My Lord Devere?' I wondered why my husband had let go of my hand and I fished around for his strong arm in the darkness.

At my feet, a great blue-white stripe of light appeared and grew wider to expose the churning water beneath the transparent floor of the glowing dwelling. As the light level rose I began to make out the immensity of the huge round chamber I stood in: the structure must have been twenty times larger than the exterior denoted! I felt dwarfed and humbled by its size; but of course, if we were moving through realms otherworldly, then neither space, nor time, had any meaning here. I lifted my eyes to the transparent domed ceiling, where illuminated clouds churned with brilliant colour — a celestial fresco of breathtaking beauty. Huge white gold pillars supported the dome, all around the perimeter of the circular space. Before me stood a huge and ominous-looking gate. In the wall behind me, the door I had entered through had disappeared. My companions were mysteriously absent, but I was not alone. Zalman was there, waiting patiently for me to recover from my awe.

'My associates . . .?' They were my first concern.

'They will be aware of moving through a space to your next destination and nothing more. You shall be reunited with them upon your leaving here. It is not my intention to alarm you,' he reassured me, 'but it has become imperative that we talk, alone.'

The fingers of my left hand enfolded my ringstone, for as long as I was wearing my treasure, Albray was following my movements.

'Not even your disembodied guardian can perceive your experience here,' Zalman said.

162

Clearly this being was aware of my every thought. A chill of discomfit crept over me — I was accustomed to having the psychic advantage, but my mind-reading ability did not aid me to detect the thoughts of my host. 'And where is *here*, Zalman?'

'Nowhere you will find on any map … save one,' he corrected. 'But that is another story.'

'Is that why you brought me here — to tease me and make riddles? Is this Set Amentet or not?'

He became more frank. 'Set Amentet is where human souls go to be judged between lives. This is a place where angelic souls go to remember all they knew before life on Earth ever existed.'

I was rendered speechless.

'Welcome to Signet station number ten, Ta-She-Ra El Amun,' Zalman continued, 'the healing station dedicated to transmuting darkness to light. It is one of twelve such power stations, each dedicated to a different purpose within the ancient Signet Grid that, as a whole, forms the interdimensional core energy system of this planet. Each of the twelve Signet stations has its own inherent portals, ley lines, stargates and guardians. Before the demise of Atlantis, this matrix powered the Amenti system and all the cities of inner and surface Earth.'

Hundreds of questions fought for precedence in my mind; before I could formulate a single one, Zalman went on.

'There are twelve and two souls living in this Earth scheme who are not of this planet. They incarnate in order to learn, to suffer and to love, but, unlike all the other humans evolving here, these twelve and two souls chose to come here. Why? To see through to completion a project they designed and built: the Amenti porthole system. These twelve and two souls are the Staff of Amenti, and as part of their task here, each staff member is responsible for resurrecting one of the twelve Signet stations in preparation for the reopening of Amenti's halls to all mankind.'

I recalled what I had learned of the history of the Dragon Queens; it seemed that my mother might not have been insane after all. 'These twelve and two souls, they are angelic in origin?'

'As we originated from the dimensional universe above this one, humans would consider us angelic, yes,' Zalman concurred.

I realised where this little heart-to-heart was leading. 'And I am one of these twelve beings. And so is Levi.'

'And Charlotte,' Zalman added.

I could not say that news surprised me. 'But if the halls are closed, then why does my son seek to go there?'

'Staff members have a secret access key built into their genetic code. Once they have fully matured as a human being they can, *and must*, gain access to Amenti's halls.'

'And what of your earthly commitments?'

'One must be free of all earthly entanglements before admission to Amenti will be granted,' said Zalman.

'Then there must be a mistake,' I said.

'There is no mistake.'

'If Levi has undergone some kind of massive spiritual awakening, then surely he must have known that Miss Koriche is pregnant with his —'

'He *knows* so much more than you could ever imagine,' Zalman interrupted matter-of-factly. 'And with his enhanced understanding, Levi believes it is time for him to pursue his higher calling. Your son is on his way to submit his body for repose beneath the blue flame, which will free his soul to walk Amenti's halls and eventually do the work of his silent watcher ... just as I do.'

'Your body is beneath the blue flame?' That explained his lack of shadow, which we had noticed during our desert trek.

'It is.'

'And how long shall your repose last?'

'As a male of the Grail line, one hundred years is the required period of exposure before reactivation.'

'Levi is to sleep for one hundred years!' I was beginning to see where the fairytales had originated. I wondered what my term beneath the blue flame might be. 'Is this duration more or less for the Dragon Queens?'

'Once deposited beneath the blue flame, the Dragon Queens will remain under its protection until the birth of the violet flame-bearer is nigh,' Zalman outlined, 'whereupon the Dragon Queens will rise at once to protect the only soul capable of opening Amenti for all humanity.'

'Goodness.' I was humbled by my destiny, but right now I needed to find out more about Levi. 'So why has my son given over his body to an ancient —'

'We are not here to discuss your son, or your ultimate destiny,' Zalman interrupted. 'You have other, more pressing concerns.'

'I have concerns?'

'Ignorance is bliss,' Zalman said, and smiled warmly, 'but you can ill afford to remain ignorant any longer. The powers of your blood are highly sought-after and, if gained, will be misused and squandered for the base causes of destructive beings.'

'Who are these malign beings you speak of?' I asked, my mind flashing back to the images of large lizard warriors I'd perceived via the comb found at the Ur site. I'd been doing my best to dismiss the creatures from my memory.

'Your ancient relatives and their allies,' Zalman said frankly.

I knew there were many 'underground' societies that had been manipulating bloodlines for aeons to produce super-beings, but I had failed to discover why. I said as much.

'It is not the secret brotherhoods that are manipulating bloodlines,' Zalman corrected my misconceptions. 'Such societies are but the human face of intergalactic interest in the atomic structure of the human species on this planet.'

My shock caused all my questions to become wedged in my throat.

'And something that needs to be made perfectly clear to you, Lady Suffolk, is that taking the Star-Fire substance was a very dangerous mistake on your part!'

I gasped at the reprimand. 'Why so?'

'When the source of your power is not self-generated, it is not self-controlled, which means it is beyond your control.'

Zalman's accusation made perfect scientific sense, and a stabbing pain in my heart alerted me to what lay ahead.

'The angels and demons that do battle for control of this planet and its populace come from the same stock, the same family,' he explained. 'So if those of your bloodline can act as the earthly vessels of angels, then ...' He left it to me to deduce my own conclusion.

'Then those of the blood can also act as vessels for demons,' I said, stunned.

I was momentarily distracted by the reflection of my own subtle form in the mirrored walls of the chamber. The difference between my tarnished gold auric hue and the huge glistening energy emission of my host was just enormous!

'You note the difference in our subtle forms,' Zalman commented. 'Despite your extensive psychic expertise and knowledge, true enlightenment still eludes you ... Now why should that be? Your energy centres are not blocked by any disease, so why is the current not more free-flowing?'

'Something is damming the flow of light from within my light centres?' I half-asked, half-stated.

Zalman nodded. 'When you consume the Star-Fire of the gods, it increases the capacity of your nervous system by ten thousandfold, granting superhuman strength and ability ... for a time. But the effect of the drug wears off and the frequency of the vessel drops rapidly. The energy centres of the body begin to collapse and block themselves, and more of the drug is needed to sustain a physical existence. If you had failed to integrate the higher vibratory energy into your system, you could have destroyed the divine mutation in not only your own genetic code, but also the code of all your descendants. And one of the strongest strands of the sacred bloodline of the Dragon Queens would have been destroyed forever.'

Tears began streaming down my face as a huge ball of pressure built in my chest. 'I would never have taken the Star-Fire had Albray not advised me to.' I was not seeking to place the blame for my mistake elsewhere, but I could not believe Albray knew how harmful the substance truly was. 'Surely my knight did not knowingly betray me?'

Zalman eased my heartache with his opinion. 'To the best of my knowledge, your guide did not intentionally betray you; it is not his loyalty I would question, but the source of his knowledge. You trust the good in your fellow humans, which, with your second sight, you can plainly see. But good intentions do not equal the truth, when advice can only be given from the best of one's knowledge. The enemies of mankind have perfected the art of control by belief, and were very careful to ensure that all doctrine is sufficiently corrupt to keep humanity's different religious factions at odds with each other. As it is, your highly developed light-body has been working overtime to keep your frequency above the demon threshold and out of the reach of undesirable influences, but now you must release the energy that is blocking you.'

I looked at my reflection again and this time perceived a dark ooze beginning to seep forth from all of my light centres. I felt that my belief in Zalman's words was the dispelling force. I could now plainly see the evidence of my own delusion and earthly desire for personal power, and their extraction tore holes through the very fabric of my being. The agony was all-consuming, but still I was concerned about its veracity.

'How do I know that this experience is not an illusion? How do I know you are not trying to stifle my development by instilling me with fear and lies?'

'Are you afraid of learning something that might interfere with your own little worldly agenda?' Zalman challenged, and I realised that the only person instilling fear in me and lying to me was myself. With my acceptance of my own shortcomings, my etheric purge waned and I was able to draw a comfortable breath. Nevertheless, I was bewildered to realise that I had become so embroiled in physical world events and my own negative ego.

'However, nothing is achieved by relinquishing responsibility to a higher authority,' Zalman continued, 'so it is wise not to trust my word. Indeed, you can trust no one and must question everything that is put to you.'

He went on with my lesson. 'All energy must have a channel, and if you are not the true channel for the divine energy you wield, then what or who do you think you are drawing that energy from?'

An external source? An internal source? Both?

'The Earth,' I realised suddenly. My heart weighed a deep hole in my chest with the revelation. 'So in fact I was every bit as wrong as my nemesis in the Sinai affair. The only thing that saved me from damnation was the angelic genes I carry.'

The knowledge sickened me as I recalled my fight to the death with Christian Molier, a shape-shifting, immortal vampire whose genetic code had become so mutated by his over-consumption of the Fire-

Stone substance that he could no longer feel anything whatsoever. There was no pleasure he could experience — neither mental, physical, emotional or spiritual — for his addiction to physical life was damning his soul inside his mortal body.

'It was the high resonance of your heart that saved you, Lady Devere,' Zalman corrected. 'The Isis gene is a mutation that can be as much a curse as a blessing. Yours is a bloodline of guardians with the ability to aid humanity to their salvation or their total obliteration. Compassion is the only key to controlling the ultimate centring force in the universe, gravity, and you have an abundance of compassion. Let it be understood, however, that the ORME -based substances provide a shortcut to supernatural power at the cost of your eternal soul. For ORME will make a comeback in the future and its seeming benefits will be promoted and sold to mankind on a mass level. There will be widespread praise and abuse of this substance, which will ultimately —'

'Drain the Earth and damn the entire human species!' I gasped.

My heart was palpitating so hard in my chest that I thought it would burst right through my ribcage. My breathing was completely erratic — I was going to black out . . .

FROM THE JOURNAL OF TAMAR DEVERE

I turned the page, breathless in anticipation of what might come next, and some papers fell from my foremother's Persian diary into my lap. My first excited thought was that they were Lord Granville-Devere's directions to Amenti. I was most disappointed to find that they were in my mother's handwriting — probably some of her old research notes. The content, however, was unlike anything I'd ever read of my mother's work.

Twelve keys to Signet Grid Stations (six male, six female) in place by 2017 to hold a higher-dimensional frequency on this planet so that it will be able to host the Sphere of Amenti. Two avatars of the Anu race will be born to human parents, and these souls hold the energetic key to open the Halls of Amenti for mass ascension. Born between 1992 and 2006, these souls will be found among the Indigo children (diagnosed as ADD-ADHD). They will have a dominant human soul, co-sharing a body with a fallen Anu-Elohim Nefilim soul, in order that the former more emotionally advanced soul may aid the development of its near emotionless counterpart and repair the damaged emotional body of the latter. This bi-soul conflict may cause chronic mental and emotional polarity, such as clinical schizophrenia or split-personality syndrome. The avatars will come to realise their full potential by adolescence, in preparation for events in 2017.

What on Earth was this all about? What was really disconcerting was that I was born within the dates specified in these notes, and I've been diagnosed as ADD.

My mother felt that the disorder stemmed from the extended periods I was separated from her, thanks to her globe-hopping career. In other words, my 'dis-order' was a direct reflection of my dis-ordered family life. So she took me out of school, employed a private tutor for me, and now we both accompanied Mum wherever her assignments led her. When his schedule permitted, Dad joined us too. As long as I studied for thirty hours a week, I was given complete control over my school schedule and what subjects I studied when. Mum reading to me from our family journals was what really captured my interest, and as she would only indulge in my favourite pastime once my studies were done, I'd proved to be a very diligent student. Also, I felt that to make any kind of beneficial contribution to our family's collection of journals, I needed to be well educated, just as my great foremothers were.

I reread my mother's notes, imagining that I was just second-guessing her line of reasoning. But even on a second reading, it seemed to me that, at the time of penning these observations, Mum suspected I might be one of these Indigo children who was perhaps an avatar. I didn't really know what an avatar was, so I went to find Mum's psychic dictionary.

Basically, I discovered that an avatar was a human being who had perfected its soul-mind via thousands of earthly incarnations. Another theory was that these soul-minds stemmed from a higher dimension of awareness, which tied in with what Zalman had told Ashlee in the journal about angels involved in the Amenti Project. Whatever the soul's origin, it was agreed that avatars were soul-minds of supreme wisdom and psychic ability who reincarnated into a human form to perform some super-selfless service for humanity. In the rendering of this service, they lifted the consciousness of the masses and advanced the evolution of civilisation.

Wow! Still, I couldn't see how any of these traits applied to me. If I was a perfect soul-mind with thousands of incarnations of experience, I sure didn't remember much about it, nor did I have any recollection of a higher-dimensional existence. I did like to think I had supreme wisdom, although my parents constantly disputed this, but I'd yet to show any glimpse of psychic skill, even though my foremothers were most proficient in the art. My life was so lacking in the supernatural for one of my ilk, that it could be considered super-unnatural! Still, my mother gave me hope: she admitted to not having tapped into her own psychic inheritance until she was in her late twenties. And I couldn't say that performing a super-selfless service for humanity would be my first choice of vocation, even if my sacrifice did lift the consciousness of the masses and aid the evolution of the world. I'd rather be a journalist!

I heard the front door closing: my parents were back from dining out. Quickly, I hid the research notes in my pocket; I didn't really know why. Perhaps I didn't want my delightful little delusion of grandeur being shattered just yet? I certainly didn't want Mum taking the notes away from me before I'd had the chance to do some research of my own.

Within moments there was a knock at the study door. Mum stuck her head into the room. 'Can I come in?'

'Sure.' I yawned and bookmarked the journal. It was a quarter to midnight.

'Which one did you choose?' Mum asked, and something in her tone told me she'd been curious about my choice all evening. 'Ah ... Persia, I knew it.' She clapped her hands together and gave a laugh that, in my opinion, sounded a little forced. 'Are you enjoying it?'

'Yeah, it's good,' I said, placing the journal on a side table as Mum took a seat. I didn't want her to ask if I'd come across any notes in the diary, so I changed the subject. 'Did you decide to publish your novel?'

'Oh ...' She appeared a little bemused by the sudden shift in topic. 'I'm still uncertain.'

'God, you're hopeless!' I playfully shoved her.

Mum forced a smile. 'It's ... complicated.'

After having read the notes now shoved deep in my pocket, I could well understand that it might be. 'Oh well, I'll still love you whether you become a famous author or not.'

Mum's smile was more sincere now and she kissed my forehead. 'So, where are you up to in the tale?'

'I'm in the middle of Lady Devere's audience with Zalman inside his Signet station,' I replied. 'Do you think Zalman was telling the truth about the damning effects of ORME in humans?'

In today's marketplace, what the ancients called Manna, Star-Fire and Ormus is known simply as ORME — Orbitally Rearranged Monatomic Elements — and the superconductive metallic substances it produces form the basis for drugs that heal a myriad of once fatal illnesses; in fact, pharmaceutical companies claim there isn't an illness that can't be cured by the miracle agent. Of course, the medical profession, which only acknowledges the physical body, would therefore be unable to see the kind of damage — if Zalman's claims are true — their miracle drugs are doing to the emotional, mental and spiritual bodies of their patients.

'If ORME is a blocking agent for all consciousness on this planet, then Earth is being laid to waste on many more levels than just the physical,' I said.

My mother gazed at me, a look of amazement on her face.

'How old are you again?' she said, plainly proud of my comprehension. 'If I had to make a ruling on the matter based on my current understanding, then I would have to say that I believe Zalman was telling the truth.'

'So you believe that there are extraterrestrials interfering with the evolution of mankind?'

Mum's expression became more serious and she took a moment to consider her response. 'Well, if that's not the case then where did the line of the Dragon Queens come from? Where did all the different genetic codes and human races come from? Science still hasn't found a satisfactory explanation for these mysteries now that we know that Darwin was way off the mark.'

That was a very good point. 'Do you know the origin of the Dragon Queens?' I asked.

Mum's eyes widened and I realised just what a huge question I was asking. When she did answer, she tried to skirt around the issue. 'Due to the nature of the subject, most of the research in that area is esoteric, or so historic as to be considered myth.'

'However ...' I knew there was more, and waved my hand to encourage her to get to the point.

'I don't want to spoil Ashlee's tale for you,' she said, attempting to close the subject. 'Most of what I know, I learned from investigating the claims in her journals.'

'And what did you discover?' I wasn't giving up.

Mum served me a look of exasperation, then caved. 'Okay ... this is the simplest version of the story as I've come to understand it. A long time in the future, in a galaxy in a higher dimension, there is a planet known as Tara. There, the perfect human race thrives in cooperation with many other beings from different planets, both humanoid and not. One of the non-human races is the Anunnaki, who tend to be a power-hungry lot; through association with them, some of the elite Taraeans are persuaded to misuse the natural power grid of the planet. Their meddling causes an overload on the system which results in a huge explosion.'

'Not unlike some of the tales about Atlantis,' I commented and Mum nodded.

'The explosion causes parts of the planet, along with its grid system and morphogenetic field, to be ripped off and cast towards the sun.'

'Morphogenetic field?' I'd never heard the term before.

Mum took a moment to consider how best to define it. 'It's the cosmic blueprint for the evolution of life on Tara. Without the complete blueprint, the souls on Tara can't ascend to the dimension beyond their own. During the explosion, many souls are torn away from their soul group and those remaining can't hope to become of one consciousness with a part of their soul-mind missing. Not to mention that there are beings from other planets visiting Tara at the time of the disaster, which are also torn away from their soul groups, so many evolutions are hindered by the disaster.'

'But wouldn't the people involved die in the explosion and then reincarnate back to their soul group or something?' I reasoned.

'But what if there is no such thing as death in the dimension beyond our own, and therefore no need for reincarnation?' Mum suggested.

'I see.' I was eager to hear more. 'So what happens to the stranded souls and the missing part of the planet?'

'The breakaway portion of Tara is sucked into the vortex that lies at the core of every star, crushed and fragmented, then spat back out into the physical universe as a gaseous substance that eventually forms a mini solar system around that star. The soul-minds connected to this fragment of Tara also fall in frequency and, cut off from their original soul matrix on Tara, have no means to evolve back to their source. This incident becomes known as the Fall of Man.'

'So what's this got to do with the Dragon Queens?'

'I'm getting to that.' Mum seemed mildly annoyed by my impatience. 'A group of highly evolved beings from Tara's dimensional galaxy get together to salvage the situation. They have the technology and the desire to rescue the lost souls of Tara, yet from their base in the next dimension they can do nothing without the aid and cooperation of beings already existing in the same dimensions as Earth's universal scheme. Now in Earth's galaxy alone there are billions of star beings, humanoids in the main, but not all of these races exist on the physical plane.'

'So there are races of beings evolving in the astral, mental and lower causal planes of our universe?'

'Correct,' Mum said, 'however, at the time of the Fall, the humanoid beings genetically close enough to humans to be of aid are the Anu, from the rogue planet Nibiru that traverses through our solar system and the next star system of Sirius. The Anu are a highly intelligent race of astral beings possessing great genetic knowledge, which is why they are chosen for the Earth mission. Also, they are the descendants in this universe of the Anunnaki in the harmonic universe above ours — the same Anunnaki that contributed to the destruction of Tara. So the idea is that if some of the Anu come to Earth, the lost souls of the Anunnaki from Tara can incarnate into the Anu bloodlines in order to evolve beyond this universe and return to their higher-dimension existence. The Anu who come to Earth are

173

also called the Anunnaki, which in Sumerian translates to mean "the Heavenly, or Lordly, who fly to Earth". The planet had already been acclimatised for habitation by the twelve Ancient Watchers, who are the Staff of Amenti.'

'Like Zalman.' I suddenly realised that I'd been reading about a conversation between my foremother and one of the oldest souls on the planet; it was all a bit overwhelming.

Mum nodded. 'They introduce various species of animal and planet life via the Amenti stargate system, and after many aeons of evolution the Anunnaki arrive and begin genetically slicing their astral DNA with the physical DNA of the different animal species, with the aim of creating an Earth being in their likeness. After many horrible abominations, the Anunnaki finally manage to create a physical form in which humanity can evolve on this planet.'

I had a hunch. 'Something went wrong?'

Mum nodded again. 'In the process of developing the perfect Earth human, the Anunnaki also discovered a new application for one of their most ancient and treasured substances —'

'Star-Fire,' I guessed.

'The Anu had long been producing the superconductive substance to fuel a planetary shield on Nibiru, which kept the surface conditions of their planet stable during its huge orbital transit through two solar systems. The Anunnaki discovered that exposure to ORME granted them the ability to physically manifest and retain that state indefinitely so long as they continued to ingest the substance. One by one, all the Anunnaki became addicted to ORME and physically manifested on Earth, as they were never meant to do. They became known as the Nefilim, meaning "those cast down". Because they'd become physical beings via unnatural means, they suffered from a lack of emotional maturity. The frequency bands of their subtle bodies were incomplete and therefore easily severed from their soul source on Nibiru once the ORME worked its blocking effect on the light centres of their chakra system.'

'Which is what nearly happened to Ashlee,' I commented.

'Yes, you don't have to be a villain to be seduced by such power,' Mum concurred. 'It happens to the best of us.'

'Us?' I queried. 'Grail Princesses?'

'Human beings,' Mum clarified, suppressing a smile. Was she mocking my belief in our family secret?

She went on: 'In time, the Nefilim discovered that they had created a genetic disaster. They had become so addicted to the physical form that they could no longer reproduce it naturally. Their reproductive eggs were scrambled, as it were.'

'So if the Nefilim weren't reproducing, where did the lost Anunnaki souls from Tara go?'

Mum gave me a stern look, which I assumed meant that she was coming to that.

'Gold was in plentiful supply on Earth, but the Nefilim were few, and as elitists they certainly weren't going to get their hands dirty. So, in addition to their genetic work on the human project, they began a covert genetic operation — to create a slave class of lizard-clones, different from humans and more adept at working underground.'

'Clones? Do you mean they had no mind of their own?' I asked.

'They were of a hive-mind mentality, controlled initially by the far more psychically advanced Nefilim. The Dracon, as the Nefilim named them, were mindless, soulless creatures — or so everybody thought.'

'But the souls of the lost Anunnaki were trapped inside the lizard-clones?' I guessed.

Mum nodded.

'Eventually, the clones rebelled, jealous of the favoured treatment that humans were receiving from the Nefilim. They drove the Nefilim from the planet and slaughtered the humans.'

'Gross.' I screwed up my nose. 'And the Dragon Queens?'

Mum gave me her 'be patient' look again. 'On Tara, it was decided by the Amenti Council that they, the twelve master architects of the Amenti ascension scheme, should incarnate into the human species in order to guide and speed the human evolutionary scheme. But in order to do this, they required physical human bodies strong enough in genetic frequency to hold their charge.'

My mother stopped and shook my knee. 'Remember, this is all probably fiction,' she said. 'I don't want you having nightmares.'

'As if!' I protested. 'I am a teenager now, I can handle it. Keep going.'

'Okay then, the line of the Dragon Queens began when a human female was raped by a Nefilim male that had been spiritually possessed by one of the Anu.'

'Sama-El?' I remembered the name from Ashlee's Persian journal.

'The Sumerians knew him as Enki, Lord of the Earth. It is said that during the human betrayal by the Nefilim, he was the only one among the Nefilim brave enough to speak out on humanity's behalf. His concept of the ideal of human rights was known as Kianism, and resulted in him being branded a traitor, banished and set adrift in space. Kianism was banned and it was considered treasonous to study it. It was expected that without access to ORME, the former Nefilim ruler would endure a painful withdrawal and an agonising death, followed by complete soul fragmentation. Enki did not die, however. On the contrary, his compassion for his human children sparked a genetic advancement within his DNA, whereby his missing emotional frequencies were repaired and he reconnected with his soul group on Nibiru. He was subsequently welcomed home by the Anu, who had assumed all their Anunnaki had been lost aeons before. Enki's report of the state of affairs on Earth was shocking, and the Anu Council appealed to their Anunnaki gods in the next harmonic universe to give them the means to save their fallen brethren on Earth. The Queen of the Anunnaki in turn appealed to the Amenti Council. Keep reading Ashlee's journal and you will learn that a deal was struck between the twelve members of the Amenti Council and the Anunnaki queen and her prince.'

'What kind of deal?' I was too impatient to wait and read about it myself.

Mum rolled her eyes. 'One that saw the Staff of Amenti reincarnate, and Enki father the line of Dragon Queens and their Princes of the Grail bloodline. And that's all I'm going to say.'

It was all rather mind-blowing. 'So what happened to the lizard race — how did they perish?' I was guessing they must have died out as I hadn't seen too many lizard people walking around on Earth lately.

'The lizard warriors, known as the Dracon, were left alone for thousands of years, and the Nefilim were confident that the dreadful mistake they'd created was extinct. But the popular theory is that they never did die out completely. By the time the Nefilim returned to Earth to resume their mining and genetic projects, they had realised that due to the blocking effect of the ORME their soul-minds were no longer connected to their Anu soul group on Nibiru. Without direction from their morphogenetic blueprint, the beautiful Anu bodies that they'd once possessed began to mutate into ugly demon-like forms worse in appearance than the Dracon. It's said that they still move freely among mankind, using mind-control and programming techniques to alter our memory so that any knowledge of the past remains buried in myth and legend. Whoooo ...' Mum made a spooky noise to emphasise how sucked into her story I was.

'You're messing with me?' I realised and slapped her on the shoulder. She'd been really starting to scare me.

Mum grinned. 'No nightmares now, you promised,' she said, and got up to go to bed, rubbing me on the leg to indicate that I should do the same.

I was still smiling at my own gullibility. 'At what point of that conversation did you start leading me up the garden path?'

'Who really knows the truth?' Mum said. 'But I intend to keep looking.'

'And that's all any potential reader could ask,' I said, bringing us back to the start of our conversation, when I'd asked about whether or not she was going to publish her novel.

Later, in bed, writing all this up, I realised those words could just as easily apply to me some day.

With one parent a published non-fiction author and the other published in fiction, this could pave the way for me to be published no matter what form my first masterpiece might take. In fact, just recording my thoughts now, I realise that my journal entries are growing more interesting by the day.

REVELATION 12

THE DESTRUCTOR

I have just had the most hellish night of my life! I had a nightmare about aliens, which is really no surprise after my bedtime chat with Mum, then awoke in a panic to find blood all over my bed. I have never felt cramps like this before — welcome to womanhood! I feel truly gross. Then, to top it all off, I opened my locked diary, to which only I know the combination, to find the following paragraph in a handwriting very different to my own and in a language I don't even understand. I scanned the piece and ran it through a translation program, which identified the characters as Sanskrit. This is the translation:

I AM. I am the destructor of the great unreality and the liberator of the perceivers of illusion who seek eternal bliss. I am death to the ignorant who fear for their lives; the ego shudders and recoils in my presence, seeing in me its own demise. I am the blackness that awaits the deceivers of cosmic law. I am Time and none shall escape my all-consuming march. Demons heed my proclamation: your demise is nigh, for I AM.

Who on Earth would be writing in my diary in ancient bloody Sanskrit? My mother is the only person I know who's familiar with ancient languages, but it's not like her to invade my privacy and vandalise my treasured belongings. Surely she knows how much this journal means to me?

Still, that didn't stop me confronting her in a blind fit of superhuman rage and accusing her of tampering with my diary. Mum was clearly deeply hurt that I could think her capable of doing something like that, but she stayed very patient with me and calmed

178

me by pointing out that my body's hormones were no doubt having a fit at present and so I could be forgiven for being a little over-emotional and irrational.

'Do you swear that it wasn't you?' I believed my mother, but who else could have gained access to my diary?

'I swear upon my soul.' She held a hand to her heart and looked me square in the eye. 'I have not touched your journal and have no intention of ever doing so.'

Inwardly I knew before I even made the accusation that I was placing blame in the wrong quarter, and my mother's sincerity confirmed this. She even offered to take a look at the offending entry and lend her expertise to the mystery. But as the entry in question seemed to be heralding the arrival of 'the destructor', and I had no idea who that might be, I decided my mother might find the piece too disturbing.

'That's okay,' I said, 'I'll figure it out.'

She seemed a little sad that I didn't want to confide in her further. 'Well, I'm here for you if you need me.'

'I know.' I kissed her cheek. 'I'm sorry I went ballistic at you. Maybe the diary entry is just another facet of my nightmare. Hell, maybe I wrote it myself!' I was joking, but the idea caused a large lump of anxiety to wedge in my throat. What if it *was* me who wrote it?

'Perhaps you did.' My mother's tone became more positive and reassuring as she reached for her psychic dictionary, a permanent fixture on her desk. 'There is a psychic art known as automatic trance writing.'

She found the reference she was looking for. 'Here we go ... "The medium becomes a channel for the writings of etheric world intelligences ... The information perceived is usually previously unknown to the medium".'

I tried not to gulp when she said this.

'"The script could even be written in a language unknown to the channel." Is that —'

But I was already on my way back to my room.

Mum's notes hidden in Ashlee's diary had said something about a split-personality syndrome. I rushed to retrieve them from the pocket of the pants I was wearing yesterday, but Mum had taken them to be washed. I was about to bolt out the door, when I recalled that I had copied the notes into my own journal, so I ran to open that instead.

This bi-soul conflict may cause chronic mental and emotional polarity, such as clinical schizophrenia or split-personality syndrome.

What if I was sharing my body with another soul-mind, some kind of alter ego? And what if the key to my unlocked psychic talent lay in this other, darker side of myself?

'But why now?' I wondered aloud, and was answered by an excruciating lower abdominal cramp. 'Okay, so what if my raised hormone levels have sparked some cosmic chain reaction in my DNA? And what if that's awoken the ET soul within me, which only emerges when I am asleep?'

A shiver ran through me and then another. Now I was really scaring myself.

Then my mind's eye hit upon a segment from my dream. It was so blindingly vivid that my reality melted away and I found myself gazing out of a large curved oblong window ...

The room I was standing in was quiet, calm and dimly lit. But beyond the transparent barrier protecting me, a war was raging and our enemies were claiming victory. From my high vantage point, I saw all my healthy and intelligent human hybrid children rounded up and devoured by packs of lizard warriors.

'They were the last hope for our immortal souls,' I said, devastated. An unusual pain welled in my throat. When I placed a hand over the afflicted area I noted how smooth the skin was on my exceptionally long neck.

'Some will survive.'

It was a male voice that replied, and I knew via the person I was in the vision that he had been largely responsible for this rebellion. I could not bear to look at him.

'We shall return and start again,' he added rationally.

I was well accustomed to the sight of blood, and yet it turned my stomach to see the tiny angelic forms of my human children ripped apart. My chest began to ache. 'We created the ultimate beings of beauty and the ultimate creatures of destruction,' I said. 'We are worse than these beasts, for if not for our great lust for gold, this planet would have been paradise.'

'Until your soul frequency theories are proven, gold is still our only means of survival.' The male warned me against voicing such views too openly.

'Then we are damned,' I uttered, and to my great shock my eyes moistened and a trickle of fluid ran down my face. I had witnessed such an occurrence in humans when they expressed excessive emotion, but my kind had been clinically incapable of feeling anything for aeons. Could it be that my compassion for my children was reversing the damage I had done to my genetic structure and the spiritual bodies that were intrinsically attached? Was I to be the living proof of my father's theory?

'You do not look well,' my companion noted. 'You must be due to ingest.'

'I will never ingest again,' I retorted. That would be my protest against our blatant abandonment of potential angels to their slaughter. 'I would rather perish than cause the like of this holocaust again.'

'We need you, Kali,' he said, and I believe I detected a slight undertone of worry in his tone. 'Your devotion to these mortals could almost amount to Kianism, and you know what became of our father for his beliefs!'

'Enki was right!' I stressed, knowing my view was considered treasonous.

My company chose to ignore my words. 'The Council will never allow you to abstain from ingesting,' he said.

'I know,' I replied. An unpleasant sensation gripped my heart at the realisation of what I must do. Its invisible tentacles extended upward to my throat and down to my stomach; I was held paralysed in its clutches. This was fear, the same fear that my human children were experiencing — fear of imminent death.

The Council would do all within its power to keep me alive and producing humans for them to rule and abuse. But even if I had begun the long road towards developing my emotional body sufficiently to reconnect to my soul source on Nibiru, I had to accept I would not live long enough to complete the process and prove my theory. Either I faced eternal damnation now, or aeons of seeing many more horrific slaughters just like this one. My ancestors had denied me any chance to aspire to a higher cosmic service, as I was one of the final few of the Anunnaki born with and damned by the ORME addiction.

My only hope was that some of my human creations might somehow survive this terrible day. My research had revealed that humans were far more emotionally adept than we Anunnaki, possessing a capacity to master the key emotions required for spiritual advancement: love, joy, compassion and empathy for each other. That was why I called my theory the 'em-bed-path'; for only empathy and compassion attuned human beings to their higher emotions, whereby they underwent a massive genetic evolution. For when a human becomes truly self-aware, he or she attains an internal command of gravity. This balance is the key to steer the fields of molecules that compose all there is, and effectively gives the individual the capacity to remodel reality according to their will.

I gazed upon my human children's suffering, and rather than resisting the agony, grief and remorse, I embraced it, for indeed it was better to feel the most excruciating pain than to feel nothing at all. I acknowledged the ignorant, self-obsessed social climber I had been, and I forgave myself for I had known no better. Now, however, I did know better and with my resolve to self-terminate for the greater good of all came the most amazing feeling that filled my heart to bursting point. My entire being was levitated to a state of bliss where fear could no longer touch me.

'Kali?' my companion called.

I did not acknowledge him.

Instead, I held both my hands out before me and, drawing on all the power vested in me from my aeons of abusing the Elixir of Life, I willed my cold heart into my clutches.

'Kali, no!'

I retained consciousness long enough to see the organ still pumping in my hands, my thick blue blood running in rivers down my arms.

* * *

'Huh!' The gruesome sight startled me from the vision. I felt like I was going to throw up and made a dash for the bathroom, but recovered after splashing my face with cool water. I gazed at my pasty reflection in the mirror; boy, did I look like one of the living dead!

I wondered if all women had bad dreams with their periods. I sure hoped it wasn't going to be this horrendous every month!

A bath and some lunch made me feel a little more human, and as I nibbled at my food I looked up the name Kali in the psychic dictionary. Although the reference was rather brief, I discovered that Kali was a female etheric world intelligence in charge of destruction. This information seemed to link my dream with the mysterious paragraph in my journal. Could the tall, smooth-skinned being in my dream be writing through me? If this was the case, it certainly put a whole new slant on the idea of keeping a dream diary!

I looked up this Kali character on the internet, which was rather more helpful.

Kali comes from the Sanskrit word 'kal', meaning time. She is a Hindu goddess, who is greatly misunderstood by the Western world as being associated with sex, death and violence, but in the Hindu text she kills only demons. For humankind, she represents the death of the ego and the will to overcome the 'I am the body' idea. She reminds us that the body is only temporary, and through this realisation she provides liberation to her children. To the soul who aspires to greater spiritual endeavours, Kali is receptive, supportive and loving. It is only a person filled with ego who will perceive Kali in a fearsome form. Her black skin represents —

Black skin?

I recalled my vision once more and realised that the hand that had risen to comfort my sore throat was indeed as black as it was smooth, and my fingers were extremely long.

Interesting.

I went back to my reading.

Her black skin represents the womb of the quantum darkness, the great non-manifest from which all of creation arises and into which all of creation will eventually dissolve.

Whoa ... she sounded rather awesome. If this was the being that was now co-sharing my body, then I was honoured!

I could hardly believe my own imagination. Yesterday I'd never experienced a single psychic moment, and today I believed I was in cahoots with an ancient Hindu goddess. And why a Hindu goddess, when my bloodline seemed to trace back to Sumerian roots? I pondered this a moment and an interesting theory came to me. What if the Sumerians' Genesis account was actually a retelling of an even earlier text? Could the ancient text of India and that of the Sumerians be derived from the same archaic source?

I knew someone who could answer that for me.

'As far as we know, Sanskrit came along after Sumerian, and Sumerian is the oldest written language so far found,' my mother said.

'But ... there might be a language from which they both derived?' I ventured.

Mum shrugged. 'Only if you believe in the theory of Atlantis.'

'Do you?'

Mum gasped and turned it into a laugh. 'Why are you so curious about ancient languages today? Does this have something to do with your mysterious journal entry?'

Time to withdraw. 'No,' I lied. 'But thanks.'

I raided the kitchen then retreated to my room.

I felt I'd done enough soul-searching for today, and as I still felt wretched I decided to simply curl up in bed with Ashlee's Persian journal. Lady Ashlee always seemed to have some great insight to impart; it could only be beneficial to spend some time in her head.

I opened the journal, found the purple ribbon that marked my place, and continued reading.

FROM THE JOURNAL OF LADY ASHLEE GRANVILLE-DEVERE

I awoke to the most incredible sound resounding around the chamber of Zalman's Signet station; its vibration penetrated to the very core of the pain within my heart and ripped out my dis-ease, roots and all. The release took my breath away and I was washed by wave upon wave of euphoria as every single one of my subtle light centres popped and cleared in sparkling bursts. When the sound died away, I felt lightened of a great load; my entire centre of gravity had shifted to a state of utter bliss.

'What a miraculous acoustic,' I said.

'In the beginning there was the word, and what you just heard was a lower vibrational interpretation of a very distant echo of it.'

Zalman referred me to my reflection and I gasped with wonder to see that my aura was now sparkling gold — that was exactly how I felt. In the mirror I noticed another anomaly behind me and I spun around to view the domed ceiling.

The moving fresco of celestial cloud above had faded to transparency, revealing the huge pyramid of deep blue suspended high above us. Great streams of electricity were being drawn from the pyramid, down over the Signet station and into the external pool of water. The giant body of liquid acted as a conductor, drawing the energy down into the huge crystal deposits at its bottom.

'Are you powering up the Signet Grid?' I asked, fascinated by the glowing water beneath the transparent floor.

'The Signet Grid can only be fully activated once all twelve of the stations have been unlocked,' Zalman explained. 'At present, the power being absorbed by the grid is helping to clear the huge build-up of negative frequency here in the cradle of civilisation, a place that has seen more conflict than any other point on the globe.'

'So we are still in Persia?' I asked, puzzled by the time and distance inconsistencies my party had experienced in the past few days.

'In the etheric equivalent of that region of the world, yes.' Zalman smiled. 'And yes, I did toy with your perception of time and space in order to see you and yours to safety as swiftly as possible. When it comes to our would-be staff, we of Amenti can exploit our influence and station systems in order to bend reality just a little.'

'And who is Denera?' I wondered.

'My partner,' he said.

'And a Dragon Queen?' I prompted.

'The first,' he replied proudly.

'Lilith,' I said, then realised I could sense a romantic attachment between Zalman and the woman who had been so solicitous of our comfort.

'You should find that your psychic senses are far more acute now,' Zalman advised with a grin.

'They certainly are,' I confirmed. 'I am beholden to you, and vow to be more vigilant of my inheritance in future.' My apology was sincere but rushed, for despite all I had learned from Zalman, I had yet to question him about the whereabouts of my son.

He read my mind. 'In the Valley of Hebron, beneath a labyrinth built by the Master Scribe himself, there is a complex of catacombs,' he told me, although his tone implied that he felt the information would prove of little assistance in my quest to find Levi. 'Therein is a porthole to the primary grid station beneath Giza.'

'Why does Levi need the aid of an ancient Sumerian scribe?' I wondered.

Zalman seemed amused by my question. 'Perhaps the reason he has co-joined with this entity is quite the opposite.'

'The scribe needs Levi ... why?' I asked. 'Is my son in danger?'

Zalman chuckled. 'I hardly think so.'

'But if you are unsure of my son's relationship with the scribe, then how can you be so confident of his wellbeing?'

'He is, who he is,' Zalman said simply. The light shields in the floor and dome above began to close over. 'Go home, Lady Suffolk, there is nothing more you can do for Levi.'

'I cannot.' Tears welled in my eyes. 'I must hear my son's resolve from his own mouth. I have to see for myself that he is all right.'

The closing of the chamber's shield doors cast my host into shadow.

'Wait!' I appealed, but Zalman merely bowed and the chamber fell into darkness.

I am unsure of how long I lingered in the silence of that dark, otherworldly sanctuary, but I do know I had no desire to depart. If life was an express train ride, then this place felt like an unscheduled stop in the wilderness between city stations.

After some time of grace, a door opened in the chamber where there had been no door and sunlight flooded the room. I moved tentatively towards the opening, shielding my eyes as they adjusted to the light. I beheld a dirty backstreet in an ancient Near Eastern town — which town I could not tell at a glance. It seemed to be very early in the morning as there was not a soul to be seen — perhaps there was a curfew in place here? As I looked down the row of small, humble dwellings, five front doors opened and out stepped Lord Devere, Miss Koriche, Mr Taylor, Raineath and Cingar, each of whom appeared as euphoric and bemused as I felt.

'Well …' My husband piped up to speak first, even though he appeared rather distanced from reality. 'It seems we have had another shift in location.'

We all nodded, except for Taylor, who was staring at the one distinctive landmark that rose above the city — a mosque.

'That is the Holy Imbrahimi Mosque!' he informed us, dumbfounded that we had somehow left Persia and were now in the heart of the Holy Land.

'We are in Hebron?' Lord Devere clarified, whereupon it was my turn to gasp, for this was where Zalman had told me I might gain access to the porthole and tunnel system that would lead to the Amenti complex.

'Unbelievable,' Taylor murmured.

'This is right where we need to be,' I said, and hugged my husband excitedly. 'Somewhere around here are a labyrinth and catacombs containing the holy remains of some very spiritually significant people.' When Taylor smiled at me, amused, it clicked. 'Imbrahimi Mosque … do you mean as in Abraham?'

Now Taylor was laughing; he nodded to confirm my guess. 'It is said that in the Cave of Machpelah below the mosque lie the tombs of Abraham, Isaac and Jacob, and their wives Sarah, Rebecca and Leah — figures revered by Jews, Christians and Muslims alike.'

'Machpelah?' I repeated the word, wondering after its meaning.

Miss Koriche filled me in. 'Double cave.'

I wondered if she had read my mind, or if my intonation had invited the explanation. 'Referring to the labyrinth and the catacombs beneath?' I guessed, and she nodded.

'There is an ancient dispute regarding whether Machpelah is the true resting place, as there is no hard archaeological evidence as yet,' she added.

Cingar raised his hand, confused. 'And we are so interested in this mosque because …?'

'Because the reputed complex of tunnels that is around here *somewhere* is a quick route to Levi's destination, and if I don't make contact with him before he enters Amenti, there will be no contacting him for a century,' I explained.

'What!' My husband was shocked by the news. 'How do you know this?'

'I met with Zalman en route to here,' I informed him, shocking everyone all over again.

'How is that possible?' Lord Devere didn't know how to react to the news. 'Why were you singled out?'

'Zalman is on the Staff of Amenti,' I enlightened him. 'He needed to bring a couple of home truths to my attention.'

'And he spoke to you about Levi?'

Our discussion was broken by Taylor, who herded us all into a small empty dwelling. 'So sorry to interrupt,' he said.

'Is there a problem?' I inquired, wondering why he felt the need to hide us.

'If you plan on entering the mosque, yes, there is a *huge* problem.' Taylor was beginning to sweat. 'For starters, we should have permission from the Governor even to be in the city.'

'But I need to get into the catacombs, so who —'

'Impossible,' Taylor decreed. 'A thirteenth-century decree by the Mameluke Sultan Baibars barred Jews and Christians from entering the structure. It would require a special *firman* from the Sultan for even the Prince of Wales to enter the mosque! And no one enters the catacombs, but no one!'

'Hence the lack of archaeological evidence,' Miss Koriche concluded.

'I wonder if Levi gained access to Amenti from here?' I mused, more to set my mind in motion rather than raise a response from my companions. 'And if he did, how would he have gone about it?'

'The entity he has co-joined with is very powerful,' Miss Koriche said. 'It undoubtedly has means beyond most human capability.'

Taylor appeared decidedly uncomfortable with the cosmic direction of the conversation and felt the need for a reality check. 'I think the very first thing we should do is notify the authorities of our presence here.'

'But then they'll be watching us,' Cingar said, 'which means we won't be able to break into their mosque.' I knew Cingar would have no problem with such a deed as he had no faith in religion.

'Why did Zalman release us inside the city walls?' I pondered. 'He must have known we would be in trouble for illegally entering the city. In fact, he advised me to go home, so why aid me to do exactly the opposite?'

Lord Devere stated the obvious. 'Perhaps it is a test.'

'Surely Zalman did not think we would stoop to breaking into a holy monument to achieve our goals?' I said.

'We wouldn't?' Cingar queried, and when I scowled, he added sternly, 'Of course we wouldn't.'

'Perhaps we have another means at our disposal?' Lord Devere pulled his notebook from his pocket and produced the instructions to achieving an out-of-body experience in order to reach Amenti. I would have kissed my lord were we not in the company of four individuals who were all having relationship issues.

It was clear to me that Mr Taylor had taken rather a shine to my would-be daughter-in-law: his light-body was constantly shifting in order to be near her. Miss Koriche, however, was still pining for my son and was ignoring Mr Taylor's subtle advances. Raineath's light-body was doing a similar energetic dance whenever Cingar came near her, but my old gypsy friend was completely oblivious to her feelings for him.

'We really should let someone know we are here,' Taylor said, clearly uncomfortable with the situation. 'Anything could befall us, and no one would come.'

At that moment the door of the small dwelling opened and in walked my son.

'Levi!' Lord Devere, Miss Koriche and I exclaimed at once, all rushing to meet him.

'How did you find us?' Lord Devere asked, moving to embrace Levi.

Miss Koriche gently grabbed my husband's arm to delay him, for she, like I, had noted the unearthly glow in the eyes of the new arrival.

'This is only your son's vessel, my Lord Suffolk,' she explained.

Lord Devere backed up a few steps, looking horrified.

'I arranged to have you brought here,' our visitor informed us. It was Levi's voice, although the tone lacked the vibrancy of my son's personality. 'As you will insist on pursuing me all the way to Amenti, your son thought it best I delay my own journey to assure you we are safe. In so doing, I must warn you against following any of the instructions to access Amenti that you retrieved from the tablet room at Ur.'

'We were just about to try that very thing,' I said, and wondered why Thoth would be warning me away from doctrine he himself wrote.

'You cannot disengage your astral form from your physical body,' he explained. 'All such activity in mankind has been curtailed for over a century by an astral seal. This frequency shield acts as a net, designed to capture any fish who jump out of the primeval waters of ignorance. Once reeled in, that fish will be gutted and bled of all spiritual potential. The word that the text would have you recite to reach Amenti is in reality a sonic designed to draw the attention of the fishermen to you.'

'Why on Earth would your writings contain such a word?' Miss Koriche took a step back from the entity, a look of disgust on her face.

'He is a turncoat,' Taylor guessed, seeming rather pleased to have Miss Koriche's love interest associated with a traitor.

'You betrayed the human race into the hands of our enemies? But why?' Miss Koriche looked bewildered; she was clearly realising her entire life had been a lie. I also sensed that she realised she had made the right choice regarding the father of her child being human. 'How many other half-truths have you left scattered around your many temples and shrines?' she asked.

'Only one text contains the whole truth,' the demi-god explained, 'and I was just on my way to destroy it when your son insisted I come and prevent his mother from exposing herself to undesirables.' He sounded annoyed, but strangely his annoyance was not directed at me.

'The book of Thoth?' Miss Koriche was horrified. The reputed text had never actually been discovered; all knowledge of it came from legends. 'You cannot destroy the only text that could shed light on all the half-truths of the ages!'

I agreed, although I could also see the sense in it. 'The truth would benefit an enemy as well as an ally.'

'My full cooperation with the destruction of my life's major work is the only way I can prove where my loyalties truly lie,' the demi-god clarified.

'Or whether you just lie,' Taylor jeered.

'One side of my family were super-beings and time lords, of which there were few; the other side were, by comparison, a multitude of witless, clueless, weak individuals. Now who would you have allied yourself with?' He sounded regretful.

I was intrigued. 'Why the change of heart then?'

'As irony would have it, my godlike relatives are damned, and my human family turn out to be the only beings in this holographic universe with the genetic potential to lead all on this planet to divine greatness.' A deep frown formed on my son's forehead; our questions were frustrating him. 'However, be that as it may, if you do not wish to be genetic fodder within the hour, I suggest you hold your questions until we are a safe distance from this place.'

I was perplexed. 'I have not done the meditation, so how would the enemy know of our whereabouts?'

'In order to bring you here swiftly, Zalman led you in and out of the etheric world,' the demi-god explained. 'Such occurrences cause disruptions in the quanta of the time–space barrier between worlds, which are monitored by the Nefilim and the Dracon of the Old World order.'

'And how do we know that you won't lead us straight into the arms of the Old World order?' Lord Devere challenged.

'Albray.' I clutched tight my ringstone in my palm to ask my knight a direct question. *Do you think this being is telling us the truth?*

He is, in so far as you should distance yourself from the vicinity at once.

I turned my sights to the fair face of my son. 'How do we distance ourselves from this place without risking being seen by the authorities and locked up?' I asked.

'You are not going to trust him?' Miss Koriche was alarmed.

I refrained from answering, awaiting an answer to my query.

'I can shield you, just as Zalman did in order to get you out of Baghdad,' he replied, attempting to restrain his impatience. 'Then I shall take you to a safe place where you can rest whilst I complete my quest.'

'I do not think so.' Lord Devere was almost amused by the proposal. 'Better that we accompany you to complete your quest and make sure that you do not have any second thoughts about where your loyalties lie.'

'Hear, hear.' I could not have agreed more.

'There is no more time for argument,' the entity decreed. 'Follow me now or perish. I cannot be discovered before my task is done.'

He turned and walked outside.

For us, it was a matter of chase him or lose him.

In the street, doors and shutters had been flung open and people were trickling out into the street to be about their business. As we hastened along behind my son, Mr Taylor warned us all to be sure-footed, for if anyone fell into the slippery muck beneath our shoes, not all the exotic scents in Arabia would make them sweet again.

We made our way through the city unseen by all we passed; we kept silent too, although in all probability the locals couldn't hear us either. We exited through the gate of the city that led towards Jerusalem, past guards and officials and into the outlying lush green hills and valleys of Hebron. The landscape was clad with vines and orchards of olives, pomegranates, figs, quinces and apricots. So thick was the morning dew upon the earth that the instant our guide led us off the road and across country, our lower garments became soaked.

'Not really what I was expecting,' I commented, taking in the lovely fresh air after the stench of the narrow city streets. The mountains of Hebron were a vast contrast to the desert of Persia.

Mr Taylor played tour guide. 'Nowhere in Judea, bar the Jordan valley, will you find such an abundance of water.'

The sky above us was mainly blue, but in the distance a storm was fast approaching. Levi watched it warily as he strode on at a steady pace. 'There is a cave three hundred good paces from here,' he said. 'It would be advisable to take shelter there before that storm arrives.'

I wondered aloud why an ancient demi-god would be wary of a little bad weather.

'Fishermen,' he explained to me in a word.

In the storm? I looked to my husband, who was just as bemused by the comment.

Miss Koriche kept pace with our guide, curious about the entity. 'Do you communicate with Levi?' she asked.

'He oversees my mission.'

'But everything you've told us could be a lie.' She eyed the pendant that hung around Levi's neck, which she had given him on behalf of her order. 'You could have snatched Levi's body and left his soul to flounder in the ether for all I know.'

'What an adventure.' He smiled at her bafflement and strode on ahead.

'I would like you to return my necklace,' Miss Koriche called after him.

'It is not *your* necklace, it belongs to me,' he said without turning back.

Miss Koriche was curious that Thoth should claim ownership of the pendant.

'Then how did my order obtain it?' she challenged.

He turned to enlighten her. 'I left it in their safekeeping before I was to face a terrible foe, just in case I perished. The gold contains a relic of my biological form, by which my soul can be summoned forth from oblivion into a conscious form again.'

'You perished in the battle then?' Miss Koriche assumed.

He raised both brows to query this. 'I thought so for a time, but, thanks to Levi, my consciousness lives to awaken my allies and fight another day.'

REVELATION 13

THE SLEEPERS OF MAMER

'It is said that the body of Hermes, formerly Thoth, was buried in the Valley of Hebron, in a cave near the Oak of Mamer — the tree made famous by Abraham's meeting with three angels beneath it. The divine knowledge of Hermes, the scribe, was reportedly buried with him. Ancient Jewish legends tell of Abraham's wife-sister, Sarah, encountering the sleeping scribe in a cavern, which she fled when the sleeper began to stir. It is said that many centuries afterwards the cave was uncovered by Alexander the Great and, by means of the powerful knowledge he found within, he conquered all of the then known world.'

Miss Koriche shared with us what she knew about the place where we were likely bound.

Mr Taylor seemed rather overawed by Miss Koriche's educated guess as to our destination. 'That doesn't sound like somewhere you should be taking me,' he joked. Miss Koriche appeared briefly amused by Mr Taylor's awareness of his own shortcomings.

'Interesting that Abraham met angels there,' I said to my husband as we considered the implication of fishermen approaching within the storm — a supposition that seemed to have extraterrestrial connotations. Personally, I had always felt that many historical accounts of gods, angels and demons were in fact extraterrestrial encounters. I had never encountered any being in the physical world that was not terrestrial in origin, but if it was true that humans were blocked by a seal within our astral form, then perhaps this hindered me from perceiving such higher-dimensional beings? Or maybe I had simply never been in the wrong place at the right time? There was also the possibility someone or something was shielding me from the malign forces that Thoth had spoken of earlier. I recalled a very comforting presence that visited me in my dreams as a child, but all I could remember of the being was its wonderful energy; whether it was some sort of guardian I could not say.

Levi came to a stop in front of a couple of large boulders set in the side of a hill.

'Have we arrived?' Cingar queried.

'We can't have,' Taylor objected. 'Where is the famous oak?'

'Further yonder.' Levi pointed off over a rise. 'Do you think I am stupid enough to leave an easily definable landmark near a site of such significance?'

'But this rocky hillside looks practically identical to all the others around here,' Taylor said, sceptical.

'Not to my eyes,' Levi assured, reminding us of his unearthly gaze.

Cingar moved to test the sturdiness of the boulders blocking the alleged passage into the earth. Finding them, well, solid as rocks, he grinned. 'If there is a cave behind that lot, you'll need the wisdom of Hermes to get to it.' He chuckled at his jest.

Levi looked to the sky as the clouds came over. He uttered something under his breath and the two large boulders simply vanished into thin air. He turned to Cingar, who had ceased to be amused. 'In Hebron every stone has a story.'

A useful thought, I mused. The walls inside this ancient cavern might have a tale or two to tell about our questionable new friend.

'Inside.' Levi beckoned us to follow him into the dark depths beyond the narrow opening — it was a good thing we were all on the slim side.

'This is as far as I go.' Raineath stepped backwards. 'I shall not be held captive again.'

Cingar looked concerned, his loyalties divided. 'I cannot leave you to find your way back to Italy alone,' he objected.

'Then come with me,' she suggested. I knew that Raineath was well aware of how Cingar prided himself on his loyalty to me. If he chose her cause over mine, then perhaps she stood a chance of capturing his heart within this lifetime.

Levi granted them leave to depart. 'The gypsies are not in danger.'

'You mean they are not prized genetic fodder?' Lord Devere was clearly wary of a trap.

'I have done all I can,' Levi said, and entered the narrow opening.

Miss Koriche did not think twice about following him.

Mr Taylor shrugged. 'Could anything be more challenging than what we've already endured this past week?' He followed his love interest into the unknown. After hearing of his previous terror from my lord, I was surprised to see he seemed only a little unnerved by the confined space. Clearly Taylor had undergone some transformations of his own.

Lord Devere appeared to be in a mental quandary about our next move.

'We shall keep watch,' Cingar told us. I could see he wanted to maintain his services to me as long as possible. 'If anything unusual happens, I shall raise an army and come after you.'

I smiled at my dear friend and hugged him. 'Do not loiter here, it could be dangerous. Return to your kin.'

'You are scaring me.' Cingar was clearly reconsidering his position.

'Fear instead for those who cross me, for I am well protected,' I said, then added quietly, 'Raineath needs to escape this region; I have kept her from her freedom long enough. And I feel sure that she is the reason Chiara sent you, so your quest will not be over until she is safely delivered into the loving arms of your kindred.'

Cingar nodded, conceding to my view, too choked up to say anything more.

Lord Devere slapped the gypsy's shoulder. 'Cheer up, we shall meet again, my friend.' Then he took my hand and led me inside the cave.

'Good luck, Raineath,' I called back. 'Be spectacular!'

'Like you,' she returned, forcing herself to smile despite her concern.

*   *   *

Once Lord Devere and I were inside the cavern, the two huge boulders reappeared to block our point of entry.

Lord Devere made light of the development. 'That's probably for the best. Now Cingar cannot change his mind.'

'Lucky Raineath,' I added. She had managed to gain enough of Cingar's affection to sway him from my service.

Along the darkened passage we perceived a light and steadily made our way towards it.

We entered a large antechamber that appeared to have been carved out of the rock; it was painted an ORME shade of gold and all sorts of artefacts were scattered about the floor: shields, armour and weaponry from the Crusade period, other shields and weapons from a much earlier time, broken pots, jugs and old burnt-out torches. Our guide, Miss Koriche and Mr Taylor awaited us there.

Upon sighting the weaponry, Albray was fast to point out that since I had left my sword back at Ur, we now had only a pistol, which was not his weapon of choice. He quietly advised that I retrieve a sword and scabbard from one of the dead, and directed me to the sword of a fallen crusader knight.

'What are you doing, Mrs Devere?' My husband knew immediately that my actions were at Albray's request.

'There is nothing wrong with being prepared,' I told him.

My husband gave me a discerning look and moved in close. 'Could you please put him aside for a while? I'd rather he wasn't whispering to you on the quiet.'

'All right.' I decided I could appease them both. I removed my ringstone from my palm and put it in my pocket and then when Lord Devere moved on, I strapped the scabbard to my belt.

'This labyrinth contains the biological forms of some of the great visionaries and leaders of the ages,' Levi explained. 'There are such caches in caves all over the planet. These remains are only relic fragments of the great ones who are no longer living, but even the smallest remains still hold enough "living" genetic material to sustain a high vibrational frequency at specific points of the Earth grid. Via their genetic consciousness, these sentinels support and guide the spiritual nature of the planet and the human race at large.'

'So why are your relic fragments buried here?' Miss Koriche asked. 'Wouldn't the vibration of a traitor be detrimental to the other pure energies herein?'

'All roads lead back to the Sovereign Integral eventually, Miss Koriche. Even a traitor can unwittingly benefit the greater scheme, and in fact sometimes treachery is required to bring about a specific outcome. Someone must volunteer to play that role. I repented my misdeeds before I departed this world, although by then it was too late to rectify the damage.' He sounded a little more human now as I detected traces of hurt and guilt, but perhaps the show of emotion was purely for effect.

Taylor looked surprised at Miss Koriche's attack on the man she was supposedly in love with. 'Dear gods! Why do I get the feeling that I have missed something of vital import?' He turned to Lord Devere and myself. 'And why are you two so wary of your son?'

'Not now,' Miss Koriche advised her associate, her eyes firmly fixed on our host. 'Is Levi another incarnation of you?' she went on. 'The young Mr Devere was such a fine being, it seems hard to believe.'

The entity got a good laugh out of that premise. 'No,' he said, eventually sobering. 'The entity you know as Levi is my human sponsor, set in place by karma to oversee my mission. Should my will to complete my quest falter, he shall strengthen my hand.'

'I see.' But Miss Koriche didn't sound entirely convinced. 'Down which of these tunnels are your relic fragments to be found?' she asked rather callously.

Levi conjured from his hand a bubble of light, which floated off down the tunnel straight ahead. We followed the light source and Levi along many twists and turns, passing by some tunnel openings and entering others.

As we walked, I ran my hand along the walls, probing for atomic memory. There were mostly long stretches of darkness at first, then I began to get flashes of occupation: various bands of soldiers; a terrified woman running past; holy men of an ancient order, hooded and hidden beneath long robes. The torches of the priests lit the cavern for a long period, then more darkness until I came to a place where the passageways and chambers were lit by stationary balls of light, much like the light bubble we were currently following. And all around were humanlike lizard warriors, angry and aggressive. I was focused on the two closest to me, curious about their appearance, when suddenly one of them broke from the conversation to stare me straight in the eye. It hissed, as if it had spotted me. I gasped and withdrew my hand from the wall.

'What is it?' Taylor was jumpy, his nerves set on edge by the confining spaces we were moving through.

My husband gave me a stern look; the last thing he needed right now was for Mr Taylor to have another episode.

'I thought I saw a snake,' I explained. 'I am so sorry if I unduly alarmed you.'

'You are forgiven.' Nevertheless, Mr Taylor loosened his collar; he was beginning to sweat. 'I feel I am handling this rather well,' he said shakily.

Miss Koriche turned back on hearing the distress in his voice. 'You are doing very well,' she said with much encouragement. Taking hold of his hand, she gave him a reassuring smile.

'Won't your boyfriend be jealous?' Taylor whispered, although I wondered why he bothered as we could hear every breath of every person in our party.

'That entity is not my beloved,' Miss Koriche told Taylor, annoyed by the suggestion. Still, she did not withdraw her aid or favour, but led Taylor through a low doorway and into a white marble hall. As my lord and I followed, I was astounded to see that the walls therein were painted with beautiful and intricate symmetrical designs, very much like the mandalas of Tibet. Some were spiralled, others were round, star-shaped, interlocking triangles and so forth, but within each basic symmetrical design appeared myriad intricate symbols of breathtaking colour.

'What are they?' I asked, looking around me in awe.

'The twelve time codes of the primal sound fields,' Levi said. When I looked at him, none the wiser, he added, 'These are the photosonic mathematical programs that clear all unnatural seals from the light-body systems.'

Now he was starting to make a little more sense. 'So the astral seal we all have, which prevents us from engaging in astral projection, could be dispersed with one of these?' I asked. I leaned in closer to study the symbol directly before me.

Levi nodded. 'And your soul-mind will be aligned to the divine blueprint locked inside each of the twelve chakras of your light-body.'

'Twelve!' Miss Koriche and myself echoed. I had only ever learned about seven.

'Seven activated chakras will get you beyond the three-dimensional holographic illusion that is life on Earth. Twelve activated chakras will connect you to every consciousness that exists in this dimensional universe and the next.'

'Whoa,' we gasped, turning circles in a vain attempt to absorb all the designs in an instant.

'But that would take far more time than we have today,' Levi said, and sent the floating light source further along the hall. He turned on his heel and followed it.

'Just one moment longer,' I begged, desperate to be left with enough light and leisure to admire this entrancing art, painted in colours so vibrant I could literally feel the atoms in my eyeballs becoming excited by their rare brilliance.

My lord took my arm gently. 'We don't want to lose him in here, my love.'

I knew my husband was right, but before we ran to catch up with our guide, I could not resist the opportunity to peek into the past of this intriguing place. I placed my hand on the wall.

This hall had stood since before the time of the lizard people, in darkness for the longest time. Then came a great explosion deep within the Earth and the hall shook violently. Pieces of damaged metal supports and glass appeared all over the floor, then flew up to reset a long arched roof. The entire hall began to glow as if it were spirit, but appeared no less dense or vibrant. The glass set within the arched ceiling allowed the rays of the sun to dance upon the stunning works of art and science, and the sky beyond the windows was a beautiful shade of violet. Then people appeared in multitudes, as if the Hall of Time Codes had been opened to the general public and not just the holy orders. These people appeared human but were extremely tall, slender and graceful and their heads were more elongated. The colours of their skin and hair represented all races currently known on Earth, plus there were some of pastel hues. They were so beautiful, so perfect in fact, that I knew in my gut that they represented what the human race once was and what we would again become.

'Who built the time codes hall?' I asked Levi as I caught up with him in the labyrinth of corridors, doors, rooms and stairs, which were reinforced with marble arches, tiled floors, walls and ceilings.

'It was built before the Fall by a race known as the Ur-Tarranates,' he said. 'The priesthoods of Ur were a product of this race of beings who developed after this complex manifested on Earth.'

Perhaps this was the priestly order I'd seen embedded in the memory of this place?

'The Fall?' Lord Devere sought clarification on that point.

'Of Tara,' explained the ancient being.

'Tara?' Lord Devere was still lost, as were we all.

I could tell the entity was becoming frustrated by our ignorance, but then he had been one of the main catalysts behind humanity's lack of universal knowledge.

'Tara is the name of this planet's body on the next level of existence up from here,' he explained, 'the second harmonic universe, if you will, in this five harmonic universal system. In the third harmonic universe this planet is call Gaia, and in harmonic universe four it is Aramatena.'

It seemed the tutorial ended there, but Taylor was curious. 'You said there were five harmonic universes, so what is planet Earth's name in the fifth?'

'The Sovereign Integral, the source of all there is.' Levi seemed to think that went without saying.

'Are you implying that those codes have been standing since before this planet even manifested in the physical world?' I asked.

'No. That hall was built on Tara and then manifested here when part of Tara's light-body was forced down into this physical level to merge with Earth.'

'But wouldn't the guardian beings have seen the disaster coming?' Taylor rationalised, not sure if he believed the tales our guide was spinning.

'Indeed, which is why the Sphere of Amenti was created and placed within the Earth in this harmonic universe before the catastrophe happened in the next.'

'But . . .?' My mind struggled to absorb all the information.

'When you have access to the time matrix such tasks are not as complicated as they sound,' Levi said. 'How can you expect to grasp the mechanics that exist beyond this universe, when you do not even fully comprehend the mechanics that exist within this one!'

Miss Koriche was quick to take advantage of the pause in the conversation, undeterred by the demi-god's irritation. 'What is the Sphere of Amenti?'

The entity sighed, clearly expecting his explanation to raise more questions than it would answer. 'The Sphere of Amenti is a time portal linking Earth to Tara's distant past; through it the lost portion of Tara's consciousness can ascend to its original soul matrix. This re-evolution was intended to be a speedy affair; however, interfering forces have caused the project more than a few setbacks.'

The entity paused a moment, looking grave; perhaps deciding whether or not to expand on these setbacks. He chose to continue his tutorial on Amenti. 'Within the Amenti system are portholes that have become known as the Halls of Amenti, but in truth they are inter-time passageways that one must pass through in order to ascend from Earth back to Tara.'

'And the portal to Amenti is at Giza?' I clarified.

Levi, having led us to a double doorway at the end of a corridor, came to a stop and turned about. 'The entrance to the Amenti system is to be found beneath Giza, yes.' He looked back to the doors and raised a hand.

The doors parted wide to reveal a huge circular shrine of cathedral-like proportions, carved out of the natural rock. Absolutely every feature had a slight curve to it. There was a round altar in the centre, in the middle of which stood a large metal bowl filled with oil — a light source. However, as Levi had supplied us with our own light we didn't need to ignite it.

Near the central altar stood an oval-shaped sarcophagus, adorned with a full-body sculpture of the occupant encased in solid gold. The hands of the sculpture held a book with a cover of solid emerald.

Miss Koriche inspected it.

'*The Emerald Book of Thoth*!' she gasped. She moved closer, unable to resist admiring the treasure. 'How do you intend to destroy that?'

'The value of this work is not in its appearance,' Levi warned. 'Becoming bewitched by its beauty is the first step down its dark path.'

'It is the knowledge therein that I will regret the loss of,' Miss Koriche assured the entity. 'Women are not like men: we see value in very different things. But of course you know that; it is why you chose to direct all your doctrine towards men! *Mankind*, my *brothers*, my *fathers* and so on,' she quoted. 'Not one mention of the special place the female plays in the higher order of evolution!' Obviously Miss Koriche had experienced a quiet wake-up call since learning about Thoth's corruption of ancient doctrine and was now keen to serve the entity a piece of her mind. 'It was such a subtle mutation of information, but it planted the seed for a division that has grown like a thorny briar within humanity, elevating man to be a son of God and crippling womankind to this day! And thus began the male elitist rule of this Earth, and all of the male-dominated secret societies and religions. Women became an inferior slave class, and yet it is she who carries the sacred genetic codes in her blood. The balance must be restored!'

The scribe's focus again settled on his treasure. 'The higher echelons agree with you,' he said.

'Wait one moment.' Taylor spoke up. 'I am wondering … if you were repentant before you died, then why did you not destroy the dangerous text back then? Why run the risk of the wrong person finding it? Could it be that you were not supposed to destroy it?'

'With all due respect to your cunning mind, Mr Taylor, I believe that if you wait just one moment, you will see why this particular period was chosen for the termination of this treasure.' Levi looked to Miss Koriche, who was closest to him. 'Are you ready to see how I shall dispose of this?' His tone implied he was about to perform a favourite party trick.

Miss Koriche merely nodded, unwilling to expose her anticipation.

'Then,' he glanced to each of us in turn, 'quiet, please.'

The entity within Levi again focused on the book of Thoth and muttered something at lightning speed under his breath that was inaudible over the sound of his deep, rhythmic breathing. The treasure dissolved into light, which gathered in a sphere before Levi whilst the physical composition of the book crumbled into a pile of ash.

'This is the truth, the whole truth and nothing but the truth,' the entity intoned. He seemed to struggle with his intent a moment, then he abruptly cast the sphere towards Miss Koriche. The ball of light turned to a stream in transit and fed itself into the woman's subtle energy system via her heart centre. 'Let us see if womankind will fare any better at producing an uncorrupted translation,' he said.

'What are you doing?' I cried, alarmed for both Miss Koriche and my yet-to-be-born grandchild. We had only this entity's word that his book contained the whole truth; he could have been instilling the Satanic bible in the woman for all I knew.

The entity completely ignored my request for information; I needed to do something else to secure his attention. The only thing he seemed to care about was the necklace Miss Koriche had given him. I reached out with the right arm of my subtle body and gripped the pendant on its chain about my son's neck, but before I could rip it from its mooring, the arm of Levi's subtle body reached out and clutched the pendant too. Now it was suspended in mid-air, just short of snapping the chain that bound it to my son's body.

'Without the pendant your son loses his perception and all influence over me,' the scribe warned, straining under the duress of performing two psychically challenging tasks at once. 'I am trying so very hard to adhere to my mission.'

I did not let go, for how was I to know that the pendant was responsible for locking Levi out of his own form? Perhaps it was a trigger to aid the great scribe to remember some other cause he might have, pertaining to his Old World agenda?

'I was instructed by the Staff of Amenti to bequeath this knowledge to the closest human to me once I held the text in my hands,' he went on, 'and fate has chosen this woman as the recipient, not I.'

He sounded rather convincing, but still I held onto the pendant.

'Would you allow this knowledge to be lost for all time at the risk of trusting me for a few moments?' he pleaded.

I let go of the pendant and it dropped back into place. The light stream vanished completely into Miss Koriche's light-body and Mr Taylor ran to catch her as she passed out.

'I am not afraid of you, scribe,' I warned.

'Your anger will only feed the problem,' he warned me back.

'I do not take kindly to being played for a fool. Miss Koriche and her unborn child are my concern, and when you threaten those in my charge, I am bound to protect them.'

'I have not harmed them,' he replied. 'Miss Koriche is perfectly well.'

I moved to check Miss Koriche's vital signs as Taylor gently lowered her body to the ground. 'And we are expected to believe that all is as you say?' I challenged the entity.

'What choice do you have? It is done.' The scribe moved towards the only door in the shrine.

'Where do you think you're going?' Lord Devere demanded.

'We have an appointment at Giza,' the entity replied, not breaking his stride.

'We do?' My husband was curious about the 'we' in the equation.

'This body and myself.'

As Levi passed by, Lord Devere took hold of his arm and brought him to a standstill. 'That body is not going anywhere without us.'

The entity looked to his restrained limb, then up the arm of the culprit to stare him in the face. 'This vessel is vital to the stability of the Earth grid at this time. Some are most eager to see it put in place . . . and others are just as eager to *prevent* placement. Which are you?'

Lord Devere considered this a very good question, and allowed his hold on Levi to lapse. He looked to me, and I nodded that I was satisfied that Miss Koriche seemed to be breathing normally, despite her fitful slumber.

We knew so little about this interplanetary genetic war that had apparently been waging beneath the surface of the Earth since before recorded history, that neither my husband nor myself could give an answer.

'So you see,' said the scribe, in the absence of a response, 'if you could accompany me to Giza — which you cannot, as I intend to utilise subatomic shortcuts that are not open to you because of the seal you all carry within your astral bodies — you would find nothing to reassure you of your son's wellbeing, nor would you be awarded the opportunity to converse with him. For all I am doing is delivering his body to an interdimensional regeneration station, where it will remain until such time as it is again needed by its owner.'

'I cannot and *will not* entrust the safekeeping of my son's earthly vessel and spiritual wellbeing to you.' Lord Devere was adamant.

Levi indicated Miss Koriche's gift to him. 'As long as I wear this pendant,' he said, 'it is I who am in your son's safekeeping. But I have ancient genetic information that the Staff of Amenti need to complete their quest, so, please, I must depart.'

But my Lord Devere was still not prepared to trust the demi-god, and neither was I. 'What would happen if Levi's body did not join the grid?' he asked.

'Pole shift,' the entity replied bluntly. 'The Earth will tilt on its axis and all surface life will cease to exist.'

'Surely you are joking?' Mr Taylor rejected the suggestion as outlandish. 'I cannot believe —'

'I wish I had the luxury of indulging your beliefs and concerns,' the entity replied, clearly fed up. 'But it is not beneficial to my mission for you to put the decoder at risk by accompanying me.'

'The decoder?' Lord Devere frowned, wondering what the entity was on about now.

'No more time,' the scribe decreed. 'You must rest.'

The light that had been guiding our movements through the labyrinth suddenly flared and stunned us all into joining Miss Koriche in the land of slumber.

It was Miss Koriche who awoke first, and in more than one regard. For while she slumbered, she had been translating and processing massive amounts of ancient esoteric information, as we were all soon to discover.

'The scribe has left us,' she advised as she shook me to consciousness. Her claim certainly served to wake me with a start.

Lord Devere prised open his weary eyelids. 'But he left the light, I see.'

'How long have we been unconscious?' I asked once we had helped one another to our feet.

Lord Devere checked his pocket watch. 'It can't have been long,' he noted.

I swayed, tempted to collapse back to the floor for more rest. 'What hope have we of catching him when we cannot reach Giza via the same otherworldly shortcuts he has taken?'

'I believe I know of a way we can use the said passages,' Miss Koriche advised. 'However, we are, as you suspect, pushed for time.' She reached down a hand to aid Mr Taylor to his feet.

'But the astral seal —' I began.

Miss Koriche held up a hand to allay my concern. 'Fear not,' she said. 'I'll explain en route to the Hall of Time Codes.'

'Of course!' I uttered, for the scribe had stated that the codes could remove all the unnatural seals from the subtle bodies. 'But how do you know how the time codes work?'

'We only need to utilise one of the codes to achieve our goal in this instance,' Miss Koriche explained. 'So, if you will all follow me.'

As we moved through the underground maze, following the light sphere and our new guide, Miss Koriche described how she was now aware of the information within the Emerald Book. 'Nevertheless, I have much clearing and realignment work to do on my subtle bodies before I will be able to translate all of the information that has been bestowed upon me,' she finished.

'So you are the decoder the scribe spoke of?' Mr Taylor asked, his tone one of awe.

Miss Koriche merely winked in response and kept us moving.

I had to admit that the scribe did not seem to have harmed Miss Koriche; in fact, I had never seen her so vibrant and jovial. The universe may have taken the love of her life from her, but it had also awarded her the opportunity to rewrite history and correct the imbalance of the sexes that she felt so passionate about.

Once we reached our destination, Miss Koriche moved down the centre of the huge hall, eyeing each code. When finally she reached the far end of the hall, she was confused. 'I don't understand; I felt sure the code was among these.'

'His royal godliness said that there were only twelve codes,' Taylor reminded her. 'And all twelve are plainly visible.'

'That's it!' Miss Koriche gasped, startling us all. 'So sorry,' she said. 'I didn't mean to scare you. It's just so exciting when I remember things I didn't know I knew.' She strode into the middle of the hall. 'In response to your statement about the twelve codes, Mr Taylor, the thing you have to consider is that our friend the scribe has a reputation for telling half-truths.'

In between the two sets of three codes displayed on the right-hand side of the hall was a large blank space, and it was here that Miss Koriche focused her concentration.

THE THIRTEENTH PILLAR

'In addition to the twelve time codes, there is an additional code,' Miss Koriche explained, 'the thirteenth pillar. It is an activation code known as Ec-ka-sha, which means void, pre-light, pre-sound. The Eckasha must be re-embedded within the genetic memory before any of the other codes can be integrated and utilised.'

'And how does this re-embedding occur,' Mr Taylor asked. 'It sounds painful.'

Miss Koriche held up a finger to beg his patience. 'First things first.' She looked back to the blank wall before her and began to chant in a foreign dialect. Her voice was lovely and very powerful. She repeated the chant exactly the same each round, so I felt I could safely assume that it was designed to create a very specific sonic vibration — much like the 'Om' chant, only longer.

'Unbelievable,' Mr Taylor murmured under his breath as the light-filled lines of the colourful code manifested upon the blank wall before us.

This code took the shape of a teardrop, which was also a flame; its primary outlining colour was brilliant blue with a pale shade of green beneath.

'The blue flame,' Lord Devere breathed. 'This was mentioned in the tablets at Ur as representing the key to evolution. It resides in Amenti, or something to that effect.'

Miss Koriche broke from her chanting. 'Yes, the blue flame represents the Staff of Amenti and grants access to the frequency bands of the dimensions of the harmonic universe where Tara resides. So, in effect, this code opens the gateway home to Tara.'

She returned her focus to the fully manifest Eckasha code and resumed her chant. To the naked eye, nothing more transpired, but via the perception of my third eye I saw some major construction taking place within and around Miss Koriche's form.

With one last deep breath, Miss Koriche turned to us and said, 'There, my vehicle is in place. Now, who shall be next?' When we all appeared a little overawed by the task at hand, she added, 'I can talk you through the procedure step by step.'

Her assurance was met with sighs of relief, and we each assured Miss Koriche that we were more than eager to try our hand at this new esoteric science of photosonics — particularly Mr Taylor, as there was no way he was being left behind in this underground maze alone.

As Miss Koriche led me through the visual and mental exercises that were required to embed the Eckasha code and clear the seal that was binding my astral form, the blanks of my perception of Miss Koriche's activation exercise were filled in. The drawing-in of the code into the subtle bodies was all done through will and visualisation.

Once Lord Devere and Mr Taylor had been led through the activation exercise, we were all rather euphoric, but there was no time to stand about discussing the wonder of our new state of being. Every second we wasted reduced our chances of catching the scribe, who now had over an hour's start on us.

Miss Koriche led us back into the underground maze, clearly confident about our destination. After some time, she pointed to the end of the corridor we were following, where a large archway opened into a huge cavernous region. 'Not much further now,' she said.

When we reached the archway, we saw that the roof rose so high above us that it wasn't clearly visible in the light of the floating orb that illuminated our way. It was the same with the floor of the cavity. From the archway where we stood, stairs led down to a long, thin bridge of earth; it looked to be a natural formation, despite its neat situation between the descent stairs and the archway located on the far side of the great dark void. There was light beyond the opening on the far side of the bridge, but we could not make out the source from this distance.

'Well, I think I can safely say that I have shed my childhood phobia at last,' Mr Taylor announced. 'That stint through the maze did not inspire the slightest dread.'

'That is because the subtle shield you have placed around yourself has released you from the delusion of physical mortality, which is the root of all fear,' Miss Koriche informed him, smiling. 'Unconsciously you are already making contact with your interdimensional counterparts, all the way back to the source, and with that inner confirmation your being can no longer fear for this life. For you instinctually remember that your time here on Earth is but a precarious, yet vital mission, which, once completed, will allow your soul-mind to rejoin your consciousness vessel on Tara.'

Taylor was enchanted by her claim. 'Then I can hardly wait to achieve my objective and go home.'

'Hear, hear,' Lord Devere and I agreed; it seemed that Miss Koriche and Mr Taylor had both made great leaps upon their chosen paths of late.

'Beyond that arch is the intersection we seek,' Miss Koriche told us, and carefully began the descent down the steep rocky stairs that led to the bridge. Seeing her difficulty, Mr Taylor gripped hold of one of her hands to steady her passage.

The increasing goodwill between these two was obvious, and despite my grandchild growing in her belly, I had to wonder if Miss Koriche was pursuing the wrong man.

Mr Taylor, excited by his new fearless disposition, decided to negotiate the bridge first. My Lord Devere took the time to stop and inspect the support structure of the path before he would allow Miss Koriche or myself to pass.

'My friend,' he called to Taylor to prevent him being too rash. 'This does not appear to be the sturdiest of structures.'

'And yet we must chance it,' Taylor reasoned with a carefree attitude, continuing on his merry way. Upon reaching the middle of the bridge, he jumped hard to check the stability of the construction.

We all gasped at his brazen action, but the path remained firm beneath his feet. 'I have a feeling this bridge has stood for a very long time,' he called back to us.

'It has indeed,' Miss Koriche agreed, smothering her relief.

'All the same, we should not push our luck,' my lord suggested. 'We shall proceed one at a time.'

Aware of our urgency, Mr Taylor made haste to the far side and then waved Miss Koriche forward.

I had a terrible feeling in my gut as Miss Koriche set off across the divide. 'Something doesn't feel right,' I whispered to my husband, wondering if I should delay her until the cause of my unexpected dread could be determined.

'I feel it too,' Lord Devere concurred, and our fear turned to panic. 'Miss Koriche,' we called out to her.

She was now a quarter of the way across and the look of dismay upon her face as she turned to us verified that we were confirming her own negative premonition. She did an about-face to head back to us, but then her attention was drawn upwards and she began to run in the other direction, towards Taylor, who, upon sighting the cause of her dismay, shouted to her to move faster.

My lord and I looked up to see a large winged humanoid-lizard creature launching itself from the corridor at the top of the stairs above us. Spreading wide its bat-like wings, it swooped down upon Miss Koriche.

I retrieved the pistol from my holster, took aim, fired, and missed my target — but the creature was forced to change its course. It turned for another pass at Miss Koriche, who had now made it halfway across the bridge over the chasm.

Lord Devere headed off across the bridge himself, waving his arms in the hope of distracting the creature from its target. Mr Taylor was also making his way back to aid Miss Koriche to fend off her attacker.

I focused my will upon the creature in the hope that I could control its movements, if not its intent. The beast drew to a halt mid-flight and looked to me; I spied the horns on the creature's head that gave it a devilish appearance. It laughed in mockery of my attempt at manipulation; clearly it functioned beyond the realm of my psychic influence.

The winged reptile resumed its dive towards Miss Koriche; this time it was on a collision course and not to be deterred.

It was obvious to Mr Taylor that he was not going to reach Miss Koriche in time to deflect her attacker. 'You shall take her over my dead body,' he snarled, and flung himself onto the creature's back as it flew past him.

'Taylor!' Miss Koriche cried out. 'You're not a hero . . . what are you doing?'

Taylor, one arm securely fastened around the neck of the flying lizard, looked to the woman he would die for. 'Finish the mission so we can all go home,' he told her.

The creature, thrown off-balance by the unexpected additional weight, plummeted into the abyss, still struggling to rid itself of its passenger. Mr Taylor disappeared from our sight with it.

Miss Koriche sank to her knees on the narrow bridge, moved to tears by Taylor's selfless act. My lord urged her to keep moving.

'No, there must be something we can do,' she appealed.

'We can keep going, as he requested,' Lord Devere impressed on her. 'The information you have stored in your being is infinitely more valuable than one man's life — and he knew that.' My lord took hold of Miss Koriche's arm to help her to her feet. 'And you know it too.'

The responsibility of her higher potential was suddenly a heavy burden. Repressing her own feelings, Miss Koriche completed her passage across the chasm. Once on the other side, Lord Devere quickly ushered her through the archway and into the greater safety of the sheltered annex.

I was not far behind my companions, but before I reached the archway I glanced once more into the black abyss below. There was little hope that Mr Taylor had survived, but still I uttered a wish for his wellbeing.

Beyond the arch was a round domed chamber that, much like the first room we had encountered upon entering the Cave of Mamer, appeared to have been carved out of the rock and reinforced with a coat of ORME gold. There were three other archways in the chamber, illuminated by cascades of liquid-light — a little like waterfalls of light — except, unlike water, the liquid did not pool once it reached the floor and was not lit from behind, but from within every single droplet.

'Which archway leads to Giza?' my lord asked Miss Koriche.

Miss Koriche, unable to summon the will to speak in the wake of Mr Taylor's sacrifice, pointed to the middle of the three.

'Do you know what that creature was?' I said. My curiosity would not wait.

'Not now, my love.' Lord Devere grabbed my hand to urge me towards the porthole, and before I had the chance to become apprehensive, my husband had taken up Miss Koriche's hand too and pulled us both into the watery light phenomenon.

The passage was as immediate as if we had just walked through a doorway. Bone dry and intact, we found ourselves in a large stone chamber that ascended before us in several long, curved stepped levels. On the highest of these was a rounded-off altar block. Levi's body stood before it, his back to us.

My entire being was tingling, as if every atom in my body had been immediately charged upon setting foot in this chamber — the same kind of euphoria that a beneficial chant might induce, but far more intense. I was completely buzzing from the crown of my head to the tips of all my extremities; and despite how it tickled, I felt decidedly queasy.

'We have a bone to pick with you, scribe,' Lord Devere announced strongly, but I could tell from his body language that he was feeling a little strange too, as was Miss Koriche.

The demi-god turned to address us and I noted he held an object in his hand, which vanished before I could perceive what it was. 'As fate would have it, here you are,' he said, sounding disappointed but not surprised. 'Did I not warn you that to bring the decoder here would be dangerous?'

'You did,' my lord confirmed, 'but you failed to explain why.'

'Your personal sonics are not yet developed enough to be of benefit here; you are all feeling the pressure of the higher sonic right now. I have just been injecting this antechamber and those that lie beyond it with frequencies high enough to protect this vessel from being sabotaged by undesirables. Your very presence here is jeopardising our mission.'

The foreboding I had felt prior to the appearance of the strange winged creature over the chasm washed over me once again. My being ceased to buzz, seeming to indicate that the sonic frequency of this chamber was suddenly plummeting. My pistol needed reloading and so was useless to me, as was my sword without Albray. Quickly I took my ringstone in my hand and mentally summoned my knight. As I had not been wearing the ringstone next to my skin, Albray had no idea of my location and was completely bemused when he joined us.

My dear lady, where are we?

Beneath Giza, I suspect.

Giza! Albray looked to the vessel that had once been my son. *We should not be here.*

No sooner had my knight voiced his fears than several lizard warriors, identical to those I had seen when probing the atomic memory of the labyrinth of Mamer, appeared out of thin air.

Draconians, gasped Albray. *Molier is a saint compared to these creatures!*

Five reptilian humanoids were ranged around the chamber and toted weapons I had never before seen. However, one of the intruders I recognised from my perception of Mamer's history, for it was the very lizard warrior that had spotted me and hissed at me. These lizard beings had distinctive individual features, just as humans do. They were large in stature, seven to eight foot tall, and extremely muscular. Their feet and hands were clawed, and their skin was smoothly scaled in a rusty brown to deep evergreen shades. Their eyes had a cold glare like that of a snake or a shark, but the rest of their facial features were humanlike, except for their fleshy brow that curved around their forehead like a headband. They were dressed in a skintight uniform made of what looked like dull grey rubber and they wore chest armour. Most of the intruders bore the insignia of a flying serpent on the left shoulder of their uniform; however, the warrior familiar to me bore the insignia on a large medallion that hung on a gold chain around his neck. From this I assumed he outranked his company. All the insignia slowly pulsed with light.

'How nice of you to deliver the decoder and the biological remains of the latest key-holder into our possession,' the leader said. 'What fine angelic specimens.' His reptilian eyes raked us disconcertingly, but he appeared most interested in Miss Koriche. 'And the decoder is already impregnated with a little genetic delicacy ... yummy.'

'Traitor!' Miss Koriche cried out to the scribe, fearful for her unborn child and angry that she had played right into the hands of the enemy.

'I told your associates to keep you away!' Thoth pointed out in his own defence. 'I don't know how we were discovered, but I was not the informant.'

The lizard warrior seemed amused by our confusion. His dark, cold eyes turned to me. 'Does he lie, princess?'

All eyes turned my way. I was rendered mute by the implication that I was the one who had sabotaged this mission.

'Mrs Devere?' My husband knew I was suppressing something as I was too slow to refute the implication.

'I suspect that I may be to blame,' I confessed reluctantly, not wanting to believe I had unwittingly betrayed us all.

'Only maybe?' the lizard taunted, confirming my fears.

It was now horribly clear that if we had trusted the scribe, Levi's body would be safely on its way to residing in the Signet Grid.

'But how is that possible,' I wondered, 'unless ... unless you are immortal?' An even scarier thought occurred. 'Or you are inter-time intruders.'

'Right on both counts,' the beastly warrior confirmed. 'But it is your kind who are the intruders; we were here first!'

'This planet was never destined for your habitation,' Thoth corrected, and looked to us. 'Do not be intimidated. These beings are not immortal; they live off human fear and use the dark arts to absorb the vitality of their victims.'

'And who was it that taught us that little trick?' the reptilian taunted the scribe. We all gasped at the extent of Thoth's treachery.

The demi-god nodded, shamefaced, to confirm the truth of it. 'Still, without the use of technological gadgets and misguided demons,

Taejax and his friends would be back in the pre-Stone Age where they belong! Their cosmic violations have nothing to do with me.'

'I belong to the past, the present and the future of this planet!' the lizard hissed back.

'If you and your kind get your way, there will not be a future for this planet beyond the year 2976,' the scribe retorted.

'That is a lie!' The reptilian, riled, aimed the barrel of his weapon at us.

Although we knew we were in danger, Lord Devere, Miss Koriche and myself were mesmerised by the lights around the barrel of the weapon that pulsated as the creature fired upon us. Instead of harming us physically, whatever invisible amunition the weapon fired struck us motionless as statues.

The lizard warrior focused on the scribe again. 'So, old friend, it seems you have a decision to make. You can defend this key-holder's body and also suffer the fate we have planned for him, or you can depart his form and hand it over to me without a fuss.'

The rest of the reptilian warriors moved in to surround the scribe, but he seemed amused by the ultimatum rather than afraid. He laughed in Taejax's face.

I was distracted from the scene by Albray's voice in my mind.

I need permission to join with you, my Lady Suffolk, for I operate beyond the laws of the physical realm and therefore —

Just do it, Albray! I stressed; he could explain the physics to me later.

Your psychic aptitude is not constrained either, Albray advised as he slipped into my form and I was freed to move again.

But I tried enforcing my will upon the winged reptilian that attacked us on the bridge, and it laughed at me, I said.

I felt Albray's shock like a bolt through my being.

You confronted a winged Dracon on your own? Why did you not call me?

Now is not the time for a lecture, my friend.

I sensed Albray's nod of assent, and he turned his attention to the problem at hand. *If you held no supernatural sway over the reptilian, then the Draconians must have developed a psychic shield of some description,* he mused.

The scribe discreetly enlightened us as to our adversary's weak spot. 'You and I both know, Taejax, that all that prevents you from going mad in this chamber and in our presence is that snake charm you all wear.'

'And all that prevents you from joining us is that sentimental trinket you wear around your neck!' the lizard warrior retaliated. 'Without it you would lose all devotion to your masterful friend and betray him just as you have all the others who were foolish enough to trust you.' The creature sounded like it was speaking from personal experience. 'Betrayal is something you taught me, scribe, and I shall not hesitate to return the favour if you do not disengage from that vessel.'

I was about to try willing the insignia of all the intruders into my possession, when I spotted, via my third eye, an etheric demon emerging from the reptilian leader's person.

There is the source of their mysterious psychic immunity, Albray and I both realised at once. The demon would prevent me removing the insignia via psychic means; we'd have to physically remove their shields if we wanted them to leave.

Meanwhile, the demon had snatched the pendant from around Thoth's neck. When the demi-god used his astral hand to prevent the theft, as he had when I tried the same stunt, the demon bit it. Thoth, not having felt physical pain in quite some time, was taken by surprise and the demon managed to secure the pendant and return it to its host's possession.

My son's face suddenly filled with alarm as Taejax swung the trinket before his eyes. 'Now, what say you, great architect?'

Tears flooded my son's eyes and silently rolled down his face. 'I can help you, Taejax,' he said. 'None of us need be left behind.'

'I have heard that before!' snarled the reptilian, and, angered that the removal of Thoth's charm had not softened his resolve as expected, Taejax cast the trinket aside and made a grab for Levi, who literally slipped through the creature's clutches by levitating into the air.

It was the distraction we needed. In a heartbeat, Albray used my body to separate two of the lizards from their left arms. Divorced from their protective insignia, they fell to the ground shrieking in torment and pain.

Taejax turned his attention towards me and flicked a switch on a small device attached to his wrist. Out shot a long thin needle.

'Beware,' the scribe warned me. 'That device is filled with liquid ORME. If you are injected, the overdose will not only kill you but fragment your soul into tiny pieces!'

What! Albray was confused. As far as he knew, a daughter of the blood could not overdose on ORME. He wasn't allowing any of the reptilian warriors the opportunity to get close to me in any case. Their technological prowess had made these warriors lazy and the other two reptilian thugs fell as quickly as their comrades, leaving only Taejax still upright and of sound body and mind. The lizard warrior circled me, unable to discern how I had defied the paralysing effect of his weapon; clearly he did not possess any true psychic talent, just as Thoth claimed.

How does one best a demon? I inquired of Albray.

With love.

With love? The tactic was rather perplexing to me in this instance.

Not to worry, I shall separate that pendant from its chain, my knight assured me as we narrowly avoided the reptilian's stab at us. *If what the scribe said is true, without the insignia the harmonics of this chamber will drive the Draconians from our midst.*

But his friends haven't departed, despite their obvious torment, I pointed out.

It is my guess that they cannot retreat before our friend here. Albray found the opportunity to slide his sword under the chain around Taejax's neck and yanked with all his might. He nearly succeeded in choking our opponent, who was heaved right off his feet, but the chain did not snap.

ORME, I deduced. *That makes things a little more difficult.*

Not really, contested Albray as Taejax quickly found his feet. *I'll just have to take off his head.*

'Wait!' For a split second the scribe distracted our attention as he floated down to Earth, eager to prevent any more bloodshed in this sacred place.

This proved time enough for Taejax's demon to stretch out and snatch the sword from our possession. I was quick to will it back to us before it reached our opponent's grasp, stretching out my astral arm to grip its hilt. The sword was suspended mid-flight, but then the demon lunged forth and bit into the extended wrist of my subtle form. Its teeth burned into me upon contact and a blistering welt erupted on my wrist. Despite the torture I hung on and tugged the demon from its host, who was racing towards us with his needle-device held high.

With my free hand, I willed the pendant bearing the winged-serpent insignia into my possession. The chain slipped over Taejax's head and flew into my grasp. The reptilian immediately dropped to the floor at my feet, where he squirmed in sonic agony.

Now that I held the pendant that shielded Taejax from the high frequencies of this chamber, the demon vanished, unwilling to share the physical pain Taejax was experiencing.

'No! We had a deal!' Taejax wailed as his last shot at redemption dissolved into thin air.

Thoth came to stand over the reptilian. 'Surely you did not expect loyalty from a demon! All your relationships are destined to end thus, Taejax, so long as you remain faithful to the Old World order.'

The scribe removed the warrior's weapons and, fiddling with the switches on the side of the pulse gun, fired upon my associates and myself, releasing us from our confinement. I regained control just as Albray stepped out of my body and left me tottering.

The lizard creatures lay on the ground vomiting black muck, their blood turning the floor a new shade of slime green. The sight and the smell was horrendous.

'Just leave,' I appealed to the reptile in charge. I could not bear to watch his men suffer any longer.

'I cannot,' Taejax forced out, his sharp teeth gritted together. 'I need the pendant.'

It is a trick, Albray advised me. The pendant could have other functions, and besides, the death of this lot could only be beneficial.

'That is precisely the attitude that has fuelled the age-old conflict on this planet,' the scribe pointed out, clearly aware of Albray's presence. He leaned over the reptilian to ensure he had his attention.

'I too was once led to believe that I was beyond redemption and bound to employ the dark arts to survive. But I am here to tell you, Taejax, it was just a control tactic based on a huge web of lies.'

Taejax managed to take a swing at Thoth, who was quick to step out of range. 'Go serve the Sovereign Integral and be with your angels, but you will never convince me to join their cause!' He began vomiting up the same black muck as his associates.

'Their cause is every soul's cause,' Thoth lectured his fallen opponent. 'I thought you would have worked that out by now.'

'As though I would believe any of your theories, traitor!' Taejax hissed.

'Such is my lot: whichever path I choose, I must betray someone,' the demi-god said, glancing between Miss Koriche and the reptilian. 'But if betraying your physical being means that I can ultimately save your immortal soul, then one day you will thank me for that betrayal.'

The reptilian appeared more hurt by these words than the physical torture he was feeling. 'I have no soul, half-breed, and well you know it!'

The scribe did not seem to agree. 'That would be convenient, wouldn't it? That would justify all the torture and murder of innocents! But suppressed as it is, and despite what you have been led to believe, I can assure you that you do have a soul — and the willpower to free it from its fated fragmentation.'

The lizard attempted to block its small ears. 'Your words are poison!'

'A poison taken in small quantities may prove extremely beneficial, old friend,' the scribe concluded.

As I gazed at the hapless creature, wondering what was to be done with him, I was blinded by a vision of a beautiful young human girl under Dracon attack, and Taejax leaping to her rescue. The vision passed instantly, but in that moment I realised this was our opportunity to secure a future ally.

I walked towards the ailing warrior and, crouching at his feet, I reached out and touched his boot.

'Mrs Devere ...' My husband made it clear that he was not comfortable with my being in such close proximity to a creature that had just attempted to damn me to hell.

But the old saying that one can never judge a person until you have walked a mile in his shoes sprang to mind, and upon making contact with the creature I sampled the pain of being exposed to a frequency that was way beyond my capacity to process. The atomic structure of my entire body was being violently shaken apart, whilst all my fear and hatred imploded inside me, manifesting as a dark liquid slime that burned a path through my interior as it was expelled from me via my mouth, nose and ears. But all that physical pain was nothing compared with the underlying spiritual anguish this being felt at knowing that one day he would cease to exist on every level of awareness.

'Save yourself and your men,' I said and, the protests of my companions ringing in my ears, handed Taejax his pendant.

The creature immediately regained his equilibrium and spat the remaining black gunk in his mouth into my face.

He was weak, however, and the foul-smelling bile dripped onto my clothes instead. 'Like all females, you are a weak fool.'

I was tempted to withdraw yet I did not. 'Is there not a female among your kind whom you deem worthy of respect?' I asked.

'There are no females of my kind,' he informed me bluntly.

No wonder the Dracon had a problem feeling love. 'Well, you may count on the fact that I shall not flee at the first sign of danger,' I said.

'If you think you are going to incite my gratitude, you are even more deluded,' he snarled. 'Show me mercy and I shall hunt you down and all those dearest to you. I will drain their vital fluids and scatter their souls to oblivion, until your entire line has been wiped from the evolutionary blueprint.'

'Ashlee, no!' My husband implored me to reclaim the pendant before it was too late.

Was I prepared to bet the lives of all my kindred that Taejax was bluffing? I glanced around those gathered in the chamber and in a split second appraised the consensus: my husband, Miss Koriche and Albray were clearly against trusting the reptilian. Then I looked to Levi, who was shaking his head, urging me not to reclaim the gift. Whose side was Thoth really on? It seemed to me that he wanted to be on everyone's side, and so did I.

I stood and backed away from Taejax. 'You do what you feel you must. I shall be waiting.'

The four warriors under his command were beginning to lose consciousness and yet Taejax was hesitant to use the escape route I had provided for them all. He had one last stab at inducing fear in me. 'I mean what I say.'

'So do I.' I smiled warmly, whereupon he snarled in frustration. He returned the missing limbs to his fallen comrades and the intruders vanished from our midst.

'Why?' both my husband and Albray implored me at once.

Miss Koriche spoke up, having rethought her position on the matter. 'Because the healing has to start somewhere.'

My husband embraced me, having feared for my soul during my duel with Taejax. His eyes turned to Albray, whom he again had to thank for saving our lives. *You have my sincerest gratitude.*

I don't want your gratitude, I want your trust! Albray was furious that he had been left out of contact during our recent perils.

I swear I shall never doubt you again, my lord promised. *I realise my jealousy is a curse, but I am only human after all.*

I am your wife's servant, Albray insisted, then saw fit to humble himself a little. *Although it seems I have steered you both wrong in the past with regard to ORME consumption.*

Thoth held up his palm to intervene. 'That would be my fault. It was I who presented the secrets of ORME to the priesthoods as a means of speeding up the genetic blueprint of mankind's angelic races, thus causing them to unwittingly damn the very souls that could save all humanity.'

Albray was utterly bewildered by the news. *Then all those teachers I respected and served without question were wrong?*

'Something we have in common, warrior.' Miss Koriche stepped forward to reassure the ghostly knight and let us all know that she was also aware of his presence.

Thoth attempted to ease the knight's remorse. 'In choosing to serve the Ladies of the Elohim, however, at least in death you have been in the service of the righteous.' He turned to the rest of us. 'And it is to the service of the Elohim that I must go now. This antechamber has been violated and we must all depart before Taejax has the opportunity to send forth a larger force to ambush us.'

I got the distinct impression that this would be as far as we would be permitted to accompany Levi's vessel; indeed, it was now plainly obvious to me, and to all in my company, I suspected, that we were a liability to Levi's cause. I had always thought myself well versed in the psychic arts and their dominions, but plainly I knew nothing in comparison to all there was to know, learn and practise. And the sad truth was, if I was so very ignorant, then how much more ignorant was the rest of humanity?

Thoth wandered towards where the necklace Miss Koriche had given to Levi had been cast to the ground by Taejax. Retrieving it, he rose and approached Miss Koriche. 'This has served its purpose so far as my quest is concerned, and I believe Levi wants you to have this, to give to your child.'

Miss Koriche was rather moved by the gesture, and accepted the gift graciously. 'Thank you, lord,' she spoke reverently to the being, having borne witness to his true character. 'My child will wear it with pride.'

'There shall be no threat to my mission beyond this point,' Thoth said, stepping away from Miss Koriche to address us all, 'provided you agree to accompany me no further. I will give you one of my light orbs to lead you back to the surface. The passage I must take is of a frequency that is agony to the uninitiated. Not even a demon can breach the outer defences of the Amenti complex.'

This moment was a test; a test I had failed several times during my search for Levi. I had to trust in my son's choices and let him go so that he may be of aid in the great conflict I was only just realising existed. I had always assumed that humanity was its own worst enemy, but it seemed we had far greater obstacles to overcome than just our own selfish desires and ignorance.

I left my husband's side and approached the body of our son, my heart welling to bursting point at the thought of never seeing him again. 'I believe I understand your treachery now,' I told the entity within him; for I had returned Taejax's pendant, which could be considered treachery in the eyes of my kindred, despite the possible benefits to the greater cause of humankind.

I looked back to Miss Koriche, whose eyes were full of tears as she nodded to confirm that she believed it was time to let Levi go so he could fulfil his destiny. She too was struggling to maintain her composure, for she finally had to face the fact that she would not be seeing her beloved again.

Although I knew that my son's soul was no longer attached to his physical form, I had to hold him close one last time. My gesture perplexed the demi-god, but he made some attempt to return my sentiment. Then my Lord Devere gently eased me away from our son's vessel. Despite the fact that they would never see their loved one again, neither Lord Devere or Miss Koriche felt compelled to embrace Levi's physical remains.

'Give our boy our love,' Lord Devere told the entity. 'Apologise on our behalf for not trusting that he knew full well what he was doing when he joined with you.'

My lord's little compliment made me smile; we would not part with this being on a sour note.

'Peace go with you both,' Lord Devere concluded, his voice hoarse. The emotion of the moment was choking us all. He put his free arm around Miss Koriche to comfort her too.

The scribe nodded that he would pass on our tidings. 'Now, follow the orb,' he instructed, then waited for us to take our leave.

The sphere of light was hovering by an arched passageway on ground level, which I could have sworn was not there when we entered. Beyond it rose a stone staircase for as far as the eye could see.

HARMONIC ACTIVATION

As I sit here in our hotel suite in grand Cairo, several days after the events I have recorded above, it is hard to believe our adventures in the Holy Land were not a fabulous hallucination. But the large welts on my wrist, where the demon fastened its teeth around me, serve as proof that it did actually happen — I did not imagine it, I did not dream it. The elation that the journey inspired in me has been swallowed up by a gaping void of sorrow that has opened in my chest — I will never revel in Levi's company again. My only hope lies in my experience in Ta-She-Ra El Amun: I can now aspire towards perfecting genetic structure naturally, through Miss Koriche's photosonics. Perhaps one day I will be adept enough to make contact with my son.

I have to wonder if Lord Malory knew about Levi's hidden agenda when he sent us off on this eye-opening quest. It is my intent to seek out the Sangreal brotherhood's Grand Master immediately upon my return to London — which may not be for a little while yet.

Our exit from the antechamber of the Amenti complex beneath Giza was a similar experience to our arrival in Hebron from Ta-She-Ra El Amun. The light sphere led us to a door and then dissipated, leaving us in utter darkness. Upon opening the door we found ourselves in a backstreet of Cairo in the middle of the day. When we looked back, we saw that our passage had transformed into an earthen wall, so we could not retrace our steps to the underworld complex.

We sought accommodation in a hotel, but despite the fact that we had not slept in days, we were all so shell-shocked from our adventures that sleep would not come. Instead, Lord Devere, Miss Koriche, Albray and myself loitered in the sitting room of the private suite that my Lord Devere had secured for the two of us, and for a long time we were each borne away on our own silent reflection.

We had all lost someone dear to us during our flight from Persia; we mourned Levi and marvelled at the reckless abandon of Mr Taylor's heroic deed.

'I should never have agreed to this assignment,' I said, breaking a long silence.

You are right, Albray retorted, *our continued ignorance would have served the world far better.*

'But what good are these insights?' I felt the cost I had paid was too high. 'Even if I knew the whole truth, who would ever believe it? Who would want to? I have witnessed some of the dark hidden history of this planet and even I do not want to believe what I have seen.'

'Everything happens for a reason, my love.' My lord entered the debate. 'There is good to be drawn from every adversity.'

This was my own philosophy being quoted to me and I realised I was not being very constructive. 'But if all doctrine, ancient or otherwise, is corrupted, how can we as human beings ever hope to discover the whole truth?' I mused.

Miss Koriche voiced her view. 'If there is adversity in our lives, it is an energy we have projected there, for evil, goodness and every attribute in between are but a matter of frequency and it is only we who can transform that sonic vibration to resonate more positively.'

Perhaps that is the only truth worth knowing, Albray pondered, *and whatever truth or reason we hope to extract from our lives, and beyond, is dependent on that one simple premise.*

'Hear, hear,' Lord Devere agreed. 'And judging from recent events, it would seem that we all have our work cut out for us in that regard.'

'An exhausting thought, my lord.' I smothered a yawn as my need for rest finally overwhelmed me.

Well, if you have no further need of me, I think it time I took my leave, Albray suggested.

We thanked the knight for his aid during our journey, and he made us vow to summon him the moment we had need of him again.

I may not be as all-knowing as I once thought, but I am committed to your safety and wellbeing, he told me.

'I never doubted that,' I assured him; for in my heart, I never had — and I never would.

For many days, Miss Koriche locked herself away in her hotel room, writing and painting her translations of the data passed on to her via *The Emerald Book of Thoth.* I was offered a glimpse of her illustration of the Ec-ka-sha code, which appeared exact in every detail, so far as I can recall; she has been meticulous in keeping the colours true to their depiction in the Hall of Time Codes. Her written work is equally inspiring and I can hardly wait to begin a serious study of her data.

Lord Devere and myself are not the lady scribe's only eager pupils.

It took less than a day for Miss Koriche's order to learn of her return to Cairo. Three veiled women came to visit her, dressed in white from head to toe bar a small slit in their head-cover that allowed them to see. I was with Miss Koriche when the party was announced, and although I offered to stay by her during the visit, she graciously declined, assuring me that she was no longer threatened by her past.

Miss Koriche was not the only one whose presence in the city had been noted. Whilst she was in conference with her sisterhood, Lord Devere and I received an invitation cum summons from the representative of the Holy See in Cairo, Cardinal Guarino Antonazzi — the very same Church dignitary who had left my husband to rot in a hole at Ur. As the invitation was addressed to both my husband and myself, it appeared that his Holiness knew of Lord Devere's deliverance. There was little point in attempting to evade the audience, as the Church of Rome was far too widespread to hide from for long; better to allow the cardinal to air whatever was on his mind. We took the precaution of making our presence in the city known to the British consulate in Cairo before proceeding, just in case we mysteriously disappeared. It wasn't much of a safety net, for as we well knew, when the church wanted information to go missing, it was as if it had never existed.

Our audience with the cardinal was to be conducted in a church dedicated to Saint Mercurius. This was the largest church in the district known as the Abu Sayfayn Cloister, just to the north of the Fortress of Babylon in Old Cairo.

Upon arrival at the appointed meeting place, Lord Devere and I were escorted into the church proper. After much genuflecting and crossing of themselves by our guides — which my lord and I did not participate in — we were led straight to a door in the north aisle of the structure, which granted entry into a courtyard. Within the courtyard we were confronted by a handful of the cardinal's guards and some dignitaries, who stood outside a small building that hosted several intimate sanctuaries and a baptistry. We were escorted into one of these small sanctuaries to find Cardinal Guarino Antonazzi seated in a throne-like chair, with only his personal bodyguard in attendance.

'Lord and Lady Suffolk,' he acknowledged as the door was closed behind us. 'What a surprise it is to see you both safe and well.'

'God's compassion must be shining on us,' my husband replied.

'Indeed,' said his Holiness, seeming slightly vexed by the fact. 'I have requested this meeting to question your intent regarding your archaeological investigations in Persia.'

Typical, I thought, the man's not even the least bit concerned that we might accuse him of attempted murder; all that matters is suppressing the find.

'We are not obliged to answer your concerns,' my husband pointed out, beating me to the mark.

'Oh, but you are,' his Holiness insisted, suppressing a smug grin. 'For although the peril for you in Persia has passed, my Lord Suffolk, I believe your wife is currently being hunted by the Shah for several offences.'

'This is blackmail,' I said, infuriated by the predictability of the proceedings.

'I like to think of it as cooperation, Lady Suffolk,' the cardinal replied.

I inhaled deeply to control my rising temper. After one glance at me, my husband took over the negotiations.

'Whether you silence us this day or not, that site is going to be unearthed sooner or later, and the texts of those tablets will be made available for public scrutiny.'

'You really have no idea what you are dealing with,' Cardinal Antonazzi cautioned.

'Whether you refer to the source of the tablets, or the church's attempt to suppress them, I am well aware on both counts,' my lord corrected.

'I doubt that very much.' The cardinal seemed altogether too confident.

'I realise that the text is but half-truths,' my husband persisted, 'but that is better than no truth at all.'

'And what is *the truth*, Lord Suffolk?' his Holiness queried. 'Would you know *the truth* if it was staring you in the face?'

I was becoming increasingly angry with this man, and it wasn't just that I deplored all that he stood for; there was something about his personal presence that bothered me.

'The truth *is* staring me in the face,' Lord Devere said, as if suddenly enlightened. 'And my understanding of it is vastly different from that which you are putting forward ... or at least my truth is far more extensive.'

'There is only one truth, Lord Devere, and that is the truth according to God,' the cardinal said dryly.

I focused my third eye upon the cardinal to see what his light-body had to say about him. I was shocked to discover a sparkling golden aura with no sign of any light centres. This man was an abomination, just as Molier had been, for this kind of light-body was the by-product of an ORME addiction! Only in this case, the subtle body hiding within the cardinal was several feet taller than its physical host. I couldn't make out the details of its appearance, but I was fairly certain it was not human, and yet it did not have the characteristics of a Dracon either. *Could he be one of the Nefilim?* I was terrified even to consider the possibility, for I knew not the extent of their power and influence.

'God has not penned a definitive work of truth, so far as I am aware,' Lord Devere was saying. 'God's truth is set to paper by men, none of them perfect.'

The cardinal was not interested in debating matters of faith. 'I am a busy man, my Lord Suffolk. Do we have an understanding?'

'We do,' I was quick to reply, for I felt the need to distance us from the presence of this dark being.

Lord Devere was only momentarily surprised by my reaction; perhaps he had also psychically perceived the truth about this being and had come to the same conclusion to withdraw. And it was clear that I would be safe from persecution by the Shah only so long as we kept our discoveries in Persia a secret. My husband seconded our agreement. 'We shall keep our observations to ourselves.'

'Very good,' the cardinal concluded. 'And you need not worry yourselves about the text in your find being circulated in the future. His Holiness the Pope is currently rewriting the guidelines for the funding bodies behind Europe's thriving archaeological enterprises.'

I could not believe the man's arrogance. 'Most excavations are funded and controlled by the universities,' I countered.

'And the most prestigious universities are answerable to whom?' Cardinal Antonazzi replied.

It was true: the church controlled the universities, and any scholar who desired to advance in society needed at least to appear to be a devout Catholic. Forty years ago the work of Lord Hereford in the Sinai had been completely banned and discredited in England, and suppressed throughout most of Europe, because it conflicted with the accounts of the Old Testament.

The cardinal did not question us about Miss Koriche; perhaps as a young woman she was not a threat, for anything she said could be easily dismissed or discredited. But we were surprised when his Holiness made reference to our other companion.

'I was very sorry to hear you misplaced Mr Taylor. He was such a helpful fellow.'

I wondered how the cardinal could know Mr Taylor was missing. Perhaps it was merely the fact that he had not been in our company when we entered the city. Yet the cardinal did not ask about his current whereabouts.

'I feel sure you will not find him so helpful upon your next meeting,' my husband said, giving nothing away.

The cardinal looked amused by the comeback. 'I feel sure Mr Taylor has learned better than to challenge me.' And he waved a hand to dismiss us.

I was very relieved to depart the cardinal's company for his personal sonic frequency was literally making me sick.

'Are you all right?' my husband inquired as we exited the church; I feared I looked as ill as I felt.

'That man is not human,' I said, taking deep breaths to control the fear that had been incited by exposure to a low-grade presence.

'I noticed,' my lord confirmed. 'I couldn't make out its true appearance, but I am guessing it was one of the Nefilim.'

'I second that.' I looked at my husband with a worried frown. If the enemies of humankind had infiltrated our society and in such major positions of power, how could we hope to steer humanity in the right direction? 'What do we do?'

My lord smiled. 'Well, we never said we wouldn't document our finds.'

'Do you think he knows something about Taylor's fate?' I asked. It was a question I found most troubling.

'For Taylor's sake, I hope not.'

Miss Koriche spent twelve hours in conference with the women from her sisterhood. They had food and drink brought to them in the room, which was across the hallway from our own.

Lord Devere and I were starting to fret that something might be amiss, when we heard Miss Koriche's three visitors finally departing. We rushed to open our door and witnessed the sisters bowing to Miss Koriche in gratitude; this was not quite the exit we'd been expecting.

Miss Koriche was absolutely beaming, and my third eye vision confirmed that her three visitors were far more cheerful in comparison to the three sullen, repressed souls who had arrived. I was so relieved that there had been a positive outcome.

'What did you do to them?' I asked as Miss Koriche invited Lord Devere and myself into her room.

'I told them the truth,' the young woman informed me with glee, 'and nothing but the truth. Give me a few years and I shall restore our ancient doctrine to what it always should have been.'

'Does that mean you intend to stay in Cairo, Ajalae?' I had hoped she would consider our proposal for her and our grandchild to come and live with us in England.

Her large brown eyes apologised. 'This is my home,' she explained.

I held up a hand to assure her I understood her reasons; she did not have to justify herself to me. 'Then we shall stay until the birth,' I said, and nodded firmly when Miss Koriche shook her head in protest.

'No, I cannot keep you from your family,' she insisted.

'You are our family too,' my Lord Devere said, and his sincerity brought tears to the young woman's eyes. 'Do you think we are going to miss the birth of our first grandchild?'

'Not on your life,' I seconded. 'We can help you find a new living arrangement here.'

'Indeed,' my husband said. 'I, for one, shall not be leaving Cairo until I see my daughter-in-law and grandson happily settled in their own home.'

Miss Koriche appeared overwhelmed; clearly she hadn't thought that far ahead. 'I am really not in a financial situation to —'

'Our grandson's allowance will cover all your expenses.' Lord Devere's statement stunned Miss Koriche into speechlessness.

'Any idea on a name yet?' I asked to fill the silence.

'I have given that some thought.' The young mother-to-be found her voice and her eyes turned to my husband. 'I would like to name him Earnest.'

This was my husband's given name and the suggestion took him quite by surprise. 'After me, Ajalae?' Clearly he was touched by the sentiment.

She nodded. 'You are the only man I have ever trusted, Lord Devere.' Her emotions welled with the confession and tears trickled from her eyes. 'You promised, many times, that you would see me to safety and you have. I want my son to be just like you.'

As my lord embraced the emotional young woman, my own tears began to roll. I so empathised with her reasons for the name choice, for during the twenty years we had been married, my dear Devere had saved me in every sense of the word.

'You came to my rescue a few times too,' Lord Devere told Miss Koriche, not wanting to take all the credit for their survival. These two had obviously formed a very close bond during their ordeal and I was glad of it, for it made Ajalae feel more like family.

'Quite a team,' she sniffled; then she smiled and released my husband to take hold of both his hands. 'Even Taylor had his moments,' she concluded sadly.

The smiles fell from all our faces, and Miss Koriche drew away from us to take a seat at the small table she had been employing as a desk.

'I feel sure that Mr Taylor did not confront and overcome his lifelong phobia for no good reason,' I offered, attemping to be of some comfort on the matter, for I sensed that Taylor was also part of the reason Miss Koriche was choosing to stay in Cairo. If our friend had survived the fall, managed to slay the beast and found his way through the outer labyrinths of the inner world, then he would most likely surface in this city, just as we had.

'Taylor is a survivor, to be sure,' my husband agreed.

'His contribution to the pursuit of truth will bear great fruit, I shall see to that.' Miss Koriche took up her quill, dipped it in ink and continued with her transcription.

By the time young Earnest was born, Miss Koriche had transformed the face and mind-set of her sisterhood, written three volumes on soul genetics and painted all twelve of the remaining time codes. She had been determined to get at least this much doctrine recorded before she went into labour, in the event that the birth of her child did not go well for her. My and my lord's presence was also a reassurance; should the worst happen, young Earnest would be well taken care of.

It was well that the young mother-to-be had worked so vigilantly, for young Earnest took us all by surprise by deciding to arrive a month early. Miss Koriche was justly distressed for the child, as babies born so prematurely rarely survived. Still, the blessed little soul did not leave us worrying too long: he was born after only a few hours of labour, weighed in at a healthy eight pounds, and was kicking, screaming and functioning perfectly well.

'It is a miracle,' Miss Koriche told us and burst into tears at the sight of her dark-haired, fair-skinned, blue-eyed baby boy.

Suddenly I sensed there was more amiss with Miss Koriche than just post-labour stress. I looked to my Lord Devere.

'You are exhausted, dear daughter,' he told her. 'We shall leave you to rest.'

'No,' she said, 'please do not go. I cannot go through with this now that I know for sure.'

My lord knew immediately what was on Miss Koriche's mind; the premature birth had aroused his suspicions. 'This child is Mr Taylor's, isn't it,' he said.

You could have knocked me over with a feather when Miss Koriche nodded to confirm my lord's words.

'He forced himself upon you?' Lord Devere attempted to ease some of her difficulty.

Miss Koriche shook her head. 'At first his attentions were unwelcome, it is true. But I cannot deny that I became attracted to him, despite the fact that he was not my designated target ... so I am not entirely blameless. It only happened once, and when I met Levi I cursed my brief impetuous moment with Taylor, for I was truly enamoured of your son. When I discovered I was pregnant, I so wanted the child to be Levi's, conceived in love and tenderness, not in a wild, irrational moment.'

I sat beside Ajalae and gave her a shoulder to cry on, whilst my husband relieved us of the crying newborn. 'I'm going to show off my grandson,' he told us.

Miss Koriche raised her tear-swollen eyes to Lord Devere. 'Did you not understand me?'

'I have legally adopted this child,' my husband said, allaying her concern. 'Thus I have a perfect right to call him my grandchild.'

'I do not expect you to honour our financial arrangement,' Miss Koriche insisted. 'That is why I confessed my shame. My Lord and Lady Suffolk, you are the best of souls, and now that I know the truth I cannot deceive you into providing —'

Lord Devere cut in and ended the argument. 'Taylor, despite his faults, was a dear friend of mine and I will not hear of his family going wanting in the wake of the sacrifice he made for all of us.'

Indeed, this turn of events shed new light on Taylor's reckless and heroic act on the cavern bridge, for he had no doubt suspected that he was saving his own child from the clutches of the alien creature. And I was delighted to realise that Levi had not abandoned his child, after all.

I smiled as my pride in my lad was fully restored. I really should have known better than to doubt Levi's motives, for clearly he was infinitely wiser than I.

Lord Devere and I left for home a few weeks later. Miss Koriche promised to send us copies of everything she wrote and painted, and we assured her that we would always appreciate her correspondence.

We chose the long sea passage that took us via many islands all the way back to France. Upon our arrival in the port of Marseilles, my lord heard word of a band of gypsies that were camped outside the city whose captain was to be wed this very night. Could it be the Choron clan? Had Raineath managed to capture Cingar's heart? Lord Devere and I could not curtail our curiosity; we hired a carriage and went to investigate.

I was so glad that we acted upon impulse, for it was indeed the Choron band whom we found frequenting one of their preferred camping sites overlooking the sea. We were warmly welcomed by many old friends — most of all by Cingar, who was astonished and overjoyed to see us alive and well.

'I have been cursing myself every day since I did not follow you into that cave at Mamer,' he said.

'But you obviously made the right decision,' Lord Devere pointed out, 'for we hear you are to be wed this night.'

Cingar nearly choked, then began to laugh. 'I am not the one to be wed this night; it is my son, who has been captaining this band in my absence, who is to marry. Surely, you did not think that I would seduce the young woman in my care?' he finished, sounding both insulted and flattered.

Poor Raineath, it seemed Cingar was still blissfully unaware of her adoration. Perhaps he would never love again, after all. I knew that if anything were to happen to my dear Devere, I could not imagine ever finding anyone who would suit me quite so well.

'Who is the lucky bride-to-be?' I asked. 'Was it an arranged match, like Jessenia and yourself?'

'It is Raineath!' he announced, as if I should have guessed. 'The moment she laid eyes on my son and he on her, *bam*, they were in love. Funny how destiny weaves her will, is it not?'

This seemed to explain why Chiara had sent Cingar to me in the first place, so that we could go together to rescue his future daughter-in-law from the harem of the Persian Shah. I found it curious, however, that Cingar referred to destiny as a female and I queried him on it.

'Only a female could be as calculating and have the foresight that destiny requires,' the gypsy explained. 'Now fate is a man,' he went on, 'no planning, just go with the flow and see what tomorrow brings.'

Both Lord Devere and myself found his reasoning most amusing. Of course, we were both invited to the wedding and were delighted to extend our stay in order to attend. Truly joyous moments had been far and few between during this journey, so a moment to celebrate and to forget all the problems of the inner and outer world was an unexpected gift.

With the merriment of the wedding behind us, we were heading home to inform Levi's three adoring siblings that they would never see their dear brother again — news that neither Lord Devere nor I was eager to impart. However, before we returned to family life in England, there was one loose end to tie up from our Persian voyage: our debriefing with Lord Malory.

It was a dark and inhospitable night, pouring with rain, when we arrived in London. We took a carriage directly to Lord Malory's private residence; I did not envy our driver's exposure to the elements. Paying no heed to the unfashionably late hour, Lord Devere and I demanded that the Grand Master see us at once.

'That is quite out of the question, I'm afraid,' we were told by one of Lord Malory's underling knights as we were led to the private library where the Grand Master and I usually met.

'We have just travelled halfway around the world on Lord Malory's account, and lost a family member and a dear friend in the process.'

My lord made his irritation plain. 'If Lord Malory will not see us now, then we shall take what we have discovered to the grave and the Sangrèal's secret agenda can go to hell!'

'Please wait here. I shall pass on that message.' The young knight quickly retreated.

We waited, and we waited. Weary from our travels, we were of a mind to leave when the door opened and in walked the one member of the brotherhood whom I truly respected.

'My Lord Derby, what a marvellous surprise.' Lord Devere was shaking the man's hand before I had even found my tongue.

Lord Cavandish, the Earl of Derby, was the father of my dearest friend, Lady Susan Devere. He was also the nephew of my great mentor, Lady Charlotte, and had practically adopted me after I used my psychic skills at the age of eight to save his family from ruin.

Lord Cavandish turned his attention my way. 'My Lady Suffolk, travel always did agree with you, how well you look.' He took hold of my hands and kissed them both in turn.

'Whatever are you doing here at this late hour, Lord Derby?' I asked. The earl was a family man and not renowned for frequenting clubs in the wee hours.

'You do not miss a thing, do you, my dear?' He grinned, expecting nothing less. 'I have been called here at this ungodly hour to set the affairs of our late Grand Master in order.'

A gasp caught in my throat and suffocated me a second.

'Lord Malory is dead?' Lord Devere was horrified, for he had known Lord Malory for some thirty years.

'How did it happen?' I asked. 'When?'

'I myself arrived shortly before you did. The doctor tells me that Malory died only hours before he was found.' The earl invited us to be seated once more and lowered himself into an armchair. 'As for how Lord Malory died, that remains a mystery. The doctor suspects —'

'Apoplexy,' I cut in, never surer.

Lord Cavandish nodded, knowing I would not like the verdict. My dear Lord Hamilton had been pronounced dead by the same cause some twenty years ago and I had never truly believed the diagnosis. Fear permeated my being now as a whole new murder theory began to take form in my mind. Was our return to London and Lord Malory's death just a sad coincidence? *There are no accidents*, I reminded myself.

I leapt to my feet. 'I need to see the body.'

My Lord Devere stood too. He knew I suspected foul play; the timing was just too neat.

Lord Cavandish clearly thought my request inappropriate, but knew better than to doubt my motives. He frowned to express how perplexed he was by the request, but nevertheless got to his feet and led the way to Malory's last resting place.

A few grave-faced men were standing about outside Lord Malory's private sitting room; all looked stunned by the sight of a woman being escorted to view the body of their Grand Master, so unexpectedly deceased.

The scene that awaited me inside Lord Malory's private chamber was almost a direct replica of the scene of my Lord Hamilton's death. Lord Malory was hunched forward over his desk, his arms stretched either side of his head, a glass of wine spilt alongside him.

'Do you suspect poisoning again?' my husband queried softly.

I shook my head.

The investigating constable, who had been speaking with the departing doctor, approached to protest at our presence in the room. 'What do you think you are doing?' he demanded. 'I do not want anything disturbed.'

It seemed fate was a man indeed, because as fate would have it, the constable was the very same man who had been called upon to investigate the death of my Lord Hamilton.

'Constable Fletcher.' I smiled in greeting.

It took a moment for him to place my face, but I was flattered when he succeeded. 'Miss Granville,' he said. 'I have often wondered if we would cross paths again.'

'You have an extraordinary memory,' I commented.

'Only for the extraordinary,' the constable returned. 'Do you have an interest in this gentleman, my lady?'

'I do have a business relationship with Lord Malory,' I replied, my eyes turning again to the scene of Malory's demise.

'Business of what nature?'

'We shared a passion for archaeology,' I explained, and took the opportunity to make a circuit of Lord Malory's body, in order to discern all I needed to before anyone had the chance to protest.

'Lord and Lady Suffolk have just this moment returned from an assignment in Persia,' Lord Cavandish enlightened the constable, at the same time offering my watertight alibi. 'It was commissioned and funded by Lord Malory.'

My gut was churning at the very thought of my hunch proving valid, and when I spied the bloody spot at the base of the lord's neck, it was a battle not to react adversely. Pretending to be interested in what Lord Malory had been reading when he passed, I took a closer look at the small wound. It could have been dismissed as an infected insect bite, but my recollection of the needle on Taejax's soul-sucking device led me to suspect a different cause.

I saw how Lord Malory's head had been pushed forward onto the desk in order to extend the back of his neck. The Dracon would have inserted the needle of the wrist device straight up through the neck cavity, stunning his victim into submission. The target area was the pineal gland in the centre of the brain, where the ORME overdose was administered. The resulting excess of vital pineal fluids produced to combat the blocking solution would then be automatically extracted and injected into the reptilian attacker, giving him a vitality boost.

My vision of this pineal fluid cum soul-extraction process was so vivid that it seemed more like a memory than a product of my imagination.

'Have you some supernatural insight to offer us, Lady Suffolk?' Constable Fletcher let me know that he was aware of my reputation as a notable psychic.

'No,' I said vaguely, nauseated by the visions that my private theorising had produced.

I did not want to believe that Malory had been murdered to prevent my Lord Devere and I discussing our Persian findings with him, or questioning him about the true reasons for the quest. For if Malory had been murdered via the mode I suspected, not only had he suffered an agonising death, but his soul had been shattered to oblivion in the process.

I swayed, overwhelmed by the thought, and my husband rushed to support me. 'Mrs Devere, are you all right?'

'I fear that the events of this day have taken their toll,' I said, offering an excuse for my faint-headedness. I turned to Constable Fletcher. 'I'm afraid I cannot be of any help to you in this case,' I said, for it was true that the conclusions I had drawn would be impossible to prove or even explain. 'Best go with the doctor's diagnosis.'

Those present could hardly believe their ears.

'That is not like you, Lady Suffolk.' Fletcher had expected a battle of wits.

I shrugged. 'You recall my philosophy in such cases, surely, Constable Fletcher?' My view had quite insulted him when first we'd met.

The constable cocked a brow as he nodded. '*If there is no case for murder, why look for a suspect,*' he quoted. 'I'll have you know that I am endeavouring to reform that attitude.'

'Bless you, Constable Fletcher,' I said; he was plainly a good man. 'We shall let you get on with your investigation unencumbered.'

My Lord Devere and I made our apologies and left the premises. Inside our carriage, the pelting rain on the roof thankfully drowned out the sound of my emotional outpouring to my husband regarding all I had observed and feared. Once I had relayed all I knew, we both sat in silence, overwhelmed by our thoughts.

Was this the first move in Taejax's private war on my kin? When he made his threat, I had suspected that it was already his life mission to hunt down humanity's hidden angels, and thus I and my kin were at no more risk than we had ever been. I was not as confident about that now. But after all that Lord Malory had put us through in the past, I could not say that he was one of my favourite people in the world. So perhaps his death was not connected with Taejax's threat at all. What I did feel certain of was that someone didn't want us to speak with Lord Malory again. Perhaps Lord Malory himself had had contact with the lizard warriors — heaven forbid if he'd been taking his cues from them!

I leaned back against my husband's arm, thankful that it was only a short carriage ride home. I was most eager to embrace my three remaining children.

Our children were in bed and sound asleep when my lord and I arrived home that night, and so we had to wait until the next morning to make our presence known. We were very warmly received indeed, and spent the morning giving out the exotic presents we had picked up during our return voyage and catching up on all the London gossip.

Rebecca, our eldest daughter, was full of news about her pending 'coming out' into society and, along with her cousins, had been collecting information on all the eligible young lords who might be awarded the pleasure of courting her. Thomas had obviously heard enough of the social news in our absence and was more eager to hear about our adventures. It was Charlotte, however, our quiet fairy child, who raised the subject that my lord and I were avoiding.

'I know about Levi,' she said, stunning us both.

Rebecca rolled her eyes.

'Charlotte has been spinning tales about Levi being an angel,' she explained. 'I have endeavoured to get her to curtail her silly stories, but you know she will not listen to me. Won't you talk to her, Mama? It is frightfully embarrassing.'

I focused my attention on Charlotte. 'How do you know about Levi, sweetness?'

'The fair folk work with angels,' she explained, as if it were elementary.

I looked to Lord Devere, who appeared as astonished as I was. There we were, searching the globe for information pertaining to Levi's whereabouts, and it seemed our best and most reliable source had been at home the whole time.

'The fair folk know of everyone who moves through their plane of demonstration,' young Thomas added; he had obviously been following Charlotte's news bulletins more closely than his older sister had.

Charlotte nodded to confirm this was true enough.

'Have you spoken with Levi?' I asked. My heart leapt into my throat when Charlotte nodded and continued eating her breakfast.

'*Mama.*' Rebecca sounded surprised at me. 'Must you humour her?

Could you not tell us where Levi really is and put an end to Charlotte's silly speculations?'

I looked to my husband. 'Could you inform Rebecca and Thomas of Levi's decision, please?' I asked him. Then I turned to Charlotte. 'Would you come with me, sweetness? We need to have a little chat.'

'Not before time,' Rebecca said, assuming I was finally going to give that reprimand.

'Of course, Mama.' Charlotte slid off her chair and served her sister a defiant glare before following me into the drawing room.

Once we were alone I asked Charlotte to tell me of her encounter with Levi. She shook her head. 'Why ever not?' I said.

'Levi requested that I not speak to anyone of it.' The sincerity and apology in her manner was adorable.

'But surely he was not referring to your own mama and papa?' I implored her again, sure that she would take me into her confidence.

'*Especially* you.' She remained apologetic but also adamant. 'Levi said that you still have a few lessons to learn about trusting in the ability and choices of others.'

The reprimand from my missing son, coming via my young teenage daughter, was very sobering and I felt quite hurt that I did not measure up to my ideal of myself in my own children's eyes.

'However,' Charlotte added on a cheerier note, 'he said to remember what your quest in Persia was all about. Seek your roots, and if you are very patient and study as hard as you are able, putting into practice that which you preach, then all of the answers you seek shall be forthcoming.' My daughter finished with a nod and a wink of encouragement, which restored the smile to my face.

'Is Levi well, do you think?' I hoped I was permitted to know this much.

Charlotte grinned broadly, a little surprised I had to ask. Observant of the lessons I was bound to learn, she replied, 'What do you think?'

I inhaled deeply and consulted my instinct on the matter. Tears welled in my eyes from the pride and excitement I felt upon receiving an answer. 'I think that, in his own cheeky style, he is off saving the planet from certain doom!'

My daughter chuckled and placed a hand on my shoulder to congratulate me.

'Gosh, Mama, I think you have more psychic power than Levi gives you credit for.' She placed her arms around my neck and gave me a squeeze.

'Will you be seeing Levi again?' I felt a little ashamed to be pumping Charlotte for information when she'd promised Levi she wouldn't talk to me of their meeting, but I could not resist.

'In this lifetime?' she asked. I nodded, tickled by the way her mind worked; she was so like me at her age. 'Hard to say.' She screwed up her nose. 'Most likely not, I think.'

'And you are not saddened by that?'

She frowned at the notion, thinking it odd. 'What kind of friend would I be if I were saddened that Levi is pursuing the quest that he came to Earth to do?'

I was again put in my place as I realised that my own fear of being hurt was at the root of my desire to find Levi and hold him here with us.

'I am overjoyed that he is not a walking dead person like ninety-five per cent of the people living today,' Charlotte continued; another very good point. 'Are you feeling better now, Mama?'

I nodded, my smile far broader than it had been for days. 'Much better, thank you, my sweet.'

'I fear Rebecca will not come to terms with Levi's choice so well as we have,' she said. 'She is still ruled by her ego, and thus I fear she shall grieve Levi always and begrudge his leaving without saying farewell.'

'But we shall not.' I supported Charlotte's wise resolve, instilling the order into my own consciousness in the process. I *would* learn my lessons. I *would* question and study and accomplish all I was put on Earth to do.

FROM THE JOURNAL OF TAMAR DEVERE

I turned the page to find that the next section of Ashlee's Persian journal began some ten years later. It was entitled 'The Search for Amenti'.

244

I so wanted to surrender to the beckoning relief my pillow promised, yet my eyes and mind desired to read on. But I had been reading for nine hours straight at this stage, minus short dashes to the bathroom and the kitchen, and the prospect of launching into another grand adventure, which I was sure I would be compelled to finish in one sitting, was more than my exhausted body could cope with.

I marked my place in the heavy volume, set it aside and switched off my reading light. I snuggled down into my bedclothes and drifted into a fitful sleep.

I am moving through the house — from my resting place, I head towards the room of references. I do not bother turning a light on, I can see perfectly well in the dark. Upon entering the room I approach the picture on the far wall — the only piece of wall, apart from the window, that is not occupied by bookcases. I reach up and take hold of the outside of the frame and tug. The magnetic seal gently gives way and the picture opens outwards, on a pair of hinges. Behind it is a safe. The lock mechanism is triggered by a fingertip identification scan-pad — no obstacle for me as I am able to morph into the form of any living thing I touch. My hand transforms into my mother's hand and I sink my fingers into the gel-touch pad. The door to the safe unlocks and opens. Inside is a journal, thicker than any of those on the shelves. I reach inside and reverently bring the book forth to admire the great treasure. It is The Book of Codes, *created by Ajalae Koriche and collated by Ashlee Granville-Devere for the benefit of her descendants. I have no need to read the text, all I need are the pictorial codes to focus upon. I existed before the time when all doctrine was corrupted; I know exactly what must be done. I turn to the Ec-ka-sha code and I begin the chant — I will activate as many of the time code clearings as is safe for this vessel in the course of one night.*

When I awoke, I felt as if I were adrift upon a cloud, basking in the sunshine of a new dawn. I couldn't remember what I'd dreamt about, but it sure made me feel one hell of a lot better than I had yesterday morning. I looked to the journal beside me on the bed and was very tempted to open it up and keep on reading, but my tummy rumbled in protest. 'Food first,' I said, and assured my gut with a pat as I rose.

I was pouring myself some cereal when Mum came breezing through the kitchen to say that she was off to a meeting with her publishers.

'*Your* publishers?' I clarified.

Mum screwed up her face then nodded. 'I think it's time to share the stories. I never told you this, but it was actually predicted that I would publish the tales of our bloodline in the future.'

'Really?' I was very curious about the prediction. 'When were you told? By whom?'

'An old soul I met in Giza told me, around the time I found out that I was pregnant with you.' She smiled at the memory.

'Did they make any predictions about me?'

'Oh, yes.' She grinned to tease me.

'Well, what did they say?'

'That you would have a very lovely singing voice.' Mum kissed my forehead and reached around me to grab her bag and keys off the table. 'And after hearing you singing last night in the study, I'd have to say that prediction has proved quite true.' She blew me another kiss, waved and rushed out, leaving me aghast.

Singing? The notion brought back snippets of my dream ... I'd been trying to unlock something. 'Unlock ...' I muttered, 'the safe!'

In a flash, I was entering the study. Did I seriously think there was a hidden safe in here that I had never known about? Not really; I just needed to prove my memory of the dream wrong.

But my recall was perfectly sound: the picture did unseal from the wall, swinging open to reveal the very safe I had dreamt about.

'Oh ... my ... Goddess!'

I so wanted to unlock it and see if *The Book of Codes* was within, but when I held my fingertips to the scan-pad it didn't transform into my mother's as it had in my dream. Locked out. That was rather disappointing.

I sat down to think it through. Why hadn't my parents ever mentioned this amazing text to me? Perhaps they had been waiting for me to read the Persian journal as an introduction to the divine genetic tool? Were the secrets of the ancients truly locked inside our study?

Neither of my parents were home at present. Dad would have left for the college early, as always, and Mum had just gone out to her meeting, so I couldn't quiz them about it. Anyway, how would I explain how I knew about the safe without telling them about my alien penpal alter ego?

My journal!

The thought sent me dashing back to my room.

The night before last, Kali had left a cryptic message in my journal. Had she been as prolific last night? I unlocked my journal and opened it to the next blank page; only it was not blank any more.

There was no translation required this time; my alter ego seemed to have grasped English overnight and was now writing in it fluently. I began to read:

I am moving through the house — from my resting place, I head towards the room of references . . .

I realised it was a description of the dream I'd had last night. Only this seemed to indicate that it wasn't a dream at all, but a record of my alter ego's exploits whilst my own consciousness slept.

Well, at least my other half has found a way to keep me up to speed on what she gets up to, I thought, trying to make light of my horror. These activations she spoke of meant nothing to me, bar the reference to the Ec-ka-sha code that Ashlee had mentioned in her journal.

Twenty years later! With great excitement I recalled how the last section of the Persian journal had begun. I'll bet Ashlee had done heaps of work with the codes by then!

I dived onto my bed and grabbed the journal, ready to head back into the late nineteenth century. 'Take me away, great-great-grandmamma.'

PART 3

THE
SEARCH FOR AMENTI

REVELATION 16

THE HALLS OF AMENTI

FROM THE JOURNAL OF LADY ASHLEE GRANVILLE-DEVERE

The Halls of Amenti have remained a mystery to mankind for aeons, but it is my understanding that they are time portholes. These halls serve as an outer defence system for the Sphere of Amenti, which houses the divine blueprint of humanity and is itself a porthole to the higher-dimension universe we once called home — Tara. Amenti's halls permit passage between space–time locations on this planet, and must be negotiated by any soul seeking to return through the Sphere of Amenti and home to Tara. The Halls of Amenti link to the seven eras of evolution, in which the seven root races of mankind manifest, although not all of the races are manifesting on the physical plane of awareness. Each fallen soul-mind from Tara is required to incarnate into each of these root races many times in order to fully re-form their damaged human blueprint, for the Halls of Amenti are protected by a genetic lock system — so that if a soul has not successfully evolved through each root race, then the required co-resonance (or genetic frequency) to pass through each hall in Amenti will not have been achieved. Direct passage through Amenti has been closed to humanity since before the downfall of Atlantis, after one of the many attempts by dark forces of the era to abuse the Sphere of Amenti for unsafe energy practices. The Sphere was removed from the Earth and placed in the central sun of the Pleiades system until such time as the Signet Grid could be reactivated to restore a satisfactory vibratory rate on Earth to again house the Sphere of Amenti — an event that has yet to come to pass by this the year 1865 AD.

251

I paused from my transcription of Miss Koriche's texts, which I was compiling into one great volume for my descendants. I had dubbed this English translation *The Book of Codes*.

I had learned quite some time ago that the Sphere of Amenti had been sealed off to prevent direct human soul-mind passage for many an age, which had given me cause to wonder how my son Levi could gain access to the halls of this grand connecting station to the cosmos. The whole purpose behind moving the Sphere was to prevent access via Earth, but if the Staff of Amenti were still to be recruited, the masterminds and protectors of Amenti must have built a staff entry point into the Amenti system — an intergalactic back door into the fourth-dimensional realm within our Earth.

My contemplation was interrupted by my youngest daughter, Charlotte, the only one of our children still residing with us. She burst into the library in a state of alarm. 'Mama, come quickly, there is a man at the door who claims Papa has had an accident!'

My heart leapt into my throat, pounding with a vengeance as the heat of my fear burned its way from my chest to my cheeks. 'How bad is it?' I ran to my daughter, struggling to remain calm and reasonable.

'Mama,' she held my hands in support, 'it does not look hopeful.'

The news shot an invisible dagger into the burning core in my chest. 'Where?'

'Near the Abbey ruins at Bury St Edmunds.'

'That is not so far afoot.' The carriage would take too long to prepare. 'We must ride.'

'The horses are being saddled as we speak,' Charlotte advised, keeping pace with me as I made haste to the stables.

I have never ridden a horse to such speed in all my fifty years upon this Earth, and the ailments of my aging body paled in existence as I rode with reckless abandon. Each time I considered life without my dear Devere, my tears became a deadly obstruction to my vision and so I was forced to rise above the crippling despair. The farmer who had found my husband had cautioned me to prepare myself for the worst; a doctor had been called to the scene of the accident, but he feared there was little to be done for any man who had been thrown from his horse so violently.

My husband had been returning from a visit with Lord Derby — a somewhat mysterious meeting as the peer had refused to enlighten Devere as to the subject he wished to discuss. We often visited the Cavandish family at their country estate in Derbyshire, a trip that took us through Bury St Edmunds, although usually by carriage. In this instance, however, my husband had insisted on riding. As I had plenty of transcribing to do, I had been happy to stay in Suffolk whilst my lord journeyed unaccompanied to Derby. Had I not been so absorbed, would the accident have been avoided? Our love had kept us young, despite the mounting years, and Lord Devere was a fit and handsome man who, like me, had barely known a sick day in his life. We had always fancied ourselves as invincible, having survived vampires, entombment, bandits, plague and interdimensional transit! Today, however, all our delusions of being superhuman had been shattered. Life would be colourless and meaningless without my husband's humour-filled, intellectually vibrant presence. I spurred my horse on faster.

As we neared the site of the Abbey ruins, our guide took the lead. We followed him to one of the outer walls of the ruins, where a doctor, a constable and several other people were locked in conversation. We pulled up our horses by my husband's steed, which was grazing nearby. I turned about in search of my love but was unable to see him. I looked to my guide, who appeared as bewildered as I, as he motioned to the blood-splattered stone wall where he had last seen my husband's body.

'Has he been moved?' I queried, and our guide redirected my question to the doctor and constable.

'Not by us.' The constable was perplexed, and seemed ashamed to introduce himself as the man in charge of the investigation now that its subject was missing. 'One minute his lordship was here, and the next ...' The man gestured helplessly at the ancient site now falling under the tranquil shadow of evening. 'There were quite a few of us near Lord Suffolk at the time of his disappearance, but no one witnessed the abduction. We have not spied anyone loitering although a thorough search of the area is still in progress.' He pointed to various groups of men around the perimeter of the crime scene, searching through scrub.

'Was my lord still living when he vanished?' I asked the doctor, desperate for some hope that the diagnosis I had received had been blown out of proportion.

The expression on the doctor's face stifled my hopes before he spoke a word. 'I am very sorry, Lady Suffolk, but his injuries claimed him shortly after I arrived.'

The shock constricted my throat and lungs; I gasped for air, fearing that my grief would burst my internal organs if I did not release it. The burning ball of soul-shattering energy that had lodged in my heart chakra only intensified and I wailed in agony.

'Mama.' Charlotte embraced me.

My entire body was suffering for the ride I had just endured, and now, with the complete collapse of my emotional body, I fell to my knees.

'Mama!' Charlotte cried again, and crouched before me, as did the doctor. He opened his case.

'I can give you something to help ease the pain,' he said.

My youthful experiences in a mental asylum had given me a distinct aversion to painkillers. 'There is not a drug known to man that will dull the loss of my dearest companion,' I said. I knew that if I numbed the pain it would only fester into disease. I needed my wits about me if I was going to find my Lord Devere's body. I was aware of supernatural possibilities at work here far beyond the reality of the average county constable, and I had psychic expertise to bring to the investigation.

Taejax had never made good on his threat to my kindred and myself, but Dracon were time-hopping entities and I had never stopped expecting that he might show up at any moment to fulfil his promise.

'Did you have the opportunity to examine Lord Suffolk's body before it went missing, Doctor?'

'I did,' the man advised, 'and if you want my professional opinion, he died from internal injuries.'

The invisible knife that seemed to be lodged in my chest twisted; I took a few deep breaths to maintain my composure. 'Were there any wounds to the back of my husband's neck?'

The doctor frowned, clearly reluctant to elaborate. 'I do not wish to be too descriptive, my lady, but his injuries were quite severe in that area.'

I nodded. It was obvious that the tiny red mark I wished to question the doctor about would not have been apparent. I turned to my daughter, to find that she was no longer at my side. Charlotte briefly hovered around the scene of her father's death, then her attention was drawn to the crumbling Abbey ruins and she moved off in that direction.

I had a little trouble getting to my feet, but the doctor kindly lent a hand. 'You should rest,' he instructed.

'I shall rest when my husband's body is found.'

I approached the wall that had sealed my beloved's fate and dipped my fingers into the pool of his blood there. His body may not be present for me to probe for answers, but his genetic memory was contained within every tiny cell of his body. *What caused this great tragedy to befall you?* I focused the question upon the sticky liquid between my fingertips.

An apparition seized control of my senses ...

My husband was racing home from Derbyshire to Suffolk, in a pressing hurry to share the news that weighed heavily on his heart and mind. Lord Derby — a man who had been more of a father to me than my own — was dead and my husband knew the event would sadden me greatly. My lord had been given a private audience with the dying man and fragmented memories of their conversation filtered through his mind as he rode.

'I fear our Ashlee is in danger,' Lord Derby had warned. 'She was bred for a purpose.'

'A purpose, my lord?' Devere had queried.

'She carries the genetic code of angels and demons, both of which will seek her loyalty.'

My Lord Devere feared that the dying man had taken leave of his senses.

'She already knows the truth ... she possesses her own mother's confession to it,' Lord Derby went on. 'Tell Lady Suffolk, from me, that her destiny will not go away. She must seek her father's counsel.' The outburst weakened the dying man and he closed his eyes as he strained to keep breathing.

'But Lord Granville has long passed,' my husband said, failing to understand the instruction. 'Are you suggesting we have a séance?'

Lord Derby shook his head, annoyed that he was too weak to get his point across. 'Thomas ... was ... not ...' But Lord Derby had breathed his last.

My Lord Devere felt saddened and frustrated by the recollection as he sighted the ruins of Bury St Edmunds up ahead. He favoured a short cut through the dilapidated Abbey as the crumbing outer walls provided some good jumps for the horse. As his steed cleared the stonework of the outer wall, my lord's upper body collided with an invisible horizontal obstruction that knocked him backwards from his horse and cast his body upon the jagged rocks of the ruins. The impact was bone-shattering: his right shoulder, left leg, lower back and head all screamed in agony. It took a moment to register that he'd been ambushed and that his attackers now stood gloating over him.

My husband had not seen Draconians for many years and had often wondered if he'd dreamt their existence. Was he dreaming now?

'Do you recall when you showed me mercy?' said one of the four reptilians present.

My husband, hauled to his feet by the other three warriors, was sorry to concede that he recognised the speaker. 'I remember you, Taejax,' he gasped, straining to draw air into his winded lungs. He squinted to prevent the blood from the graze on one side of his forehead flowing into his eye.

'I just wanted to be sure that you realised your mistake.' The lizard commander made a fist, and from the knuckles of the electronic gloves he wore four long glowing knives protruded. They did not seem to be made of solid matter. 'Etheric blades,' Taejax explained, displaying them before my husband's eyes.

Devere grinned at the creature, which was used to inciting fear in its victims. 'Do you have so many friends that you can afford to kill one?'

'We are not friends,' Taejax growled, irate. 'Give this to your wife from me.' And the warrior drove the unearthly blades into the gut of my beloved.

The otherworldly weapon drew no blood, nor left a physical wound, but the internal organs pierced by the weapon went into seizure. The damage felt very real — the shock of the injury began to numb my lord's physical senses.

'The physical body cannot function without its etheric double,' Taejax explained as he withdrew the blades back into the electronic glove. He activated the ORME injection needle of the module connected to the inner side of his right wrist. 'Fear me now, human? Say goodbye to existence as you've known it.'

An abrupt gust of wind knocked Taejax from his feet. Rocks began to hurl themselves at his comrades, whereupon Devere was released and collapsed to the ground to nurse his injuries.

'It's the Anu,' one of the warriors snarled. Taejax growled and the four Dracon vanished.

My lord looked about for his rescuers. Outlined by the early rays of sunlight streaming over the Abbey ruins, the silhouette of first one man, and then two more, approached. As the figures emerged from the morning light they solidified into tall, fair-haired beings.

'We are not too late,' said one. 'His soul is still intact.'

'A good thing,' said another. 'We can ill afford to lose Sinclair at this late stage of the game ... and Devere's essence is urgently needed to fortify the grid.'

My husband was fast fading from this world, but he resented being spoken of in the past tense before his time was done.

'Mathu, shall I go and inform his wife?' the third lofty fellow asked the being in charge.

'I shall go,' Mathu replied, and transformed his angelic appearance into that of a mundane farmer — the same farmer who had led Charlotte and myself to the site of my lord's accident.

I broke from the trance and looked around for our escort, who was not within eyeshot. I struggled to my feet and began a frantic search for the only being who might know where the body of my beloved had been taken.

As I neared the main ruins, into which my daughter had disappeared, I picked up on the high-frequency energy that emanated from the old structure. A grid crossing, I deduced. From my own investigations into the Earth grid, I understood that the sacred sites of this planet had been erected by the ancients to fall into alignment with each other. All across the globe these sites marked the trackways of the Earth's energy grid. Many of these energy pathways crossed at ancient sites, marking doorways between the Earth's dimensions. Some of these doorways reportedly led to higher dimensions, some to lower, some to parallel Earth, and yet others led to time–space and inter-universal portholes, like the legendary Halls of Amenti. The crossings in the grid became positively or negatively charged in accordance with their history, and it took psychic skills to deduce which side was currently in control of the crossing during inter-time war.

The high vibratory rate of this site sent my entire atomic structure into a state of buzzing excitement, hence I felt safe in assuming that it was a positively charged crossing. Had the site been negatively charged, my being would have felt the drag induced by a lower atomic frequency.

As I passed through the stone arch that led into the main body of the ruins, I spotted Charlotte engaged in a rather heated debate with our escort.

'I know who you are, Mathu,' I called out. 'You know where my husband's body has been taken.'

The farmer looked to me. 'Then you must also know why his body has been taken.'

'Could you not have waited long enough for me to bid him farewell?'

'I was just explaining to Miss Charlotte that we waited as long as we could.' Mathu's appeal was of little comfort to me, although my daughter appeared appeased by his words.

'I beg you to take me to my Lord Devere,' I half-appealed, half-demanded.

'His vessel is devoid of his human essence now and will be of no comfort to you,' Mathu advised calmly, 'but his soul-mind awaits you in Amenti.'

This was the straw that broke the back of my patience with ancient doctrines, secrets and hearsay. My grief turned to anger. 'I am growing tired of cryptic promises.'

'I understand that you are angry, hurt, and also very powerful on this plane of demonstration,' the disguised being warned. 'But while that road will surely see you into the company of your husband's murderer, it shall not lead to salvation for anyone involved.'

He was right. I drew a few deep breaths to calm myself and find some clarity. 'Who is Sinclair, and why should the state of my husband's soul-mind have any bearing on Sinclair's wellbeing?' I asked.

My daughter looked perplexed by my query, but Mathu grinned at the extent of my perception. 'He is a past-life incarnation of your husband, and is very important to the plan,' he replied. 'If Lord Devere's soul-mind had been fragmented to oblivion, then we would have lost Sinclair's aid prematurely.'

'Sinclair is in the past?' I queried.

'Time is simultaneous,' he offered by way of an answer. ·

'But my husband is not so important to "the plan" that you should save his life?' I wondered why, if the Fey were time-hopping beings, they could not have arrived sooner and saved more than just Devere's soul-mind.

'It was your husband's predestined time,' Mathu explained, sympathetic to my feelings. 'He would have died whether or not he'd been attacked. But when we learned he had been targeted for termination by the Dracon, we took measures to save his soul.'

'Was my husband targeted because of me?'

'Only in so far as the attack may embitter you and promote your dark side.' I recognised the warning beneath his words. 'The real reason Devere was targeted was that the Dracon knew that the high frequency of his physical remains would reinforce the Earth grid beyond hope of their sabotage. An attack was imminent, and that is why your husband's remains were spirited away so quickly. Also, Sinclair is causing the Dracon quite a bit of grief — to have him and all his righteous incarnations out of the inter-time war would be very beneficial to the Old World order.'

'So why didn't Taejax kill Lord Devere at Giza ten years ago?' I reasoned out loud. 'He had the opportunity.'

'The Dracon have only just discovered the connection between Sinclair's soul-mind and Devere's. There is an incident in your future —' He cut himself short, clearly feeling it unwise to enlighten me.

'Are you saying I am to meet this Sinclair fellow?' I was delighted, yet perplexed. 'But he is in the past, you said, so how can I meet him in my future?'

'It is ... complicated.'

Mathu declined the opportunity to expand on this explanation, but he had already succeeded in lightening my heartache a little. The prospect of meeting a past life incarnation of my beloved restored my hope that I would some day again be graced by his presence. Clearly, pursuing this topic was going to be futile and there were other pressing questions.

'Do you know my immortal father?' I asked.

'I should do, for he is my father also,' Mathu replied with a grin.

My heart began pounding in my chest with excitement. 'You are my brother?' An only child, I had never had any blood siblings.

He smiled warmly. 'I am but one of the many half-brothers and sisters you have littered throughout inner and outer time.'

'Oh my!' Charlotte covered her mouth to hide her awe.

I gasped with joy, which mixed with my sorrow to cast my emotions into turmoil. 'Why have I never been told this? Why has my true father never revealed himself to me?'

'You were not ready. And,' Mathu spoke over my protest, 'you are still not ready to stand in his presence and execute your true role in the plan.'

I was insulted and disappointed, but I humbled myself to request more information. 'Then what must I do to gain an audience with our father who art in heaven?'

'Once you have set your earthly affairs in order and your demons to rest, he will send for you,' he assured. 'Nothing can be done before then, lest the rest of history be altered due to the shortfall of your actions in this lifetime.'

'But I —'

'Shh.' He directed our attention to the sound of footsteps approaching through leaves; company was imminent. 'Listen to me ...

there is no test in getting what you want when you want it; the true test of character transpires in the waiting. Dwell on this in moments of despair.'

Mathu vanished an instant before the doctor and the constable entered the Abbey ruins, and I had an inkling that this was not the last I would see of my Fey brother.

My Lord Devere's funeral and burial went ahead without his body, the disappearance of which is a vexing mystery for the poor constable in charge of the investigation. He assures me that the search will be ongoing and I can hardly tell him he is searching for a body that will never be found; I can only thank him for all his efforts on our behalf.

Our youngest son, Thomas, has inherited the Lordship of Suffolk at the age of twenty. As he is yet to marry, I know he will make himself a fine match. It would have been Levi inheriting the Granville-Devere title and estates, had he not been officially missing, assumed dead, for many years. I miss my eldest boy now more than ever — he was so like his father.

I hold myself together during the daylight hours, remaining strong for my grieving family. At night, alone in our bedroom, I wail my grief into my bedclothes, until exhaustion overcomes me and I sleep.

My Lord Devere and I made a vow long ago that even in death we would not abandon each other. I have been seeing ghosts since before I can remember, and yet I have had not an inkling nor a glimpse of my husband's presence, despite my appeals and tears. I miss him so very much, and I fear I am falling into a deep pit of sorrow and brooding anger from which I shall never be able to rise. Before and during my marriage I was full of purpose and ambition, but now, as a widow, life holds no meaning, no interest, no joy.

Not even the company of my dearest friend, Lady Susan Devere, has been able to lighten my inner darkness. Susan is hard pressed for cheer also, having recently lost her father, the Earl of Derby. We supported each other through the funerals of our menfolk, and although Susan warmed my frosty exterior through the ordeal, as soon as I was alone at night the self-destructive thought processes resumed.

I am angry at the Anu for denying me the opportunity to see Devere once more. I hate the Dracon for my beloved's painful death. I am annoyed at myself for having shown Taejax compassion. I am even furious with Devere for failing to make contact and leaving me alone and miserable in his wake.

Last night I was sunk deep in my pit, brooding on all the wrong emotions, when in my thoughts I heard the Dracon taunting me.

Weak woman! You have so much power at your fingertips but your compassion and restraint render your talents useless! Your breeders have you well controlled with their ingrained sense of morality. Your compassion has already cost you your mate. One by one we will destroy every soul you hold dear until your hatred and lust for revenge drive you to us.

My conscious perception was engulfed by a vision of myself in a subterranean cavity amid a throng of Dracon warriors. They were cheering as I unleashed my bloodlust upon Taejax; I used my psychokinetic ability to implode his vital organs, to ensure he suffered as my love had suffered. But the act only left me frustrated, for I felt no satisfaction upon taking the life of my enemy. I extended my revenge to the next lizard warrior, and the next, until I had laid waste to an entire battalion. My fury expended, I looked down at myself. My human body, stained with the blood and guts of my enemies, had transformed: I had become one of the Dracon.

'No!' I rose from the bedroom sofa panting in horror and desperation. 'I do not wish any being harm!' I recited the statement over and over until I believed it.

Who could I approach for help with regard to the protection of my family? The Anu had saved Devere from obliteration, but would they save other family members who came under threat? Would they even be aware of their plight if they were not connected to great human incarnations who had become embroiled in the inter-time war? I had lost all my close connections within the Sangreal Knighthood, and most of my close friends and family were not privy to my esoteric endeavours. Then I recalled the advice my otherworldly brother had offered me as an aid in times of despair. *There is no test in getting what you want when you want it; the true test of character transpires in the waiting.*

He was referring to my wish to contact my real father and hopefully learn of this 'purpose' that so many believed I'd been born and bred for. The test that was to transpire in the interim was beginning to become clearer to me now. Zalman had told me that both angels (the Anu) and demons (the Dracon) came from the same Nefilim stock. Did it not stand to reason then that both the Anu and the Dracon were waiting in the wings to see how I would process this great tragedy in my life? Would my hatred send my frequency spiralling downwards into the ranks of the Dracon, or would I rise above my personal suffering and continue to contribute to the positive evolution of humanity?

I must be constructive, I realised. A little wise counsel would not go astray, however. I missed my mentor, Lady Charlotte, and I pined for my husband and for Levi. Still, I did have one friend who shared my esoteric interests, who was versed both in the psychic arts and in the art of self-defence.

I held my ringstone and spoke his name: 'Albray.' The sound was sweet relief to my battered sensibilities. 'Albray.' His stone felt like the hand of an old friend in mine. 'Albray.'

His smile was a wondrous dawning on this dark night of my soul. *Alone at last*, he said, and frowned sympathetically.

I sniffled back my emotions and smiled at my old friend. 'I fear I am not handling that reality very admirably.'

Adversity arrives and all your beliefs and training fly out the window. My knight came to sit on the lounge beside me.

'I do not know what I believe any more ... all my study, investigation and research has only confused me —'

Then stop reading what other people would have you believe about life on Earth, Albray interjected, *and get out there and start living it again! I cannot claim to know what your true destiny is, Lady Suffolk, but you are not going to find what you are looking for chained to a desk.*

'I cannot *leave* — my family may be in danger. My Lord Devere was targeted —'

Because of Sinclair, yes. Albray sounded as if he knew more than he was saying.

'Do you know who this Sinclair is?'

I believe the fellow in question might be Captain Henry Sinclair, Albray advised.

'You knew him?'

Albray shook his head. *I knew of him, as he was a relative and close ally of Marie de Sinclair, the Grand Master of the Priory of Sion during the course of my service to them. Henry was an extraordinary seaman, and something of a pirate from what I heard. But we digress. There is only one member of your immediate family that will be of interest to the Dracon, and she is more capable of defending herself than you realise.*

'Charlotte!' I was immediately panicked for her welfare.

You are not listening to me! Albray grew frustrated. *And you wonder why your destiny has not come for you? Listen to yourself. On the one hand you are saying you want to move on and claim your destiny, and on the other you are saying . . .*

'. . . I cannot leave,' I concluded, having grasped his point. Mathu had said that only once I had set my earthly affairs in order and my demons to rest would my father send for me.

Your will must be clear, Albray added.

I nodded firmly in encouragement to myself. All I really wanted now was to seek the truth about myself. How could I expect to comprehend the greater universal truths if I was not even sure where I came from? I expected my new-found resolve to raise my spirits, yet my sense of foreboding deepened dramatically. Suddenly I understood what was causing the sensation and shockwaves of fear resonated through my being.

'Taejax is here.'

Speak of the devil. Albray was immediately alert and on his feet.

Trepidation welled inside me, for I realised why the reptilian had come. 'Charlotte,' I gasped, racing for the door. 'She has been targeted.'

I rushed to the library, where Charlotte was usually to be found working on her own journals. I entered to find Taejax frozen like an ice sculpture and my daughter speaking intently with Mathu, who was not wearing a guise today. His fairy-like features and tall stature were plain for all to see and he appeared as physically solid as I did.

'I am fine, Mama,' Charlotte was quick to reassure me. 'But it seems I have made a frightful error by setting the elementals upon this warrior, believing that he meant me harm.'

'Indeed he did,' I assured her.

'No, he did not,' said Mathu.

'This creature was going to wipe my husband's soul-mind from existence,' I argued. Mathu knew this; why was he contradicting me?

'But he did not do it,' Mathu said, continuing to plead the reptilian's case. 'My brothers and I arrived in time to prevent the event. And the only reason that we knew Devere had been targeted was because Taejax forewarned us of the event.'

I was completely bemused. 'But I saw him ready to deal the soul-shattering blow. He —'

'He had to play his part in the mission and make it look real, otherwise he would have been exposed as a traitor.' Mathu whipped up a small warm whirlwind with a wave of his finger, which swirled towards the reptilian. 'I believe that Taejax has come to Miss Charlotte with a warning.'

'Are you positive?' I watched anxiously as my old adversary went into rapid defrost inside the mini tornado.

'Nothing is certain,' Mathu replied, 'but in this case my suspicions are more than likely correct.'

I looked to my youngest daughter, who appeared so waif-like and defenceless. 'You did this, Charlotte?' I gestured to Taejax's frosty coating.

She nodded. 'I have not spent all these years studying and communicating with elementals without making a few friends in the process.'

My gaze turned to Albray; he was right about Charlotte's ability to protect herself, and he smiled to imply *I told you so.*

'There … is … no … time …' Taejax forced his frozen mouth to articulate the warning. 'You … must flee … the … Earth plane … tonight!' His eyes were fixed on me, which was confusing.

'Are you referring to Charlotte?' I queried.

'No, you!' he hissed. 'You have been identified as a key-holder.'

I was bemused. 'So why did you seek out my daughter?'

'To give her these.' The reptilian stiffly opened his four clawed fingers to reveal two glowing rings in the palm of his hand. 'They are made of Ormus and will telepathically link the consciousness of the two people who wear them.'

'Why would you give these to me?' Charlotte was intrigued.

'So that you might link with your mother and finish journalising her discoveries beyond this world. Knowledge of her quest will be vital to the flame-bearers of the future.' The reptilian glanced past me as he spoke and I wondered if he could sense Albray's presence.

'Key-holder? Flame-bearers?' I drew his attention back to me. 'I do not understand.'

'That is restricted information at this time.' Mathu cautioned Taejax against saying more.

'Well then, how do I know these rings aren't a trick that will disclose my every movement beyond this plane to the Dracon?'

'Taejax is a trusted ally of the Anu,' Mathu assured me.

'How can you know that for certain?'

Mathu smiled and referred me back to the reptilian.

'You set me on this path,' asserted Taejax, his physical features softening before my eyes to become more akin to the Anu. 'No one has ever shown me mercy, nor cared if I lived or died.'

As he spoke, the four clawed digits on his hand turned to five fingers, his tough green scales to fair skin, and his dark empty eyes a pale soulful grey. His transformation from demon to angel was not complete, but it seemed his personal evolution was well underway.

'This could be an illusion,' I said. 'The children of shadows can assume the form of any man.'

'Any man, yes,' Mathu concurred, 'but the Anu are not human.'

'Your act of compassion was a revelation to me,' Taejax explained eagerly. 'The more I pondered it, the more I felt and the more I drifted beyond the control of the hive-mind that had controlled my every movement. I began to think for myself. My thoughts and new-found emotions were hard to process at first ... the pain, guilt and remorse I felt for my past treatment of humanity was agonising. I had never understood that a passive being was actually braver than his aggressor ...

266

how strong and resilient one has to be in order to transmute such emotion into a positive force.'

I was stirred by the great feeling in his voice, and taking a peek beyond his physical form, I could see that many of the energy centres of his subtle body had been activated and cleared of their blockages. I recalled the scribe's prediction. 'That would suggest Thoth was telling you the truth,' I said. 'He betrayed your physical being to ultimately save your immortal soul, and the day has come when you are thankful for his past betrayals.'

'And he has thanked me, many times,' said Mathu.

The implication of these words grabbed my attention. 'You are Thoth?' I had never seen this soul-mind wearing his own body; I had only seen him in Levi's form.

'Sometimes,' he admitted. 'I have many names throughout time and space, as do you.'

'Time is wasting,' Taejax said, reclaiming my attention. 'You are going to die tonight. We must —'

'Is that a prediction?' I queried his certainty.

'It is fact.' The lizard warrior reassumed his Dracon guise. 'I know because in another interdimensional reality I murdered you.'

I gasped.

'And in another reality again, you committed suicide.'

I stared at him, shocked.

He stared back at me, with those soulful Anu eyes that had yet to resume their dark disguise. 'We cannot afford to get this wrong again,' he said. 'Our window of opportunity to access this century is closing. If you do not take your position amongst the Staff of Amenti this time, chances are the Anu will lose this war.'

The conviction in his voice compelled me to place all my questions and doubts aside. 'What must I do?'

'Mathu knows.' Taejax placed the two rings in my hand. 'When we meet again I will appear as your enemy, but remember that you are more powerful than the most adept of my ilk. You were created to lead the Dracon, not to be subject to them.'

I was overawed by his conviction, but nodded to confirm I would remember his advice. Taejax placed a hand over his Dracon pendant and vanished.

'Time to get you organised, key-holder.' Mathu placed a hand on my shoulder to guide me towards the door.

'But Charlotte ...' I was still concerned for her safety.

I shall stay and watch over Charlotte, Albray advised, *until she finishes penning your tale, and beyond if necessary.*

'And if you leave me the ringstone,' Charlotte added, plainly aware of Albray's presence, 'I shall see it returned to your secret journal so that your knight may complete his quest in the future.'

'How do you know about the ringstone?' I said, surprised. I had certainly never told her of it.

'You are not the only mind-reader in the family,' grinned Charlotte as she approached and took hold of both my hands. 'Your time has finally come, Mama. This is not a once-in-a-lifetime opportunity; this is a once-in-a-soultime chance to leave your mark upon this universe.' She took one of the rings from my palm and slipped it on her finger. 'I shall be with you all the way. Have no concern about leaving this life behind; your call to arms is of vital importance to the plan.'

'Is that what this is — my conscription to join the inter-time war?' The idea incited such anticipation in me that I could hardly breathe.

'You are not being conscripted,' Mathu corrected, 'you volunteered. Did you not just decide that all you really want now is to seek the truth about yourself?'

'Indeed.'

I looked to Albray, who had aided me to this resolve.

Be clear, he instructed me, both to reinforce the lesson and hide his welling emotions. He clearly believed this was to be the final parting of the ways for us.

'You shall see each other again,' Mathu said, feeling we were wasting time. 'We shall all meet again in Amenti.'

His eyes drifted to Charlotte and suddenly I suspected that there was more to their relationship than had been made apparent to me.

THE GREAT
EVOLUTIONARY DIVIDE

CHARLOTTE GRANVILLE-DEVERE JOURNALISING ON BEHALF OF LADY
ASHLEE GRANVILLE-DEVERE

Mathu and I awaited the approach of dawn in the lower drawing room. The gateway between the third dimension and the fourth was only accessible in the twilight hours. I had changed from my regular clothes into my green velvet adventuring garments and was now ready, in body at least, to leave my family home in Suffolk, England. Many memories, good and bad, haunted my leaving. I regretted that I would not have the opportunity to say farewell to my other two children. Yet if I had been murdered this night or compelled to take my own life, then I would not have had this chance to say goodbye to Charlotte either — and my journals would end without any reference to the Halls of Amenti, preventing my daughters and their daughters from ever gaining access to the mystery.

During the hours beforehand, I had brought my journals up to date in preparation for handing over their writing to Charlotte. My daughter was already wearing one of the ORME rings Taejax had given us. I was still toying with mine, shy of awarding her full perception of my thoughts whilst still in her company.

'Should we not test the rings?' Charlotte invited, opening my journal and dipping her pen into the inkpot. 'I should really capture your last perceptions of your home in Suffolk, England, 1866.'

'A fair request.' I swallowed my reservations and placed the ring on my finger. The telepathic connection was only one way — from my mind to Charlotte's — so that I would not be distracted from my quest by her ponderings. The connection could be broken at any time by the removal of the ring, which meant any events occurring in my conscious perception whilst Charlotte was not wearing the ring would be lost. I would have to bear in mind my chronicler's physical need to rest, eat and refresh herself if I wished my tales to be told in their entirety. If my quest did not allow me to make rest time for my scribe, Charlotte could hand the ring to someone else who was willing and able to record my movements, whilst she took some repose. There was no one in the house at present who fitted the criteria, but Charlotte had already sent word to my dear friend, Lady Susan Devere, who had supplemented my journals with her own work before. Susan had only just left us for home so we were confident of her return within the day.

'Are you perceiving me?' I stared at Charlotte to gauge her reaction.

Her eyes were closed as she homed in on my thoughts. 'How odd,' she said and grinned, 'I can see myself — but underlying your perception . . .' Then she put her head down and began to write.

Her concentration was disconcerting; what could she be writing? But I didn't wish to block her flow by asking, so I turned my attention to quizzing Mathu. 'Tell me more of the cosmic order and my Anu kindred,' I requested.

'The souls of the Anunnaki who have learned compassion, love and divine wisdom are spared from spiritual fragmentation upon death via a secret passage known as the Hall of Amorea,' he explained, 'which was built by the Staff of Amenti specifically to accommodate the soul-minds of the Anu. You see, the Anunnaki, the Nefilim and the Dracon are not human and therefore cannot evolve back to Tara via the Sphere of Amenti, which contains the human morphogenetic blueprint. The Anunnaki need to evolve back through a soul-mind consciousness akin to our own — like that of the Anu, whose Amorean system, located in the astral realm on Sirius B, serves the same function as the Amenti system does here on Earth. The Hall of Amorea is the bridge between the lower etheric realms of Earth and the astral planes of Sirius B. Once we are sufficiently emotionally evolved, we are permitted to descend through the Hall of Amorea back to Earth to amend our karma on this planet and guide the development of humanity to speed the return to Tara for all. As an astral race of beings, we Anu can only assume an outward physical form that feels nothing, lest the Anunnaki genes inside us be seduced by the pleasures of the physical world again. We would then be compelled to ingest ORME to descend into true physical manifestation, where our souls will be damned once more,' Mathu continued. 'We can share the physical form of select humans incarnate, those of the Grail bloodline. Only their human bodies are equipped with the potential to accommodate our high sonic frequency.'

'And if a human son of the blood does not have a vibratory rate high enough to accommodate an Anu soul-mind, then some brotherhoods, disposed towards your cause, might feed him ORME so that he may serve as a temporary host for you,' I said sharply, for I knew this had been the case with my own father.

'Mama!' Charlotte broke from her writing, shocked at my rudeness.

'Desperate times have called for desperate measures,' Mathu admitted, shocking Charlotte still further.

But then her expression changed to one of interest. 'Really? So, in that event, you feel what your human host feels?'

Mathu nodded, his eyes intent upon Charlotte, whose heart chakra was fast flushing the deep pink shade of attraction.

'Human beings are not cattle!' I said sternly, infuriated on my father's behalf and annoyed by the amorous interest that was building between Mathu and my daughter. 'Papa could have been genetically damaged by the process. He never did manage to impregnate my mother again, despite his desire for a son — not to mention the psychological damage.'

'You had to be brought into the world, and that was the only way to create a body that could withstand hosting your soul-mind.' Mathu tried to justify my real father's actions. He looked from Charlotte to Albray and back to me, and added, 'None of the blood could ever hope to achieve earthly greatness without what our father gave of himself to

271

advance human development. So when judging him, first consider that to aid mankind he gave up his own evolution and the physical rulership of the Earth in order to gain spiritual rulership of Amenti. And if we fail to open Amenti and raise the spiritual frequency of the collective consciousness of this planet by the close of the year 2017, the Dracon will finally succeed in destroying the Earth in the year 2976.'

From the picture Mathu had painted of our father, it seemed he could well be the entity known in esoteric circles as the Sanat Kumara, the Lord of the Earth. I felt Mathu was being over-dramatic.

'I would hardly say that I had achieved a greatness befitting a daughter of the blood,' I said.

And I certainly haven't, Albray scoffed with me.

'Yet,' Mathu emphasised, which made Albray laugh. Being dead, he felt his chance to achieve worldly greatness had passed. 'Trust me, you shall all have your chance to save the world,' Mathu went on.

Even me? Albray wanted to be convinced.

Mathu was happy to oblige. 'I assure you, Shining One, that the best days of your life still lie ahead of you.'

My knight seemed stunned by the response, so I seized the opportunity to ask a question of my own. 'What did Taejax mean when he referred to me as a key-holder?'

'Once you have negotiated the Halls of Amenti your soul-mind will resonate a sonic code that will unlock one of twelve stargates on the Earth grid system, all of which must be opened by December 2017. You each hold one of the keys to the planetary grid.'

'But I shall be dead by the nominated time?' I hated to state the obvious.

I am dead already! Albray echoed my confusion.

'You have a lot of trouble seeing past that event,' Mathu said, and Albray looked taken aback by the flippant comment. 'I have said more than I should already, but in time you will know that I was honest and sincere in what I told you this day,' Mathu concluded. Then, having given us all food for thought, he glanced out the window at the night and decided it was time to deliver me to my destiny.

*   *   *

272

I had mixed emotions in the wake of farewelling my youngest daughter and my knight, but Mathu kept telling me that we would all meet again in Amenti, and as that was where I was bound, my inner excitement began to override my heavy heart and fill me with a sense of myself in my younger days. As Mathu led the way across the chilly moonlit gardens of our family estate towards the outlying woodland, I considered what he had told me of the Anu's capacity to manifest on the Earth plane. 'So you cannot physically feel anything right now?' I asked. The cold night wind had seeped through my attire and was starting to chill my bones.

'Not a thing,' he confirmed.

I was tempted to test his claim, but I refrained. Still, I could not resist prodding him regarding the connection I had detected between him and my daughter.

'You still experience emotion, do you not?'

'My entire evolution is emotional,' Mathu told me, as we entered the woodland area. I looked down, forced to tread more carefully. 'Human beings are fortunate in that your physical evolution awards you many experiences to advance your emotional understanding. Your emotions grow through feeling, whereas mine develop via empathy, perception and intuition. So yes, I experience emotion but without any physical sensory enhancements.'

He sounded mournful about this fact. I imagined how it might have been to know my dear Devere without ever feeling myself enfolded in the warmth of his embrace, or never savouring the sweet all-consuming pleasure of his kisses and lovemaking.

'I asked because you have the aura of a star-crossed lover,' I went on. 'Would your doleful insight have anything to do with my daughter?'

A look of shock crossed my half-brother's face, yet he seemed shyly disposed towards confiding in me. Were the Anu not accustomed to speaking of the affairs of the heart? I wondered. If there was no death beyond the physical, then there was no birth, and probably no reason to be intimately involved with another; perhaps there were rarely affairs of the heart to be discussed.

But as Mathu replied his voice trembled and I realised I had put a crack in a mighty dam that was about to flood all over me. 'My complete devotion was hers long before she was ever your earthly daughter,' he said. 'She was the first of the Anu to follow the path of our father, whom the Nefilim Pantheon banished from Earth as a traitor. She was the first to break free of the ORME-induced soullessness inherent from our Nefilim parents. She sacrificed herself to prove that the Anunnaki had souls just as humans did, and that the key needed to reconnect to our soul-minds was the emotion of compassion. She is the Great Mother of creation and the only Anu who has the ability to fully integrate into a physical form. She has had many incarnations but her time of reckoning is yet to come.'

'Charlotte is the flame-bearer that Taejax spoke of?' I guessed.

Mathu shook his head. 'Not in this life. As your daughter, she is here to pave the way for her next and final human incarnation, who will be born into your family when the time for Amenti's opening is nigh. She will fling open Amenti's door and —' Mathu broke off, suddenly alert.

'What is it?'

'Shh!' he urged, and his form decomposed into a breeze and blew away in the wind, leaving me astonished and alone.

I looked around. The cloud cover partially exposed the full moon, which shone upon a huge old oak tree that stood in the centre of a clearing before me. *I know this place*, I thought. I'd often played here as a child, and according to my mother's written confession I had been conceived here too. This place had always held a comforting and protective energy for me, so why did I feel so apprehensive now? Was it just the darkness and the cold? My skin prickled to warn me of danger as I observed many more large rocks scattered over the ground in the clearing than I recalled. The moon cleared the cloud completely to reveal that the huge obstructions were not boulders but bodies. I cautiously approached and crouched beside the closest to me and was shocked to find it a Dracon. I rose again to count twenty or so warriors sprawled unconscious before me. After seeing how easily the Anu had dispersed the Dracon who attacked my husband, it was not hard to imagine that this might be their handiwork.

The moon was lost behind cloud again and the clearing fell into darkness. It bothered me that I could not discern whether any of the fallen were showing signs of life. Where had Mathu gone? I froze to remain silent, yet the sound of my breath and the thumping of my heart in my throat seemed loud against the sudden eerie silence of the woodland. Even the chilly predawn wind had retreated — any sound would surely be amplified through the darkness and my senses were on full alert. A moan some distance ahead drew my attention and heightened my fear. In that instant, a sense of someone standing nearby increased that fear tenfold. I looked to my right and saw the outline of a reptilian against the first dawn light; he was standing not a foot from me.

'You have been identified, Solarian.' It was Taejax and the name he spoke rang bells at the very nucleus of my being.

Solarian. I heard the name in my mind and my heart leapt for joy. In my mind's eye I remembered a beautiful sentient being imploring me to reconsider a mission I was volunteering for. *Are you sure you want to do this?* she warned. *You will remember nothing, and risk everything you have achieved spiritually.*

Everything is already at risk, I'd replied.

'Obviously we cannot allow you to join the staff of your treacherous father.' Taejax's words broke into my vision and in the same moment he struck at me, his claws making a nasty gash across my cheek. Was our secret ally prepared to kill me, as he had my dear Devere, in order to maintain his cover?

A rock flew out of the darkness to my right and knocked my attacker to the ground.

Make haste to the tree hollow, Mathu called in my mind.

A light began emanating from within the old oak tree. Between myself and my destination, the sea of Dracon bodies stirred and rose to life.

'You cannot defeat us all by yourself, Mathu!' Taejax launched himself forward to latch onto my foot and restrain my advance.

Defeat you and your men on my own! Mathu's voice and laughter echoed around the clearing, although he was still not visible. *Why on Earth would I be required to do that here?*

Up through the leaf-littered ground shot the roots of the great oak, latching themselves around the reptilians to bind them and keep them from my path.

Did you forget about our outer defence system? Mathu taunted.

'If it lives, we can kill it, Fairy!' Taejax let go of me to activate the deadly spike that extended from the gadget on his right wrist. I scampered beyond his reach but was unable to tear my attention from discovering his intent. The reptilian inserted the sharp metal spike into the thickest of the roots restraining him.

NO! Mathu cried, but was not fast enough to prevent Taejax administering a fatal dose of ORME to the ancient tree. The poison had a petrifying effect on the root and spread like wildfire through its system. Mathu materialised, a large axe in his hand, and amputated the infected root before the poison could spread into the rest of the tree. Taejax broke free from his now-dead restraint to come after me. I turned to run.

Ahead of me, the root-bound reptilians were following Taejax's example and activating their death spikes. A ball of energy welled in the centre of the tree hollow, spitting forth a dozen streaks of light energy that manifested into male and female Anu warriors who promptly set about with axes to combat the threat to the timeworn guardian of this passage to the otherworld.

My fourth-dimensional brothers and sisters did their best to remove the Dracon from my path as they urged me towards the illuminated tree hollow. The Anu did not fight the reptilians directly, but rather summoned the elements, using fire, whirlwinds, quicksand and any other natural force of the physical world to distract their opponents without permanently harming them.

I was lashed at and struck down by my floundering attackers yet I continued to propel my aging body forward, numbing myself to the physical pain and focusing solely on reaching the light ahead. I knew Taejax was right on my heels as I made it to the hollow, and when I felt myself lifted off the ground I feared he had caught me. Then I heard his growling voice behind me — 'She's escaping!' — and the distance between us sounded wider.

I dared to look aside and saw it was Mathu who had snatched me from the horror. He launched me headlong into the swirling interdimensional light passage. 'Welcome home, Solarian.' His smiling face vanished in a blur of light so intense it forced my eyes to close.

Every atom in my body was excited beyond any physical thrill I had ever felt. I lost nearly all sense of myself during the passage, as if I had been broken down into tiny particles and merged with the light filling the passage, yet I felt my half-brother's arm about me for the duration. I placed my complete trust in his guidance as we were propelled at lightning speed through the inter-time gateway.

I gradually became aware of the many wounds to my body that now throbbed and smarted with a vengeance. 'Am I alive?'

'Just.' Mathu sounded perturbed.

I parted my eyes to behold him staring down at me, clearly concerned for my wellbeing. 'We will move swiftly,' he advised, 'for you will need this body in the future.'

I moaned, wearied and battered. 'Can I not have a new one?'

Mathu laughed. 'A hundred years under the blue flame and this body will be better than new.'

The way I felt at present I found this hard to believe, but a hundred years' repose did sound inviting. 'I think I see where the legend of Sleeping Beauty was derived from. Will my Prince Charming be there when I awake?'

'That's how the story goes.' Mathu was non-committal. 'And hopefully we shall have a happy-ever-after ending.'

As I looked around me I recognised the dim chamber. Large stone stairs ascended in long, curved levels to a platform and an altar block. The light-filled liquid portholes behind us fell in a constant downward stream, which illuminated the entire chamber with its vibrancy.

'I bade my son's body farewell in this place. We are beneath Giza,' I said.

'The way to Amenti is found here,' Mathu replied, and flew in one great bound up the stairs with me in his arms. For once, I was thankful to be carried, as I had sustained quite a battering during the panic of the escape.

Mathu set me down on the top stair and retrieved a large metal ankh from amongst his robes. He held the tool up before the stone altar and a blue beam of energy shot from its centre and into the ancient stone block. The wall directly behind the altar vanished to expose a tunnel.

'This is the last port of call in the physical world for all Amenti's staff,' Mathu told me.

'One of those would certainly make the life of an archaeologist a lot easier,' I commented, as Mathu swirled his hand around like a magician to produce an orb of light. It floated up to guide and illuminate our passage.

'Due to the Dracon's theft and misuse of ankhs in the past, such interdimensional tools are now banned from surface Earth use,' Mathu explained, and took me up in his arms once more to continue our passage down the exposed tunnel, which was constructed from huge red granite blocks.

'So why do you still get to wield an ankh in the physical world?' I inquired, amused to note that Mathu was not walking but rather gliding along with me.

'As a guardian of humanity, I am an authorised ankh-wielder,' he bantered.

The tunnel entrance reconstituted behind us. This was the last path Levi had walked in this world. Being here, I could not help but wonder what had become of him.

'Have you seen my son since the last time we were here?'

'In the past or the future?' Mathu asked in all seriousness. 'In this dimension or the next? He is everywhere.'

Our light orb slowed to a hover as we approached a rather unusual set of doors: in the shape of a triangle cropped at the top. They were constructed from an ORME-based metal — both doorway and doors had that telltale eerie glow. There were no handles or locks to be seen.

'Touch it.' Mathu urged me to satisfy my curiosity about the substance, and as I reached out my fingers and made contact with the doors, they abruptly opened.

'Dear Goddess,' I uttered, astonished by the interior of the tunnel ahead. It was completely round and constructed from a dark metal. Silver metallic ORME strips ran along both sides and the ceiling, lighting the long passage. Mathu dismissed his orb with a thought and proceeded into the tunnel with me.

'Who built this place?' I asked, stifling a yawn. The alien environment was astonishing yet I was struggling to keep my eyes open.

Mathu noticed my tiredness and willingly launched into a lecture in the hope of keeping my mind engaged and awake. 'The Amenti complex was constructed on Sirius B,' he explained. 'But the schematics were supplied by the Ceres Council, who oversee the Amenti Project from Tara's plane of demonstration. The Amenti complex is fully mobile — hence the confusion that Amenti is still located beneath Atlantis. It was in fact relocated to Giza thousands of years before the great deluge, as the build-up of low-grade energy in the Earth grid centres beneath Atlantis threatened to destroy the Sphere if it wasn't removed.'

'And how was the complex relocated?' Just asking the question exhausted me, and I closed my eyes to rest.

'It flew.' Mathu gave me a shake as he increased the speed of our passage. 'Stay with me, Solarian, you are so close to home.'

Home? With my consciousness fading, I was at a loss to recall where that was. A vision of the young and vibrant smiling face of my dear husband served to remind me where home was to be found.

You are my home and I am yours, he said, looking more splendid than ever I had seen him. *You return home, Solarian,* he said sweetly. *We can do this.*

Polaris. The name sprang forth from my subconscious, igniting my will to live as I fell into a fitful slumber.

FROM THE JOURNAL OF CHARLOTTE DEVERE

I put down my pen and stretched. I had been writing my mother's experiences into her journal for half the night and the better part of the morning. Albray, my mother's ghostly knight, looked relieved.

I promised your mother I would watch over you, he said, *and I cannot, in good conscience, say I've done that by allowing you to go on without food, drink and rest for so long.*

'Mama lost consciousness a little while ago,' I informed him, 'I can afford to take a break.' I stood and shook out the stiffness in my joints, then approached the breakfast tray that had been left for me many hours before.

What has happened to cause Lady Suffolk to lose consciousness? I could tell from Albray's concerned tone that he held my mother in considerable affection.

My curiosity got the better of me. 'Were you lovers?'

Albray looked stunned and mildly amused by the question. *Such as I am, that is rather impossible.*

'Not really,' I pointed out frankly. 'She could have astrally projected herself into your realm to join with you.'

Really? Albray looked fascinated to learn this.

'Oh yes,' I assured him. 'Or you might have had a lustful encounter during an episode of possession.'

I never thought of that, he answered dryly, but I suspected it was a lie. *And how is it that you have such a broad knowledge of interdimensional sexual relations, Miss Charlotte?*

I merely smiled in response. 'You haven't answered my question.'

I have had the honour of being your mother's protector for a good part of her life, he said, *and I can tell you surely that your father was her only lover.*

I have a talent for detecting lies, and the knight's sincerity warmed my heart and stirred my romantic streak. 'You love her nevertheless.'

It seems it is my fate to be attracted to women I cannot have. He shrugged. *Although, considering what I have learned from the lustful acts you have accused me of this day, the future is looking brighter.*

I had to smile; it was easy to see why my mother never left home without him. 'Mama is in good hands,' I assured him as I picked at my food. 'I do not fear for her safety.'

That is well. Albray appeared satisfied and relieved. *That leaves only the question of your wellbeing.*

'You have no need to worry on my account,' I said. 'I thrive on experiences that most would consider extreme. A trait we share, I suspect.'

Albray saw the humour and a chance to make a point. *Could it be my* deceased *status that gave away my extreme tendencies?*

There was a knock on the door and our head maidservant entered with a fresh tea tray.

'Perfect timing, Mrs Mills.' I was grateful for her excellent service. As she placed the tea tray beside me I noticed two cups.

'Lady Oxford has arrived, Miss Charlotte,' Mrs Mills explained.

'Please show her in,' I instructed. 'See,' I said to Albray when the maid had left, 'you can stop worrying. I now have someone to share the burden.'

Indeed, Lady Susan is as valorous, committed and capable as any of her ilk, Albray agreed, and I detected a hint of intimacy in his voice again.

'You do get around,' I commented. His cheeky grin did nothing to disperse my suspicions. 'How much does Lady Susan know about you?'

We merged to fight our way through a few rounds of swordplay with a Melchi warrior once. Then Albray wiped the cheeky grin from his face. *But we have never been formally acquainted, as Lady Susan has not developed her psychic skills in this incarnation and so remains unaware of me.*

'I shall bear that in mind,' I said, and wondered how on Earth I was going to manage to explain everything I needed to in order to recruit my Aunt Susan to the cause. Still, as she had gone to great lengths in the past for the sake of her friendship with my mother, I held no doubt of securing her aid.

'This is just like one of your mother's stories, only far more immediate,' Lady Susan commented as we took tea by the fire in the library and she absorbed all I had told her. 'So our last farewell was truly our last,' she added, and shed a single sentimental tear.

'We shall all meet again in Amenti,' I consoled her, although in truth it probably confused her further. All I could hope was that we would all understand and confirm this claim before our task was done.

'I am honoured that you would call on my aid in this affair,' my aunt ventured. 'I've never had much psychic aptitude, but your mother incited in me a keen interest in the spirit world and a yearning to become more adept.'

Anybody else would have laughed in my face after such a wild tale, or called the asylum, but not my aunt. 'You are a godsend,' I told her. I removed the thought-conductor ring from my finger and placed it in her hand. 'You'll find everything else you need on the desk.'

'Of course.' My aunt put her cup aside. 'Go and rest, child, you must be exhausted. I shall read through the journal before I begin — I feel sure it will answer any queries I might have. My only hope is that I can do the account justice.' She slipped the ring onto the ring finger of her right hand.

'Just record what you see,' I advised.

'And if I do not perceive anything?' Lady Susan voiced her worst fear.

'I have no idea how long Mama will remain unconscious,' I said, 'so if you perceive nothing, I dare say it is because there is nothing to perceive. I shall be back to relieve you as soon as I have slept.'

'Take all the time you need,' my aunt insisted. 'I am well rested and ready to begin.'

She moved to the writing desk and started to read all that had unfolded so far in my mother's quest to find Amenti, Levi and the court of the Dragon Queens.

SUSAN DEVERE JOURNALISING ON BEHALF OF LADY ASHLEE GRANVILLE-DEVERE

I passed the next few hours reading of Ashlee's adventure in Persia ten years ago, and was fascinated by all her discoveries there. Then my conscious perception was distracted from my reading by a hazy vision that was forming in my mind. It took a moment for me to realise that this was the telepathic transfer I had been waiting for: Ashlee was waking from her slumber. Feeling inspired and excited that I was indeed able to perceive her, I quickly found my place in the journal, dipped my pen in ink and prepared to record my observations. I need not have worried about my journalising prowess, as Ashlee's stream of consciousness was as concise as a dictation.

REVELATION 18

ANGELS

'All is clear to angels except in war.
When I awoke to this truth, it was from a dream I had last night.
I saw two angels conversing in a field of children's spirits,
rising like silver smoke.
The angels were fighting among themselves about which side was right
and which was wrong. Who started the conflict?
Suddenly, the angels stilled themselves, like a stalled pendulum,
and they shed their compassion to the rising smoke
of souls who bore the watermark of war.
They turned to me with those eyes from God's library,
and all the pieces fallen were raised in unison,
coupled like the breath of flames in a holy furnace.
Nothing in war comes to destruction but the illusion of separateness.
I heard this spoken so clearly I could only write it down
like a forged signature.
I remember the compassion, mountainous,
proportioned for the universe.
I think a tiny fleck still sticks to me
like gossamer threads from a spider's web.'

I awoke to find myself lying in a very comfortable white pod, open at
the top, its rim trimmed with a thin tube of intense violet light. My
fair, otherworldly brother was leaning over me reciting this poem
about angels.

'And now, when I think of war, I flick these threads to all the universe,
hoping they stick on others as they did me.
Knitting angels and animals to the filamental grace of compassion.
The reticulum of our skyward home.'

Mathu finished his recitation and smiled warmly at me.

'That was beautiful.' I thanked him for his waking gift.

'I'm glad you like it,' he replied. 'You wrote it.'

I was astonished by the claim, but Mathu nodded to assure me he spoke the truth. 'Way back when you still remembered your mission here,' he said. 'It speaks of the time of the Draconian rebellion. You wrote it to remind yourself of who you really are and why you came here.'

But where was I?

I cast my sights about the huge round chamber. It contained many pod-like beds, which were arranged in a circular formation around the central point of the chamber and gave the appearance of what Thoth had so beautifully described in his writings as a flower. In the petal-shaped pods were placed the bodies of the Staff of Amenti, to be bathed in the radiance of the blue flame. The advanced interdimensional power source pulsated inside a tube of light that extended from ceiling to floor in the chamber; its blue-green glow felt like ecstasy to my battered body.

'This place is known as the Chamber of Life,' Mathu said, and grinned. 'How are you feeling?'

'Sedated,' I replied, straining to raise my head and look down upon myself. I was shocked to find I was dressed in very little — just a small band of glistening white fabric strapped around my breasts and hips. My wounds had been cleaned and my body smeared with a glistening light-emitting oil.

Mathu calmly encouraged me to lie back. 'The oil protects your mortal skin from the effects of the blue flame, whilst acting as a superconductor for its healing energy,' he explained.

'You did this?' I referred to my new attire.

My concern made him chuckle and he shook his head. 'The Priestesses of Ur prepared you for your slumber, just as they have prepared all the Dragon Queens before you. Just as the Priests of Ur tend the Grail Princes who reside here.'

'Levi is here?' I looked to my right and left. Although the lids of the pods alongside mine were transparent, they were in darkness. The band of ultraviolet light that ran around the rim of my pod prevented me from identifying the occupants of the others, or much of the architectural detail of the chamber I was in. The central tube of blue flame energy, which was so radiant to the senses, cast only an eerie soothing light. I felt my physical awareness dulling once more.

'You are safer here than anywhere on Earth,' Mathu assured me. 'Go now, walk the Halls of Amenti. Remember all you have been, all you are and all you will be again.'

'Watch Charlotte ...' I was not able to complete my request, but I knew Mathu would protect my daughter regardless. My eyelids felt suddenly leaden, as did my body, and my consciousness dropped loose from my earthly burden.

A great limestone hallway stretched out before me filled with luminous air. I myself was glowing! I had shed all physical density, but my subtle body was glowing with a rich colourful vibrancy. I realised I had not yet arrived at the Halls of Amenti, but in an outer chamber that, if legend was correct, led to the famous Hall of Records. Etched high up on the wall to my left were many geometrical symbols; as I advanced down the passage I counted forty-nine in all. I felt I should know the significance of this number, but it eluded me at present.

At the end of the passage, which veered around to the right, I entered a much larger hall, also constructed of limestone, with many other halls branching off it. As I moved down the main thoroughfare of this labyrinth I glanced into the halls to either side of me, all of which hosted many other doors and passages. I was not distracted from my course, however. I had been here before; the memory was like a dream, and yet I knew that the chamber I sought lay dead ahead. As I neared my destination, I heard the sound of running water. The limestone hall ended, although the pathway underfoot did not — it extended into a bridge across a vast cavernous chamber that had no bottom, or at least not one that could be perceived from my vantage point. High above, the ceiling of the chamber was composed of huge, glowing crystal clusters — quartz in the main, but also others of varying colours — set into the stone like stars scattered across the fabric of space. Water ran down the chamber's inner walls and down into the black void below.

The bridge led me to a large, round mound, and awaiting my arrival on this central platform was a solitary robed figure who lowered his hood upon my approach. 'Welcome back, Solarian.'

I gasped upon recognising my company and my heart leapt for joy and lodged in my throat. 'Devere?' I quickened my approach across the bridge, eager to be near him.

'I was once,' he admitted, and I detected a Scottish accent.

I slowed to a stop as he swung his robe back over his shoulders to reveal the attire of a pirate. 'Sinclair,' I realised.

'My key incarnation is known by that name,' he confirmed, seeming a little disappointed by my sudden reserve. 'Still, you have known me by many different names in many different lifetimes, not all of which have been upon this Earth.'

He certainly was as charming as my husband, and his broad accent was delightful on the ear. I resumed my approach, noting the subtle differences in his appearance, which were too minor to deny that Sinclair and Devere were one and the same soul-mind. *Of course!* That was the name he wanted me to remember. 'Polaris,' I ventured, whereupon he smiled broadly, delighted by my recognition of his spiritual identity.

'That is my goal,' he said.

'I have had a few fleeting visions since entering this complex,' I explained, not wanting him to think I was more knowledgeable than I actually was. 'None of which made any sense to me.'

'Allow me to help you correct that.'

His dazzling smile and friendly demeanour encouraged me to relax, and as I stepped off the limestone bridge and onto the central platform, the pathway behind me vanished. There was a large golden disk in the centre of the island we were now stranded upon, and it appeared to be divided into six segments. 'Please.' Sinclair invited me to stand upon the segmented circle.

I stepped onto the plate, whereby each segment of the disk lit up in turn. When all the golden segments were glowing brightly, my guide's smile broadened. 'Do not be alarmed,' he said and stepped onto the plate with me.

'Why should I be alarmed?' I asked, then looked down to see the golden disk beneath our feet vanish. We dropped into the void. I felt a surge of panic until I realised that I was spirit and therefore in no physical danger. As my fear lessened so did my speed, and after a long period of a pleasant floating descent, I touched down beside Captain Sinclair.

Shockwaves of recognition pulsed through me as we entered the Amenti chamber. It contained six perfectly rounded doorways, each crafted from a different shade of gold. 'I know this place,' I was stunned to claim.

'You ought to,' Sinclair laughed. 'You helped design and build it.' Then he smiled at me in my beloved's endearing way. 'And now you are going to remember everything.'

'You have traversed Amenti's halls already?' I asked, and he nodded to confirm. 'And you remember our life together?' Hope made tears well in my eyes, for I felt distanced from my love as I addressed this other incarnation of him.

'Aye,' Sinclair said, observing me fondly. 'But you speak as if our time together is done, when it is only just beginning.'

He was so very like my dear Devere when first I had met him, and his view encouraged me to complete the quest at hand. I turned to examine the six doorways.

The first porthole, directly beside the archway through which we had entered, had a frame of red-gold. Beside it was one framed in orange-gold; the next was yellow-gold, then pink-gold; blue-gold; and the last was a stunning and rare violet-gold. Each passage beyond appeared filled with liquid-light that reflected the colour of its doorway.

'Should there not be seven doors?' I asked, for the seventh porthole of the Amenti system was the one that would lead to the Sphere of Amenti and home to Tara.

'Only once you have traversed the first six halls will the seventh door be revealed to you,' my guide clarified. He escorted me past the pool inset into the middle of the floor of the circular chamber, to the closest of the portholes. 'Would you like me to explain the mechanics of the portholes before you begin your travels?'

'I would be much obliged,' I replied, fascinated by the advanced appearance of the Amenti system.

'There is a pair of electromagnetic spirals inside each of these portholes, which counter-rotate and merge to form a passage where time continua pass through each other —'

'On second thoughts,' I interrupted, 'a picture is worth a thousand words.'

I stepped up to the red-gold porthole, assuming that as this colour was at the lowest end of the spectrum it would relate to my root chakra and connect to the very earliest root races of mankind.

'Know that you will not relive all your lives, past, present or future,' Sinclair warned, 'only those pivotal events that activated the frequency keys that allow you access through Amenti.'

'I understand.' I felt a rush of excitement and trepidation.

As I faced the liquid-light porthole, I took a moment to calm the expectation welling within my being, then I made my first step into a much larger world. As I stood upon the red-gold disk, I felt a great explosion of calmness and certainty welling within my lowest chakra. My root chakra began to vibrate with a sonic tone, and as this amplified the sound resonated up through my light centres and caught in my throat, where my larynx echoed the mighty note. I felt a deep shift take place within my subtle body as the oscillation of my atomic consciousness altered to match that of the porthole before me.

The red waterfall that cascaded down over the opening of the porthole began to swirl clockwise into the centre, like water rushing down a plughole. Then another spiral of water, this one rushing counter-clockwise, joined with the first and the centre of the swirling torrents opened wide. A great rush of red light erupted from within the vortex and my conscious being was sucked forth to return to the very beginning of my human evolution on this Earth.

FROM THE JOURNAL OF CHARLOTTE GRANVILLE-DEVERE
Before I had even parted my eyes from slumber, I knew Mathu was in

my room; I sensed his exalted, otherworldly presence. 'How long have you been returned from Amenti?' I asked.

'Many hours,' he replied.

I rolled onto my back to see my Fey friend standing at the end of my bed, wearing his physical outer layer. I smiled and stretched, relishing the mutual attraction I felt between this being and myself. Since first meeting Mathu I had been infatuated with him, but as the Fey showed so little emotion I had imagined that my romantic fantasies about him were in vain. Yet in light of what the angelic warrior had told my mother about me, I had been given fresh hope.

'You have watched me sleeping all that time?'

'Yes, my lady.' His tone implied this was a pleasure, not an obligation.

I was amused by his incorrect, formal address. 'My name is Charlotte, for unless I marry a lord, the title of Lady is not for me.'

'My mistake,' Mathu granted winningly, 'your Highness is far more fitting.'

I had to restrain myself from laughing out loud. 'So you truly think I am a Mother Goddess of the Anunnaki?'

'I would recognise your soul-mind anywhere,' he assured, 'for it is unique ... like you.' He seemed awkward, which I thought strange for a being supposedly lacking in emotion.

'Why am I the only Anunnaki able to incarnate into human form?' I asked, for this part of Mathu's explanation to my mother baffled me.

'In truth, I too have the ability to incarnate into human form, but I have not proved as adept as you at integration,' he said. 'Before I learned compassion from you as an Anunnaki, I was egotistical and self-absorbed, and after enlightenment I was too selfless and, due to my great intellect, had something of a god complex. The object of being human is to master emotion; instead, I became so engrossed in teaching humans that my true mission here was overlooked. I considered any relationship that was not a teacher–student interaction beneath me.'

'I do not agree,' I said and sat upright to argue. 'I am no different from you. Humans have never interested me in a marital sense, and due to my extrasensory abilities, how could I fail to feel like an advanced alien intelligence amid herds of mindless cattle? But ...' I paused to gather my nerve '... I see how you look at me and I know that your true mission here has not been entirely overlooked.'

'Lust is not one of the higher emotions,' he said weakly, clearly relieved to have our emotional predicament out in the open.

'Lust?' I queried gently. 'Mere lust could never inspire such devotion as you hold for me.'

He frowned, perplexed, as he came to sit rather heavily on the bed beside me — with no sense of feeling in his physical form, he could not gauge his own force and weight. 'So you think love is my motivation?'

'Generally speaking, if all you feel for someone is lust, a sexual union with your desired will often make that attraction disappear ... but love lingers on.' As I stated my view I felt an intense magnetic energy building between us.

He stared at me with his lilac eyes, appearing baffled by my comment. 'But we have had no physical union that I am aware of.'

I smiled at my own folly; he had no understanding of emotion, so I could hardly expect him to know I was flirting. 'That was an invitation, not an observation,' I said. My anticipation welled as I leaned forward and kissed him — but of course only I really experienced the event.

'I cannot lay claim to you as I am,' he said regretfully, and gently urged me back. 'I can feel nothing, which would be most unpleasant for you.'

'Then shed your physical form and enter mine,' I suggested brazenly.

'I ... I would not know what to do. I have never ...' He shied away from saying more.

This only ignited my desire for our union, but I did not want to force myself upon him. 'As I have had no interest in a human relationship, I am well aware of how to pleasure myself,' I said, hardly believing my own impudence. 'Join with me and my pleasure shall become your pleasure and you will know human love.' I felt that if he was still hesitant I would die of humiliation for being so wanton.

Mathu's physical form faded to reveal his beautiful semi-transparent

Fey being. 'I am honoured by your gracious invitation and I humbly commit myself into your capable hands,' he said softly.

He reached out to me, and although I could no longer feel his physical touch, I felt a warm tingling sensation that excited my senses more than the caress of any human hand. His presence moved further into alignment with my own and the tingling intensified, heightening my sexual arousal. My nightdress was quickly dispensed with, and under the warmth of my bedcovers we explored the hidden depths of our passion. I was so consumed by him that it was hard to determine just who was guiding my hands. My body shuddered in delighted climax too frequently to define one orgasm from the next. The intense emotional and physical stimulation sent my consciousness into a euphoric dream of faraway worlds. I could hear Mathu whispering to me in my mind, his groans of pleasure and release making me all the more aware of my delight. I had never before had cause to consider how truly sacred the male and female union was, but somewhere in the midst of our delirium Mathu and I discovered love.

When Mathu's soul-mind departed my body, he was as giddy as a schoolboy and grinning from ear to ear. 'Happiness,' he said, and pointed to himself to indicate another higher emotion that he was experiencing for the first time as a result of our union.

I rolled on my side to face him as he lay on the bed beside me. He was still dressed in his green Anu attire — belted pants, shirt, vest and boots — which seemed either too old-fashioned or too modern for this age. 'You have never experienced happiness?' I asked.

He shook his head, his new and thrilling emotions made plain in the way his eyes adored me. 'You have again set me on the em-bed-path. Long ago, you taught me what it was to be compassionate, and now you have taught me what it is to feel love.'

I was flattered by his adoration, but I could not accept it. 'You made the choice to feel.'

'Because you inspire me,' he argued as I rose to dress. I wanted to remain shut away in my room with my new lover, but I had to relieve Lady Susan from her shift recording my mother's experiences in the Halls of Amenti.

'You inspire me too,' I said, pulling on a warm dress over my nightshirt, as had been the fashion decades before Victoria's rule. 'What is the em-bed-path?'

My mother's ghostly knight unexpectedly appeared in my room before Mathu could answer, discovering me still buttoning up my dress. His glance flew to Mathu, still floating on my bed.

Why are you here? Albray demanded of my lover.

'He is here at my invitation,' I answered. 'Why are you here?'

I promised your mother I would protect you. The knight's displeased expression was still aimed at Mathu.

'Mama may have allowed you to meddle in her private affairs, but I would rather you did not meddle in mine,' I stated bluntly, finally gaining the knight's full attention. 'You are not my father.'

Not yet, Mathu uttered in amusement.

'I gather my aunt is ready for a break?' I asked, attempting to ease the tension.

If you would be so kind. Albray backed off and vanished through the wall of my room.

'My reprimand might have been a little harsh,' I considered in retrospect. 'Still, what right has he to judge me, having lusted after my mother all those years?'

'He was only recognising a kindred spirit in her, and in you,' Mathu said.

I thought back to Mathu's jovial comment. 'He's not my father yet … are you implying that Albray will be my father in a future life?'

When Mathu nodded I did not believe him. 'But the knight's soul is trapped in the afterlife by a vow he made to the Ladies of the Elohim.'

'Your next mother will release him from that obligation,' Mathu assured me. 'Half of your perfected human incarnation lies within him.'

'I had best start being a little nicer to him then,' I grinned.

'Me too,' joked Mathu, 'if our love is to be realised in this life and the next.'

The suggestion was so romantic that I shed a tear. I had been waiting so long for love to come my way that the idea that not even death would separate us was deeply comforting.

'So even once I've died and been reborn again, with no memory of you, you will still be watching over me?' I said.

'Yes, I will,' Mathu vowed, and then grinned at the irony. 'And so will he.' He nodded towards the spot on the wall where Albray had taken his leave.

ARCHITECTS OF EVOLUTION

SUSAN DEVERE JOURNALISING ON BEHALF OF LADY ASHLEE
GRANVILLE-DEVERE

ROOT RACE ONE — ETHERIC (NO TIME)

I am compressed in utter darkness — motionless, powerless, formless — and yet semi-conscious and without fear. This is only a state of transition, an etheric membrane between my angelic existence and the lowest etheric world of the lowest dimensional universe, where all life must endure and adapt to the primordial elements that compose a physical existence. I am now to become a participant in my own experiment, but I am not alone. All eleven of my collaborators on the Amenti Project believe as strongly as I do that we can protect the lost souls of Tara and show them the way home.

I have yet to pass fully through the membrane between dimensions for I still remember that I am one of the Ceres, a race evolving on Tara's astral globe, who have progressed through physical evolution to become spirit beings and guardians to the human beings still living on Tara. The Ceres existed long before the cataclysm on Tara that now occupies all our time and effort.

In the wake of the planetary disaster my people selected a council of technologists and scientists to work in conjunction with the Elohim's Interdimensional Association of Free Worlds to create the technological and biological means to salvage the missing part of

Tara's morphogenetic blueprint and rescue our lost soul-minds from the lower-dimensional universe into which they had been cast during the cataclysm.

Up until recently the members of the Amenti Council were overseeing the salvage mission from Tara. We were able to execute the construction of the Amenti system by will alone, so our personal presence in the lower harmonic universe was not required, nor even considered. There were many complications involved in the descent of a being from the second harmonic universe into the denser, primal universe below ours — as Tara's lost soul-minds had discovered. It had been a mistake on our part to trust the lower harmonic manifestations of our Anunnaki adversaries, the Anu, with the task of perfecting the physical bodies for our kindred, but the Elohim senate had demanded this cooperation, believing it was integral to avoiding a repeat of the war between the humans under our guidance on Tara and the Anunnaki settlers on our planet that had led to Tara's partial destruction.

The twelve members of the Amenti Council, six male, six female, decided to take matters into our own hands. I, Solarian, made a pact with my partner, Polaris, and our fellow council members, Dexter and Vespera, Arcturus and Meridon, Levi and Thana, Castor and Talori, Zalman and Denera, that we would commit our souls to the Sphere of Amenti in order to incarnate on Earth and lead our people home.

We were none too eager to welcome the Anunnaki Queen, Kali, and her prince, Mathu, when they arrived on Tara to discuss a salvage proposal for the Nefilim. This scheme involved building a direct porthole between Earth's etheric realms, that could be accessed via the planet's core and the astral realm of Sirius B that bypassed the physical plane altogether. Through this porthole, dubbed 'the Hall of Amorea', the souls of the fallen Nefilim, Dracon and Anunnaki might be channelled back to their rightful evolution through their Anu soul group on Sirius B. Kali and Mathu hoped to incorporate their Hall of Amorea into the Amenti Project.

'What will set you apart from any of the other human souls floundering through the primordial darkness and despair on Earth?' the Anunnaki Queen asked. 'You will be as lost as the mortals you seek to save. But build our Hall of Amorea and we will draw the Nefilim and the Dracon back to their Anu soul group in the subtle realm, from where they will assist you to remember your quest and provide you with the means to carry it out.'

However, the twelve members of the Amenti Council were not yet ready to trust the word of an Anunnaki.

'Your Nefilim have damned themselves to oblivion and are abusing every human being they can breed!' Polaris voiced what we were all thinking. 'What makes you think the Nefilim can be persuaded to give up their ORME addiction and return to their Anu soul group?'

'We propose to commit our soul-minds to the blue flame at the same time as you do,' Kali explained, gesturing to her prince and herself.

'But that would alter the morphogenetic code in all of us!' Castor, our chief genetic engineer, protested.

'Only from where the Blue Flame of Amenti resides in the astral realm downwards, and this mutation would affect us fourteen only,' Kali pointed out.

'And we can borrow from each other's morphogenetic code in order to gain an advantage over our adversaries on Earth,' Polaris mused, following the Anunnaki Queen's train of thought.

Kali nodded. 'You will be able to draw on Anunnaki intellect and psychic expertise, which your kind do not possess on a physical level. And we will be awarded a more highly developed emotional body than any of the Anunnaki souls who currently reside on Earth.'

'Not to mention that you'll be the only Anunnaki with the ability to incarnate into the human race,' the more spiritually minded Denera pointed out.

'A necessary event to allow me to pass back through the Halls of Amenti,' Kali replied.

I needed to know if this offer was worth considering. I turned to our genetic engineer. 'Castor, how will we unscramble our genetic codes upon our return through the Sphere?'

Castor thought a while. 'I could create a smaller flame of higher frequency that could be placed inside the blue flame to house the morphogenetic information of just us twelve plus these two extra souls. If we take a snapshot of our individual morphogenetic codes before our departure, the Amenti system will be able to restore the code to normal upon our return.' Castor looked pleased, until he considered a possible complication. 'However, we would all have to pass back through the blue flame together — if any one of us was missing, we would all be stuck in the lower harmonic universe indefinitely.'

Kali nodded. 'This, then, is how you can trust the word of the Anunnaki, for if you all perish, then so do we.'

'But how do you plan to fulfil that promise?' I asked. 'You will forget who you really are, just as we will.'

Kali smiled. 'I have an ally in the lower harmonic universe who will remind me. He will father and protect us all.'

I knew the ally to whom she referred — we all did, for mankind had only one true advocate among the Nefilim, and that was Enki.

So Kali's Hall of Amorea was built, and now I find myself in a dark limbo between worlds, wondering if I will ever find my way back home.

You are my home and I am yours. We can do this, I recalled my beloved Polaris saying.

Polaris! I wanted to call through the darkness. *I want to be delighted by your presence once more. I will not forget you.* I clung to an image of him, attempting to burn it into my soul, as my conscious memory of my previous existence was swept away in a rush of movement and light.

ROOT RACE TWO — SEMI-ETHERIC/SEMI-PHYSICAL (300,000 YEARS AGO)
Beyond the stifling blackness of density
are my crude elementary beginnings.
Large, sexless and gossamer am I,
and completely etheric in nature.
I am really nothing more than a gigantic phantom,
swaying and drifting in the dense atmosphere
of the seething primordial seas.
My form is not fixed in shape or colour,
but it holds the promise of what will become a human being.

Clumsy, passive and near-senseless, I hold only a vague consciousness of fire as it warms my being into activity, inspiring an aspiration to communicate with my outer world. Many ages pass and my form develops an ability to stand, walk, run, recline and fly, but even so I am but a shadow with no rational mind.

Over time a great transformation occurs and the imperishable form of my first root race incarnation splits into two distinctly different forms: one active, one passive; one electric, one magnetic; one of water, one of fire; one white with a connection to the moon, one yellow-orange with a connection to the sun. Thus, the bodies of my second root race incarnations are born.

I take on a vaguely human-like form, which is still gaseous in appearance and completely sexless. I develop a sense of touch and thus I feel the lapping of the waters, the roar of the winds and the warmth of fire. My hearing is more acute now and my fellow incarnates call to me in flute-like notes, stirring in me emotions that well from a mysterious spring hidden deep within me, within us all. A dreamy enjoyment of life fills me with delight, but neither pleasure nor pain is stimulated by external sources for I am still a product of above and not below.

I drift, I float, I glide and climb through the sunlit creepers of dazzling, vibrant blooms, and over many aeons the elements of nature harden my outer shell.

The oscillation rate of my atomic consciousness altered and I was deposited back into the entrance chamber to the Halls of Amenti.

'That was horrific!'

I leaned forward to clutch my knees and steady myself. My subtle form had undergone a massive expansion; I truly felt I had been stretched across aeons and robbed of my individuality and sexuality.

'The first porthole leads to the etheric existence of the first two root races, which are the most alien and unfathomable consciousnesses in comparison with your own, so the experience is bound to be a little uncomfortable,' Sinclair explained as he waited for me to regain my composure. 'The first hall also spans the greatest period of Earth time. Be assured that your next experience will not leave you feeling so ... stretched.'

'But I felt so powerless, so ineffective and will-less,' I exclaimed.

'Of course you did. You were little more than a sexless, shapeless, elemental phantom beginning to develop a sense of the world around you.' My handsome friend smiled sympathetically; perhaps he had felt this same doubt at this stage of his journey through Amenti's halls, I thought. 'But you will never be will-less again,' he went on. 'You developed and perfected that attribute many, many lifetimes ago and it can never be taken from you.'

As the experience played out in my mind's eye, I realised that the first porthole had taken me much further back in time than I had expected. 'I remember being Solarian,' I gasped, excitement welling in my chest, 'before I even came to Earth.'

'What do you recall?' he asked.

I struggled to focus on the memory. 'A meeting ... between the Queen and Prince of the Anunnaki and the Amenti Council ...' I paused to smile as in my vision I saw myself glance around the conference table at my fellow Council members. 'I recognise most of the Council members, for they are souls I knew in life,' I said, and tears of happiness rolled down my cheeks. 'You are there, and Levi, Albray, Zalman, Susan —'

'Is your daughter Charlotte present?' Sinclair prompted.

'No,' I said, disheartened.

'Are you sure?' the captain teased.

'Oh my,' I gasped as I spied her. 'She is Kali, the Queen of the Anunnaki.' Just as Mathu had claimed. 'And Mathu is her prince.' My heart jumped into my throat upon knowing that Charlotte, who had never been interested in marriage, would find love after all.

'And what of the meeting?' Captain Sinclair gently guided me towards drawing the more relevant data from my experience.

'Do you remember it?' I asked, wondering if I was being tested or pumped for information.

'Yes,' he confirmed. 'And it is my aim to see if you recall all that I did ... or more perhaps?'

'The meeting took place following the Draconian uprising on Earth,' I said.

'Yes.'

I walked over to take a seat on the side of the pool in the middle of the chamber and the captain joined me. 'A deal was struck,' I remembered. 'It was a dangerous proposal, for souls had never descended through the Sphere of Amenti before, as I designed it for —'

I broke off, shocked to realise that I had been one of the master architects of this place.

'Amenti was designed for ascension *from* Earth,' I continued, 'so in order for our angelic souls to descend *to* Earth, another flame of a higher frequency had to be created. This violet flame was inserted inside the Blue Flame of Amenti to house our twelve souls plus the two Anunnaki souls.

'Did I forget anything?' I asked, wondering how my memory had stood up against his.

'Only that because we twelve plus two souls descended through into the Amenti scheme together, we must also return through the porthole together.'

I gasped, realising the implications. 'So if even one of us is lost, our morphogenetic structures will not re-separate properly when we try to return to Tara via the violet flame, and we will all be stuck here!'

'Fortunately, we are all still doing well at this time,' the captain reassured me. 'That is what is meant by the term flame-bearer: Charlotte will be the violet flame-bearer, which is the key to Amenti for all of us.

'There are three flame-bearers needed to unlock the Hall of Records in preparation for the opening of Amenti. The carriers of the orange and blue flames are Amenti Council members, which ensures that the Anunnaki cannot betray us again, for they cannot open the Amenti complex without those two flame-bearers, and the Sphere of Amenti cannot be accessed without all twelve of our Signet stations being activated first.' Sinclair sounded very proud of our safety measures.

'All for one and one for all,' I concluded, and looked to the next porthole.

REVELATION 20

AMAZONS

FROM THE JOURNAL OF TAMAR DEVERE

I allowed the journal to drop into my lap. All of my fears and aspirations were reaffirmed: I was the violet flame-bearer, destined to open the great Hall of Records and Amenti. That is, if my father truly was the ghostly knight of these tales remanifested on Earth. But the coincidence of the Anunnaki queen being called Kali and my sudden bout of automatic trance writing in her name just couldn't be ignored.

My parents had both read these journals, and since they'd given them to me to read on my thirteenth birthday, I could only assume they were trying to scare the life out of me, suck me into an elaborate practical joke, or that they really were attempting to awaken my subconscious awareness of who I really am.

And what of Mathu's vow to watch over Charlotte in her next life? Was he here watching over me now? Could he have been my mysterious caller, who warned me of danger? The idea was both disconcerting and exciting. I'd never had a boyfriend — I'd never really been interested — and if I proved to be anything like Charlotte Granville-Devere, then perhaps I never would be interested in a human mate. The idea of a celestial admirer was quite a turn-on though.

It was approaching midnight and my eyelids were drooping, but still I took my personal journal in hand to record the events of the day whilst they were still fresh in my mind. By the time I had completed my account it was fast approaching one o'clock. I snuggled under my bedcovers and allowed my weary eyes to close, wondering what Kali had planned for this evening — more coding work most likely. 'Fine with me,' I mumbled, so long as I could sleep through it.

I access The Book of Codes *as easily as I did last night, but am interrupted in my work by the male of this house. Do not fear, our work is not exposed: with a wave of my hand, I will our father back to his slumber; he shall not recall our confrontation. As a result, I do not accomplish as many activations as hoped, integrating only the next three time codes. This amounts to six codes now integrated. Our sixth DNA strand is braiding — the human consciousness and extraterrestrial subconsciousness are beginning to meld. Soon Tamar and Kali will be one. Only two more nights of encoding and our full potential will be realised and our being safeguarded.*

'What!' I sat upright in bed, my journal in hand, gaping at Kali's overnight entry. My eyes were very sensitive to the sunlight streaming through my window, as if I hadn't had enough sleep. Not surprising, as it seemed my body wasn't really getting any rest at all. In fact, I felt like I was coming down with something: I was in a cold sweat, my breathing was laboured, my skin felt like it was crawling over every aching muscle and bone in my body, and my head hurt at the base of my skull. I touched the area: it actually felt swollen.

'Christ, what the hell's happening to me?'

Perhaps my symptoms were a reaction to what I'd just read and I was in shock, or maybe it was simply the flu? It wasn't until I stood that I felt the cramping in my intestines — was this just more of the joys of having my first period? But then I noticed something very strange — my pyjamas had shrunk! The legs now rose up well over my ankles, the sleeves were too short and the top felt tight across my chest. In the process of trying to stretch the fabric back out to fit my body, I noticed that my inconsequential breasts were somewhat enlarged this morning.

I rushed to the mirror and opened my pyjama top: sure enough, I exposed a pair of rounded, pert breasts — not huge, but definitely bigger compared to those I'd been sporting yesterday. My face too had altered slightly: my features were more refined and slender; in fact, my entire form seemed to have slimmed down and become curvier at the same time — I was BEAUTIFUL! I'd never really thought myself ugly or anything, but *wow!* — it was hard to believe the transformation.

Leaning towards the mirror to take a closer look at my face, I realised that my dressing table sat lower on my body, as if someone had trimmed the legs overnight. That's when I realised it wasn't my PJs that had shrunk, but that I had grown several inches. I confirmed this by trying on every pair of trousers I had — none of them covered the full length of my legs any more. How on Earth was I going to hide this? I could temporarily get around the problem by wearing a skirt, but that sure wasn't going to hide my rapidly developing form for long. And come to think of it, why would I want to hide it? I looked fabulous, even if that wasn't how I felt.

A hot bath soothed my numerous ailments and made me feel quite sensual. My body felt more like a woman's; the young, underdeveloped teenager was gone forever. Afterwards, as all seemed quiet in the house, I headed for the kitchen to make some breakfast. I planned to return to my room to eat, read and avoid my parents as much as I could until Kali had finished her work on us. She obviously had a plan, and didn't seem to have any problem dealing with adults.

My father's 'good morning' nearly startled me out of my skin. 'You look very nice today,' he commented, placing a hand on my shoulder to reassure me. 'Have you done something different with your hair?'

'It's the skirt, probably,' I said, grabbing hold of it and swishing it about to distract him from the rest of me. As I rarely wore a skirt, Dad nodded to accept that must be it.

He didn't mention anything about seeing me in the library last night, so I guessed Kali's claim that he wouldn't remember was good — it seemed she was powerful indeed. Secretly, the idea of being able to wield all that power was very inviting, and despite my underlying fear of the rapid changes manifesting in my body I was eager to become one with my tenacious, confident alter ego.

I didn't grant much of an opportunity for Dad's memory to be jogged — I finished making my breakfast and, with a kiss on the cheek, wished him a good day and retreated to my room. Phew, that was close, I thought. Thank goodness I'd chosen to wear a big sloppy jumper or Dad might have noticed more than just my change of attire.

I returned to the journal, eager to read more about Charlotte's new romance, and was a little disappointed to note that the next entry was Charlotte's chronicle of her mother's journey through the second of the Halls of Amenti. I was tempted to skip ahead for passages about my new love interest, but guessed these episodes from various journals had been intermingled in this volume in a very specific order, and if I didn't wish to lose the continuity I'd best just keep on reading.

CHARLOTTE GRANVILLE-DEVERE JOURNALISING ON BEHALF OF LADY ASHLEE GRANVILLE-DEVERE

'Take all the time you need to prepare for the next passage,' Captain Sinclair said kindly. 'Time is not an issue.'

'It can only get better from here,' I said, assuring myself that I was ready to move on.

Sinclair frowned, clearly not wishing to lie. 'Not very likely. The third root race manifested into the physical world and their forms were perishable.' Then he grinned. 'Even so, you are bound to witness many amazing things, for the Lemurian races were truly a wondrous breed who became the substance of the great myths and legends that would inspire every root race that came after.'

Now I was curious, and stood tall to indicate that I felt ready to embark into the next hall.

Sinclair motioned to the orange-gold plate. 'Lemuria awaits you.'

I hesitated a moment. 'And shall I be seeing you there?' I gazed into Sinclair's blue eyes and his smile was answer enough. 'So who was my key third root race incarnation?' I continued. Sinclair had already walked the Halls of Amenti, therefore I assumed he knew all that had happened in this second hall.

It seemed I was wrong for he was shaking his head. 'Although you and I have incarnated together in all of our lifetimes in order to aid each other to greatness, we did not necessarily reach enlightenment in the same lifetime,' he explained. 'When I entered this hall, I only bore witness to my own key Lemurian lifetime; your key incarnation may have been born in another lifetime altogether.'

'I see.' I gave up trying to siphon information from my host and turned to face Amenti's second porthole.

When I stepped onto the activation plate, I perceived a great welling of energy within my navel area. The whirling force extended to my spleen, where the second chakra of my subtle form was located. The chakra began to vibrate with a sonic tone, and as the note grew deep in my belly, the sound resonated up to my larynx and became a deep vocalisation. The particles of my subtle body went into an excited frenzy as they brought themselves into alignment with the glowing orange-gold porthole before me.

The water within began to swirl clockwise into the centre, and the second counter-clockwise water spiral penetrated the swirling column from behind. Orange light erupted from the vortex and my consciousness was drawn into the otherworldly passage, back to the time of the first physical manifestations of humanity.

ROOT RACE THREE — PHYSICAL (45,000 BC); THE HA-MAZON

I am Antiope, daughter of Otrera, of the Ha-mazon. Our enemies have come to call us the *Antianeira* — 'those who fight like men' — or the *Androktones* — 'killers of men'; both are well founded. We Ha-mazon are a tribe of warrior women, the progeny of gods and queens, legendary for our prowess in battle and despised by every kingdom in the known world for our independence from the shackles of male bondage. No Ha-mazon has ever married, nor will ever do so. We seduce any prisoners of royal blood, then kill them to prevent any attempt to claim us or our offspring. Our daughters are raised to be warriors; our male progeny are slaughtered at birth.

Today we have two captives: Herakles, whom it is said has the blood of the Lord of the Sky in his veins, a man of Lilian stock belonging to the clan of the god, Enlil; and Theseus, the son of Queen Aethra of Attica and a fair specimen of Kian stock. Both are of bloodlines that could empower our race. Our warriors ambushed them on the shores of the Euxine Sea, before they could begin their attack on our capital, Themiscyra, with the aim of possessing the legendary girdle of invincibility worn by our queen, my older sister, Hyleana. Their quest is folly, however, as the only way the treasure can be transferred is if it is given freely. And as our queen is renowned for her chastity and her skill in combat, any man

305

believing he will one day possess the girdle of power is the greatest of fools.

Herakles and Theseus are brought before Queen Hyleana in the High Temple of Lilith, the great founding mother of my tribe.

Our great foremother was not of Lillian stock, as her name suggests. For although the god Nergal, a son of Enlil, raped Lilith's human mother, her mother claimed that the spirit of the Lord Enki had come over her attacker just before Lilith's conception to transform the base act into one of love and healing. Because of this, Lilith considered herself Kian. Her father, Enki, had been cast out of the Nefilim city of Eden long before Lilith's birth and branded as a serpent traitor thereafter. Due to Lilith's insistence that she was the daughter of Enki and not Nergal, she was branded a serpent also — the Dragon Queen — and considered a lowly creature, giving the gods the perfect excuse to use her for their pleasure and for the breeding of other demi-god daughters to abuse and exploit. They even tried breeding Lilith with a man, Adama, but as a demi-god Lilith refused to take a subservient role to a human. For twelve thousand years the gods held her captive, first on Earth and then in the heavens. During the course of her long suffering, Lilith's spiritual father spoke to her in her sleep and eventually she came to realise that the legacy of her spiritual parentage had instilled in her many superhuman talents: the ability to read minds, to see spirits, to predict the future, to comprehend different languages, to move objects with her mind, and the art of levitation. When the Nefilim returned to resume their mining and scientific projects on Earth, Lilith and her many daughters rebelled against their oppressors and fled. They founded the Ha-mazon race — 'Ha-mazon' being our word for 'warriors' — and for thousands of years Lilith ruled the Ha-mazon, nurturing the superhuman talents of the women in her company and teaching them how to use these talents for the construction of cities and to make war on those who tried to take what was ours. Once the Ha-mazon were well established and prosperous, Lilith, weary of her earthly burdens and battles, called upon her father, Enki, asking that he show her the way to her repose. It is said that the Lord of the World sent his seraphs to escort Lilith to his heavenly house of many halls, where she sleeps peacefully in a flower beneath a healing ray, where she will remain until the end of days, when

Enki shall recall all his spiritual warriors to battle for the redemption of this Earth and her human children.

Today our Queen Hyleana is dressed as a goddess. Her golden hair hangs in long ringlets and the crown of our foremothers is upon her head. A veil covers her face, but many necklaces, rings, anklets and bracelets adorn her person and her prized girdle of gold bands the top of a fancy flounced skirt — a plainer version of which is our warriors' uniform. Every Ha-mazon wears a metal vest that exposes one breast and flattens and protects the breast of our bow arm. It is rumoured among our enemies that we Ha-mazon burn one breast in infancy to more fully develop our weapons arm, but those men who learn the truth never live to tell.

'I live in the opulence of Athens and I have seen the splendour of Troy, yet never have I witnessed architecture so remarkable and elegant as this,' Theseus compliments her, on being introduced to our queen.

'Women are by nature constructive,' our queen explains. 'Men have proved more efficient at deconstruction.'

'A sweeping generalisation, your Majesty.' Herakles speaks up in defence of his sex. 'Indeed, your entire tribe proves that there can be an equal amount of creator and destroyer in one person, so does it not stand to reason that some men are gentle and creative by nature too?'

Our queen is more amused than insulted, thus Herakles ventures to expand on his argument.

'Take young Theseus here,' Herakles motions to his companion, 'he did not come to Pontus to make war. He is here purely to admire and learn about your culture and history.'

'So that he might better know how to conquer us once he is King of Attica,' Asteria, head of our armies, interjects, and the laughter from our troops seems to indicate that they agree.

'That is not my intent,' Theseus insists. 'I am compiling a book on the belief systems of different nations in an attempt to draw parallels and establish some understanding and respect of foreign cultures. I hope that people might learn to cooperate for the mutual benefit of trade, rather than destroy those lands we covet or do not understand.'

'That is a noble pursuit,' Hyleana grants, although all we Ha-mazon know Theseus will never have the opportunity to complete the work.

I will be the warrior who seduces and kills the Prince of Attica. My sisters have instructed me in the art of seduction, but this is the first opportunity I have been awarded to test my comprehension. Killing, however, is second nature.

'And why are you here?' Hyleana turns her attention back to Herakles.

'I come to ask if I may borrow your girdle of power —'

Laughter drowns him out. It takes our queen a few moments to compose herself before she makes a signal to restore silence in the temple. 'You would have to kill me or seduce me to take my girdle,' she explains, 'and as I am invincible in battle and sworn to chastity ...' She shrugs in conclusion.

'There must be some task I can perform for you so that I may merely *borrow* the girdle,' Herakles suggests gamely.

'Why is it so important to you?' Hyleana sounds genuinely interested.

'I am doing penance to my sworn enemy as punishment for the deaths of the two souls who meant the most to me in all the world.' Herakles looks pained by the fact and to my people there is nothing more attractive than a man in pain. 'As part of that penance he has ordered that I bring to him your girdle of power ... but he did not specify that I must leave the girdle in his possession. My only hope is to somehow win this favour from you, and then return the girdle when my task is done.'

Hyleana looks thoughtful. 'There is only one thing you could achieve that I cannot ...'

'Name the task, your Majesty,' Herakles encourages.

'Impregnate all my troops,' our queen says jovially. A loud cheer rises from the thousands of women in attendance.

Herakles seems overwhelmed by the prospect and his face takes on a bemused smile. I have seen many a man led to his death wearing just that smile.

'That could take some time, your Majesty, and I have several more tasks to perform before my penance will be done,' Herakles barters, believing that he still has choices.

'Then you had best get started,' Hyleana advises him. 'Take them away, ladies.'

Before either man can protest they are hit with several tranquillising darts and drop to the ground immobilised.

Hyleana rises and removes her veil to smile at me. 'Theseus is all yours,' she says encouragingly. 'Enjoy yourself, sweet Ann, and bring me his head when you are done.'

I bow; it is my honour to perform her will.

I bathe in scented oil and drape myself in a fine fabric of crimson red. In my bedchamber I find Theseus, stripped to his loincloth and strung between two support pillars; he does not look happy.

'So the rumour that you rape and murder your royal captives would be true?' he says.

'I am here for your pleasure,' I assure him as I approach. 'You are bound for my protection.' I bury a kiss deep into the nape of his neck.

He seems to find my justification amusing. 'Look at you,' he admires my warrior physique, 'you could crush me with your little finger.'

It is true that Theseus is slighter than your average hardened warrior, but he is prettier too.

'I am no threat to you,' he whispers, so tenderly that I almost believe him. 'Cut me loose and it will be my pleasure to indulge you.'

I push away and let the red cloth fall from my body; it billows to the floor at my feet. It is arousing to have his eyes so intent upon me.

'I guess the mutilation rumours were false,' he says, referring to my unscathed breasts.

I lie down on the bed before him and, stretching out, run my hands over my naked, oiled form. 'I know how to pleasure myself.'

Theseus is aroused by my display. 'Pleasuring yourself will not get you with child.'

'Oh, I think I can persuade you to rise to the occasion,' I say, amused, and slide my fingers deep into my pleasure zone, expressing my satisfaction with a moan of delight.

Theseus closes his eyes tight. 'And if I do not cooperate?'

I rise, approach and rip the loincloth from his body. 'Fortunately, men have no control in this matter.' I press my naked form against him.

He strains to focus on resisting my will, but his member hardens with my every caress. He knows that surrendering to his desire will be the death of him and yet the event is inevitable.

'You do this a lot, don't you?' he whispers, hurt evident in his tone.

I smile at his misconception. 'What do you think?'

'I think that men are like cattle to you ... and I am just another piece of meat to be bred from and slaughtered.'

'Which is exactly what I am to you,' I counter.

'That is not true, Antiope.'

I am shocked that he knows my name, for we have not been introduced.

'Yes, I know you,' he goes on softly. 'You are the reason I accompanied Herakles on this quest. I have heard rumours of your beauty and prowess in battle and I was curious to see if the stories were true.'

'And are you disappointed?' I ask, even though I know I am leaving myself open to emotional attack. One of the first rules of sexual engagement we learn is: do not allow the act to become personal by indulging in idle talk.

'In appearance you are every bit as beautiful as reported,' he assures me. 'But true beauty comes from the heart, Antiope, and your heart is closed.'

My body is wrapped around Theseus and so he cannot see how hurtful I find his remark. I cannot resist telling him the truth — not only because it will be a rude shock to him, but because it will inflame his desire. 'I have never lain with a man,' I utter softly in his ear. I pull back to look him in the eyes, and the passion I see there sparks a fire in my chest.

'And I am a dead man,' Theseus replies. His member jumps to attention as he kisses me, and the emotion conveyed through our bodily contact sets my head and senses reeling. I pull myself up to mount him.

'Wait,' he pleads. 'I want to hold you — could you not free just one of my arms? Please?'

My state of arousal sends me searching urgently for a blade — with two legs and one arm still bound, he is hardly a threat to me. I spy a knife and my mental summons brings it flying across the room and into my grasp. I slice through the leather strap that binds Theseus's right arm. When I look into my imminent lover's face I am moved, for I have never witnessed such adoration before.

'You are extraordinary,' he tells me, his voice rich with tenderness as his freed arm enfolds me and pulls me closer. 'In another life I would marry you.'

I am not insulted, for I understand it is meant as a compliment. 'To the Ha-mazon, marriage is an act of treason,' I say.

'And sex is an act of war,' he adds regretfully.

'And war is an act of love,' I conclude.

Theseus is frustrated by our creed. 'So in order to prove my love I must make war with you?'

'Indeed.' I smile to encourage him. 'So what are you waiting for? Make war with me!'

Submerged in a kiss so involved and all-consuming, I am unaware of anything beyond the pleasure within my body. This experience is more intense than battle, and more exciting than a covert mission. New and powerful emotions rush through me like the waves of a stormy sea; I am drowning in a state of bliss previously unknown to me. By the time my objective is achieved and the seed of Theseus flows inside me, the Prince of Attica is free of all his bonds and our bodies lie entwined on my bed of padded skins.

'Again,' I urge playfully, and the source of my pleasure laughs and rolls on his side, propping up his head with one hand to speak with me.

'Sweet Ann.' He uses my sister's pet name for me and I realise he must have still been conscious when she gave me my final orders. 'Do you not have other plans for me?'

All the new emotions I am feeling weaken my resolve to carry out my orders; the thought of never knowing such pleasure as this again fills me with dread. Even though I am well aware that this prince's fond words and caresses are merely his escape plan, I am willingly enchanted.

'You would kill me if given half the chance,' I say.

'Is that right?' His challenge is a little unnerving. 'Do you recall cutting my other bonds in the course of our lovemaking?'

311

I do not, and shockwaves rock my body as I see him produce my blade from behind his back.

'I have had it the entire time.' He hands me the weapon and all I can do is swallow. 'I can hardly kill the most beautiful thing I have ever seen. Still, you have a job to do,' he positions the knife in my hand so that I might take aim at his heart. 'If you are the last thing I see, then I die a happy man.'

My entire life has centred around one premise: that men are mindless, self-centred, murdering perverts. But if they are not, then how many good men have I killed?

Tears of protest well in my eyes. 'I can hardly kill the most beautiful thing I have ever seen.' I turn the blade towards my own heart instead.

'No.' Theseus stays my hand.

'They will kill me anyway,' I say, struggling for possession of the weapon.

'Come with me back to Attica,' he begs and I cease to battle him.

'They will pursue us,' I tell him, releasing my weapon into his possession. 'You will start a war over me.'

'Your queen started that war when she ordered my death,' Theseus corrects. 'And you may well be carrying the heir to the throne of Attica. I will not have him slaughtered at birth, or before.'

A voice interrupts us from the doorway. 'Get dressed, we need to depart.' It is Herakles, and he slaps his hands together to rally us.

I stand, naked, and will the knife back into my hand. 'How did you escape?'

He shrugs. 'I am Herakles.' The knife is snatched from my possession and flies straight to the huge warrior's grasp. 'Did I mention we are in a bit of a hurry?'

He turns to face in the other direction while we dress. 'Is there a back way out of this city?' he asks.

'I can get you out,' I assure them, for our city is riddled with secret passages and escape routes and I know all of them.

There is no chance to engage in conversation until we reach the Mycenaean army still camped by the sea. As the troops prepare to depart, I ask Herakles about the sack he is carrying. He produces from it the golden girdle of the Ha-mazon queen.

My labrys — my double-headed axe — is in my hand faster than I can think to draw it from where it rested against my back. 'What have you done?'

Herakles backs up to plead his case and avoid a swipe from my axe. 'I just put her to sleep,' he says.

'Please do not kill my best friend.' Theseus appeals for me to calm down.

'Give it back!' I swipe again but Herakles evades the blow.

'I'm just going to borrow it,' he assures me.

'No, you are not!' I lunge at his stomach with the blunt end of my labrys, and wind him momentarily. 'While you have the girdle, my queen is vulnerable!'

'I have friends in high places looking out for her,' he says cockily. 'No harm will come to her, I promise.'

The rage inside me begs to be unleashed. 'Are you insane? Your "friends in high places" are the very reason we have isolated ourselves from men and your godly friends for centuries!'

I prepare to strike, but for the second time this night Theseus stays my hand from killing.

'I believe him, Antiope,' he says calmly.

'I will abandon my people, but I will not forsake them, Theseus,' I reply, my weapon still poised. 'You ask too much of me.'

'Herakles is doing this penance to save his soul,' he reasons. 'If the betrayal of your tribe is on his conscience, that would seem to defeat his purpose.'

I stare at Herakles, trying to divine the truth for myself.

Herakles makes a final appeal. 'Beyond this world I have a divine purpose, but if my penance is not done before I die …' He shakes his head. 'I will be damned like most of my relatives. So please, Antiope, have mercy on my soul by trusting me.'

'All right, you may borrow the girdle.' Why do I care? What am I thinking? I back away from the warrior and look to Theseus. 'I will stay and help guard my queen.'

'No!' Theseus protests. 'They will kill you!'

'Not before it is known whether I carry the next Queen of the Hamazons in my belly,' I say, and continue to back away from them. Our

313

queen will never mate and I am her next of kin, so it is my daughter who will become heir to the throne of Pontus. 'So you have nine months to see the girdle safely returned.'

'And what if you are not with child?' Theseus reaches for me, despite my weapon warding him off.

'Then I shall be dead when you get here,' I conclude coldly and push him away, although the fire he started in my chest is burning a hole right through me. I want to stay with him.

'Please come with me.' Theseus brushes my double-axe aside to take hold of me.

But I am resolute about my decision; neither his sweet words nor his touch is going to sway me. 'You wanted to prove your love, so now fate has awarded you the chance.'

'Theseus, time to go!' Herakles calls from a rowboat.

Theseus sadly resigns himself to the situation and my challenge. 'You live up to your legend while I am gone, and take good care of our son,' he instructs and then kisses me.

The moment is gone before I realise and he walks away from me. *You will forget me*, I say in my mind. *I know it.*

'I am going to marry you, Antiope,' he calls back.

'Time will tell,' I reply. I am sceptical: is it possible to place my faith in a man and trust his love for me will save my life? Death seems far more likely.

I am dragged before my queen as a traitor and discover my crime in releasing the hostages is far greater than I had imagined, for Herakles failed to mention that he had killed Asteria while making his escape. I am so gullible! Herakles has no intention of returning the girdle, and Theseus has charmed his way to freedom, just as my sisters warned he would. The head of our armies, my mentor and dear friend, is dead and I am sentenced to join her in the afterlife. But in the meantime, my queen will wait to see if I am with child, and if so, whether I am carrying the heir to her throne.

I am indeed pregnant. I am imprisoned in a tower of the palace and isolated from all contact with my sisters. From my high window I watch them happily enjoying the life I used to share. My only company is the child in my belly, to whom I have become more attached than I could have imagined. I do not intend to allow anyone to murder my only friend through this trial; I intend to fight to the death and then sail the seven seas to see this child to safety, if fate decrees it to be a boy. Occasionally I find myself imagining that Prince Theseus will come to our rescue and steal us both away to safety. It is a foolish dream, for nowhere is safe for us now that I am marked as a traitor; the Ha-mazon will hunt me down.

Months roll by and as my time draws near, I begin to formulate an escape plan for my child, should I need one. I have not allowed my condition to let my warrior skills wane — I have all day, every day, to train. Yes, I will be weak from delivering my baby, but I have been badly wounded many times and fought on, and never before have I had so much incentive to triumph.

On the day my labour pains begin, I am sitting at my tower window and notice some strange metallic objects moving across the sky. My heart fills with terror for this can herald only one thing. 'Nagas!' I yell to my sisters down below. The Nagas are the lizard people who were servants and slaves of the Nefilim before they rose up in rebellion against their masters.

At any other time my sisters would ignore my call, so I am relieved to see women rush to the warning horns to put our city on high alert.

My next contraction takes hold and is stronger than those before it. The door to my tower opens and my younger sister and midwife, Melonippe, enters. 'Anything?' she queries impatiently.

'No, nothing.' I smile and struggle to right my cramping body; I ignore the pain — a discipline I am well used to.

'I am needed to mount our defence,' she advises. I see the fear in my sister's eyes; of all our enemies, the Nagas are the only foe we dread. 'I shall be back to check on you when I can.'

'Leave me a weapon, Mel,' I plead.

She shakes her head. 'I'll make sure the tower door is locked.'

'I know I am bound for execution and not worthy of protection, but I am the last line of defence for your future queen,' I reason.

Melonippe reluctantly reaches for the dagger on her hip.

315

'That will be useless against the Nagas,' I object. 'I need my labrys.'

The Nagas are the reason that the labrys is the Ha-mazon weapon of choice for hand-to-hand combat. When Lilith and her daughters first wandered the face of the Earth in search of a new home, they were attacked by a swarm of the Nagas, who had not died off as the Nefilim had thought. As the lizard race had no females of their own kind, they raped the women. They did not succeed in taking hostages, as Lilith used her superhuman powers to drive the creatures away, but many of the women, including Lilith, were left impregnated in the wake of the attack. However, the battle had taught them much about their enemy. They knew arrows and blades could not penetrate the reptilians' body scales, and that the only way to kill the Nagas was to behead them. And one needed an axe or a good sword for that. The women designed the labrys and used it to fend off any further attacks, and when the half-breed creatures the women were carrying were born, they too were beheaded with the labrys. All except Lilith's spawn: he was born with superhuman strength and cunning. He escaped decapitation to establish himself as the ruler of the Nagas.

'Please, Mel.' With my final plea, the contraction passes.

She glares at me, despising me for my betrayal, yet loving me still as her sibling. 'I'll see what I can do,' she says, and leaves.

I look to the objects hovering high above our city and I pray to my great foremother Lilith to deliver us from this attack. Surely it cannot be coincidence that we have not seen these creatures for hundreds of years and yet they choose to visit us now, when our queen is not protected by the girdle of power. Are they aware of her vulnerability? Could it be that Herakles and Theseus were the source of this information? The probability stabs at my heart with more intensity than the labour pains that aggravate my body. My illusions of love are fading fast, and I accept that I shall probably pay with my life for the compassion I showed those men. Until then, I will kill any creature that gets between me and my child's freedom. The Nagas will not attack until nightfall, which, judging by the shortening gaps between my contractions, is when my child will enter this world.

The door to my tower opens and Melonippe places my labrys on the floor. 'I wish you were fighting with us, Ann . . . I miss you.'

I rise and waddle to the door, which is closed and locked before I reach it. 'I miss you too, Mel,' I call through the heavy barrier. Tears of regret and sentiment well in my eyes. 'I will not forget this kindness. May the Goddess be in you this day. You know where I am if you need me.'

I retrieve my weapon and keep it close. Now that my labrys is in my hand, my child's future is assured.

The pain is so intense that my consciousness has withdrawn inside of me, focused on nothing but dispersing the cause of my agony from my body. Some time ago I heard the battle cry. I know my people are under attack but I am hard pressed to be of aid or even to care; death would be a welcome relief. The tower has fallen into darkness, which, in my defenceless position, I prefer. I hang from a crossbar in an upright position, bearing down with all my might. My grip on the bar is weakening and my legs are beginning to fail me, but to lie down will slow the birth process and I need to have this baby now! Not in all my days have I felt so exhausted and never has it been so important for me to endure.

I summon all my strength for one last attempt at birthing this baby from my vertical position. Before I can even push, I feel my child bursting its own way into the world. I crouch in the darkness to assist and catch my babe, and wrap its body quickly, then struggle to deliver the afterbirth. It is a long and arduous task, for I am sore. Once I have shed my burden, the cramping subsides and I cut and tie the cord that once bound my babe to me. I make a sling from some fabric I have been storing for just this purpose, and hold my babe to my body. It locates my nipple and begins suckling.

I am reaching into the sling to check its sex, when I spy a creature at the window of my tower, the moonlight at its back. It must have scaled the wall. My pain has lessened and again I have my wits about me and am aware of the battle taking place below me in the city. Now it seems the battle has come to me. I silently take my labrys in hand and back away from the bloodied birth site.

The creature stands upright as it reaches the floor — it is a good foot taller than I am. Then it drops to all fours and, nose to the floor, follows its hunger to the afterbirth. As the creature devours it with relish, I bring down my weapon and sever its head. The body falls and twitches on the floor.

There is a banging at the tower door. At the same time, a second reptilian crawls in through the window. I draw a deep breath for strength. If the Nagas knock down the door, I will have my escape route.

'Antiope!' My heart skips a beat to hear the voice of Theseus just beyond the door. 'Are you alive?' he begs to know.

I dare not answer and betray my position to my enemy, who has spied his companion's corpse on the floor.

'Stand clear!' my prince yells in warning, and the door bursts open. Herakles stumbles into the dark tower room to confront the reptilian warrior. The Nagas lashes out, making several nasty gashes in the arm of the huge warrior. Herakles looks mildly annoyed. Grabbing the lizard from behind by the chin and around the shoulders, he tears its head clean off.

I have never been so pleased to see anyone in my life; this is my dream come true!

'Antiope!' Theseus enters carrying a torch, which he passes to Herakles, and rushes to embrace me.

'Careful.' I hold him at bay, lest he crush the child strapped to my front.

'Our son?' His worried expression transforms into wonder and expectation.

'I do not know the child's sex,' I tell him honestly.

'Shall we see?'

At my nod, he unties the sling. Herakles brings the torch closer, but we hear someone climbing the tower stairs. Theseus reties the knot and we all stand with weapons poised.

Melonippe appears in the doorway. 'You're still alive,' she says, seeming as surprised as I am that we both survived. 'The queen wishes to see all of you in the temple. You are to drop your weapons and follow me.'

'You brought back the girdle?' I ask Herakles and he winks at me.

'It is already in your queen's possession.'

The relief is incredible, although it is doubtful that this will change my sentence. I whack Herakles in the jaw with the blunt staff between the blades of my weapon. 'That is for killing Asteria,' I tell him.

'You killed one of her kinswomen?' It seems this is also news to Theseus.

'A truly regrettable accident,' Herakles admits.

Theseus is clearly not happy. 'That changes everything! Why did you not tell me?' Now it is the prince who wants to kill his best friend.

'We would never have come this far if I had,' Herakles replies.

Melonippe whistles, drawing their attention to the fact that she has an arrow aimed in their direction. 'As much as I would love to see you tear shreds off him,' she tells Theseus, 'my queen awaits.'

The men file out peacefully and I follow.

'What sex is the child?' my sister asks as I pass her.

If it is a boy, she will slaughter him this instant. 'It is a girl,' I say. 'You have your queen.'

'You must give her up to me,' Melonippe says.

I delay the inevitable. 'But she is feeding.'

'Then we shall find her a nurse.' Her voice hardens with annoyance.

'No!' Theseus turns back to assist me.

'Yes!' I say, holding up a hand to stop him in his tracks. 'I am a security risk to her now; we all are.' I hope that he will not question my bluff.

Melonippe exchanges her bow for a blade, and waits for me to undo the sling holding the baby and tie it about her instead.

'Now move,' she says, and motions us all down the stairs ahead of her.

In the temple, Hyleana waits to take possession of her heir. Melonippe delivers the babe into the arms of our queen. I wait alongside Herakles and Theseus for our fate to be decided. The queen admires the sleeping babe in her arms and, peeking under the cloth, checks that my claim of a girl child is true. I hold my breath to pray that my faith in the Holy Mother is sound — that she has delivered unto me a girl who will live!

319

Theseus silently takes hold of my hand and squeezes it for strength. Hyleana lowers the cloth, still appearing enchanted with the child, and I breathe a great sign of relief. No matter what happens now, my child is safe.

'Antiope.'

Fatigued and injured, I step forward and bow deeply before the queen, then wait for her to pass judgement on me.

'You betrayed your people by releasing these captives who trespassed on our land, murdered your kinswoman and stole our most sacred treasure. I have decided that death is too good for you, dear sister, thus I sentence you to marry your prince and return with him to Attica.'

I gasp with a mix of welling joy, relief and sorrow. I raise my eyes to view my sister and queen, and I know she is smiling behind her veil. 'Your mercy is great, your Highness.'

'You will not think so in ten years,' she warrants, as I step back and take my place alongside the other accused.

'Herakles.' Hyleana summons him forward and he goes down on one knee before her. 'You saved my life this day, but had you not stolen my girdle from me, my life and city would not have been at risk for you to save.' Her tone hardens. 'My primary grievance is that you killed our champion and most trusted adviser. Do you have anything to say in your own defence?'

'I am guilty as charged, your Highness.' Herakles sounds remorseful and humble. 'Is there any way I can make amends for her death?'

Hyleana does not have to consider the notion very long. 'As Asteria was the equal of ten Ha-mazon warriors, if you father ten Ha-mazon babies, I will consider the debt repaid.'

'And what if I father boys?' Herakles queries. 'Would they be given to me to raise?'

Hyleana dwells on this a moment. 'I agree, but only on the condition that they are never told of their origins, for if they ever set foot in Pontus, they shall be killed as surely as they would have been at birth.'

'I look forward to enjoying your hospitality for some time yet,' Herakles says, and steps back to join us. 'It will be a refreshing change to love my way to freedom.'

'The pleasure will be all ours, I am sure,' Hyleana returns.

She calls forth the last of the accused with some affection in her voice. He kneels before her, even though he is not subject to her rule nor looking for her pardon.

'Theseus, you are the first man ever to capture the heart of a Hamazon. You escaped our custody fairly, without crime against or injury to any of my people. This day you brought your forces to aid in the defence of Pontus against a formidable foe, at the cost of many Attican fatalities. Thus I believe I owe you a favour. Ask of me what you will, Prince of Attica.'

Theseus, formally excused of any crime, assumes his rightful standing position. 'I have only two wishes, your Majesty. One, you have already realised.' He glances back to me and his devotion fills me with joy. 'My other wish is that Antiope and I may raise our child together in peace.'

I can hardly believe he would be so bold. The queen will never agree.

'Ask yourself, Theseus,' the queen poses, 'what is in the best interest of my daughter? Here she will be raised as a goddess, to become the independent leader of her own mighty nation. Can you offer her that?'

Theseus looks to me for my advice.

'We can have other children,' I say, my words shooting daggers into my heart for the thought of parting from my new babe is agony. 'Her destiny is here, and ours lies elsewhere.'

The prince swallows his disappointment and pain and turns to respond to the queen. 'Then my wish is that you take great care of our daughter.' He bows as tears overwhelm him, but is composed when he rises and steps back to join me.

The queen sighs, moved by Theseus's resolve. 'I never thought I would meet a man who is as selfless as a woman,' she says. 'You would honestly put aside your own wishes in favour of what might be better for your female offspring?'

'Is that not wise, your Majesty?' The banter is taxing on Theseus's heavy heart.

Hyleana leans forward on her throne. 'It is most wise, Theseus.' Her voice is gentle and filled with admiration. 'You are a beautiful aberration among men, and I cannot bring myself to destroy a babe with the potential to be another such wondrous exception to the rule.'

Hyleana holds high my sleeping child, allowing the cloth to fall away to reveal a boy child.

The gasps of all present are near deafening. I am bombarded by shock and relief at once.

'I will spare the life of your son and heir, Theseus,' Hyleana decrees. 'Come and claim him.'

The sight of my son being delivered into his father's hands brings an end to my endurance. The shock of the birth, the Nagas attack, my rescue and absolution overpower me and I collapse onto the cool stone of the temple floor . . .

The rotation angle of my atomic structure altered direction and my conscious self was delivered into the central chamber amid Amenti's halls once more.

This time the experience was more bearable, just as Sinclair had promised, and yet there was so much information to digest now that my consciousness had been freed of the all-consuming effects of the hall.

'I recognised so many of the players in Antiope's tragedy,' I said with some excitement. 'You, of course; and Melonippe was Susan; and although I never saw Lady Charlotte Cavandish in her younger days, I feel I recognised her soul-mind in Hyleana, Queen of the Ha-mazon. I met her once before: she was the healing lady of the desert, Denera,' I suddenly realised. It was no surprise really that such a highly acclaimed psychic as Lady Charlotte Cavandish would turn out to be the first of the Dragon Queens, Lilith, who was indeed Zalman's partner on the Amenti Project. This revelation pleased me immensely, for it meant that one day in the future I would be reunited with my old mentor.

Now that I had regained my third root race consciousness, I remembered the story of the founding mother of the Ha-mazon race. 'Is it true that Lilith gave birth to a half-breed Draconian, who went on to claim leadership of the Dracon?' I asked.

'That is unfortunately true,' Sinclair said. 'The beast took the name Poseidonis for a long time, but has had many other names. And what other pearls of wisdom did you glean from your latest experience?'

'Are you testing my comprehension again, Captain Sinclair?'

'I merely wish to demonstrate some of the effects Amenti's halls are having on your conscious memory,' he replied winningly. 'For example ...' He held out his hand and a labrys manifested there, the double-headed axe favoured by Ha-mazon warriors for its ability to decapitate a Dracon opponent.

He handed the weapon to me and I laughed. Then I noticed how comfortable the large axe felt in my hands and realised I knew how to wield it. I began to execute one of Antiope's training exercises and Sinclair took a few steps back. 'I am doing it!' I cried, filled with excitement. 'I killed Dracon with this weapon.'

'You did?' Captain Sinclair sounded surprised.

I was puzzled. 'The way you have been talking, I assumed you knew what had transpired.'

'It is true that this was a key lifetime for me also, and we did fight a common enemy together, but I did not spot a Dracon during my entire incarnation as Theseus, King of Attica.'

'What?' I lowered my weapon, confused. 'Are you saying history has been altered?'

'I couldn't say.' Sinclair glanced to the next porthole, which was yellow in frequency. 'When you have traversed all of Amenti's halls, I will investigate the anomaly.'

The next porthole led to the age of Atlantis and I eyed it with reserve. 'Do you think I will be fortunate enough to be deposited at the height of the continent's golden age of learning?'

Sinclair winced. 'You and I did not come to Earth to take part in the good and prosperous times.'

'So ... it's back to chaos and catastrophe I go,' I said, taking a step towards the third, yellow-gold, porthole.

The captain grinned. 'Look how much knowledge and awareness you obtained from your Lemurian debacle.' He had a valid point.

REVELATION 21

POSEIDONIS

ROOT RACE FOUR — PHYSICAL (11,000 BC); THE ATLANTEANS

I stand in line with my parents behind a host of other hopeful aspirants waiting to be presented to the Master Scribe, Hermes, as a candidate for his instruction. Master Hermes, the architect of the Pyramids and many other monuments, is something of a mystery. He has been alive for as long as my people can remember, teaching those in the civilised world — beyond the borders of Poseidonis — the many things necessary for a useful and purposeful life. Some say he is the son of a god, as old as time itself, who has assumed human form. Others claim he is a mortal who found the secret to eternal life, and yet others think that the Master is so enlightened that he has reached an everlasting state of being.

Master Hermes rarely takes on students, but he has travelled across many nations this season to canvass all children aged thirteen. It is said the Master seeks two particular individuals, one male and one female, prophesied by himself to be his protégés for the foreseeable future — a position that holds the promise of being a future counsel to kings and pharaohs.

My people are the Pelasgian, a Mediterranean tribe who inhabit the land from Argos to Dodona and the Strymon. I was born into a rich, landowning family and am considered bright for a female. Now of an age when I must marry or pursue some other gainful pursuit, I am grateful for the Holy Decree that orders my parents to present me to the Master Hermes, for marriage interests me not.

To my surprise, and my parents' delight, the Master greets me as an old friend whom he is well pleased to see after some time apart.

'Praise the great plan, I have found one of you at last! And the other must be close, for you are never far apart.' The Master takes hold of both my hands and peers deep into my eyes with his own of pale violet; I feel that I am staring at an angel. 'I know your destiny, dear sister,' he tells me, 'and if you will come with me to Egypt, I foresee that we will be of great aid to one another and to all the known world.'

I cannot imagine what aid I could offer to Master Hermes and the world at large, but I am very excited by the opportunity. My parents are thrilled, both with the honour bestowed upon me and the financial compensation they receive for the loss of their daughter.

'Your name from now on will be Aleka, which means the defender of mankind,' Master Hermes announces, and I am promptly handed over into his care to begin a new life of learning across the sea. I am not at all apprehensive about my future, for with such a mentor it can only be a wondrous experience.

Our departure is delayed whilst the Master interviews boy after boy in search of the second soul he has prophesied. Only when the temple priests assure the Master that he has seen every thirteen-year-old boy in the district does he finally concede it is time to move on — but not back to Egypt as hoped. We must head for the next town, and the next, until the Master's prophecy is fulfilled.

'Why is it so important that your prophecy be realised?' I ask as we make our way along the seashore towards the next town.

He stops still and I stop beside him. 'I hope to avert a terrible disaster,' he tells me, then walks towards something that has caught his interest. I follow his line of sight to see a young man crouched down on the sand, scaling fish on a board.

'How old are you, son?' the Master asks as we approach.

The boy continues about his task without looking up. 'I am thirteen years old.'

'And why were you not brought to see the Master Hermes in the temple, as requested by your priests?'

'There was no point in taking me to *see* the Master as I am blind.' The lad finally looks in our direction; his glassy blue eyes are confirmation of his disability. 'The Master would surely not consider a blind boy worthy of his time and knowledge.'

'Quite correct,' agrees the Master as he places his hands over the lad's eyes. 'See me now?' He takes his hands away and when the boy parts his eyelids I see that his pupils have turned a vibrant blue.

'Yes,' he gasps, his shock and excitement landing him on his behind. He squints and shades his eyes from the soft evening light. 'I see light, my lord . . . I see colour! I see . . .' he looks my way and strains to focus harder '. . . shape.'

'Very good,' says Master Hermes. 'Now you must come with me to Egypt. Have you any parents I need to consult?'

The lad shakes his head. 'I have brothers, but they will not argue against a holy decree.'

'Then why the concerned look upon your face, lad? Is your current life so satisfying?' Neither the Master nor myself can understand the boy's reluctance.

The lad gets to his knees to beg the Master's pardon. 'No, your Holiness, I am greatly honoured by your interest, but I am not worthy for I cannot even write my own name.'

'Of course you cannot,' Master Hermes says, 'as I have not yet told you your name. From now on, you will be Manetho. In hieroglyphics this means "gift of Thoth" and I shall teach you how to write it myself.'

At first I like Manetho: he is humble, studious, friendly and good company. During the course of our ten years of study together, however, he becomes increasingly competitive, secretive and proud. We are both made privy to secret structures, doctrines and powers that not even the High Priests of Memphis are aware of. Answerable only to the Pharaoh and Master Hermes, Manetho and I are revered as servants of the gods wherever we go. The Master awakens dormant superhuman powers in us, which are realised by undergoing a series of ancient activations that the Master refers to as time codes. These giant, ultra-colourful works of art are located underground in a cave across the sea to the north-east of Egypt. There is a shortcut to the hall of codes from beneath the Great Pyramid, which we utilise often. By concentrating on the geometry of the complex symbols within these ultra-colourful pictorial codes and invoking the compatible mantra, a conscious recognition of super-conscious memory is eventually triggered. A side effect of this process is the unlocking of our psychic potential.

There are rare times, like today, when I find Manetho tolerable. He is excited and in good cheer because the Master has requested that we meet him in the hall of codes and this can only mean one thing — today we finally integrate the last of the twelve time codes. We know that this event will mark the end of our training with the Master, for with this initiation we will make contact with our super-conscious selves and discover our true destiny in this life, as prophesied by the Master when he first came in search of us.

Master Hermes looks very grave when he joins us in the ancient subterranean hall. 'Time has caught up with us,' he declares, 'there is not a moment to waste.'

He directs us towards the final time code painting and I follow him obediently. Manetho is not so pliable.

'What has happened?' he demands.

'Afterwards,' Master Hermes says, but Manetho is already probing our Master's mind for answers. 'Manetho!' the Master growls in warning, for he is not focused on suppressing what he knows. By the time he has psychically shielded his knowledge, Manetho has his answer and his face fills with horror.

'The dark forces of the Emperor Poseidonis have launched an attack on the peaceful merchant nations that border our homeland,' he cries out in shock, already retreating from the chamber. 'I must go to their defence!'

Master Hermes forestalls Manetho's departure. 'I foresaw this event,' he says. 'It is why I went in search of you, why I trained you. Integrate the final time code and then will you know how you may best be of aid in this affair.'

'You knew this would happen and yet you warned no one?' Manetho is incensed. 'I have brothers who will be called to arms —'

'Until a situation manifests, it cannot be construed as reality,' the Master says, endeavouring to calm his student. 'In telling the nations involved that they may be attacked by the forces of Poseidonis, I would not be telling them anything that they haven't been aware of for thousands of years.'

'And yet our training timed out fairly neatly.' Manetho refuses to be pacified.

'Will you not trust me just one more day?' Master Hermes appeals. 'Let us finish what we started all those years ago.'

Manetho does not look well disposed towards the suggestion. 'For all I know, that last code might relinquish my will to you, or some other alien being!'

'Manetho, you go too far!' I was horrified that he could imply the Master was not human.

Manetho ignored my protest. 'There is only one thing I wish to know,' he said to our mentor. 'Does your divine plan involve saving my brothers?'

'Their mortal lives you cannot save,' the Master says regretfully, and Manetho heads straight for the nearest exit. 'But you can help save their immortal souls and the lives of all those who will be embroiled in the forthcoming holocaust!' Master Hermes calls after him.

I run after Manetho and catch him by the arm, pulling him to a standstill. We may be rivals but we are also friends. 'Watch me do the activation,' I plead. 'Then you will know if it is safe.'

'I do not have the time,' he says.

'Surely a few hours will not —'

'The warriors of Poseidonis are black magicians!' he interrupts. 'The Nagas are with them, plus their low-density spirits, summoned forth into the world by the blood sacrifices of innocents! Who can help my brothers, our homeland, if not I?' He gazes into my face, and the frustration and determination I see in his eyes stifles any further protest I might like to make. Is this stabbing pain in my chest my own heart breaking, I wonder.

'I shall miss you, Manetho.' Tears well in my eyes as I realise the truth of my words.

'You never needed me,' he says, and I am surprised as he is usually so full of himself. He moves to depart, but then returns to embrace and kiss me.

'I always wanted to do that,' he says, then lets me go and leaves me dumbstruck.

As I watch him vanish into the labyrinth that leads to the porthole back to Giza, I sense the Master come to stand behind me.

'I pride myself on my psychic aptitude and I never even suspected an attraction,' he muses.

'Will his training keep him alive?'

'Perhaps.' Master Hermes seems no more certain of the outcome than I am. 'Now, however, the fate of the human planetary consciousness rests firmly upon your shoulders, Aleka. Time to contact your super-conscious,' he suggests.

With a deep intake of breath for courage, I nod that I am ready.

The last time code is the most complex to integrate and the process is a lengthy exercise of visualisation and harmonic stimulation. Afterwards, I feel I am on sensory overload and am quite euphoric.

'Rest now,' the Master instructs. 'You have done very well.'

'But I do not feel as if I made contact . . .'

My knees give way beneath me and I collapse. The Master catches me and lowers me to the ground.

'Do not resist the influx of consciousness,' he advises.

Wave after divine wave rushes into me via the energy centres of my subtle body and I am filled with a greater awareness of being than ever before. Manetho was right to fear that this activation would submit his will to an advanced alien being, but he did not fathom that it would be his ultimate self.

My eyelids part and I see the Master through my new multidimensional perspective and recognise him as Prince of the Anunnaki. 'Mathu.'

'Solarian.' He seems greatly relieved to be addressing my true self. 'We have a serious security issue that only the scientific acumen of the Amenti Council can avert. I suspect that we need to change the frequency codes protecting the Arc Porthole passage.'

Half of me is shocked by his suggestion, and the other half is shocked that I know exactly what he is talking about.

During an attempt by the Emperor of Poseidonis in the distant past to abuse the Sphere of Amenti for unsafe energy practices, the Sphere was moved from the inner Earth realms of the Anu to the heart of a planet in the Pleiades system. A bridge between the worlds was incorporated into the Amenti system, and this passage was known as the Arc Porthole. This bridge would enable the Sphere to return to Earth when it again held a consciousness high enough to host the Blue Flame of Amenti.

'Can Amenti's staff isolate the main crystal generator beneath the City of Poseidonis,' Mathu goes on, 'leaving only Poseidonis with a direct link to the Arc Porthole?'

'Only if we decommission all the surrounding generators,' I reply. 'But without these power sources, civilisation will be cast back into the Stone Age and the resulting hardship is going to have a very detrimental effect on the human evolution project.'

'So will not having a planet to evolve on,' Mathu points out.

'Have the agents of darkness become a security threat to the Sphere of Amenti?' I ask, wondering why the need for the upgrade on the Arc shield codes.

Mathu shakes his head. 'But I suspect a threat at any moment.'

I recall the news that sent Manetho rushing off: that the Emperor Poseidonis's seafaring force has attacked the nations surrounding Egypt. Mathu knows that the real prize Poseidonis seeks is the ultimate power source — the Blue Flame of Amenti — access to which can only be gained from beneath the Giza plateau.

Two phases of the moon after his departure from Giza, Manetho does return, grieving the deaths of his brothers, but glad to bear news of the defeat and retreat of Poseidonis.

'Are you sure about this?' The Master is wary for he knows the Emperor is cunning; like Master Hermes, the Dark Emperor has been in existence for as long as anyone can remember, proof that he is not pure human.

'I find it hard to believe and I was there!' Manetho emphasises. 'When Poseidonis sent only half his fleet into combat against my people and we were outnumbered two to one, I thought our aim impossible. Still, our vessels were smaller and easier to manoeuvre, and despite all the strategies and sorcery of our enemies the weather was with us and our adversaries suffered an overwhelming defeat. When the rest of the Emperor's fleet was sent into battle, again we drove them back, but this time with heavy losses to my people.'

Manetho did not mention his brothers, but I perceived mental images of how he had lost them all to terrible deaths.

'With the second wave of ships came the Nagas and their transparent otherworldly creatures,' Manetho continued. 'They possessed weapons the like of which I have never seen and were relentless in their use of them. They inject a spike into their victims, by which they can literally suck out their life!'

I am horrified by this, but Master Hermes does not look at all surprised.

'I nearly fell victim to one of the death spikes myself,' Manetho tells us, 'but my attacker spotted this.' He grabs the glyph of his name hanging from the chain around his neck. 'After inspecting it closely, the serpent warrior retracted the deadly spiked weapon, slapped me on the back and announced to his brothers-in-arms, "This one lives". Whereupon one of them clobbered me over the head with a plank of wood. When I awoke, the Emperor's force had retreated. I was told that the Emperor himself had been forced ashore and, with only a small band of warriors to support his retreat, had fled overland back to his island.'

I applaud Manetho's bravery, but the Master appears concerned. He turns Manetho around and pulls a small metal spike from his cloak.

'What is it, Master?' I ask.

'It is a means to find me,' he replies. 'We must act swiftly. Aleka, you must put our evacuation plan into immediate effect.'

'But why?'

'The fault is all mine,' Master Hermes assures Manetho and myself. 'But we have no time for discussion. Do exactly as I have instructed ... I am depending on you both.'

Then he notices a weak vibration emanating from the tiny metal spike in his hand. He points us towards one of the pillars in the temple and commands, 'Hide!'

I grab hold of Manetho's hand to speed his compliance.

'I am so sorry,' he tells our mentor, horrified at having brought danger to him.

'Fear not, Manetho, I foresaw this also.' Master Hermes waves him to hide and Manetho conceals himself close to me behind the pillar.

A company of lizard-like warriors appear out of thin air! I understand the theory of superconductive teleportation technology, but this is the first time that I have seen it in practice. Our Master stands tall in the face of the enemy.

'A direct route, my friend,' the reptilian says once he is fully manifest, indicating the spike still in Master Hermes' hand. 'Much easier than fighting through several nations to get to you.'

'Why do you seek me, Taejax?' The Master is polite but to the point.

The reptilian lowers his weapon, although his companions keep theirs trained on Master Hermes. 'I want to give you the opportunity to make up for your treachery. Tell me the frequency codes of the Arc shields and I will forgive you for abandoning me all those years ago, for betraying the rebellion that you helped to start!'

'I must try to be fair to both my human tribe and my reptilian brothers,' the Master reasons.

'Save the speeches,' hisses Taejax. 'All I want from you is the codes.'

'How many catastrophes must you live through before you learn this lesson, my friend?' the Master asks. 'How many more times will your kind try to abuse the power of the blue flame before you realise that it cannot be used for base purposes?'

'As many times as it takes to achieve our objective!' Taejax grabs hold of the Master by the collar of his robes. 'Poseidonis will get the codes out of you, *old friend.*'

The intruders and the Master vanish from sight.

My heart pounds in my chest as I mentally run through what I must do. I move away from the pillar to find Manetho still pressed hard against me. 'I must be about the bidding of the Master,' I say and shrug him off.

Manetho pulls me around to face him. 'Before I left, Master Hermes said something about not being able to save my brothers' lives but that I could save their immortal souls,' he says. 'Do you know what he meant?'

'I do,' I say, and a kiss is my reward. 'Stop that!' I put a little distance between us in order to maintain my focus. The memory of his last kiss has been distracting me for months! 'We are a little pressed for time.'

He suppressed a grin. 'What do you need me to do?'

'Report to the Pharaoh on the Master's behalf and tell him to evacuate every soul he can to the inner Earth territories before dark and then seal the portholes closed.' I look to the sun beyond the temple and note that I have the better part of the afternoon to achieve all I must. 'Then meet me in the Hall of Time Codes,' I tell him, and start towards the Master's quarters beneath Giza.

'Where are you going?'

'To fetch a few items that I must deliver into safe hands,' I call back. 'I promised Master Hermes that, if all else fails, I will see these treasures to their appointed places of safekeeping before it is too late. So hurry — we have much to do!'

'But what will happen if the Emperor gets the information he desires from the Master?'

I realised that Manetho hadn't really understood the reptilians' demands, which meant he was going to find it difficult to convince the Pharaoh that such an evacuation was necessary. I began to explain.

'The Master suspects that Poseidonis has pirated some ankh tools and plans to use them to channel fifth-dimensional energy into the main crystal generator under Poseidonis. This will create a massive electromagnetic pulse that will shoot through the Earth's crystal grid and into the Arc Porthole. With the Arc shields deactivated, the massive pulse will be channelled towards the Sphere of Amenti. When the Sphere is destroyed, the Emperor and his allies plan to extract the blue flame back down through the Arc Porthole and use it as an inexhaustible energy source.'

'What?' Manetho is perplexed, for he has not integrated the final time code and so has no knowledge of his work on the Amenti Project; something I hope to remedy before this day is out.

'Trust me,' I urge him, as time is wasting. 'If the Sphere of Amenti is destroyed, humanity's evolutionary blueprint will be erased forever. Every soul on Earth will be trapped in the lowest three dimensions of creation and continue to reincarnate as part of a slave class. Poseidonis and his minions will use them as miners to dig up the minerals they need for their potions of immortality and their technologies. They also use humans for genetic cross-breeding, and to feed to their drones to keep them strong.'

'That doesn't sound good,' Manetho grants. 'But what should I tell the Pharaoh?'

'Tell him that by nightfall the known world will have disappeared. The Master will give Poseidonis false codes and the Arc Shields will deflect the blast back to where it came from, but this means Atlantis will be destroyed.'

Over the last couple of months, since my full integration of the time codes, Master Hermes and I have been working on ways of isolating the damage of the forthcoming disaster and reinforcing the Amenti system from future attack.

Via my super-conscious contact with Solarian, I was able to instruct the Staff of Amenti to decommission all the remaining power-generating crystals in the Earth's power grid. These giant super-conductive crystal clusters were set in place beneath the twelve stations of the Signet Grid to form an artificial energy matrix to distribute blue flame energy around the globe. Unlike Amenti, which grants access to different time–space locations upon Earth, the twelve stargates of the Signet system lead to different time–space locations on other planets within our universe. The matrix has also powered the civilisations of surface Earth until now. The risk that the matrix might be abused by Poseidonis in the future poses a far greater threat to humanity's evolution than being cast back to a primordial existence for an extensive time. So all the crystal power centres are now concealed within the Earth or beneath the oceans or icecaps for reactivation at a later date. All twelve Signet stations have fallen into darkness, as have all the great cities of surface Earth, bar the isle of Atlantis. The residents of the Earth believe that Poseidonis is to blame for the power failures, and ultimately he is.

Master Hermes and Solarian have also devised and implemented new security measures for the Amenti system. All the passages to the inner Earth territories are to be sealed and shielded, leaving only one way for a human being to physically enter the Sphere of Amenti from this time forth.

They have fashioned two objects to link together to form a key that will lock and unlock the Amenti system. One of the objects is a coiled ring, charged with the energy of the orange-gold flame of Earth's morphogenetic field that is held in density two at the core of the planet. The second object is a staff charged with the blue flame morphogenetic field of Tara. Individually these tools can be used for healing, directing weather patterns and for construction purposes — much as the ankhs have been used in the past. The tools are stored within two lead-lined golden boxes constructed from imperishable wood, which are also batteries that serve to recharge the objects within when they are not in use.

It is my job this day to see these tools and their containers delivered into safe hiding at separate locations upon the globe, until such time as the rightful key-holders incarnate to open Amenti's doors to all humanity. The Arc of the Ring will be taken with the Pharaoh and his royal family into the inner Earth territories, where it will be safeguarded by the Priests of Ur. The Arc of the Rod will be hidden on surface Earth, somewhere beyond the time and place of the pending disaster. But first I need Manetho to integrate the twelfth time code to help me arrange transportation for the Rod.

Manetho joins me in the hall of codes and reports that the evacuation is underway. Then he curiously eyes the golden box I have with me.

'Afterwards,' I say, and point with my torch towards the time code he must integrate. 'The souls of all, including your brothers, are in peril.'

'Lead on,' Manetho says, and submits to my lengthy instruction. When it is completed, he feels as giddy and euphoric as I had. He staggers backward, then takes a seat on the ground to steady himself. 'What have you done?' he demands.

'Try not to resist,' I advise him, as the Master advised me.

'I could never resist you, Solarian.' Suddenly Manetho is acutely coherent.

I realise Manetho's integration of the twelfth code has been successful as I feel Solarian come over me and take control of the situation. 'Polaris?' I say in her voice.

'At your service, my lady.' He grins broadly and I breathe a sigh of relief.

'I need you to contact your key-holder and send him to this time–space location,' I tell him, 'at Mathu's request.'

Just as he advises the task is done, a great rumbling comes from within the labyrinth. I fear that the Master has not been able to withhold his information from Poseidonis until dusk as planned. Then silence. I strain my ears and hear the sound of hurried footsteps approaching the Hall of Time Codes. For a moment my heart is gripped by the fear that Poseidonis has tortured Master Hermes to reveal our plans and now the serpent warriors are on their way to finish us off.

'Fear not, it is the key-holder as requested,' Polaris informs me.

I gasp as a fair, strangely clad version of Manetho enters the hall of codes. But I am not as surprised as Manetho, who leaps to his feet, dumbfounded.

'Aleka.' The fair-skinned stranger tips his hat to me, then looks to my stunned companion. 'Manetho,' he grins. 'Captain Henry Sinclair at your service.'

'Who are you?' Manetho the man is perplexed, and yet his soul knows the answer.

'I am a future you, who has walked the Halls of Amenti and been given the liberty to overcome time and death. Now, I believe you have something for me?'

'Ah yes.' I snap out of my stunned state and motion to the Arc.

'There it is.' Sinclair admiringly inspects the famous treasure. 'Is the other Arc safely away?'

I nod, still in awe of this super-being.

'Excellent.' He stands, and the Arc levitates into the air beside him. Manetho and I gasp in amazement. I have mastered moving objects at will, although for me it takes great preparation and all my concentration; for this man it appears as simple as breathing in and out. Then I remind myself that he is more than human; he is an angel.

'Where will you take it?' I ask.

'Do not fear, this treasure is taking a little trip seven thousand years into the future, to the time of Akhenaton, Pharaoh of Egpyt. He will be your Master incarnate, who will come to be known by his enlightened followers as the *Mosis* — the true and rightful heir to Egypt and to this.'

'But how will you deliver it?' Manetho is curious.

Sinclair waves us to follow him. 'Allow me to show you.'

Manetho relieves me of my torch, enabling me to collect the Master's Emerald Book, and we follow the captain through the labyrinth to a huge cavern. Stairs lead down to an earthen bridge that gives access across an abyss and into the porthole chamber that grants passage back to Giza. Beneath the bridge is a huge vessel, just floating in mid-air.

'My ship, *Kleio*,' announces Sinclair proudly. 'Named for the Goddess of History.'

It is unlike any ship I have ever seen. Its body and sails are constructed from a dull silver metal and gold, and appear far too heavy for catching the breeze.

Manetho, being something of a seaman himself, is fascinated. 'How do you power this?' he asks.

'It has many different sources, but at present it is running on the blue flame energy of the Earth grid. And as the grid is about to be shut down for a very long time, I had best be going, while the going is good.' He walks onto the bridge, leaps from there to one of the metal sails and slides all the way down to the deck. The Arc of the Rod floats down to land on the deck also. 'I would offer you a lift somewhere, but the ramifications on history ... well.' He shrugs in apology. 'Besides, I believe that book needs to be somewhere else?'

I look at the Master's Emerald Book of Knowledge, which I have sworn to deliver to a tomb inside the labyrinth; the Master has left me a map to find my way. 'Dear heavens! I must hurry,' I say. Nightfall cannot be far off. I turn to leave, but Manetho is still gazing at the *Kleio*.

'I am going to be him some day,' he says proudly as, without so much as a breath of wind, the huge vessel disappears in a blaze of light. Then he realises I am about to head in the opposite direction from that which leads to our salvation. 'Where are you going?' he says.

'I promised the Master,' I call back, already climbing the steep staircase that leads to the labyrinth.

Manetho tries to reason with me. 'These tunnels may survive the forthcoming deluge, but without a society to sustain us, we will perish. We must return to Giza before the porthole to the inner Earth is closed!'

'I know,' I yell back, 'but I need to do this first.'

I pause to pull out the Master's map, and wait for Manetho to catch up as he is still in possession of the torch. The path marked leads to a set of open double doors at the end of a corridor. My heart begins to pound in my chest as we run towards them.

We enter a huge rounded shrine carved out of the natural rock. There is a round altar in the centre holding a large metal bowl filled with oil. Manetho ignites it with the torch; by its light we are able to see that the central altar is at the head of an oval sarcophagus. Its lid is inset with a full-body sculpture of the Master Hermes.

'The Master is going to die.' My tears well as I realise this truth.

'*We* are going to die if you do not dispose of that book,' Manetho says sternly, wishing to avoid a sentimental scene.

I lift the Emerald Book to place it on the sarcophagus. The stone hands of the sculpture reach out to take it from my grasp and I gasp, jumping back into Manetho's embrace.

'The Master's magic knows no bounds,' he says, grabbing my hand. 'Time to get to safety.'

I run with Manetho back through the maze, down the stairs, across the cavern bridge and into the porthole that leads to Giza.

Upon entering the altar room, we are thrown from our feet by the violent shaking of the Earth. Guards are ushering people down a staircase that runs beneath the altar block, the huge stone pushed back this day to allow passage. 'Hurry, your Holinesses,' the leader calls upon seeing us. He is ready to order the altar stone pushed back into place in his wake, but stalls the command to wait for us.

The stairs fall into darkness as the entrance is closed over, and for the longest time we descend in confined blackness, the passageway around us shaking violently. My only comfort is in knowing that these stairs have withstood this kind of abuse many times throughout history. Below, I see light and hear voices yelling warning of their intent to close the porthole.

'We are the last,' the guard with us calls out to stall them.

The light comes from an open porthole made of solid gold. We step through it into a long tubular passage with walls lined with running liquid-light, yet not one drop falls upon those who traverse it. I am running with all my might when a great rumble resounds through the tunnel and I am thrown to the ground. The passage begins to collapse behind us and the liquid-light swirls towards us at a frightening pace. Manetho drags me to my feet and I am gripped by fear as I realise we are not going to make it to the antechamber beyond the porthole.

Manetho embraces me as the pulverising force of the collapsing liquid-light field engulfs us. In an instant all the burdens of my mortal life are crushed into blissful oblivion. And Atlantis disappears forever.

'You are a time pirate!' I accused Captain Sinclair upon my return to the Amenti antechamber.

'So, now you know. But I prefer the term "time lord" myself,' he grinned.

'Where did you get the ship?' It was the most amazing form of transportation I had ever seen.

'Polaris left it on Earth for me to find when I was ready,' Sinclair explained, moving around to the next porthole. 'It was hidden within my Signet Grid station, which is attuned to my personal sonic and will therefore open only for me.'

'The Signet Grid,' I repeated, recalling what I had learned of this stargate system during my last journey. 'But Hermes had the Signet system shut down before Atlantis sank, didn't he?' I joined Sinclair in front of the pink-gold porthole.

'I found and reactivated the Polaris station many centuries ago,' the captain said, unable to resist an immodest smirk.

'In Nova Scotia?' I guessed, and Sinclair nodded, looking surprised. 'I read up on you before leaving home,' I admitted. 'Legend has it you discovered America long before Columbus.'

'Thank heavens — at least legend gets the story straight.'

Captain Sinclair was so like my Devere, but even more congenial if that were possible.

'Are you going to kiss me?' he asked, and I realised I had been gazing up at him like a lovesick schoolgirl.

'Do you think I should?' I said; the notion was rather attractive.

He grinned and indicated our spirit forms. 'Here in Amenti that is not advised. That pleasure will have to wait until we have been reunited with our physical forms ... at which time I would strongly advise you to act in accordance with any such desire you might have.'

It was a deliciously awkward moment. I ended it by turning to face the pink-gold porthole. 'Right then,' I said.

'Try not to miss me too much.' Sinclair's words made me laugh as I stepped onto the activation plate.

'Oh.' I turned back as there was one question I needed to ask about the time zone I had just relived. 'Did Hermes manage to kill Poseidonis as planned?'

'We believe so,' the captain said. 'Hermes died to ensure the creature perished with him, and Poseidonis has not been encountered since.'

FROM THE JOURNAL OF CHARLOTTE DEVERE

After penning the account of my mother's past lives in two of Amenti's halls, I was fatigued, hungry and mentally distracted. I wondered how Lady Susan was coping with the massive intake of information — we had not had time to converse, nor to read much of each other's sessions under the influence of the ring; that would have to wait until my mother's journey was over.

Once Lady Susan arrived, I withdrew to my chamber to eat, hoping that Mathu might join me for a pleasant interlude and a little conversation. I had promised Albray I would not be late to relieve Lady Susan from her chronicling shift, and so the knight had been kind enough to agree not to bother me in my private quarters — unless there was an emergency, and even then a knock of announcement was required.

'How are you holding up?' Mathu emerged from a stream of evening sunlight through my window and manifested into solid form to address me.

'Very well,' I assured him. 'I am enjoying the task immensely, as I have been writing about Master Hermes and the fall of Atlantis.' Then I continued to eat, not wanting to pursue the topic unless he chose to.

'Ah,' he said warily. 'Then you must have questions for me.'

'I understand if you would rather not dig up the past.' Now that Mathu was close, my desire to have him join with me again was taking precedence over my curiosity.

He took a seat in the other chair at my tiny dining table. 'What would you like to know?'

'We can talk later if you have more pressing concerns,' I suggested shamelessly.

'But then you might wonder whether I seduced you to avoid discussing my past.' Mathu cocked an eyebrow in challenge and perhaps he was right.

'Fair enough.' I returned to picking at my food as I considered my questions. 'Did you help to begin the Dracon rebellion as Taejax claims?'

He looked remorseful. 'It is true that I aided the Dracon to perfect the dark arts that came to be a major force in their rebellion,' he admitted. 'At the time I believed that without ORME I would cease to be — a problem shared by my materialistic Nefilim forefathers, the Dracon and their drones. I was told that only humans had the emotional potential to braid their atomic structure up the evolutionary ladder and out of this finite universe. So eventually humans would ascend to the next harmonic universe and my kind would be left behind, with no means to transcend the physical world.'

'But did the Master Enki not evolve into spirit form?' I queried.

'It was a death sentence even to mention the name of Ki back then,' Mathu explained.

'Enki?' I needed to be sure we were discussing the same entity.

'Ki,' Mathu confirmed. 'En was a title meaning Lord.'

I nodded, enlightened. 'Do go on.'

'As far as I knew, the Master had perished whilst in exile. I became resentful and jealous of my human half-brothers, just as the Dracon

341

did, so I helped devise natural and supernatural means to torture and permanently eradicate human souls.'

I was horrified by this confession, and yet I felt for Mathu as he obviously carried so much guilt. 'What changed your view about humanity?' I asked.

My lover's eyes filled with tears. 'You did ... or rather your first incarnation did.'

I was so touched I was speechless.

'You spoke to me in a ghostly visitation, after you had taken your own life. Your suicide was unprecedented among the Anunnaki, for our fallen kindred and their allies fear death above all else. I was standing right beside you when you ripped your own heart out.' His tears overflowed and rolled down his face.

'Mathu, you are crying.' I moved to collect his precious tears on my fingers — the Anu didn't usually feel emotion so intensely as to weep.

He laughed, which was also unusual behaviour for one of his ilk. 'Ever since our union, my emotions have been surging out of control,' he explained. 'I have cried out my sadness until only joy remains — the joy I have felt since finding you again, sweet Kali.'

I closed the distance between us by taking a seat on his lap facing him. 'Was Kali my name when first you knew me?'

'Kali is the name to which your soul answers,' he said. 'Our spiritual father knew this, and gave you the name during your first lifetime on Earth.'

I was fascinated to learn this. 'Would you tell me more about Kali? She appeared to you in spirit form, you say. So she proved the Anunnaki do have souls, as her spirit was not expunged upon death?' I realised now how Kali had changed Mathu's beliefs.

He nodded, with much admiration in his eyes. 'She told me that if I starved myself of Ormus and started using my personal power for selfless and positive ends, I too could be saved. So I turned to the Kian philosophy of our spiritual father and began to nurture human knowledge and civilisation. I ceased ingesting Ormus and continued to live for hundreds of thousands of years. I travelled the globe to teach mankind and became known in many different lands by many different names. I taught humans how to use the ankh tools for construction and healing, and how to defend themselves against the dark arts and the Dracon. All the while I yearned to join you in the spirit world and I waited patiently for my earthly life to be taken from me.'

'You cannot expect to save mankind all on your own,' I said, appealing to him to forgive himself.

'Why not? I managed to condemn mankind all on my own.'

'Ha!' I scoffed. 'You have had plenty of help. And do not speak of mankind as if it were some innocent child with no choice in its own downfall. From what I have learned, you are only one of fourteen soul-minds sent here to *guide*, not *command*, the spiritual evolution of all on this planet. So you can cease to be so hard on yourself: the final outcome in Tara's saga is the responsibility of all, not just you.'

He stared blankly at me for a moment. Then he said, 'It is so very good to know you again ... you always did have a way of saying just what I needed to hear.'

'Praise the universe for that.' I smiled to reassure him. 'You are a fine soul, Mathu, but you cannot do better than your best, and you have done your best since your redemption.'

'How could you know that?' He was delighted by my view, however uninformed.

'It stands to reason that if you had not been good, fate would not have led you to me, your just reward.'

Clearly Mathu liked my reasoning, for he paled into his spirit form to join with me and claim his karmic prize.

TRANSFORMATION

FROM THE JOURNAL OF TAMAR DEVERE

My eyes were hanging out of my head from reading all day and my body had various aches and pains from supporting myself in various positions as I read. I'd even taken dinner into my room, so as to stay in the story. There seemed only a couple of chapters left to go, so I felt confident of finishing the journal tomorrow.

I lay back against my pillows to muse upon all the exotic images that had been implanted in my mind by reading Ashlee's adventure. Could it all be real? The Dragon Queens, the Signet Grid, the inter-time war? Was Captain Sinclair still time-hopping around? Was Mathu still watching over me?

I wondered whether my guardian angel might be tempted to visit me, and became aware that I was caressing my newly-formed breasts. I unbuttoned my shirt slowly, as I imagined he might, then I closed my eyes and slid my hands slowly over the fleshy mounds on my chest, my nipples hardening with the excitement welling deep in my gut.

My mother knocked and entered, and I quickly pulled closed my top to hide my developing breasts.

'I'm so sorry.' My mother was shocked. I wasn't sure if it was because I'd covered myself in her presence, when normally I wouldn't have cared less, or the realisation that I had a bust worth covering.

'No problem.' I covered my panic. 'What do you want me for — the dishes?'

'No, no, I've done them,' she said.

This was odd. The dishes were my chore, and I only got to avoid doing them by going out, having a birthday or being ill.

'I was just wondering, if you're feeling better now, whether you'd like to get out of the house for a bit tomorrow?' she said.

'Um ...' I wasn't too enthusiastic about the idea. 'I really want to finish this journal.'

Mum glanced at the volume on my bedside table to see where it was bookmarked. 'That shouldn't take you more than a couple of hours,' she said. 'We can go shopping in the morning and be back by lunch.'

'You want to take me shopping?' I was almost insulted by how superficial that sounded, with all that might be going on in the world.

'Well, honey ...' Mum looked down at my pyjama pants that left my ankles exposed, 'I think you need a few new clothes ... including a bra.' She smiled as she said this, and we both burst out laughing.

'You noticed then?' I joked, a hot flush filling my cheeks.

'Sweetie, you don't have to be embarrassed.' Mum hugged me. 'If you ever need anything, please don't wait for me to notice. Your father and I are so caught up in our work that you get overlooked sometimes.'

It seemed Mum thought that my development had been gradual and she'd failed to notice it, rather than something that had happened overnight.

'So what do you say?' She squeezed my hand in encouragement.

'I guess I could use some stuff.'

'Good. Pick you up at eight-thirty in the kitchen.' She kissed my head and bade me goodnight.

By the next morning I had grown the same amount again and looked like a sixteen year old. 'Oh my Goddess!' I stared at my reflection in the mirror: I was absolutely gorgeous; how could this person possibly be me? What was more, there was no way I could hide this. I couldn't help smiling, although my head was thumping and I felt nauseous and stretched.

I checked my diary for Kali's entry for the day, but all it said was: *Tonight.*

I had a shower to ease the aches and pains in my body, but when it came to getting dressed I was stuck; absolutely nothing fitted me any more. I had to call for Mum. When she entered I got the shock of my life — she was radiating coloured light.

'What's the matter?' she asked, then took a step back when she saw that I was now as tall as she was.

By this point I'd realised that what I was seeing was her aura. I covered my astonishment, recalling why I'd called her in here. 'Nothing fits!' I said.

To my mother's credit, she didn't freak out at this point and drag me off to some doctor to find out what was wrong with me. She simply smiled and said, 'I think we might need to raid my wardrobe.'

Luckily, Dad had left the house early. I followed my mother into her room, still wrapped in a towel. 'Aren't you going to ask me what's going on?'

'I expect you'll talk to me about it when you're ready,' she said, and slid open her wardrobe doors to expose the selection of clothes. 'What about this?' She pulled out a dark brown T-shirt dress. 'It'd look great with these boots.' She pulled out her brown suede boots that I'd always admired.

I held the dress in front of me, imagining that it would look rather good. 'This is just like playing dress-ups in here when I was a kid,' I said.

'Only today my clothes will actually fit,' she joked. Then her concern came through. 'Are you in any pain?'

'I've got a few aches and pains, but nothing worth complaining about.' I pulled on the boots.

'Would you list your symptoms for me? I'm not going to take you to a doctor,' she added, 'I'll just do a little research.'

'All right,' I agreed, rather relieved that Mum was looking out for me, and ran through the list while she noted them down.

Our shopping trip was an interesting experience. I'd never seen a light-body before and suddenly I could see everybody's, as well as the light-bodies of plants and animals. The other thing that was really odd was that I'd gone from being one of the unnoticed masses to someone who was stared at by men, admired by women and flirted with by teenage boys who thought me their age. I had never felt so powerful: if I dropped something, young men stopped to pick it up for me; if I wanted help with anything, people fell over themselves to assist. It was utterly amazing and very amusing to me; but although my mother played it cool and collected, I think she was a little horrified by the attention I was suddenly attracting.

There was a darker side to all this: stalkers. I repeatedly spotted two men whose auras were unlike those of the other people around me. Their light-bodies were entirely gold, and where most people's light-bodies revolved around their light centres, these men seemed to have no chakras at all. I recalled Ashlee referring to people with these kinds of auras as abominations — vampires even. These two men seemed to be taking a keen interest in Mum and me and it freaked me out. I didn't want to point them out to Mum in case I was just being paranoid, but they hadn't escaped her attention.

'Not to worry,' she advised me with a smile. 'Time for coffee.'

I was dumbfounded by her complacency. 'Shouldn't we —'

'Trust me,' she said. 'We just need to stay in a public place until the problem resolves itself.'

We found a table in a café where we could observe our stalkers, and ordered coffee and cake. Mum's assurance had made me curious. 'You know more about what's happening to me than you're letting on,' I accused.

'I've read the journals too, Tamar,' she said. 'I can put two and two together, just as you can.'

She was right, but now that my psychic senses were more acute, I thought there was something else; something I wasn't being told.

'There we go.' Mum nodded towards our stalkers who had been surrounded by several uniformed guards. 'Security's arrived. Time to go.' She rose and collected her bags.

'But what about our order?'

Mum slapped fifteen dollars on the table. 'We'll grab something when we get home. Stay close.' She set off through the crowds towards the car park. It was all very strange, but I was happy to be leaving the mall as with my heightened sensitivity to light and sound, I'd developed a splitting headache!

I couldn't help but notice that Mum kept checking her rear-vision mirror on the drive home. 'Do you think they might follow us?' I asked.

'No, of course not. I'm sure that the mall security team has taken care of them.' But her tone wasn't convincing.

'But how did mall security even know about them?' I was confused, and that wasn't good with my throbbing head.

'Huge malls like that have massive amounts of surveillance, honey.'

'And you just trusted that those men would be spotted and picked up while we had a coffee?' I wasn't really buying her explanation.

'Well, I come from a long line of psychics.' She made light of my suspicions and so I passed on further interrogation until later, when I hoped my head would hurt less.

I noted Mum locked the door behind us when we got home, which she never usually did.

'Shall I make you some lunch and bring it to you in your room?' she asked. She knew I wanted to get back to my reading, yet I felt she was trying to get rid of me for some reason.

'Could I have an aspirin too, please?' I asked.

'Oh, sweetie.' Mum caressed the side of my face, sorry that I was feeling poorly. 'Of course you can. You go and lie down and I'll bring it right in.' She was so obviously trying to get rid of me that I obliged straightaway, going to my room and shutting the door loudly so she knew I was in there.

Sure enough, when I crept back into the hall after a few moments and tracked Mum down to her office, I heard her whispering to someone on the phone, telling them about the men who had been following us.

'Darling, I think she should know about Giza,' she went on. There was only one person she ever called 'darling' so I knew she was speaking to Dad. I didn't catch much else as Dad seemed to be doing most of the talking, so I tiptoed back to my room and closed the door. Then I sat on my bed to think.

The unusual light-bodies of those men in the mall was a result of taking too much of the ORME substance, which meant they were semi-human demons and to be feared. Mum must have known this, but surely she wouldn't think a mall security team could keep such beings in check! A cold shiver ran through my body: I was in danger. But then I calmed myself: they couldn't possibly know about my connection to Kali. Nobody did, but me.

When Mum brought me my lunch and some painkillers, my head was too sore to start drilling her about her odd behaviour at the mall. But after the food and aspirin, my headache eased and I felt well enough to carry on with my reading. I decided to leave my confrontation with Mum until later and settled down to finish the tale of Amenti.

SUSAN DEVERE JOURNALISING ON BEHALF OF LADY ASHLEE GRANVILLE-DEVERE

ROOT RACE FIVE — PHYSICAL (1244 AD); THE CATHARI

I hide alone in the darkness, terrified, trembling uncontrollably. My guardian, Pierre de Saint-Martin, has just been slain in his sleep by Sir Christian Molier. Molier claimed that he and his knights were sent to us by Marie de Saint-Clair, the Grand Master of the order of the Priory of Sion, to guide us here to the Chateau de Blanchefort, where we were to deliver a holy treasure of great significance into safekeeping. My sister, Lillet du Lac, and I, Lilitu, were aided in our escape from Montsègur by another knight, Sir Albray Devere, who also claimed to have been sent by the Grand Master. Molier claimed Devere was an impostor, and we believed him and allowed Molier's men to drag him away. When Molier informed us earlier this night of Devere's escape from his captors, I thought it was terrible news, but now he is my only hope.

I huddle in this closet across the hall from my deceased guardian's sleeping quarters. I was on my way to speak with him when I heard the sound of several knights ascending the stairs. Fearful of being cornered by unfamiliar men this late at night, I hid in the closet. It petrifies me to think that had I not concealed myself, I would now be lying dead alongside my guardian. I hug the treasure in my charge to my person — a scroll, crafted from a resilient, lightweight metal that gives off a strange glow and is a mystery to all who see it. This scroll is said to hold ancient text of vital import, but as no one knows how to open its lock, no one really knows what it contains. Still, many people have died throughout the ages to ensure the treasure's safety, and now my sister and I are its guardians.

Lillet. She is in danger. I must warn her.

I steel myself to open the closet and step outside, but then pause. My sister will kill me herself if I jeopardise the treasure in my charge for the sake of her life. She will say I allowed selfish sentiment to outweigh my better judgement; Lillet cannot abide such weakness of character.

I must stay strong.

I wipe the tears from my face and steady my erratic breathing so I might listen for events unfolding in the chateau. I feel a wetness at my feet and realise that the blood of my guardian has flowed across the hall and under the door of the closet. I shrink away from its advance.

Suddenly I hear voices: Molier's guards are everywhere, shouting orders to search every room, and I fear I shall be found. I grip the hilt of the dagger I wear on my girdle, knowing I do not have the courage to use it.

'If Devere has taken the priestess, we won't see them for dust,' comments one of the knights as they work their way down the hallway towards my closet.

Devere has saved Lillet! I breathe a sigh of relief. *But who will save me?*

'At least it gives us someone to pin de Saint-Martin's murder on,' another knight responds. They laugh at the fortunate coincidence. I am appalled by their blatant treachery, and wonder what lies they will tell about me after my murder.

'I hope we find that other little priestess,' says the first knight, 'I could do with some entertainment.'

His desire is echoed by various others and I block my ears, not wishing to hear their foul suggestions. I wriggle to the back wall of the closet and into a corner where I hope I may not be spotted. My head collides with a hard metal object and I am not quick enough to smother my pained cry of surprise.

'Did you hear that?' one of the knights asks. They know where I am; I hear them approaching.

I reach up to identify the item that has betrayed me — a long clothes hook. I grasp it for support, almost swooning at the thought of my imminent fate. *God help me*, I pray, and as I lean against the closet wall, the hook drops and a small door opens at my back. I fall through the void and land on my behind some distance below. The door closes, leaving me in utter darkness.

I am stunned by my deliverance and remain silent as the knights search the closet above. 'You are imagining things,' one of them tells the other, and they close the door and resume their search of the chateau.

I rise and turn to confront the pitch-dark space ahead of me. I wonder where the Blanchefort family stand in all this. Are they in league with Molier, or are they also in mortal danger? Then a tap on the shoulder scares me witless.

'It is I, Madame de Blanchefort,' a woman whispers. 'We were worried about you, Lilitu. Come with me, I know a safe place where we can wait this out.' The lady finds my hand in the darkness and leads me through a maze of dark underground passages.

'Sir Molier murdered my Lord de Saint-Martin,' I whisper, hoping to gauge from her response where my lady's loyalties lie.

'I am sorry,' she replies. 'But the good news is that Albray Devere has your sister safely away from here, and now you are safe with us. My Lord Comte is currently in the great hall, pretending to swallow Molier's account of the night's events. It seems the knight is eager to set off after Devere, and we intend to let him ... eventually.'

'No, you must not let him go after Lillet!'

'Your sister is in the safest of hands,' Madame de Blanchefort assures me. 'We will stall Molier as long as we can, but our priority now is to see you to safety.'

'I am starting to think there is nowhere I shall be safe from the Inquisition,' I say. 'No one who can protect us.'

'There *is* someone,' she tells me encouragingly. 'I assure you, there is light at the end of the tunnel.'

My lady pushes open a door and we enter a room bathed in candlelight and firelight. I realise it must be a secret room for there are no windows, but several doors, each giving access to a different part of the chateau, I assume. Despite the stone walls and lack of decoration, it is a cosy room with a large rug to insulate the floor, and pillows and blankets on the lounge and chairs. It seems Madame de Blanchefort knows how to wait out a crisis in comfort.

Then I notice a female hand resting on the arm of a chair facing the fire. A plain gold band adorns the ring finger, distinctive because of its unusual illumination. To the untrained eye this would pass as pink-gold, but I recognise it to be of the same super-metal as the ancient scroll in my charge. There is only one such ring in existence that I know of and it is worn by the Grand Master of the Priory of Sion. The ring was originally found beneath Solomon's Temple in Jerusalem, along with the scroll that is now in my charge.

'My Lady de Saint-Clair?' I ask tentatively. But what was she doing here?

'Your Holiness.' She turns in her chair to bow her head to me. 'Forgive my lack of reverence, Lady, but I am weary from my journey.'

I insist that she refrains from humbling herself in my presence. 'No, it is I who am honoured.'

She motions to the seat alongside hers. 'Do not fear for your sister,' she says. 'Sir Albray Devere is more reliable than an army of guards — he is one of my two most trusted allies.'

I am reassured by her words. Although I do not mean to seem rude, I cannot stop my eyes from drifting to her ring.

'Beautiful, isn't it?' She holds out her hand so we may both admire it. 'It is no ordinary ring, and for a long time after it was found no one was aware of its extraordinary purpose. It was given to my great-uncle, Henry de Saint-Clair, by Godefroi de Bouillon, after he aided him to take Jerusalem and uncover the secret treasure of Solomon.'

'And what is its extraordinary purpose?' I cannot allow such a comment to pass.

Before my lady can answer, we hear footsteps approaching from behind one of the doors into the room.

'Fear not, Lilitu,' Madame de Blanchefort tells me, 'that door leads down through the mount. It is your salvation that approaches.'

'My salvation?' I look to Lady de Saint-Clair for answers.

She nods. 'The other trusted ally I was telling you about.'

The door opens and a tall, fair-haired fellow breezes into our midst, wearing attire unlike any I have seen. The soft fabric of his shirt and the leather and tailoring of his vest and trousers is far superior to anything available on the continent; the craftsmanship of his long brown boots is also remarkable. His belt is equipped with all manner of weapons, some that I recognise and some I do not. Had our guest not been so well dressed, I would have thought him a pirate or a treasure hunter. On his right hand I spot an illuminated ring that is exactly the same as the one worn by Lady de Saint-Clair. I look back to her.

'Allow me to introduce a future relative of mine,' she says, 'Prince Henry Sinclair.'

I gasp to learn that our mysterious guest is nobility. 'A future relative, my lady?' I query as I bow my head in respect to the prince.

'I prefer the title of captain, as my Lady de Saint-Clair well knows,' the man says, dismissing any formalities. 'And in answer to your query, I will be a relative of my Lady de Saint-Clair when I am born in the next century.'

'How can it be that you are here then, captain?' I was completely confused.

He smiles to soften his stalling of my interrogation. 'My lady, I have an urgent matter I must attend to, so if you require my aid you must enlighten me as to how with all due haste.'

'Show him your treasure, my Lady du Lac,' the Grand Master encourages me. As my holy order is allied to the Order of Sion, I obey and produce my treasure for the captain to inspect.

He smiles and rubs his hands together in delight. 'And what does this scroll contain?'

'I was told it contains information that would validate my bloodline,' I say, allowing him to lift my treasure from my fingers.

'A genealogy?' He frowns, seeming confused. 'This scroll is a product of the inter-time war, which has little to do with legal kingship.'

I have no idea what the captain is talking about. 'That is what I was told,' I say.

'I am not one for hearsay myself.' Captain Sinclair kneels by a low coffee table and sets the scroll upon it. 'Let us take a look, shall we?'

'No!' I protest, sure that he will damage the treasure. 'No one has been able to get it —'

The captain touches the lock and the scroll unfurls, displaying its secret contents.

'— open,' I finish, utterly astonished. I kneel beside him at the table. 'What is it?' I ask, then I see that the page of the scroll is completely blank. I am sickened by the rush of fury I feel. 'Thousands have died for this!'

'Wait,' he urges me, and the page fills with light. I am astounded all over again. 'I have dreamt of this map's existence,' he informs me, excited by the discovery. 'And you are right — it will help to validate those of your bloodline, in a sense.'

'It is a map?' I gape at the page that now displays the picture of a globe, akin to the moon, but this globe is ablaze with colour, from deep green to burnt orange, and vast patches of blue beneath whorls of white. There are brightly coloured purple spots marked all over the globe, and as the captain touches these markers, text appears on the page; it disappears when he withdraws his touch.

'Is it magic?' I gasp, amazed and petrified.

'No.' The captain assures me there is nothing to fear. 'In a thousand years it will be easily explainable.' He retracts the map and stands, still holding it. 'I will see this to a safe place, have no fear of that.'

I felt I must protest. 'Captain Sinclair, I am not questioning your integrity, but it is my charge to see that treasure to safety and I will not allow it out of my sight until that vow is fulfilled.'

Captain Sinclair appears most put out by my protest. 'I cannot possibly take you where I am bound.'

'Why not?' I demand. 'I am not afraid to die as I have seen so many others do for this cause.'

'Indeed, captain,' Lady de Saint-Clair interjects on my behalf. 'Why not take her with you?'

'Because . . .' He stops himself short. 'It is complicated, my lady, and I have no time to waste debating the matter.'

'Then I suggest you do not debate it,' my Lady de Saint Clair advises. 'You of all people should not have trouble finding the time to return my Lady du Lac safely to us.'

The captain is getting a headache, I fear. 'As you wish,' he says and begrudgingly directs me towards the door by which he arrived. 'Ladies.' He bows his head in farewell.

'You are welcome to return here when your task is done, Lilitu,' Madame de Blanchefort tells me warmly as I follow the captain out of the room. He still holds my treasure in his hand.

'I am so grateful to you both,' I tell my lady allies, and wave a quick farewell as I begin to descend an old stairwell that spirals down deep into the Earth. The captain is ahead of me, using a strange luminous green stick to light his way.

'You had best keep up,' he calls back. 'These stairs can be deadly in the dark.'

I hurry to catch up, but the stairs are wet and I find myself falling. My heart stops as I realise I am plunging towards a deep, dark cavity in the middle of the stairwell. If not for Captain Sinclair's steadying arm about my waist, I would have toppled to my death. Instead, I watch my treasure scroll, knocked from the captain's hand, drop down into the darkness. After what seems an age, it clatters to a landing below. I am mortified.

The captain sets me back on my own feet and makes haste down the stairs. Not wanting to lose the light again, I keep pace with him.

At the base of the deep descent, we recover the scroll and I am relieved to find it apparently unscathed. When the captain attempts to open it, however, he cannot. 'Damn, jammed,' he says.

I am so devastated by the prospect of having sabotaged my own mission that I begin to weep.

'Not to worry, I have a man on board who should be able to repair this,' the captain reassures me in an attempt to prevent my hysterics. Nevertheless, I can tell he is deeply disappointed by the setback. 'Come on, we must go.'

He leads me through a large stone arch into a cavern that is filled by a large metal object — which my guide introduces as his ship, *Kleio*. The vessel is nestled tightly inside the cave and I marvel at how it came to be here and, more importantly, how the captain plans to get it out. I dare not question my saviour, however, as he seems not very well disposed towards me at present and I do not blame him. He wants me to volunteer to stay behind and save him the return trip, but I cannot, not with the future of my treasure in question.

The ship's hatch locks behind us and the captain leads me quickly down a wide passageway. As I am dragged along by the hand, I marvel at the sleek architecture and the strange materials that form the interior of the ship.

'Well, it's about time!'

I turn to see another fair-haired gentleman approach from beyond the hatchway where we entered. He seems very surprised to see me.

'Is that who I think it is?' he asks the captain.

Captain Sinclair does not answer, but continues to drag me down the passage.

'You cannot take her with us!' the other man says.

'I tried to tell my Lady du Lac just that.' The captain turns to emphasise the fact for my benefit. 'But Sion needs her hidden, so we'll just have to stow her in a cabin until after we've executed the next mission. After that, we'll take her back to base so she can see her treasure safely stored, before we return her here, allowing for a time lapse of a year or so.'

The captain shows me into a cabin and looks to me for my approval of his plan.

'I am very grateful for all your aid,' I say, although I am uncertain about that last part — does Captain Sinclair mean to imply that I will be on board his ship for a year? I suddenly realise that for the first time in my life I actually feel safe, and the idea of a whole year of this security is very appealing.

The captain's companion is still worried about my presence on board. 'But what if she meets up with —'

'*Levi*,' the captain says discouragingly, 'we will ensure that does not happen.' He hands Levi my damaged treasure. 'See what you can do with this.'

'What is it?' Levi fiddles with the lock.

'The Signet Map,' Captain Sinclair replies, and I am surprised to learn that he has a name for my treasure.

'Whoa, it exists.' Levi regards the scroll with more reverence.

'Barely. It was dropped from a very great height.'

His crewmate isn't pleased. 'How could you let that happen?'

'I lost my concentration for a second,' the captain confesses, as if it had been his fault.

'It was my fault,' I said. 'I slipped and knocked the scroll from the captain's hands.'

'I see.' Levi looks to Sinclair, who looks even guiltier than I do. 'So you had your hands full at the time?'

'Can you fix it?' I appeal, breaking the tension building between the two men.

'I'll see what I can do.' Levi serves the captain a scornful look and heads back up the passageway.

Captain Sinclair turns back to me. 'I have to leave you now and I suggest you sleep for a while. I'll come and check on you when I can, but under no circumstances are you to leave this cabin. Is that understood?'

I nod, thanking God that the captain is patient and even-tempered. 'I understand.'

'If you experience any sort of strange phenomenon while you are on board, do not be alarmed, it is completely normal.' The captain smiles and closes the cabin door on his way out.

I do not dwell on his strange words long, but decide to take his advice and lay my weary body down on the cabin bed. I wonder how my sister Lillet is faring. In my heart I know she is safe and strong; she would kill herself before she failed in her duty.

I should have taken the fall and saved the map! The realisation brings tears of shame to my eyes. *I am a coward.* I know my tears are worthless self-pity and yet I cannot stop the flow. I cry out my shame and remorse until, exhausted, I drift on the verge of sleep.

I perceive the world around me being engulfed by waves of blue-green light, the effect of which is quite stunning and beautiful. The light is calming, healing, empowering! I part my eyes a little to discern whether I am imagining the phenomenon, but the effect is so mesmerising I must give in and sleep.

*   *   *

Lillet! I wake knowing I have just heard my sister's voice. I am up and at the door before my consciousness returns to my body.

There is a lot of commotion in the passageway; I hear the voices and laughter of many women. I open the cabin door and step out to see five women standing in a line against the wall further down the passageway, with the captain attempting to direct them.

'Ladies, may I have your attention, please? The suiting room is this way.' He motions up a flight of stairs to the next deck.

'Do our suits match?' asks one of the women, who looks remarkably like a young Lady de Saint-Clair.

'That is up to you,' Sinclair replies, confusing the issue.

'What manner of suits are these exactly, captain?' inquires a red-headed woman in a flirtatious tone. She is standing closest to the captain and he appears smitten by her long red locks and her porcelain-like skin.

'The adaptable kind,' he replies. 'These suits are made by the Anu from an etheric fabric that will mould itself according to your telepathic order.'

'And are you wearing one of those suits right now?' the siren redhead asks, smiling. She is interrupted by another of the women, a buxom brunette.

'Tell me, captain, can you telepathically direct someone else's suit to do your bidding?'

Captain Sinclair appears overwhelmed by the attention and cannot wipe the silly grin off his face. 'Are the Dragon Queens angels? I do not think so, my ladies.'

Some of the women protest his opinion; others applaud it. Then the red-headed woman looks over to the doorway where I am standing and sees me watching them.

'Oh my goodness!' she cries in alarm. 'I have to go.' And she rushes upstairs without delay.

My sister emerges from the cluster of women, amazed to see me. 'Lilitu?'

'Lillet!' I rush to embrace her, ignoring the displeased look on the captain's face. 'You are alive!' I hug her as I have never hugged her before and she is surprisingly receptive to my outpouring of selfish sentiment.

'Yes, I am alive.' She strokes my hair affectionately and her eyes and voice fill with tears. 'And I am so proud of you.' She kisses my head several times.

'Why?' I cannot think of anything I have done that would make her proud.

'Ladies, you need to break it up,' the captain says. He appeals to my sister: 'It's not right for you to be meeting out of time like this; anything you say to her could affect the causality of the future dramatically.'

Lillet seems to understand the captain's plea and backs away from me, turning to head up the stairs. 'Goodbye, Lilitu,' she says sadly. 'I shall be waiting at the Chateau de Blanchefort when you return.' It is not like my sister to be so emotional. What has happened to her? Or is this an impostor?

'Where are you going?' I call after her. 'Who are these women?'

Captain Sinclair takes hold of my arm and leads me back to my cabin. 'I believe I asked you politely to stay in here,' he says. 'You must forgive me if I enforce my will.' He closes the door and locks it behind him.

I collapse on the bed, confused as to why I must stay isolated from the ship's other inhabitants, when my sister enjoys free rein and the company of other women. Furthermore, I feel unworthy of my station as a priestess among my people, for not only have I allowed the treasure in my charge to be damaged, I am now entertaining lustful thoughts of Captain Sinclair. When I think of him, I feel butterflies in my chest and stomach. Shame consumes me: my attraction to him completes my failure. As one of the Perfecti I am not permitted to feel personal emotions for another — but how can I not? The captain saved my life today, twice! Perhaps it is just admiration I feel, for he seems to hold the answers to the mystery of the treasure I have sworn to protect. Yet I am also very aware that, as royalty, Captain Sinclair is one of a few select men to whom a priestess of my faith is permitted to bear a child.

Stop! I am angered by my self-indulgent thoughts, for it is not my duty to my faith that compels me, but the image of a siren redhead who interests the captain far more than I do.

The cabin door opens and I awake. I sit up as Captain Sinclair enters, appearing far more relaxed than when last I saw him. 'The crisis is over and all is well with the world,' he tells me. 'I apologise if I caused you offence earlier, but I had good reason for alarm, I assure you.'

I nod to accept his apology, quietly considering that his smile is so charming I would forgive him anything.

'Here.' He hands me my scroll. 'Levi repaired the damage.'

The instant the scroll is placed back into my possession a great weight lifts from my shoulders. 'Thank you, captain.' I hand the scroll back to him. 'I am eternally indebted to you and your crew.'

Captain Sinclair is clearly confused by my action. 'Do you not wish to deliver this to safety yourself?'

I shake my head. 'It will be safer with you.'

Captain Sinclair is amused that I think so. 'Need I remind you that I was the one who dropped the Signet Map into the chasm?'

'To prevent me accidentally killing myself.'

The captain does not agree. 'Watch this.' He places my scroll on the bed and steps away from it. He then holds forth his hand and the scroll launches itself into his grasp. 'That was all I had to do. I was to blame for the damage, not you.'

I am too stunned for speech. Then I find my tongue. 'Why then did you allow the treasure to fall?'

'As I told Levi earlier, I was distracted.'

'By my imminent death,' I reason, willing to claim responsibility once more.

'No,' he corrects me gently. 'It was your intimate proximity that stole my focus.'

It takes me a moment to process that Captain Sinclair is implying he was distracted by me!

'I realise that your station and your faith do not tolerate personal emotion,' he continues, 'and it is not my intention to make you feel uncomfortable, but I cannot have you hate yourself for a crime that was not yours.'

My ego is so uplifted by his confession that I cannot wipe the smile from my face. 'Then I am still partly to blame for the damage,' I say, making light of the uncomfortable situation.

The captain shakes his head slowly, unwilling to let me accept any of the blame. 'I should have waited for you at the top of the stairs. I should have left the map in your safekeeping. The fault *was* entirely mine.'

He offers the scroll back to me and, feeling more confident, I decide that I will personally deliver my treasure to its new home.

'Very good.' He motions me to the cabin door. 'This way.'

'Have we arrived at our destination?' I rise, excited to learn that the end of my quest is imminent. This lifelong burden will soon be lifted from my shoulders.

We exit the *Kleio* onto a huge dry dock. Men are suspended from high frames carrying out maintenance on the vessel. They are strangely clad and speak a foreign language, but look happier about their work than any people I have ever seen.

The captain nears a set of double doors that open at his approach. I cease gaping at my surrounds and hurry to catch him up. 'Is my sister still on board?' I ask, wondering if I will be permitted to see her.

'No. Lillet and her companions disembarked some time ago.' The captain leads me into a long white corridor with closed doors either side. 'She will be waiting for you upon your return to the chateau as promised. Still ...' The captain stops to relay his thought to me. 'I would appreciate it if you did not mention your meeting on my ship to Lillet, or anything else you have seen whilst in my company.'

'I find that request puzzling, captain.'

'Lillet will not remember your meeting,' he tells me. My confusion must be apparent on my face because he continues: 'That meeting will take place in her future, but if you tell her of it beforehand it may not happen, as her knowledge of it may affect causality.'

'But it has already happened.' I frown, perplexed.

'For you, but not for Lillet,' the captain points out.

My brain struggles to process this information. How is such a thing possible?

'Who are you, captain ... really?' I ask.

Captain Sinclair serves me a rather mysterious smile. 'Follow me,' he says, and leads me off in the direction of some answers.

I reserve my questions as we walk along and instead admire the spotless, well-lit corridor and its beautiful honey-coloured polished timber floor. 'Your base is very beautiful, captain.'

'Thank you, I had a hand in the design,' the captain replies.

Turning a corner, we enter a shorter corridor. He steps beneath a sheet of light and the double doors beyond open. As I pass beneath the sheet of light, I am curious to note a gold plaque on the wall. The text appears to be moving, transforming from one language into that of my own.

> This is a Signet station,
> one of twelve pyramids of light
> placed on the Earth plane by design.
> Each station is as unique in frequency and purpose
> as the twelve Masters who are the keys.
> They are the Council of Amenti,
> who incarnate as the teachers
> and healers of their timelines
> to oppose an enemy
> that transcends time and space.
> The keeper of this station
> is the soul frequency Polaris,
> the Master of Time, Space and Realities.
> The battle of good versus evil,
> light versus darkness,
> may be viewed here.
> And you will know what you must do.

I turn to the captain, stunned by what I have read. 'You are Polaris?'

'Not at present,' he replies, 'but we are in contact.'

He directs my attention into the room beyond the open double doors. My jaw drops as I creep forward into the massive alien dwelling. 'What is this place?'

'This is Signet station number nine, known to the ancients as Sophia-Hokhmat.' He strolls in ahead of me to allay my fear. 'It is known today as Polaris Control Centre.'

The entire room is rounded, bar the floor, but inset in the centre of the flat polished timber is a huge copper disk. The walls are massive curved windows that look out into a deep chasm that appears to be composed entirely of quartz crystal clusters, both great and small. These draw endless streams of blue lightning from a source above, which I cannot see from the entranceway. Inset into the centre of the ceiling is a sparkling pool of silver water, which holds me absolutely fascinated.

'Amazing, is it not?' The captain walks into the middle of the copper disk and stares up at the pool. 'It is liquid-light.'

I am not brave enough to stand directly beneath the wonder, but I am curious to find out where all the power is being drawn from. I approach the huge windows to cast my sights skyward. 'Dear God!' I utter upon seeing the huge celestial pyramid of silver above us, which is shooting lightning down into the chasm surrounding the station. 'Is that where my treasure is to be hidden?'

Captain Sinclair moves to one of the many slanted surfaces inside the station, which are covered with lights and other intriguing objects, and begins to fiddle. This results in many strange little sounds and flashing images on a series of light-filled pages that look very much like the map on my scroll. 'The Polaris pyramid will transfer you to the Solarian station,' the captain explains. 'This would have been impossible before today, as without the Signet Map I would never have known the location coordinates of the Solarian station. From there, you will learn what is to become of the Signet Map ... or at least, that is what you told me.'

'When?' I am confused, for I have no idea what he is talking about, let alone a memory of any previous meeting between us.

'In your future,' the captain says.

'I see.' I frown, feeling I will have to take his word for that.

I look up to the blazing structure of light and lightning suspended high overhead. 'I cannot possibly go up there,' I say.

'It was frightening to me too once,' he says, attempting to encourage me. 'But if I had never taken the risk, this station would still be dormant.'

I draw a deep breath for strength, but fear forces my head down in defeat once more. 'Will you not do it?' I hold out the map, and to my great relief the captain takes it.

'You are afraid that you will not be able to conquer your fear in order to do what must be done, as so many whom you admired in the past have done,' he says gently.

Images of my brethren flinging themselves into the fire at the defeat of Montsègur flash into my mind. I retrieve my property from him. 'Where do I need to go?'

'Just stand right in the centre of that copper disk,' he tells me, motioning, and I follow his direction, forbidding my mind to entertain any fear. 'That's my girl,' he murmurs as I reach my appointed launch position.

'You appear to have many girls,' I comment as Captain Sinclair returns to the control panel. 'And from what I have seen, you prefer redheads.'

The captain finds this comment frightfully amusing. 'I will always adore you, no matter what colour, creed or race you are,' he tells me.

I am so stunned by his response that I am at a loss for a reply.

He winks at me. 'See you when you get back.'

I look up to see the silver pool above swirling towards me. 'How *do* I get back?' I ask, suddenly panicked.

'You'll work it out.'

The sparkling silver liquid cascades over me and I am drawn up into its whirlpool in a blinding, thrilling rush.

I am aware of being inside the celestial silver pyramid. Wherever I look, the walls of the huge structure become transparent and I can see through to the station and crystal cavern below. I cannot seem to perceive anything inside the pyramid, not even my own form. I feel as if I am a wisp of consciousness suspended in a glistening silver vacuum. There is a very deep sense of Captain Sinclair here: his presence permeates the space and it stirs my blood to feel his spirit seeping through mine. I hear the sound of rushing water and look up to see a porthole of liquid-light erupting overhead. The glistening whirlpool turns from silver to brilliant turquoise as it rushes down to collect me.

I am propelled further and faster this trip, and deposited on top of a glistening turquoise pool, which I hasten to walk across to reach ground that appears more solid. The structure I have entered has physical presence this time and so do I. The floor and walls are constructed of turquoise and crystal, but unlike the Polaris station, which felt highly energised, this station appears lifeless. I can see beyond the walls of this structure too and I gasp when I spy beneath me the globe depicted in the Signet Map. Clearly this station is in space! Why isn't the Solarian station on Earth, as the Polaris station is?

I recall the captain's words: 'If I had never taken the risk, this station would still be dormant.'

The Solarian station is dormant!

So why didn't the captain activate this station too?

I realise that the answer to this question was written on the plaque outside the Polaris control centre: *Each station is as unique in frequency and purpose as the twelve Masters who are the keys.* Captain Sinclair could only open the station he was attuned to. Perhaps he is the first of the Masters to activate his pyramid, and that grants him access to the other eleven stations even though they might still be dormant?

Stairs lead up to an altar of solid turquoise that glistens in the light cast from the porthole. It seems the most appropriate place to leave my treasure, so I scale the stairs, my offering in hand. I place the Signet scroll upon the altar stone, and at my touch the huge block of turquoise lights up. Inside the bright transparent block, a swirling mist manifests and forms a face. I recognise the ghostly features of the woman: it is the redhead I saw on the *Kleio*, only her features are slightly more elongated and angelic.

'Lilitu du Lac, you have done us proud in returning the Signet schematics to Solarian station. It will remain safe with us until such time as we need it.'

'We?' I question.

'You and I, our key incarnation.'

Now the captain's parting comment makes sense to me: 'I will always adore you, no matter what colour, creed or race you are.'

I am the redhead! As impossible as it seems, the premise explains so much — why the woman on the *Kleio* felt compelled to leave upon sighting me, and why the captain wanted to keep me apart from his other female passengers.

'And now you know where the Signet Map must go. Be at peace, dear daughter, until the time of the reckoning is nigh.' The face of the beautiful being disperses into the glowing mist and a luminous vapour rises up to enfold my treasure and pass it back to me.

'I shall see it done,' I say.

'Be silent about your charge, for the sake of the plan and the future.' The light-filled mist evaporates into nothing and the altar falls into darkness once more.

I feel deeply fulfilled in the wake of this meeting, for with the recognition of myself in the red-headed woman I have gained a great gift: I need fear death no more. I have never felt so at peace or so empowered — nothing would frighten me into hiding in a corner again!

I return to the turquoise water of the porthole and am whisked up for my return trip to Polaris station.

I return to the cabin of the *Kleio* to see Captain Sinclair smiling down at me. 'Where is she?' I ask, determined to deliver the Signet Map safely.

The captain motions to my left. 'She said you would be asking for her.'

I sit upright to see the stunning redhead — the woman I will be some day — quietly awaiting my attention.

'Not a word now, ladies,' the captain warns as I slide off the bunk and move to meet myself halfway.

'Thank you,' the woman says, defying the captain's advice. Once the map is in her possession, she unexpectedly embraces me. 'Your service to the plan has been greater than you shall ever know in this lifetime.'

'Enough.' The captain prises us apart and takes hold of my arm to lead me from the room.

'It was an honour to meet you,' she calls after me.

'Where are we going?' I ask.

'We're taking you home,' Captain Sinclair says and smiles.

'But you said I would be away a year before returning to Chateau de Blanchefort,' I cry.

He looks puzzled at my obvious disappointment. 'No,' he corrects, 'I said that I would return you to the chateau *allowing* for the lapse of a year, which is not the same thing, although the outcome will be the same.'

'I'm sorry, captain, I do not follow.'

Our discussion is interrupted by Levi, who pops his head into the hallway to call out, 'We've arrived.'

'I'll be right with you,' the captain returns, then looks back to me; I am still awaiting an explanation. 'Please trust me on this,' he says. 'I have a war to fight and no time for explanations that you won't understand anyway.'

I turn away, disappointed. 'I am beholden to you, captain. I shall not inconvenience you any longer.'

'My Lady du Lac, you are not an inconvenience; you are a past life incarnation of the being I love.'

I knew this, and yet his stating the fact really brought it home to me.

'Surely you can see how our association could land me in very hot water,' he continues. 'In fact, it already has. Be that as it may, you will never be an inconvenience to me. It is my honour, as always, to be of service to you, Solarian.'

His use of the name restores peace to my being. I realise I have no more questions to ask, for all the answers I seek are somewhere inside me, and I will find them in this life, or the next.

I follow the captain to the exit hatch and there bid him farewell. 'I greatly look forward to our next meeting, Captain Sinclair.'

'As do I. I shall see you on your way,' he offers, cracking the white stick in his hand, which turns green and begins to glow.

'No need.' I take the glowing stick from him. 'I will be fine on my own.'

I head off down the ramp and across the earthen floor towards the stone arch that leads into the stairwell. Halfway there, I look back to find the captain still watching me. 'Why are you still here?' I shoo him away with my hands.

'Lilitu, watch out!' he cries. Too late. A clawed hand grips my throat from behind. I attempt to turn to see what has hold of me, but the creature keeps me firmly in place.

'Take me to the Signet system blueprints or I will eradicate her soul! And we all know what that means — game over for everyone.' My attacker's gravelly voice sends shivers of fear through me and I sense a sharp instrument held to the back of my neck. Yet I do not feel like curling up in a ball. My mind is focused.

Captain Sinclair is racing towards us, his weapon aimed at my captor, but now he stops, fearful.

I am the only one who knows where the treasure is. Suddenly I know exactly what I must do and, for once in my life, I have the courage to do it. I feel around for my dagger and drive the blade into my stomach.

The pain and shock hit me immediately and my perception slips into slow motion. I see Captain Sinclair's distress at losing me, and then hear my attacker's furious screech at the fact that I have outwitted him. He slashes at me with his claws and I fall to land heavily on the rocky ground. I am vaguely aware of the fight going on around me, but I no longer have the life energy to care about the outcome.

I emerged from the pink-gold porthole shaking with emotion and awareness. In this past life, I had been sister to the women Albray gave his soul to protect, and I had taken my own life before the very eyes of Captain Sinclair.

'I am so sorry,' I said, for he must have felt terrible to watch me die like that.

'What are you sorry for?' He smiled at me, completely unaware of my meaning.

'Do you not remember saving Lilitu du Lac from the Chateau de Blanchefort?' I asked.

The captain thought hard, then shook his head. 'No, I have no memory of that event.'

I suspected he might be withholding information from me and said so.

'Not at all. The event must take place in my future,' he suggested reasonably, 'beyond my hibernation beneath the blue flame. I did some time-hopping before then, and I expect I do more of the same afterwards.' He could see I was still suspicious and added, 'I would have kept time-hopping around, doing the bidding of the Watchers on Amenti's staff, but I was aging and so Polaris advised me to put the *Kleio* away for a time and rejuvenate. And that is where my body is right now.'

'I saw all of the Dragon Queens alive and well on board the *Kleio*,' I told him. Only then did I realise that I recognised all of the women as souls I had known in this lifetime. 'Susan, Charlotte, Miss Koriche, Lillet du Lac and myself,' I said delightedly.

'How fascinating,' the captain agreed. 'But that is only five souls — shouldn't there be six Dragon Queens?'

He was right. 'So where was the other one?' I wondered.

He shrugged, as baffled as I was. Then I remembered I had seen someone else on the *Kleio* who had stirred my emotions. 'Levi was on your ship too, captain.'

Sinclair looked pleased. 'Excellent. So now both our minds can rest at ease about Levi's safety, if we know he is in our future.'

There was much comfort to be drawn from that knowledge and I smiled too. Then another wonder from my past returned to me. 'I saw the Solarian station — it was still dormant but very beautiful. You transported me there via the Polaris pyramid.'

'Did I?' Sinclair was fascinated. 'I did not realise the Polaris could connect to the other dormant stations ... I shall have to look into that.'

I grinned, happy to be of service. 'It seems we are still aiding each other to greatness.'

He gazed at me fondly. 'Yes, we are ... and always will.'

I longed to kiss him. I thought I had known all there was to know about my dear Devere; how delightful to find there were entire worlds I didn't know about him, our future and myself. The times we spent together may have often been perilous, but never boring.

'Two more halls to go.' My guide brought my focus back to the quest at hand.

I moved towards the blue-gold porthole. 'My astral evolution.' I could not imagine what it must be like to be an eternal being, as the Anu are, and I was curious about how this lifetime would play out. If there was no death in the astral realm, where would this hallway lead? Suddenly I realised how much I was enjoying the whole Amenti experience — every soul should have the chance to feel so enlightened! And that was exactly the reason why I had volunteered to be one of Amenti's staff: so that every being on Earth might walk these halls.

THE SILENT WATCHER

ROOT RACE SIX — ASTRAL (NO TIME); THE STAFF OF AMENTI

In this life I am born into a noble family, the only daughter of a baron, the Honourable Lord Granville, or at least that is what I am led to believe. But at the age of forty, I come across a confession written by my mother pertaining to the night I was conceived. Driven by guilt at seeing me locked away in a mental asylum at eight years of age, my mother reveals that I am not my father's child, but the offspring of an angelic presence that possessed my father during their wedding night. I learn that the blood in my veins is not entirely human, which offers some explanation for the fact that I am able to see things not always of this world.

My life as Ashlee Granville-Devere is filled with many wondrous events. However, the crucial moment in this lifetime, which releases the key sonic for my passage through this hall in Amenti, takes place beneath Giza as I am bidding my son's body farewell.

I and my companions are under threat from the Dracon Taejax and his reptilian warriors. Taejax threatens to hunt down my family, to drain their bodily fluids and scatter their souls to oblivion, but despite this, somehow I sense good in him. To the protests of my company, I kneel before my known enemy and hand him the pendant that will stop his suffering and allow him to withdraw from the battlefield.

From this moment, my passage through Amenti is assured.

*   *   *

The blue-gold porthole took me straight back to the antechamber to the Halls of Amenti, back to the soul who had accompanied me through all my lives on Earth. 'An astral being cannot die,' I stated the obvious, 'which leaves me here.'

'Yet there is still a porthole to go,' Sinclair said, playing on my curiosity.

'Two, if you count the porthole back to Tara.'

Although the captain must have known where the violet-gold porthole would lead, having taken the journey himself, he was more interested in teasing me. 'So where does the sixth one lead?'

I thought back to Miss Koriche's writings: according to what I had read there, the last porthole led to the part of my soul-mind that was evolving on the mental and causal planes beyond. 'This porthole leads to Solarian,' I said, making my best guess.

Sinclair raised his eyebrows, impressed by my reasoning.

Although I was thrilled to be on the verge of total awareness, I feared being consumed by the infinite all and forgetting the individuals who had meant so much to me whilst on Earth. 'Will I come back?' I asked.

'I am still here,' he pointed out to allay my fears.

It suddenly dawned on me that he had already traversed the Halls of Amenti and yet had not returned to Tara. 'Why *are* you still here?' I asked. For a brief second I had the romantic notion that he had delayed his return home on my account. Then I recalled my experience in the very first Hall of Amenti and the pact made by the Amenti Council of twelve with the Queen and Prince of the Anunnaki.

'We cannot leave without the others,' both Sinclair and I said at the same time.

In one way I was disappointed that I would not be taking the ultimate passage any time soon, but part of me also looked forward to finishing my work here on Earth, in the company of my fellow staff members.

Sinclair regarded me proudly. 'You have made your own wings, my love, and now it's time to fly home.'

His words inspired me to confront the last stage of my soul's epic evolution on Earth. I stepped up to the violet-gold porthole and allowed its liquid-light whirlpool to consume me and reconnect me with Solarian.

ROOT RACE SEVEN — CAUSAL; THE CERES COUNCIL OF AMENTI

I am in a cavern deep within the Earth, at the time when the Solarian base station was first set in place here. I now remember the physical location of the station to which I alone am the key and it is thrilling to be so close to achieving the primary objective of my mission.

I move through the intricate underground labyrinth, pausing to read an extract from Ceres philosophy that I recorded in pictographs on the cavern wall before time on Earth began:

The Sovereign Integral is the natural state of existence of the entity that has transformed beyond the evolution model of existence and has removed itself from the controlling aspects of the hierarchy through the complete activation of its embedded time codes. All entities within the time–space universes are in various stages of the transformational experience and each are destined to achieve the Sovereign Integral level as their time codes become fully activated.

My efforts were not in vain, for the images stir memories of my life beyond the Earth scheme, just as I intended, and I know what I must do in order to return to my life as Solarian.

I see that some of my work has been vandalised since I was here last, but so skilfully that only I as the artist can tell. Pieces of artificial nano-filled crystals have been deposited throughout the cavern system — a technology that is a hallmark of the Old World order — and it is therefore no stretch of the imagination to guess who has interfered with the text. Still, it matters little, as there are many other such deposits of wisdom on the planet.

I leave the extensive cavern system behind me and pass down through several layers of rock placed in the passage by design, just prior to the demise of Atlantis. The complex in the crystal cavern beyond has never been entered by a human being and has been inactive since the flood.

We Ceres are extremely accomplished at moulding the matter of the lower planes of density, able to extend our will into the dimensions below our own, where our thought forms manifest as beings of light that do our bidding. We designed and constructed the Signet stargate system by transporting the twelve pyramids through the dark void in the centre of the sun in order to create this world in the solar system where souls could evolve and where civilisation could be nurtured. Originally, the twelve pyramids formed a matrix on the Earth through which blue flame energy was drawn from the Sphere of Amenti and channelled into huge extraterrestrial crystal deposits. The resulting energy force was sufficient to establish portholes to inner Earth and other interstellar civilisations within this lowest harmonic universe, and each of the twelve different extraterrestrial races that agreed to be part of the Signet security system for Amenti donated life forms to the Earth's design.

But over time the Nefilim and Dracon began to misuse the Earth grid for selfish purposes, just as the Anunnaki had misused Tara's energy matrix. When that misuse became apparent, the Signet power stations were transformed into security stations and the Sphere of Amenti was hidden in deep space, with all connections to the Earth blocked except for the Arc Porthole bridge. Our thought forms left the Earth's surface in our pyramids, and many of these remain outside of the physical planet. Up until the fall of Atlantis, however, the Pyramid matrix continued to connect the crystal grid on Earth to the blue flame energy of Amenti via the Arc Porthole bridge. But when Master Hermes warned us of Poseidonis's intent to convert the Blue Flame of Amenti to use for his own power projects, the Pyramid matrix was shut down completely to prevent its total annihilation. The Staff of Amenti buried and submerged the crystal power generators, along with the doctrine we wished humanity to find at some distant time when it might be appreciated and utilised. For although we wish all the lost souls of Tara peace and prosperity, we cannot enforce it upon them. Evolution is a choice that can only be actualised through will.

And it is such a will that has brought me to this place; this station where my spirit will wait until the final countdown in the inter-time war. A day is coming when all of Amenti's staff will take up their superhuman forms. We will draw down the twelve pyramids of light and fortify the consciousness of the Earth. For this planet must be ready to host the Sphere of Amenti when it finishes its descent down the Arc Porthole bridge early in the twenty-first century. Should we fail to achieve the minimum host frequency, both the Sphere and the Earth will be obliterated upon contact.

As my spirit enters the pyramid, I feel I have finally arrived home. Here I will await my final call to arms.

> *Here I connect to that sound beyond sound*
> *that has stalked the night-land of my dreams,*
> *where I enter rooms of fossil light*
> *so ancient they are swarmed by truth.*
> *I hear a sound beyond being*
> *that travels the spine's invisible ladder to the Orphic library*
> *where rebel books revel in the unremitting light.*
> *Tiny words with quicksand depth,*
> *embroidered with such care they*
> *render spirit a ghost and God,*
> *a telescope turned upon itself,*
> *dreaming us awake.*

FROM THE JOURNAL OF CHARLOTTE DEVERE

I paced the library floor impatiently, waiting for Lady Susan to hand over the desk and quill to me. Her session had been a particularly long one this time, and I assumed my mother's adventures had her riveted. I had alerted her several times to the fact that I was here to relieve her, but she merely shook her head and continued writing.

Even Albray was appearing a little concerned for our scribe's wellbeing.

'What do we know about the current leader of the Dracon?' I asked Albray as I strode up and down. 'They seem far too organised at present not to have someone in the command seat.'

He did not answer, but merely shrugged.

Finally, Lady Susan put down the quill, stretched and collapsed back into her chair. 'It is done,' she said.

'But there were three portholes left to traverse,' I said, moving around the writing table to speak with Lady Susan directly. 'Surely Mama could not have covered so much ground in one session?' I was concerned to discover tears streaming down the lady's face. 'What is it?' I asked. 'Has something gone wrong?'

Lady Susan shook her head, then said with a smile, 'I want to die.'

I looked at her, confused.

'So that I may complete my evolution and join her,' she explained, pulling a handkerchief from her sleeve to wipe her face. Her hand was shaking. 'I saw myself several times during Ashlee's journeys ... in one I was Marie de Saint-Clair!' She gave a laugh of bewildered delight. 'I know for certain that somewhere in the history of this world, I have earned my right to join the ranks of the Dragon Queens.'

I feared she had exhausted herself; her senses were surely on sensory overload. 'You should rest,' I suggested.

'Rest!' Lady Susan looked amused. 'Who could rest after such an experience? I may never sleep again!' She stood and strolled around the room to stretch out her stiff limbs.

'Lady Susan, I —'

'No, Charlotte, I haven't lost my mind,' she interrupted. 'I saw myself on the Amenti Council of Tara,' she went on, her voice filling with heartfelt amazement. 'The perception stirred memories in me clearer than those I perceive of this life. My true name is Talori,' she announced. 'Your true name is Kali.'

'I know.'

'And his,' Lady Susan pointed to Albray, 'is Arcturus.'

'It is?' The knight looked stunned.

'I have been aware of you for days,' the countess informed him, smiling. 'I believe we may have met before, in the Sinai?'

Albray nodded that she was quite correct.

'I recognise your energy,' she said in a thrilled tone. I knew Lady Susan had always wished for a little of my mother's psychic talent, and I could see by her aura that she had undergone a major spiritual awakening in the past few days.

'Be that as it may, my lady, I believe you should rest and eat now.' Albray was the calming voice of reason.

'But I wish to read all that Charlotte has penned of the tale,' she objected.

Albray was firm. 'The account is not going anywhere.'

'I will make sure it is all in order for you when you awake,' I promised, and Lady Susan finally submitted to our joint persuasion and left to get some rest.

'So what has become of your mother?' Albray said the moment the countess had exited the room. After days of waiting, he was just as curious as I to read this final piece of the puzzle. But first I needed to record Lady Susan's reaction to completing her quest, while it was still fresh in my mind.

FROM THE JOURNAL OF TAMAR DEVERE

A gentle knock on my door distracted me from my reading. This time Mum waited for my invitation to enter before opening the door.

'This list you gave me of your symptoms,' she said, 'hyper-sensitivity to sound and light, hot and cold flushes, breathing difficulties, intestinal problems, a swelling at the base of the skull, and the sensation of your skin crawling — according to an article I've been reading, these are some of the side effects associated with rapid DNA activation.'

'Really?' I tried to sound surprised.

'But there are some other symptoms listed too and I wanted to see if you had experienced any of those?' Mum looked at me over the top of her reading glasses.

'Shoot,' I said.

'Have you noticed a change in your sleeping patterns?'

You could say that, I thought. 'Reading this journal has been keeping me up late, and I've been having more vivid dreams when I do sleep,' I offered.

She moved down her list. 'How about periods of extreme joy or rapture?'

Like when I saw my body this morning?

I shook my head.

'Mental confusion?'

'Not really.'

'Difficulty concentrating?'

'No.'

'Enhanced telepathic ability?'

'No such luck.' But I was interested in the possibility that I might develop this talent, and I *had* been a little more intuitive when it came to what other people were thinking.

'Seeing auras?'

'Yes,' I said, surprised. It hadn't occurred to me to write that down as a physical symptom.

'Really!' Mum smiled, proud of me. As far as she knew, this was the first sign of psychic ability I'd ever exhibited. After my nightly adventures with Kali, I knew better. 'That was the first psychic talent I acquired too. Then astral projection.'

'I haven't had that experience yet,' I told her, although I suspected I'd been doing a fair bit of walking about in my sleep.

'So what does my light-body look like?' She tested my new power of perception.

'It's mostly blue and sparkly, but you have dark patches over your heart and third-eye light centres ... are you worried about someone you love?' I said, before realising that someone was probably me. I wanted to tell her about Kali, but then I worried that if she knew about the forthcoming merger, she'd probably try to stop it. 'I'm sorry to make you worry, but I truly feel there's no need to,' I told her. 'What's happening to me might be strange, but it's not horrible or painful in any way.'

Mum came to sit beside me on the bed and gave me a hug, clearly relieved to hear that. 'It's my pleasure to worry about you,' she assured me.

'What do you think Dad's going to say when he sees me?' I asked, a little concerned about his reaction to my rapid development.

'I believe he'll think you look stunning,' Mum said, and smiled. 'Just like every other male who set eyes on you today.'

We both had a little chuckle.

'No more ugly duckling,' I commented.

'Oh,' groaned Mum, 'you never were an ugly duckling. Everyone goes through an awkward stage at your age — you've just grown out of it faster than most.' She sniffed back her emotion and pulled away.

'There's something I want to give you, now that it won't fall off.'

She pretended to pull something off her finger and placed whatever it was in my hand.

'Mum!' I said, feeling annoyed at being treated like a child again. But as I dropped my hand I felt something slide off it. 'Hey, there really is something there!'

'Don't lose it,' Mum said. She helped me find the lost item on the floor, and this time slid it on my finger.

'Holy shit!' I exclaimed. 'It's an invisible ring! That is totally sick!'

My mother looked confused.

'That means cool, Mum,' I explained. 'Where did it come from?'

'It was a gift to me from a prince, who didn't tell me where he got it,' she said mysteriously.

'What does it look like?'

Mum shrugged, as if she had never thought about it. 'I really don't know. I guess it looks however you imagine it to look.'

'But what's the point of making a ring no one can see, besides the novelty value?' I wondered out loud.

'Well, invisibility would be an asset if you didn't want anyone to know of the ring's existence,' Mum said, which only added to the mystery.

I gave her a huge hug and kiss. 'I'll cherish it always,' I said.

Mum kissed me back. 'Well, I'll let you get back to your reading,' she said.

I nodded. 'I'm nearly done.'

Mum closed the door after her and I picked up the journal again. Where was I? Ah yes, Charlotte recording Lady Susan's reaction to Ashlee's final adventures. But then I noticed the script that followed wasn't Charlotte's hand at all, and that it seemed to have been written in a different ink from the previous entries . . .

THE DARK HALF

FROM THE JOURNAL OF LADY ASHLEE GRANVILLE-DEVERE —
AN EPILOGUE BY LADY SUSAN DEVERE

A year has passed since I aided Charlotte Devere to pen the tale of my
dear friend's journey through the Halls of Amenti. It has taken me this
long to add the Amenti section to this, Ashlee's final journal. I also
found entries in Charlotte Devere's private journals that I felt needed
to be incorporated into the Amenti account, to explain what unfolded
at the Deveres' home in Suffolk once Ashlee's tale had been
committed to paper.

On that day when Ashlee's journey was complete and my
connection with her via the ring ceased, I was eager to read of the
other events of her adventure, those that Charlotte had chronicled.
However, Charlotte and Albray urged me to eat and rest first, so I
returned the ring to Charlotte and retired to my room.

I was aware that I had undergone a deep spiritual awakening
during the course of my journalising these past few days, but I had
no idea how extensive that awakening had been when I lay down to
sleep off my exhaustion in my room at the Suffolk house. What I did
know was that something inside me had been turned on, and I was
inspired, excited, liberated! I was one of the Dragon Queens and an
Amenti staff member, and so was my husband, James! The thought
of my sensible, upstanding husband, who in this lifetime abhorred
all things esoteric, being one of the Amenti Council was very
amusing to me; but I knew I need not push the issue with him in

this life, for indeed he had many lifetimes to learn of his true self, and his moment of realisation would come at the right time for him. The only thing that mattered to me was that, in the end, we would be together.

This welling sense of expectation of my higher calling made it very difficult to get to sleep, yet when I did finally succumb I slept like the dead. And then I began to dream.

I am back in the library, yet when I glance down, I do not have a physical form. I hear a cry and see that Charlotte is pinned to the desk by a strange fair-haired man. He stands between her spread legs, mauling her neck with kisses. I am surprised that she is not struggling to be free of him, for the stench emanating from him is overbearing. Then I realise she must know him, for she addresses him by name.

'Mathu, are you not afraid of hurting me?' she asks.

'I can be sensitive,' he says, grabbing her thighs and grinding himself against her.

'No.' She tries to push him away but he is too strong for her.

'Oh, come on, don't be a tease,' he says, pulling her close again. 'I have to know what it's like to fuck a queen, just once.' He wriggles his tongue in her face then sticks it down her throat.

I gag at the same time Charlotte does and suddenly I feel her emotions as strongly as if they are my own. I want to be sick! I can tell that she wants to repel him, but she has not developed her mother's psychokinetic expertise. She tries summoning fire elementals to her aid, willing them to heat his body until he relents.

'Ha!' Mathu laughs in her face. 'No elemental on this Earth scheme would dare oppose me.'

She is at his mercy. I realise that it is her very love for him that has invited this attack. 'Mathu, please —' she says.

'Thank you kindly, I don't mind if I do.' He rips her frock open and she screams at the top of her lungs as she struggles against him.

Lady Susan!

* * *

Lady Susan!

My eyes sprang open and instantly I recalled the dream. I wanted to be sick, but the sight of Albray at my bedside distracted me and I realised it was his voice that had wakened me.

Quickly, the ghostly knight urged. *I need your body.*

'By all means,' I said and clambered from beneath the bedclothes. 'Although my body is not what it used to be.' I glanced down at myself and realised I was wearing my sheer underdress and nothing else.

You look just fine to me, Albray said. *Now, grab swords.* He pointed outside my room to where a display of weapons was mounted on the corridor wall.

'No time to be modest,' I sighed, and ripped two swords from their mounts and raced behind Albray in the direction of the library and, I assumed, to Charlotte's rescue.

The swords were heavy in my hands, but the instant Albray joined with me they became as much a part of me as my arms and legs. My entire body moved with greater ease as the ghostly knight assumed full physical control.

I slipped into the library as silent as a draught. The huge fair man was ravishing Charlotte on the desk, slapping her face to prevent her passing out. With a shock, I recalled the name from my chronicling of Ashlee's journey through the Halls of Amenti: Mathu was Kali's prince, which meant he was also Charlotte's great love.

'This is what you wanted, isn't it, princess?' he jeered. 'And I'm going to make sure you don't miss a —'

From behind, Albray thrust both swords into Mathu's body. He shouted out in pain and staggered backwards as Albray withdrew the weapons just as rapidly.

'I thought your physical body didn't feel anything?' Charlotte cried.

Both Albray and I were surprised by her reaction, and even more startled when green slime began to ooze from the wounds in Mathu's body.

Charlotte burst into tears. She rolled off the table and backed away from her attacker. 'You are not Mathu,' she accused, appearing relieved.

'Sure I am.' His voice became gravelly and his body began to stretch out of shape, ripping apart to reveal a huge albino reptilian, about nine foot tall, with wings that unfurled as we watched. I recognised it from Ashlee's travels as a Dracon, except he had more skin than scales and long fingernails instead of claws. 'Didn't fairy boy tell you about me? I'm his dark half.' He let out a growl and the force of his anger sent Charlotte and myself rocketing backwards to hit the bookshelves that lined the library walls.

The first rays of dawn shone through the library windows and Mathu manifested in the room.

Charlotte was most relieved to see him. 'Mathu, where have you been?'

'In the last century,' he said. 'I am so sorry —'

'He's been making deals to save his own skin,' Pintar interjected.

'Poseidonis! I thought you perished with Atlantis!' Mathu's calm demeanour was diminishing rapidly.

'I go by the name of Pintar these days,' the winged demon grinned. 'Did you really think you could kill your own shadow?'

The beast held out a hand and willed Charlotte to him. Mathu counteracted the command and Charlotte hung suspended in the air between the two adversaries, her dress gaping open to expose her bruised body.

'Let her go!' Mathu entreated the beast.

'I claimed her, so I get to keep her,' Pintar taunted. 'Foreplay doesn't count.'

Charlotte cried out under the duress of her body being torn between two equally opposing forces. Out of mercy, Mathu let her go and Charlotte flew into Pintar's clutches. A metal spike extended from the inside of the demon's wrist — Pintar had a soul-shattering module embedded in him.

'No!' Mathu was horrified and moved to intervene.

Pintar held the spike against the back of Charlotte's neck, which stopped Mathu in his tracks.

'How did you find us?' Mathu asked.

This scene was so familiar to me: it was like watching Lilitu's death all over again. Then I found myself remembering an event I had never seen, and realised it was Albray's memory of witnessing Taejax give Ashlee and Charlotte the rings. Something Ashlee had said at the time was playing on his mind: *How do I know these rings aren't a trick that will disclose my every movement beyond this plane to the Dracon?*

Taejax betrayed us, I say to Albray, noting the ring on Charlotte's finger.

If the reptilians were able to intercept the rings' transmission, that would explain how they had tracked down Lilitu du Lac. It might also explain how the Dracon — the Nagas, as the Ha-mazons called them — had attacked the warrior tribe in Ashlee's recollection of events, for if they were monitoring Ashlee's perception of that lifetime they would have discovered that the Ha-mazon were vulnerable to attack. Perhaps it also explained how Poseidonis had escaped death during the destruction of Atlantis.

I looked at Pintar's long gnarly fingers wrapped around Charlotte's throat; staring me right in the face was the answer to many of the conundrums in Ashlee's tale — Pintar had his own ring.

'The rings' transmission has been intercepted,' I told Mathu, trying to answer his question without referring to Taejax directly.

Mathu was bewildered; he didn't understand how Taejax could keep up the illusion of evolving without truly doing so. 'That cannot be . . .'

The library door flew open and Lord Devere entered, accompanied by Taejax. Then I realised it was not Devere at all, but Captain Sinclair. Both he and the Dracon seemed startled by the scene that met them.

'What are you doing here?' Mathu asked, clearly unconvinced by the timing. If Taejax was not guilty, then his use as a double agent was at an end.

'Obviously, I am a prisoner,' Captain Sinclair said, motioning to Taejax.

The reptilian had been holding his firearm at ease, but at Sinclair's words he raised it and aimed at the captain's head. 'I spied him creeping around outside,' Taejax informed Pintar, pushing his supposed captive into the room.

'How did you know I was here?' Pintar demanded. 'I sense your disloyalty . . . your mind and will used to belong to me!'

Suddenly it was clear that Taejax had not knowingly betrayed us.

'My orders were to keep an eye on the house,' Taejax snarled. 'I didn't know you were here. I came to retrieve the ring.'

Sinclair put his hand up. 'That is also why I am here. However ...' he fixed his eyes on the beast that held Charlotte captive and, seeing the state of the girl, became irate '... it seems I have bigger fish to fry.' He pulled a sleek handgun from his weapons belt and aimed it at Pintar, in the same instant drawing another handgun to aim at Taejax.

Pintar laughed off the threat. 'You cannot hope to kill me with a gun.'

'That is probably so,' Captain Sinclair agreed, 'but liquid nitrogen darts will destroy that hideous body you are wearing.'

'Will you bet one of the souls you need to get home to Tara that you will not miss?' Pintar challenged, pulling Charlotte around in front of him as a shield.

'I am a patient man,' said the captain, raising the gun to take a better aim at Pintar. I could tell that he wasn't covering Taejax properly, which reinforced my suspicion that he knew the reptilian was not a threat. 'I will find a clear shot and I will not miss.'

Suddenly Taejax flung himself at Sinclair, overpowering him. Both guns went flying out of his hands. The captain appeared surprised by the move, as were Albray and myself. Who was bluffing whom here? Only Taejax knew.

Pintar was pleased to have the situation back under his control. 'Now this event can end one of two ways,' he said to Mathu. 'You can allow me to take my *impregnated* whore home, where I will nurture her and our pending child with a healthy ORME addiction so they may enjoy eternity at my side whilst I enslave the human race and reassume control of surface Earth —'

'I'm sure the Nefilim are just going to step aside for you,' Captain Sinclair interrupted.

'Or,' Pintar ignored the dig, 'you can try and save your precious Kali, whereupon I overdose her now and that will be game over for Team Amenti. Personally, I'd rather have your queen as my sex slave until judgement day, but the choice is yours.'

I glanced at Charlotte; she had gone quiet and closed her eyes, clearly repulsed at the idea that she may be carrying the demon's child.

As I watched, a bead of sweat rolled down her temple. Then she spoke: 'Why delay the inevitable?'

Pintar yanked her head backwards. 'What was that, sweetheart?'

Charlotte struggled to contain her wrath as she stared into the eyes of the creature. 'I said, why delay the inevitable when your pending child and I can burn in hell right now?' The young girl's body burst into flames. Pintar growled in rage and cast her aside.

'Kali!' Mathu was devastated to witness her suicide all over again. He summoned a storm inside the library to rain upon the flames and put them out, but Charlotte was little more than a muddy pile of ash by the time the storm quenched the fire, for she had combusted from within.

Mathu looked to Pintar, his eyes filled with hatred.

'That's twice you've just stood by and let her off herself,' Pintar taunted.

Before Mathu could launch himself at the creature, Captain Sinclair had dived across the floor, grabbed up his sleek gun and fired several rounds of liquid nitrogen darts into Pintar's legs. Instantly, they froze like ice and pinned him to the floor as though he were turned to stone. The creature screeched in pain and frustration.

'I'll take that.' Captain Sinclair bade Pintar's ring to come into his possession and so it did.

Furious, Pintar struck at the captain. 'I'm going to destroy you, Polaris,' he screamed. The captain easily avoided the assault, not the slightest bit perturbed by his enemy's rage.

Taejax fell to his knees beside the mound of wet ash that had been Charlotte. 'I was only bluffing!' he cried. 'I thought I was doing the right thing to protect my cover! I should have let Sinclair take the shot, but he left himself so open to me that I had to try and take him out or Pintar would have suspected something.'

Mathu placed a comforting hand on his old friend's shoulder. 'You could not have guessed she would do this, whereas I ...' His tears flowed freely. 'I should have known.'

I too was shocked and saddened by Charlotte's decision, but not half as much as Albray, who felt he had failed in his vow to Ashlee.

Pintar laughed at our sorrow. 'You fool,' he told his turncoat

Dracon. 'You betrayed them all and you didn't even know. You are an outcast, Taejax! You will fade into a mortal, die and be damned!'

Taejax did not respond, his attention all on Charlotte's remains.

'Hey, big guy!' Captain Sinclair whistled to secure Pintar's attention once more. 'I need some answers from you.'

'Go fuck yourself!' Pintar snarled.

'You are so predictable.'

The captain fired a few more darts into one of Pintar's arms and the demon cried out as it too froze. Curiously, despite his frozen body parts, Pintar was sweating; I suspected he was drawing fire elementals to himself and ordering them to defrost him — just as Charlotte had summoned them to aid her to combust. Captain Sinclair knew he was pushed for time.

'You had targeted Ashlee and Earnest Devere as Ceres operatives long before Taejax gave the rings to Ashlee and Charlotte, hadn't you? I know Taejax didn't tell you, and as he has severed himself from your control, you could not have read his mind.'

'You want to know how I tracked Solarian?' Pintar queried. The captain nodded. 'Go fuck yourself!'

Sinclair wasn't surprised by the answer. He fired another round of darts at the demon's limbs. 'I can do this all day,' he said. 'I have plenty of ammunition.'

'Solarian has made many enemies in the underworld,' Pintar snarled. 'She gave herself away by exposing the extent of her power to her enemies.'

'Molier!' Albray and I both came up with the name of the culprit.

The captain saw the truth of it, realising that Molier must still be on the loose, for he had escaped Ashlee's wrath thirty years ago and no one had seen him since. This in turn explained a mystery from Sinclair's life as Earnest Devere. 'You tried to discover Ashlee's whereabouts from Lord Malory, and when he wouldn't tell you, you killed him,' he accused the Dracon.

'I obliterated him,' Pintar gloated.

It was clear to me that the captain was having difficulty suppressing his urge to finish off Pintar once and for all. 'Where is Molier now?' he demanded.

'Go f—'

Sinclair filled the beast full of darts until he was so frozen he could no longer respond.

'Oops.' The captain realised his trigger finger had been a little over-zealous. 'Now we're going to have to wait for his elementals to thaw him out a bit.'

As the crisis seemed to have passed, Albray sat me down in a chair and departed my form.

'Are you all right, Talori?' the captain asked me, then nodded to acknowledge the ghost who now stood beside me. 'Arcturus.'

I was not used to the name Talori, but it resonated with my being. 'I'm fine,' I assured him; my only hurt was grief at the loss of Charlotte. 'But where did that monster come from? My understanding is that the leader of the Dracon is Lillian's misbegotten child, so how is it that Pintar claims to be your shadow, Mathu?'

Mathu turned from comforting Taejax to explain. 'After I witnessed Kali's suicide and then was visited by her spirit, I was so remorseful of my own heartless acts towards humanity and my Nefilim relations that I immediately wanted to start righting all the wrongs I had done or encouraged. However, I was so crippled by guilt and pain that I could do nothing. So I employed the dark arts I had perfected one last time, to draw out all that was bad from my being. I placed all this evil into a Dracon drone, which I intended to kill afterwards and thereby rid myself of my most horrid memories and feelings.'

'But once your darkness was gone, you no longer had the wish to kill,' Captain Sinclair guessed.

'Not until today.' Mathu's intense gaze turned to Pintar, who was slowly defrosting.

'Let me guess ...' I felt I had figured out the connection to Lillian. 'The Dracon you let go was the same warrior who raped Lillian, and when he impregnated her the evil thought-form transferred to her child.'

Mathu nodded. 'And once a demon has escaped the vessel of its containment, there is only one hope of destroying it. It must be returned to its original source for processing.'

Mathu relieved the captain of his dart gun and began firing at Pintar, until the reptilian's entire form was petrified. Then he focused on his disabled adversary ... slowly a whirlwind built around the beastly abomination, yet we felt barely a breath of its presence. Mathu returned the dart gun to Captain Sinclair in exchange for a regular handgun.

'What do you have in mind, old friend?' Sinclair asked, clearly concerned.

'Something I should have done tens of thousands of years ago,' Mathu replied.

He fired at Pintar and the creature's form shattered into icy splinters. The dark, angry thought-form was released, but it and the ice splinters were held contained by the whirlwind. When we saw that Mathu intended walking into the eye of this maelstrom, we tried to prevent him, but were repelled by the elemental forces under his command.

The evil entity was absorbed into Mathu's form, the whirlwind died away and Mathu was left struggling with himself. It seemed the clash of forces would drive him to madness; he cried out in agony and stumbled about the room, struggling to digest not only his long-forgotten nightmares, but all the horrors that Pintar had committed since. Then, suddenly, he cried, 'Out of the way,' and took a running jump at the great bay window, vanishing before he broke through the glass.

What the hell was that all about? said Albray in the stunned silence that followed. *What is going on?*

'I'll read you all that Charlotte and I recorded on Ashlee's behalf,' I promised him. 'That will explain a great deal.'

Sinclair crouched down by the grieving Dracon. 'Come, Taejax, we should depart.' Then he spied the ring lying in the ash that had been Charlotte Devere's body. He retrieved it and looked to me, the only living being remaining. 'Can you take care of things here?'

I shall remain as long as I am needed, Albray added, pointing out that he was not entirely useless, just because he was dead. *I know what must be done.*

'I'll be fine,' I assured the time pirate and his alien friend. 'You should both go before you are spotted and I have to try and explain you.'

And thus it fell to me to complete the journals of Ashlee Granville-Devere and Charlotte Devere.

What became of Mathu, how his struggle ended, remains a mystery to me. I have not seen or heard from Captain Sinclair or Taejax, and I do not expect to, not in this lifetime. I miss Ashlee a great deal; I miss her stories, her friendship, and all the mayhem and mystery that followed her wherever she went. I have read all of her journals now and have been enlightened and challenged by her adventures, just as I suspect future generations will be. It was my greatest honour to know Ashlee Granville-Devere and to preserve these writings in her name.

Albray has stayed with me as promised, but now my task is near complete I must dismiss him and return his ringstone to the back of Ashlee's red journal, where she always hid it for safekeeping. I will miss him too. All these journals I am committing into a large chest that I shall personally see delivered to Rebecca, Ashlee's eldest daughter, for all the first daughters of her family line to inherit.

As for myself, life will go on, but it will never be the sheltered experience it was before I agreed to help chronicle Ashlee's journey through Amenti. For now I know that the blood in my veins is not entirely human, and I have been awakened to a perception of things not always of this world. There is a war being waged outside the time frame of this planet, and somewhere in the future I am a fully aware Ceres operative, striving with the other Staff of Amenti to further the cause of human evolution in this dimension and beyond.

FROM THE JOURNAL OF TAMAR DEVERE

With a great sigh — partly of satisfaction and partly of disappointment for having finished the journal — I closed the book on the life of the great Lady Ashlee Granville-Devere. Even though I was thrilled to have absorbed an abundance of information about mysteries I would never have known existed, tears welled in my eyes. I was upset by Charlotte's death, and I wondered what had become of the enchanting Mathu and his struggle with his emotional baggage. I wanted to know more about him and was sad that my wish could not be fulfilled. There was nothing more to read.

I went down to the kitchen for something to eat and was pleased to see Mum there, drinking a cup of coffee. I gave her a hug and sat down at the table next to her. 'I finished the journal,' I said.

'So what did you think?' Her tone was casual, but I felt it was time for us to be straight with one another.

'I'm not sure what I am supposed to make of it,' I said, folding my arms. 'I think that the reason you're not really that concerned by my sudden growth spurt is because you were expecting it.'

'I know, I know.' Mum held up a hand to assure me she understood my annoyance. 'You're not stupid, and you're not a child any more, and it's high time I levelled with you.'

'About Giza?' I prompted. I had no idea what vital import this had on my current situation, but Mum had mentioned that someone had made predictions about me during her stint in Giza, shortly after my conception.

She looked shocked. 'You were listening in on my phone —'

'Giza,' I repeated, not to be sidetracked by a lecture.

Mum calmed, realising that, for once, I had right of way. 'Here.' She pulled a small notebook out of her bag and handed it over to me.

I read the title on the front aloud: '*Project Alkazar*. What is this? It doesn't look like one of your regular work journals.'

'That's because it isn't,' Mum said. 'It's kind of a sequel to Ashlee's journey through Amenti.'

I couldn't believe it: my hope to learn more was about to be realised. 'Really?'

Mum nodded.

'And you wrote this?'

'Yes,' she smiled proudly, 'I did. I'd like you to read it before —'

'But, Mum —' I opened my mouth to object to not getting my answers sooner, but Mum interrupted me in her turn.

'I promise this journal will bring you up to speed, and anything you want to know after that I'll gladly tell you. Deal?'

'Sure.' I raced out of the kitchen and back up to my room, eager to discover if there was any news of Mathu in here. I was also curious to find out just how well informed about cosmic affairs my mother and father truly were.

THE FLAME-BEARERS

FROM THE JOURNAL OF MIA DEVERE

I hadn't long arrived back in Australia following my misadventure in the Sinai with Christian Molier and company, when an archaeological group contacted me — at least, at the time I assumed they were an archaeological organisation. They called themselves the Alkazar Project and said they had discovered a way to unlock the legendary Hall of Records fabled to be hidden beneath the rear paws of the Sphinx on the Giza plateau in Egypt. They anticipated needing a translator to decipher the texts they expected to find there, and I was their first and only choice for the job. The project certainly seemed right up my alley and the money they were offering made the prospect very attractive. However, I had only just married my dear husband and was not yet ready to leave him for months on end. The project leader was very understanding and insisted that I bring Albray along — little did I realise that my husband was as integral to the opening of the Hall of Records as I was.

It was on the plane en route to Giza that my nausea and vomiting started. I was normally a very good traveller and so my first conclusion was that I was coming down with something. When Albray and I arrived at the hotel in Giza, which had the most spectacular views of the Pyramids, we were advised that the Alkazar Project leader, Jamila Paki, wished to have a private meeting with us in our suite that evening. As I was still feeling rather poorly, this arrangement suited me just fine.

After a sleep, a swim and a meal, I felt much improved. By the time reception rang to advise that Miss Paki and her associate were on their way up, I was well enough to be excited about the pending meeting.

When I opened the door to greet my new employers I nearly died of shock, for accompanying Miss Paki was a treasured friend from my Sinai adventure.

'I told you that we'd meet again,' the tall Arab, dressed all in black, said to me with a smile.

'Akbar!' I threw myself into his embrace — a mode of greeting we were both comfortable with after all that we had been through together. 'What are you doing here?'

'Inside,' he advised, indicating that we should not speak in the hall.

'I'm so sorry.' I remembered my manners and invited Akbar and his tiny associate inside. Our guests entered and I closed the door behind them. 'You must be Miss Paki.' I held out my hand to shake hers.

'Call me Jamila, please,' the woman implored.

Jamila was not at all what I'd expected. She had a very jovial, friendly face that beamed with vitality despite her age — I was guessing she was a good twenty years older than I. She was dressed in brightly patterned flowing robes and looked more like a holy woman than an archaeologist. What was more, she held my hand as a dear old friend might.

'And you are Mia,' she said. 'I have heard so much about you.'

Well, at least now I knew who her source was, and perhaps why I had been her only choice for the job.

Akbar's attention turned to my husband. He bowed. 'Albe-Ra, what an honour it is to meet you again.'

Albray was taken aback, for he had not gone by that name since the thirteenth century. 'I think you are mistaken,' he said.

Akbar smiled and looked to Jamila, who backed up his assumption. 'There is no mistaking you, Shining One, these eyes see all,' she said, gesturing both to herself and Akbar.

It seemed my first impression of Jamila had been spot-on: she was a psychic not an archaeologist, and one of great merit if she was in the company of Akbar, who was a member of an ancient brotherhood known as the Melchi.

'What is going on here?' I said warily. 'Why do I get the distinct feeling that we have been lured here under false pretences?'

'Everything I told you on the phone is true,' Jamila defended with a smile. 'If you will allow us the opportunity, I shall be happy to clarify the situation for you.'

I looked to my husband to gauge his feelings on the matter. He smiled and motioned our guests to take a seat on the lounge.

'You're not an archaeologist, are you?' I asked Jamila once we were all comfortable.

She appeared amused by the question and paused before responding. 'I am what you might call a spiritual archaeologist. I am a seeker of ancient souls — souls such as you three — sent to Earth to fulfil a specific purpose in the great cosmic scheme of things.'

'Three?' I queried; was she including Akbar in this equation?

'You, Albe-Ra and your unborn child,' she said, leaving my husband and me gobsmacked.

'You think I'm pregnant?' I asked, panicked and excited at once. Was that the reason I had been so ill?

'You *are* pregnant,' she assured me, 'and the child you are carrying is of vital import to Earth's evolution at this time.'

'What!' Too much information — I was overwhelmed.

'Why are you surprised?' Jamila reasoned. 'Consider the extraordinary circumstances by which you and Albe-Ra have been brought together across time and space. Did you honestly think that the mighty Elohim had brought forth this greatest of Grail Princes from the Middle Ages and paired him with you, a Dragon Queen, for no good reason?'

I looked to Akbar, annoyed that he had told Jamila about my little family secret.

'I said nothing,' he defended, in response to my glare. 'Jamila sought me out and she already knew all about you. It was Jamila who enlightened me as to the origins of your companion, as indeed she enlightened me to a great many truths about myself.'

If my memory served, I hadn't told Akbar how I had met Albray, nor how it was that he had come to my aid in the Sinai last year, which seemed to indicate my friend was telling the truth.

'How could you know about us?' I asked Jamila, desperate for answers.

'Your father told me about you,' she said, and I near stopped breathing.

'My father died before I was born, and my mother died before I was five,' I said bitterly.

'So you know little about your conception then?' Jamila remained calm, knowing she was treading over what was very emotional ground for me.

I had recently been reading one of my foremother's journals about her travels in Persia. In it, she had investigated her mother's claim that she was seduced by an angel on her wedding night who possessed the body of her husband in order to mate with her and produce a human body capable of sustaining an angelic soul. If the child produced by the union was a girl, she would be a Dragon Queen. In all of the history of this planet, past and future, many were born into the Grail bloodline, but the Dragon Queens numbered only six and one — just as the true Grail Princes numbered only six and one. According to Ashlee's account, twelve of these souls came from a race of advanced humans, the Ceres, who lived on our planet in the harmonic universe above our own. The other two souls were of a different race entirely, known as the Anunnaki.

'Are you implying I am a daughter of Sama-El?' I said.

Sama-El was the serpent in the Garden of Eden, which was why his progeny were known as Dragons. It was said that, through the bodies of human men, he had fathered all of these queens and their princes; it was also he who reminded them of their mission here on Earth, once they had evolved sufficiently.

Jamila nodded. 'It is he who instructed me to seek you out at this time and enlighten you as to the quest you are destined to perform.'

'Why now?' Naturally, I was suspicious.

'Your destiny had to be given time to unfold,' Jamila explained, 'for your task requires three unique souls: Albe-Ra, the holder of the orange-gold flame of Earth's morphogenetic field; you, the bearer of the blue flame consciousness of Tara; and your daughter, the holder of the violet flame consciousness of Gaia.'

You could have scooped my jaw off the ground. Ashlee's journal had predicted that her daughter Charlotte would reincarnate, and when she did she would carry the violet flame.

'How can you know for sure that we are the three flame-bearers?' Albray interrupted. 'For it will mean certain death to the three of us if you are wrong.'

I turned to my husband. 'Hold on ... you know what this is all about?'

Albray nodded. 'A very old prophecy ... more ancient than I.'

I felt rather irked that my husband had never mentioned this. 'Would you care to enlighten me?'

'My love,' he began, sensing my mood and thoughts, 'it has never once occurred to me that we might have anything to do with the legend in question.'

'I'm sorry.' I changed my tone to one more accommodating. 'This is all such a shock.'

'For me too,' he assured me.

Jamila offered me a more detailed explanation. 'The Hall of Records is a fourth-dimensional porthole passage and storage area that connects the morphogenetic fields of Earth, Tara and Gaia — it is a conduit through which data from the Akashic record of the five harmonic universes can be downloaded. The Hall of Records can only be opened by three specific individuals — a man who holds the two-dimensional orange-gold flame, a female who holds the fifth-dimensional blue flame, and another female who holds the violet flame of dimension seven. Once opened, universal memory will come "online", so to speak. The Sphere of Amenti will release this coded data into the Earth's grid, where it can be picked up by the human bio-energetic field and translated into conscious information by any being who has managed to assemble the fourth DNA strand or higher.'

I was only more perplexed. 'I still don't understand what the term flame-bearer means.'

'When I speak of the coloured flames, I am referring to the multiple bands of frequency that compose the morphogenetic fields,' Jamila said. When she saw the frown on my face deepening, she tried to simplify. 'Take your husband, for example: he holds the orange-gold flame, which is the standing wave pattern that composes the frequencies of dimensions one to three, which you may know as density, the etheric or underworld, and the physical world.'

'Gotcha,' I said, finally starting to understand.

'The blue flame-bearer — you, Mia — holds the frequency patterns of dimensions four to six —'

'The astral, mental and causal realms,' I cut in, showing off my newly acquired esoteric understanding.

'Exactly. And the violet-flame holder, your daughter, holds the frequency pattern of dimension seven, through which Tara's dimensions eight to twelve can be accessed — and this is the primary goal of evolution. Flame-bearers carry a specific magnetic base tone within their DNA — the Gene of Isis — that allows their bio-energetic system to become highly magnetic in order to activate this recessive gene. Without this gene, the human body would be ripped apart when attempting to fulfil the flame-bearers' essential role — to open the Hall of Records. Many have attempted this feat, but only the three flame-bearers combined possess the frequency codes that allow them to act as conduits for downloading the transmissions from the Akashic Record.'

'But there must be thousands of people who have the Gene of Isis in their DNA,' I said.

'Yes,' agreed Jamila, 'I myself am a carrier. However, I am not the chosen bearer of the blue flame, nor am I pregnant with the violet flame-bearer.'

I looked to Albray, who appeared as bewildered as I was.

'You both need time to process this information,' Jamila said, apparently reading our minds. 'We shall return in the morning to speak more.' She stood, as did Akbar.

'Until tomorrow.' Akbar smiled and bowed his head to us.

My Arab friend seemed happy and excited, quite unlike the serious, reserved person I'd met in the Sinai. This assignment obviously thrilled him. I could not say I felt the same. The news of my pregnancy changed everything, for if it proved true, mine was no longer the only life at risk when I entered precarious ancient places.

*   *   *

Albray embraced me the second I closed the door on our guests. 'We are with child,' he said, and squeezed me, obviously delighted by the prospect.

'My love, nobody speaks like that any more. And I don't think we should celebrate being parents until I can confirm Jamila's prediction.' I didn't want to get too excited by the possibility, yet I could not wipe the grin from my face.

'How can we do that?' he asked. Having been in the twenty-first century for only a few months, he was unaware of all it had to offer.

'I'll go down to the hotel chemist and buy a pregnancy test, I guess.'

'I'll go,' Albray volunteered, eager to run off some of his excited energy. 'You rest.' He kissed my forehead and headed for the door.

'Honey ...' I spied his wallet sitting on the table, and when he turned back I referred him to it.

'Ah, right.' He grinned at his own absent-mindedness. 'I might need that.' He grabbed the wallet and kissed me again before heading out the door.

Less than a quarter of an hour later, my pregnancy was confirmed; if we were to believe Jamila's prophecy, we were expecting a daughter. Albray was over the moon, having longed for centuries to start a family. I wanted to be excited, and was delighted by the prospect of parenthood, but the professional aspect of me regretted the fact that a child was going to curtail my professional commitments considerably. When I explained my concerns to Albray, he understood, but pointed out that until such options were put to me, I was worrying about something that did not exist.

'But what about the opening of the Hall of Records?' I said. 'You don't think such a task is going to be risk-free, surely?'

'For the true flame-bearers it will be risk-free,' he replied. 'Let us wait and hear Jamila out before we put a damper on the best chance for the advancement of planetary consciousness, hey?'

His attitude was so relaxed that it calmed me too.

'I won't allow any harm to befall you or our daughter,' he went on, then grinned, highly amused by his own words. 'Our daughter,' he repeated, 'that just sounds so peculiar coming out of *my* mouth.'

'I know what you mean … *Dad*,' I teased and my own face split in a huge grin again.

'I like the sound of that,' he said, placing his palm flat against my belly. 'In here grows the key to a higher harmonic universe and we made her.'

Albray was clearly proud to have taken part in such a conception, and his kiss conveyed his love and gratitude for the gift I was to bestow on us both.

By the time Jamila returned the next morning, alone, both Albray and myself were far more at ease.

Since I had confirmed the cause of my nausea, it had ebbed and been replaced by a huge appetite — I swear I had not stopped eating since I'd found out about Tamar. Yes, we had already decided upon a name for our daughter. Albray felt it would be nice to name her after the first child of the Magdalene, for Tamar was an integral Grail Princess that history had denied ever existed. It was also Tamar who had passed on the Gene of Isis to Albray's family line and my own.

Jamila was carrying a huge bunch of flowers, which she handed to me. 'Congratulations on your happy news, from all at project Alkazar.'

I accepted the offering graciously and admired the bouquet. 'How did this project get the name Alkazar?' I asked. 'I don't know of a god by that name.'

'*The Secrets of Alkazar* is a children's book on magic that advises aspiring magicians to pay attention to techniques of misdirection, for an audience will always look where the magician looks and treat as important whatever the magician treats as important. Hence, the magician must never look at what he wants to conceal. The Hall of Records is hidden according to the methods of Alkazar,' she said in conclusion, and smiled.

'So you believe Thoth's chamber is located somewhere away from the main attractions of the Giza plateau?' I reasoned.

'Indeed. This is why most investigations into the Giza plateau have come up inconclusive as far as the legendary Hall of Records is concerned, for it is nowhere near the Pyramids or the Sphinx — it is my belief that it is is a gross case of misdirection. However, these markers are still the means to locate the hall in question, if you think like a master architect cum mathematician might. One of the sacred names of the Sphinx is Neb, which means —'

'The spiralling force of the universe.' I couldn't resist the chance to show my knowledge again.

Jamila grinned and nodded. 'And why should the spiralling force of the universe be associated with the Sphinx?'

I knew the answer to this one too, as I had read Rocky McCollum's work on the Giza necropolis. 'The Fibonacci spiral,' I stated confidently.

Fibonacci, born Leonardo da Pisa in 1175 AD, wrote the *Liber Abaci* in which he outlined a sequence of numbers that begins with 0 and 1, and continues by following the simple rule of adding the last two numbers to get the next — thus the sequence 1, 2, 3, 5, 8, 13, 21, 34, 55 etc. This number sequence was not a new discovery, but rather a rediscovery of the mathematics of Plato's time and before. The numbers were used in a quadratic equation to find the golden ratio, which is denoted by the Greek letter *phi*. *Phi* was used as an integral part of the design of ancient Greek architecture, the most famous construction of which is the Parthenon in Athens.

'In the 1970s, Rocky McCollum noted that you could draw a Fibonacci spiral that would touch the apex of all three of Giza's Pyramids,' I said. 'That spiral folds in on itself at a spot south-east of the Pyramids between the Sphinx and the Nile. Is this where you believe the Hall of Records will be found, at the spot where the spiral ends?'

'If I wished to hide a great treasure on the Giza plateau, where only the discerning mind might find it, this spot, seemingly in the middle of nowhere and yet so carefully marked, would be my choice,' Jamila replied. 'But the Fibonacci spiral is not only the physical mathematical signpost to the Hall of Records, it is also the supernatural key to enter it.'

Now Jamila had lost me and my expression must have reflected this.

'Long ago, the initiates of Horus were trained to expand their consciousness in a Fibonacci spiral in order to separate their astral body from their physical, whereby they gained liberty to explore the subtle world hidden within our physical Earth.'

'You're talking about astral projection,' I realised. This was one of the few supernatural talents accredited to my bloodline that I did possess, although I had not utilised the ability since my husband had been awarded a physical form by the Ladies of the Elohim and had ceased to frequent the astral plane.

'This feat is familiar to you.' Jamila sounded very sure of this.

'Yes, but my talent was purely desire-driven.' I glanced at my husband who was grinning. 'I have never attempted the feat purely for the sake of it.'

'Desire-driven, you say?' Jamila decided to outline what might be of inspiration to me in this instance. 'Do you not desire that your daughter be born into a world where the will of all humankind is not dictated by a race of beings who would use us as slaves and genetic fodder in order to aid their physical immortality, and thereby damn our own souls forever?'

'What?' I had yet to read the entire Persian journal written by my foremother, Lady Ashlee Devere, and so I thought the supposition hysterical and couldn't repress my chuckle.

Jamila appeared insulted by my reaction. My husband, who had accompanied Ashlee for part of her Persian adventure, did not seem very amused either. He raised his brows and glanced at Jamila apologetically.

'You believe this claim?' I asked, bemused.

'I have personally fought off five Dracon,' he confessed, then added, 'With much help from Lady Devere, of course.'

'Dracon? Do you mean vampires, like Christian Molier?' I asked.

Albray shook his head. 'Christian Molier started out his life as a human. Dracon, on the other hand, have never been human; their genetic roots are reptilian.'

'There is no connection at all?' I was surprised.

My husband shrugged. 'They both have a taste for particular human secretions, and presumably both contributed to the vampire legends through the ages.'

I could scarcely believe what I was hearing. 'Why have you never mentioned this?'

My husband rolled his eyes at the question. 'I have been operating on the physical plane, on and off, for hundreds of years! We have been together less than six months, so there are bound to be numerous aspects of my experience that we haven't yet had the chance to discuss.'

I scoffed at his explanation. 'This is a little more relevant than just your average, run-of-the-mill, general knowledge, don't you think?'

Albray came clean with the true reason. 'Our relationship is still new. I didn't want you thinking you were marrying a lunatic.'

'I love that you are a lunatic,' I said, inciting a grin from Albray, 'but I will never doubt anything you tell me.' He looked unconvinced. 'Okay, I know that wasn't the case when we first met, but you were a *ghost* ... any human being is bound to be wary in such circumstances.'

He and Jamila suppressed their amusement, realising I was bordering on information overload again. I ignored their reaction and went on.

'Here I am, newly pregnant and being told that the planet I live on and the species I belong to are in serious threat of being overthrown by a race of reptilian creatures! So just tell me what we need to do in order to open the Hall of Records.'

'You and your husband must go to the place marked by the end of the spiral, and then use the spiralling technique to proceed into the hall itself,' Jamila advised.

'So it is only our astral forms that have to enter the ancient dwelling?' I was most relieved not to have to place my child or myself in physical danger.

'I believe so, but that does not mean there is no risk involved.' Jamila was quick to correct my misconception. 'Even using the ancient spiralling technique, people have physically died trying to open the hall. Throughout the ages, one hundred and forty-eight sets of three have attempted to enter Thoth's chamber and all have perished.'

'Did you send any of those people to their deaths?' I asked Jamila.

'No,' she assured me.

'But how can you be so sure that we three are the chosen ones?' I was feeling panicked now. 'What if your source is really some shape-shifting vampire, like Molier, posing as an angel to advise you to send us to our deaths?'

'Because I would see through such a deception,' Jamila replied calmly. 'I can clearly see both the blue flame and the violet flame that have ignited in you, due to your love and union with this man.' She motioned to my husband. 'Mighty forces that were once dormant in both of you have now been unleashed, and through your love for one another you have been granted the ability to defend and serve your cause, that of your unique daughter, and indeed the whole planet.'

'Is that what they told Jesus Christ and the Magdalene, do you think?' I asked Jamila.

'Rather interesting that you chose the name of their first daughter for your own,' she responded, her brows raised.

I hadn't mentioned our choice of name. 'How do you know what we plan to call our daughter?'

Jamila only smiled, as if to say 'Do you really have to ask?'.

'For as long as this planet has been inhabited, there has been an interstellar war raging between its past and future inhabitants,' she went on. 'This conflict has been whittling its way down to a zero point, and that critical point will be realised within the next twenty years. Whether you like it or not, you two are going to be heavily involved in the outcome.'

Albray was nodding slightly, as if conceding that her claim rang true for him. It was easy for him to be so accepting, I thought, having fought his way through so many adventures since the thirteenth century, both on the physical plane and beyond. He was already used to being an interdimensional, time-hopping warrior. But now he had a new priority and I was angered by his apparent disregard for our unborn child.

'What about the safety of our baby?' I demanded.

'Knowledge is the greatest weapon of all,' he assured me. 'We cannot protect her from what we do not know about.'

'Allow me to share what knowledge I have been given about your task, and then decide what level of involvement you will have,' Jamila requested.

I was silent a moment, considering whether I was capable of processing any more information right now.

403

'Surely it would be better to hear Jamila out, so we can make an informed decision as soon as possible?' Albray suggested, and I nodded.

The prophetess was grateful. 'I have known for some time that the chosen three would come from the Western world,' she began. 'But it wasn't until word reached me about your victory in the Sinai, Mia, that I suspected you to be one of the flame-bearers.'

'Was it Akbar who told you?' I asked. I knew that the leaders of the Sinai project had gone to great pains to bury the details of the archaeological dig; only those intimately associated with the project could have known about it.

'The Magi of Akbar's order informed me of your service to them, and once I began to investigate you in the Greater Akashic library, much more psychic information was forthcoming — about your husband, your daughter and yourself.'

'The Greater Akashic library?' I'd never heard of such a place.

'Akasha is a planetary recorder cell — a library of knowledge that is sorted in two distinct levels. The Lesser Akashic is fed by the thoughts and emotions of all human consciousness throughout the history of Earth and acts as a frequency consciousness monitor for the entire Earth grid at any given time. The purest knowledge-forms from the Lesser Akashic are transmitted into light inscriptions, which are then "flamed", or inscribed, into the heart of each crystal in the Greater Akashic field of the recorder cell ... so one could say that the Greater Akashic Record is a Light-library.'

'But if this library is a record of history, and my daughter has yet to be born, how can you have perceived information about her from there?'

'Time is simultaneous,' she explained. 'The Akasha exists in the higher etheric realms outside of time, and therefore past and future are equally realised, although are constantly changing due to developments in the inter-time war.'

I was starting to feel a little ill and really just wanted to go and lie down. 'How you found us is really not so pertinent right now as what you have planned for us,' I said, cutting to the chase.

'Of course.' Jamila smiled warmly to assure me she understood my impatience. 'To enter the Hall of Records, you must use the spiralling technique to liberate your subtle body from the physical. Once this is achieved, you will find yourselves in a room constructed of red granite, like that used in the antechamber to the king's chamber in the Great Pyramid. In the corner of this first room you will encounter a clay pot. I have been informed that this pot is a key for negotiating the way safely through to the Hall of Records. There are three passages leading from this room, and the right person will know how to read what is written on the pot in order to choose the right path. Any but the true flame-bearers will not make it beyond this point. Two of the channels lead to death. And in the case that someone who is not a true flame-bearer makes a lucky guess, the third channel will suck you in and never let you go.

'The right person will make it to the door beyond the guarded channels and, upon arrival, will produce a particular sound and this sonic frequency will open the door. Beyond is a long hall where the walls, floor and ceiling emit their own light — it will appear as though the air itself is lit up. Along one wall are etched images of the forty-eight chromosomes of Christ-consciousness, the first of which is the Flower of Life. From this hall, many rooms and passages lead to still more rooms, wherein is stored the physical proof of the technologically advanced civilisations that existed on Earth millions of years before the scope of our current historical record. Among these rooms is a gold stairway with a holograph above it that names the three persons who are appointed to enter. These will not be the names they were born with, but their soul names.'

'And what is down the stairs?' I asked as Jamila paused to sip at some water Albray had poured for her.

'I cannot say. For only those pictured in the holograph are permitted to know.'

REVELATION 26

AKASHA

I lay awake that night, mulling over all that I had learned that day. I kept coming back to the non-human enemies of mankind.

'The Nefilim are real; they are not from our planetary system, but they have a good working knowledge of the time porthole system in our dimension,' Albray had explained.

Jamila had added a more modern perspective. 'The Dracon are an affiliated group of the Nefilim, who are in contact with governments and responsible for most of the current alien abduction phenomena. The Nefilim are planning to use holographic implants to mentally take over humanity — a strategy which has been made infinitely easier by their distortion of ancient spiritual teachings. These holographic implants will bring all affected humans under the control of a frequency fence. The implants themselves are so small that they cannot be detected with the naked eye, and can be introduced into a human body via a simple injection disguised as immunisation, a flu shot or any other medication.

'Your bloodline makes you naturally resilient to disease,' she went on, 'but the Nefilim have spent many ages instilling in humans the habit of obeying overarching authority figures. You have been programmed to obey their word without question and follow blindly the ideas of others; hence you mistrust and fear your own instincts and can no longer make a personal connection to the source. The time is now ripe for the Nefilim and the Dracon to carry out their mental takeover.'

It was horrifying news, but my brain was exhausted by the effort of processing all I had been told today. Finally, the demands of my tired body overrode my excess adrenaline levels, shutting down my brain and sending me into a deep sleep.

I stand in the centre of a chamber constructed of huge red granite blocks. I understand this is an ancient place, although it appears so spotless and new that I could be the first being ever to see it complete. It is cubed in shape and the featureless ceiling is two storeys above my head. On the far wall are three doors; torches burn between them, casting light into the chamber and shadow into the passages that lead out of it. I turn around to see Albray inspecting a pot in the corner to the right of me. I join him and gaze curiously at the pot, which is engraved with words in a language I have never before seen.

'What does it say?' My husband looks to me for answers.

A great panic grips my heart as I realise I am unable to draw any sense from the markings. I sense dark forces swirling around us and suddenly I am no longer in the chamber.

I am walking along an earthen tunnel that slopes down in one direction and upward in the other. The walls are lit by a luminous green fungi that is growing all over them. Albray is no longer with me, but I carry our daughter, asleep, in my arms — a newborn babe, perfect and helpless. As I admire her I hear the sound of clattering; it is distant but approaching fast. I hesitate only long enough to pinpoint the source in the downward part of the tunnel, but even that short time is too long — several huge lizard creatures slither along the floor, walls and ceiling towards us. I turn and run, knowing I must protect my child. As the tunnel gets steeper, the baby in my arms impedes my escape towards the daylight. I have no means to defend myself; no experience to draw upon. My panic explodes into horror as my child is snatched from my grasp.

The reptilian holds my screaming babe high above his head in victory. 'The flame-bearer!' he cries.

His companions gather around, eager to rip her to shreds and devour her before me.

My scream draws the attention of the lizard warriors, their jaws now dripping with my daughter's blood. One touches a thick metal band attached to his left wrist; a long metal spike extends forth from it as he moves towards me.

*   *   *

'Mia ... Mia, wake up.'

I felt someone gently shaking me. My eyes parted with a gasp, and I was immediately aware of the cold sweat of panic that covered me from head to foot.

'You are dreaming.' Albray's smiling face was very reassuring.

'I want to know everything!' I appealed to him. 'I want to know everything that you think you know about the inter-time war.'

'I have been proved wrong in the past,' he warned.

'I don't care,' I said, and got up to fetch a towel. Stripping off my damp attire, I rubbed myself dry. 'You're right — burying our heads in the sand and pretending we're just your average married couple is utter stupidity.'

'Wow!' Albray sat up to shake off sleep. 'That must have been some dream.'

'It was a nightmare,' I said, crawling onto the bed and sitting naked before him. 'Tell me anything you think I should know.'

Albray was contemplative a moment. 'Well, you'd better put some clothes on if you want me to stay focused ... your breasts have never looked as spectacular as they do at present.' He reached out to fondle them but I blocked his advance and pulled on a bathrobe.

'Now, spill it,' I ordered.

Albray, disappointed, sat back against his pillows. 'Well, I've seen your friend Akbar before,' he began.

'In the Sinai,' I added, for it was Akbar who had aided Albray and myself to prevent Molier claiming an ancient weapon of power, hidden in the sacred site beneath Mt Serabit.

'No, I met him before that, only he was going by the name of Zalman at the time,' he said.

'The same Zalman who spirited Ashlee Devere and her company out of Baghdad?' I had read that far in my foremother's Persian journal.

'The very same,' Albray said, and grinned as I absorbed the information.

'But that event took place over a hundred and fifty years ago!'

'I was born in the thirteenth century,' he pointed out, 'so is it really so impossible?'

When he put it that way ... 'So Akbar is deceiving me — is that what you're implying?'

'Not in a bad way,' Albray assured me.

'How can deception not be bad?' I argued.

'I suspect our friend is an Amenti staff member; and if we are the flame-bearers, we are also staff members.'

I thought back to Ashlee's journal and the mention of Amenti and how she expected the Dragon Queens were somehow linked to it.

'I think the best thing you could do right now is to finish reading the Persian journal,' my husband went on, 'for certain characters did foresee my return to life at that time, and hinted at my future involvement with the Amenti scheme.'

'But what is the Amenti scheme?' I asked.

'Read the journal.' Albray snuggled back under the covers. It was obvious that if I wasn't interested in being amorous, he was going back to sleep. 'I'll answer any questions in the morning.'

The sight of his bronzed warrior form partially draped in soft white linen was a great temptation to delay my reading until morning, but the new life in my belly was demanding food now that I was awake. And my dream, so vivid, had instilled a sense of urgency in me regarding my pursuit of knowledge. *Know thine enemy.* I dragged Ashlee's Persian journal from a suitcase and retired into the lounge room with it.

By the time Albray emerged from the bedroom in search of breakfast, I had completed Ashlee's tale of Persia and Amenti, but was still confused.

'Arcturus,' I said in greeting, calling my husband by his soul name, which Ashlee's tale had revealed to me.

'You finished then,' he said, pouring himself some juice. 'I'll take those questions now.'

'If I'm one of the Dragon Queens, then why wasn't I with the other five Dragon Queens Ashlee saw assembled in one of her past lives? And how will I manage to spend a hundred years beneath the blue flame, to be as resilient as my sisters, when the day of judgement is less than fourteen years away? Is our daughter to have the fate of the world thrust upon her shoulders when she's only a little girl?'

'Whoa!' Albray came to sit beside me and gave me a reassuring hug. 'If there's one thing you must have learned from your reading it's that there's a higher plan. All twelve of the Amenti Council members planned their evolvement in the Earth scheme very carefully before coming here to rescue Tara's lost masses. Can you not trust that your higher consciousness has matters well in hand?'

'But,' I protested and stood to pace, 'you're asking me to accept that we are two of twelve angels sent to Earth to guide human civilisation back to a higher harmonic universe! I mean ... come on! That's got to be a little hard for you to digest?'

'I was a cursed ghost for seven centuries; I do not find anything hard to believe.' Albray stood and moved to admire the amazing view from our balcony. 'All the answers we are seeking are right here, beneath our feet — I have seen it.'

'Yes, you have.' I followed him onto the balcony to admire the Giza plateau. According to Ashlee's tale, Albray had indeed seen some of the inner Earth porthole system that linked to the Amenti scheme beneath Giza; he and Ashlee had battled a band of reptilians in one of its outer chambers.

'Ashlee certainly knew how to show a knight a good time, didn't she?' I felt a twinge of jealousy, which I quickly suppressed.

But Albray was more perceptive than your average fellow and he gently pulled me to him so he could caress my belly. 'It is you who will show me the greatest adventure of all.'

His kiss upon my forehead dispelled my jealousy, but my deep inner worry for our child and our future remained. I could hardly wait to see Jamila again for I had many more concerns to air.

Jamila did not arrive for our noon appointment, nor did she call to explain her delay. I tried phoning her on the contact numbers she'd given me and left messages, but she did not respond. Miss Paki was a very polite woman and did not seem the type to miss a vital project meeting without calling to reschedule. I would have contacted Akbar, had I known how, but I didn't. Finally Albray and I considered calling the authorities to report Jamila missing.

'If only I were still a ghost, I could seek her whereabouts ten times faster than the local police,' Albray grumbled. He loved having a physical form again, but it did have its setbacks.

'I could try seeking her via otherworldly means,' I realised. I hadn't tried astral projection for a little while, but this situation was an opportunity to test the one skill I needed for the job I was considering.

I decided to make a Fibonacci spiral the focus of my initial meditation as Jamila had said the mathematical signpost was the supernatural key to freeing the subtle body from the physical. Why run around looking for Jamila when the answer to what had become of her was surely recorded in the great celestial library known as Akasha? Of course, I had no conscious knowledge of the technique once used by the initiates of Horus in Ancient Egypt, but it seemed logical to expand my consciousness using the outward spiral ratio of 1, 2, 3, 5, 8, 13, 21, 34, 55, 89, 144 and so forth, which, in theory, should release the astral body from its heavy physical counterpart. To return to my body would then be a simple matter of retracing the spiral inwards to draw my consciousness back into the physical form.

Alone in the bedroom, I sat cross-legged on the bed with the blinds and windows open — despite the afternoon heat, I needed fresh air. I took a few deep breaths and imagined my consciousness as a pinpoint of light; from that point I began to spiral the light outwards at an ever-increasing ratio — 1, 2, 3, 5, 8, 13, 21, 34 ... As the spiral increased, I became lighter and lighter — 55, 89, 144 ...

My consciousness floats upwards, leaving my form seated on the bed. My attention is drawn to the open window, and my perception surges forth towards the wide-open spaces above the Giza plateau. My spirit is exhilarated by the immensity of the view from above the ancient monoliths. I fly the path of a Fibonacci spiral, passing over the apex of all three Pyramids. The speed of my flight increases as my path winds into a central point. I spin around in a vertical position and descend into the ground like a drill head burrowing for oil.

Deep into the inner Earth I descend. On my way down I am aware of passing through chambers and stairwells. More earth and I am dropping through a vast darkness. This vast darkness is the night sky of a wholly different civilisation within the Earth; I see massive cities filled with majestic Old World architecture. Then into the Earth's darkest depths I plunge.

When I cease to spin I am enshrouded by a vast oppressive darkness of isolation and loneliness. This is not like the astral experiences I have had before. Above me in the darkness I see a speck of light, which I feel compelled to follow or be lost. As I move upward I am aware of disembodied, grotesque forms moving around me in the darkness. I rise higher and the misshapen creatures transmute into deformed human beings: some are grey hooded figures that sink into the depths of the darkness; others are spirits of coloured beauty that ascend to pursue the light alongside me.

The darkness is shadowed by the outlines of houses, trees and roads, but all is motionless. The colour-filled souls disperse into the passing scenery and I continue my ascent alone. With the dawning of light, cities arise around me and there is movement, colour, rapid growth and change. The transformation speeds up to a point at which my surroundings blur into pure light and the rising din reaches fever pitch and breaks into a beautiful silence. Through the light dance streams of breathtaking colour, echoing human laughter, music and song, then all the sounds and the voices blend into a perfect harmonious crescendo.

The magnificent mists of colour form a hallway with no walls and no ceiling, only a glimmering celestial path with six giant sets of obelisks running down either side. I proceed along the heavenly passage, unable to see to the end as it is shrouded by the light-filled mists. The mists part to reveal a hooded figure holding a book, who awaits me beneath a celestial archway that leads to a room without walls and yet the interior is concealed from my sight. I approach the figure without fear, for although I have no conscious memory of this place, my intuition tells me that I have been here many times before and that the soul-mind who awaits me is an old, old friend.

'Welcome, Meridon.' He calls me by my soul name and the sonic excites my being with its harmonious resonance. He retracts the hood from his head to expose his familiar face to me.

'Akbar,' I gasp.

'In my capacity as record keeper of the Lesser Akasha, I am known as Zalman,' he corrects politely.

'Zalman?' I recognise the name from Ashlee's Persian adventure but am confused. 'Does that mean you are a past or future incarnate of Akbar?'

'Neither and both,' he concedes, amused that his answer confuses me further. 'I am the sum total of his soul-mind's consciousness before he ever ventured into the Earth scheme. I am his dweller on the threshold between this universe and the next.'

'And Meridon is my dweller?'

'Only until you walk the Halls of Amenti,' he informs me, 'then Meridon will be consciously joined unto you for the time of reckoning. For the Staff of Amenti are capable of remembering all talents and knowledge acquired during earthly incarnations, and the skills that saw you appointed to the Amenti Project are realised and reactivated.' Seeing my bewilderment, he expands his explanation. 'For example, my partner and I were brought onto the Amenti Council to adapt the Akashic record-keeping system to this lower harmonic universe. I see to the Lesser Akashic, filtering out all that is detrimental to human development, and my partner presides over the Greater Akashic Record, which she assimilates and files away to be of inspiration to the worthy.'

The mention of the Hall of Records reminded me of my concern for Jamila. 'You must know why I am here?' I ask.

Zalman nods, his expression grave now. 'I am sorry to say that your contact has become a victim of the war that lies at the root of all wars fought on this Earth.'

Panic grips my heart. 'Jamila has been killed? Why? By whom?'

'You already know the answers to both those questions,' he says. 'You are a prophetess of old, Meridon; in Ancient Egypt you were the best trance medium and dream decoder in existence.'

Last night's nightmare takes me captive once more, only this time I am an observer, not personally involved, and it is not my baby being torn apart by the Dracon, it is Jamila.

'No!' I protest; the horror too great for me to accept as reality.

'I am truly sorry,' Zalman says, but remains insistent that I acknowledge my own precognition. 'Many people die such horrible deaths every day. Impoverished countries, plagued by war, disease and famine, are the perfect feeding grounds for the Dracon and the Nefilim. Millions can go missing there and nobody cares.'

'Are you implying that Jamila was a random victim?'

'Oh no, Jamila was the product of a holy order of women who evolved from the teaching Miss Koriche left with her order. The purpose of this order was to assist our father to awaken the Staff of Amenti. Jamila was targeted for the specific purpose of delaying your mission in Giza.'

'Then why not target me directly, if I'm the one they want?'

'Even though you have not yet been activated, you are a Dragon Queen and therefore you have powerful protectors — some you are aware of and some you are not. The important thing is that your mission in Giza is not delayed.'

'But I know very little of what is required of me. Jamila did not finish —'

'Akbar is on his way to you,' Zalman assures me.

'Does he know about Jamila?'

Zalman nods regretfully. 'Akbar found what was left of her.'

Even though I did not know Jamila very well, her horrendous murder pains me to the core.

'It is very important that you follow Akbar's instructions without delay,' Zalman warns. 'Your enemies are coming for you.'

In the distance I hear my name being called. I reach out a hand to Zalman in a vain attempt to prevent my departure.

'A gift for you.' Zalman puts the book he has been holding all this time into my hands, and I clutch it tight against my body as Zalman and his library rush away from me.

TIME PIRATES

'Mia ... Mia!' Albray was shaking me, even though he knew that to pull a person out of an astral experience prematurely added to the already physically draining effects of the exercise. There had to be trouble afoot. Had our enemies sought me out as Zalman had predicted? My consciousness was propelled back into my form at great speed, making me feel dizzy and disorientated.

'The book?' I mumbled. I felt for the gift Zalman had given me, and in that instant the object seemed to meld into my person and vanish.

Albray grabbed me up in his arms. 'Apologies for bringing you out of a trance so quickly, but we have to go.' He carried me into the lounge area, where Akbar was tossing a few of our essential possessions into a bag.

'Where are we going?' I asked, feeling as though I had taken a sleeping potion.

'Amenti,' Akbar replied. 'It is time —' He stopped himself from saying more, closed the bag and rose. 'Time to leave.'

I passed in and out of consciousness as Albray carried me down the fire escape, through the kitchen and out through the hotel's staff entrance, where I was piled into the back seat of a vehicle. As the motor roared to life and the car moved off, I slipped into a fitful sleep.

'I have a wife and child to consider now.'

It was Albray who spoke and he was quite close by. I roused myself to peer out through the car window. We were in the middle of a vast, flat plain and it was nearly sunset; my guess was we'd come to the place

415

where Rocky McCollum's Fibonacci spiral ended. My husband and my friend were standing near the car, arguing.

Akbar fixed Albray with a glare of caution. 'If you do not unlock the hall this day, you will not have a family to consider much longer.'

'Are you threatening me?' Albray grabbed hold of Akbar by his robes.

Akbar did not retaliate. 'I am not the threat, I assure you.'

I grappled for the door handle and stumbled out of the car before my husband could draw the sword that was now strapped to his hip. 'We must listen to him, Albray.'

'Why must we?'

'Because I located the Akashic library during my astral projection and was advised there to heed Akbar's advice.'

Albray was not convinced.

'I can tell you what became of Jamila,' I offered as further proof.

Albray released Akbar and folded his arms, eager to hear my version of the events that had already been relayed to him by Akbar. My knight was very surprised when both accounts came to the same horrendous conclusion.

'Akbar is more than he appears to be and knows far more than he can reveal to us in our present state of conscious awareness,' I assured Albray. 'But he is a staff member of Amenti, just as you suspected, and it is imperative that we trust him.'

Albray was amazed by my conviction. 'This is quite a change of tune for you — trusting in your own psychic perceptions.'

'Actually I used to do it all the time in Ancient Egypt,' I replied, and glanced at Akbar, who knew all Zalman did about my fortune-telling days.

Akbar grinned to confirm my statement and my husband was discomfited to note the communication between us. 'Is there something going on between you two that I should know about?' he demanded.

Akbar looked floored by my husband's jealous assumption. 'No, nothing like that.'

'The librarian of the Lesser Akasha is Zalman,' I blurted out to defuse the situation. Albray's attention shifted back to Akbar, but now he was viewing him in an entirely different light. 'If anyone can predict what will come to pass, it is this man,' I finished.

'You have walked the Halls of Amenti?' Albray asked, stunned.

'Not six months ago,' Akbar confirmed, pleased that the misunderstanding had been corrected. 'That was when I first met Jamila and she enlightened me to my true identity.'

'But doesn't your body have to reside beneath the blue flame for at least one hundred years after the journey through Amenti before it is resilient enough to accommodate the connection to your higher self?' Albray asked.

Akbar nodded. 'That is true, but one among Amenti's staff is a time traveller —'

'Sinclair,' Albray and I interjected at the same time.

'— and it was he who aided me to cheat time to be here with you today,' Akbar concluded.

'So yours was only a recent enlightenment?' I asked.

Akbar grinned. 'It would seem so,' he said, 'and yet during the time I spent under the blue flame, my consciousness at one with my silent watcher in that cosmic moment that spanned one hundred years, I recalled what it had taken me thousands of lifetimes to learn.'

I realised this was why Akbar appeared so different to me now. In the Sinai he had been just like me, a human stumbling through a web of ignorance in search of some meaning to existence. Now he was at peace, for he knew his reason for being. And soon I too would know the truth behind the extraordinary life I had been given.

Hesitant though I was to risk the life of my unborn child, it seemed that not attempting this quest would be as dangerous as attempting it. After my husband and I had shared a quiet word, we agreed to tackle the task fate had landed in our lap.

When we turned to inform Akbar of our decision, the sun was very low in the sky. It was then we noticed an approaching dust storm, kicked up by the many horses' hooves of the oncoming party.

'Melchi,' Akbar advised, so that we would not be alarmed. 'They will form a guard.'

Albray was reluctant to have an audience. 'The fewer people who know of this, the better,' he said.

'Jamila's death means that somebody already knows of our intent here in Giza,' Akbar countered, 'and that same someone is sure to try to thwart our intent again.'

At that moment I sensed the presence of something malign, close by and yet unseen. I indicated as much to Albray, who drew his sword, uttering the name 'Pintar' under his breath. He recognised the presence of the low-grade entity, as he'd encountered it once before.

I remembered the name from Ashlee's account: this was the leader of the Dracon. The thought of his presence close by sent shockwaves through my being. I turned circles, focusing my third-eye vision to see beyond my physical reality, but my ability in this field was undeveloped and I was only able to catch a glimpse of a dark shadow with no definition.

'Do not be alarmed.' Akbar moved closer to us and drew his long curved sword, taking a defensive stance. 'The dark lord does not wish you harm at this time.'

'Drawing your sword does not invoke my confidence,' Albray muttered. 'Why wouldn't we expect anything but trouble from Pintar?'

Akbar glared at Albray, clearly feeling he should know the answer and that it was improper to be discussing it in front of me. 'Have you forgotten?' he said sharply, then lowered his voice and whispered the reason to Albray.

Though I could not see my husband's expression, I could tell from his body language that whatever Akbar had said weighed heavily on him.

'Tell me!' I demanded, and rested both hands over my womb, as if to protect the tiny being within. It was then I remembered Pintar's obsession with the soul-mind that was Ashlee's daughter, the same soul-mind that was now reincarnating in my belly. 'That abomination wants its mistress back,' I realised, horrified.

Albray embraced me, wanting to allay my sudden rush of fear and anger. 'We won't let that happen,' he said with certainty.

'Damn straight it won't happen!' I said and tore myself away from Albray to yell at our invisible stalker: 'You stay away from her!'

Akbar grabbed my arm to caution me against provoking one of the darkest entities ever to crawl out of the primordial ether. 'I want a weapon to defend myself!' I demanded, agitated by his restraint.

'Amenti,' he whispered and gave me a nod of assurance. 'You have thirteen years to prepare your defence, for only when your daughter reaches adolescence will she be of any interest to Pintar.'

'So why show up now?' Albray queried.

'To make sure no one else harms the object of his interest, I suspect.' Akbar looked around; it seemed to me he was straining to hear something we could not, but I was too worried about my daughter to take note.

'Who else might be —'

'Shh!' Akbar implored and I fell silent.

The sun's rays vanished completely and all of us could now hear the ominous sound of wings beating in unison. They seemed to be approaching at a faster rate than the horsemen.

'What is that?' My heart jumped into my throat and choked me with foreboding. I had read about the Dracon, I had seen them in my nightmares, but no amount of imagining could compare to the heart-pounding, cold sweat-invoking shockwaves of fear that I felt at the prospect of actually seeing one. 'It sounds huge.'

'*They* are huge,' Albray corrected, gazing towards the approaching threat.

I caught sight of the skyward intruders myself — three of them.

'I thought you said Pintar was here to protect us,' Albray complained to Akbar.

'Not all the Dracon are loyal to Pintar,' Akbar pointed out. 'Since the destruction of their leader's physical form, some serve Nefilim masters.'

The winged half-human, half-lizard creatures circled above like dragons from a medieval movie; the sight was surreal. The horsemen were approaching at full gallop but were still minutes away from our defence. I looked to Akbar, who smiled.

'I told you your enemies were coming,' he said.

'No,' I corrected, 'Zalman warned —'

I stopped as I fully recalled Zalman's words and his parting gift. In my mind's eye I opened the book he had given me and, in a blinding flash, a vision shot out from between the covers: I saw myself at this precise moment in time, and suddenly I knew what I must do.

'Come!' I grabbed Albray's hand and urged him to run with me away from the cover of our vehicle.

'That is suicide,' he said and pulled me back.

'We need to be out in the open.' I tugged him once in my direction and then let go and ran.

'Listen to her, my friend,' Akbar advised, 'she is your intuition.'

Albray, having spotted one of our airborne enemies about to target me, was up and after me in a heartbeat. Akbar did not follow us, for he knew as well as I what would unfold this night.

'Could you not wait for our defence to arrive?' my husband pleaded.

'Our best defence is not to be here,' I said, and stopped on the very spot seen in my vision.

'But only our subtle bodies will venture forth into the hall,' he began.

'Not the way I see it.' I turned to argue and was forced to dive to the ground to avoid being snatched up by the flying Dracon.

'Are you all right?' Albray squatted alongside me, and I hauled myself up to my knees and hugged him as I looked to the dark, cloudless sky for aid.

For a second I doubted what my vision had predicted, but then the Dracon, who were readying themselves to strike, seemed to run into a large unseen object and fell from the sky unconscious.

'Captain Sinclair,' I said, relieved to have my premonition vindicated.

A round, downward-facing porthole of white liquid-light opened above us and a light-stream spiralled down to engulf my husband and myself. Fast as lightning, it withdrew into the belly of the *Kleio*, taking us with it.

Inside the *Kleio*, Albray and I were deposited atop a pool of liquid-light, which hardened into crystal beneath us and continued to emit a dim glow.

Albray brushed himself over with his free hand, checking all his body parts had been safely transported. 'You could have warned me!'

'We only had a small window of opportunity before the situation would have become very messy and hindered our pick-up,' I said. I looked around the chamber, admiring the polished timber and modern brass fixtures and trim. 'This room has a very stylish, nautical feel, doesn't it?'

'Very tasteful, I'm sure,' Albray said coolly.

'That's right,' I said, realising the reason for this. 'You and the soul-mind that is the dear captain have a history of not getting along, thanks to your rivalry for the attentions of Ashlee Granville.'

Albray looked insulted, but after a little consideration found himself guilty as charged. He sheathed his sword and moved towards me. 'Well, that is hardly going to be an issue now ... I am a happily married man.'

I was charmed by his reassurance. 'And father,' I reminded him as his lips neared mine.

The door to the chamber retracted into the wall, admitting the captain himself. 'Greetings!' he called out.

'You have wonderful timing,' Albray complained.

'Payback,' the captain replied cheerfully. 'Karma is a wonderful thing.'

In his well-worn brown leather attire, Captain Sinclair was rather more modern-looking than I'd expected — but then he was a time lord. He was just as Ashlee had described in her journals: long blond locks and bright blue eyes that sparkled with mischief. It was easy to see why Ashlee loved him; he was a very attractive man indeed.

'Mia Montrose, it is a pleasure to make your acquaintance again.' Sinclair approached and kissed my hand.

'Her name is Mia Devere these days,' Albray reminded his old rival.

'Have we met before?' I asked tentatively, not wanting to be rude but at the same time uncertain of the captain's claim.

'Many, many times,' he assured me, 'as you will soon see.' He did not let go of my hand, and I felt so comfortable with him that I did not withdraw it — an oversight Albray corrected for me by stepping between us.

'Where are you taking us?' he demanded of Sinclair.

'To Amenti, one hundred years and one week ago,' the captain said.

I understood the one hundred years part. 'Why the extra week?'

'So you can return to Giza last week and open the Hall of Records before anyone realises that you intend to.'

Sinclair's explanation blew our minds.

'So, in actuality, we had already completed our quest before we even set foot in the country,' Albray said, impressed. 'That *is* brilliant.'

'Thank you.' Sinclair seemed rather impressed by the plan himself. 'That is why the Amenti Council hired me.'

'But what about the week's crossover?' I was perplexed by the conundrum this posed and held my head as it was starting to hurt. 'Are you saying there are another two of us hiding out in Giza when we arrive here?'

'Of course not,' Sinclair assured us. 'I will drop you both home after your quest here is complete.'

'So if I were to call home right now, *I* would answer the phone,' I said. The premise made me laugh. 'I wonder what I'd say to myself? I'd probably reassure myself that everything went okay.'

'I'm sorry to say that you won't have time to make that call.' The captain looked up at the ceiling and the light in the room began to fluctuate; blue-green waves engulfed the interior of the ship in a stunning and beautiful display. Despite increasing to a blinding intensity, the light was both calming and empowering. Then the room faded back to normality.

'Good lord,' Albray murmured, still frozen in awe and bliss.

'Welcome to 1906,' Sinclair announced, shocking us out of our delirium. 'The year Rolls-Royce was registered, Mount Vesuvius erupted and devastated Naples, and an earthquake flattened much of San Francisco. Due to our aforementioned tight schedule, you won't be able to do any sightseeing up top, however.' He headed for the open hatch door.

I had expected being dragged back through time to be a little more uncomfortable. 'Up top?' I asked. 'If you refer to surface Earth, then where are we now, captain? Underwater?'

'Underground,' he grinned, knowing that as an archaeologically inclined linguist, I would be most excited by our location.

'Truly?' I joined the captain at the door. 'Underground where?'

'We are parked in the Cave of Mamer,' Sinclair advised and my excitement trebled — I had read of this place in Lady Ashlee's journal.

'It exists,' I whispered, overwhelmed by the prospect of seeing it for myself.

'Well, of course it exists!' Albray was annoyed by my lingering scepticism. 'I keep telling you: everything Ashlee wrote in her journals was true!'

I could only smile. The supernatural had scared me once, and I'd never wanted to believe Ashlee's tales because they seemed far too full of promise and excitement to be true. But now I knew I was not going to be disappointed: the captain was real, my psychic ability was real, and for the first time, I dared to believe that the Dragon Queens and Amenti were real.

'To hell with sightseeing up top!' I said, and headed down the spacious passageway. Just as I realised I had no idea where I was going, I collided with a fellow exiting another cabin.

'So sorry,' the dark-haired gent said, and reached out to steady me on my feet. Then he gazed at me, stunned. 'It's you!' he said.

'And who might that be?' I queried with a smile, for he was very dashing with his straight shoulder-length dark hair and deep blue eyes. His neat beard and moustache, along with his English accent, made him seem something of an upper-class rogue. I was quite sure I'd never met him before. 'Who are you?'

'Taylor!' Albray yelled from behind me, and my new acquaintance immediately unhanded me.

'Ah, you must be Ashlee's mysterious ghost,' the man reckoned, noting my husband's choice of weapon. 'The swordsman.'

'But you cannot be who you appear to be,' Albray said, wondering if *he* was addressing a ghost. 'Ashlee saw you perish in this cavern, in the claws of a winged Dracon.'

'She saw me fall; she did not see me die,' the man pointed out.

'But how —'

Albray's query was cut short by my gasp, for in the cabin Taylor had just exited was a reptilian. The sight, coming so close to my recent horrendous visions of the lizard warriors, sent shockwaves through my system; for a moment I could hear nothing over the pounding of my own heart in my ears.

'Mia!' I realised Albray was trying to tell me something. 'It is Taejax,' he said.

My fear ebbed a little as I recalled that this particular Dracon had managed to free himself from the reptilians' hive-mind long ago. He had also lent a hand to destroy the unnatural physical form of Pintar, the Dracon leader and mastermind.

'The enemy of your enemy is your friend,' Taylor reasoned, attempting to bring me out of my shock.

'I am so sorry,' I apologised, my eyes fixed on the Dracon warrior. 'I have never been so close to one of your kind before.'

'I am the one who should apologise,' Taejax granted, 'as this is merely a disguise I wear for missions.' And before my eyes his form morphed into that of a tall, slender, fair-haired being of exceeding beauty.

'You have become one of the Anu,' I realised.

The Anu appeared in the ancient legends of every culture, just under different names — in Britain they were the Fey or the Fair Folk, and in Ireland the Tuatha De Danaan. This otherworldly race claimed to owe their existence to one Great Mother goddess, Danu, Don or Diana. It was she who provided for their evolution in the subtle realms of this world, where they could observe and aid mankind without being seduced and corrupted by the desires and emotions of the physical world. For the Anu — like their lesser-evolved physical manifestations, the Nefilim, Draconian and Anunnaki races — could not fully comprehend emotion.

'I am not of the Anu yet,' Taejax explained, 'but upon my physical departure from this world I feel confident that my soul-mind will have developed enough to ascend, via the Hall of Amorea, which the Great Mother Goddess designed for the very purpose of allowing repentant Anunnaki souls, like mine, to transcend into the Anu evolutionary scheme on Sirius. It was the personal sacrifices made by your pending daughter that assured my spiritual evolution,' Taejax informed me. 'She has offered a spiritual alternative to damnation for all the fallen Nefilim, Anunnaki and Draconians who choose to break free of their selfish ORME addictions and their lust for human domination.'

I remembered something about this from Ashlee's journals, although the references were very vague. I realised that not even she had known the full story behind the earthly mission of my daughter-to-be. Still, it was clear that Taejax believed the child I was carrying was the human incarnation of the Great Mother Goddess of the Tuatha De Danaan.

'And Taejax is the reason I am not still locked up in an oubliette in the Dracon underworld,' Taylor said, finally answering Albray's question. Then he turned his attention back to me. 'As to who you are to me, well ... we have met in many lives, but back in the days of the Amazons we had a clash of wills and you were killed, an error for which I am eternally sorry.'

I had read this part of Ashlee's tale only this morning, thus it was still fresh in my mind. But Ashlee hadn't mentioned recognising Taylor's soul-mind. He filled me in.

'I was the warrior Herakles at that time, and you were Asteria, champion and commander of the Ha-mazon armies.'

I was absolutely stunned at the idea that I had been one of the greatest warriors of the ancient world! Taylor found it delightfully odd that I was so amazed by the news of my murder at his hands.

'And Ashlee could not have recognised me in her past life, as we have yet to meet in this one,' I said, mostly to myself.

'But what is more important,' Taylor went on, 'is that you are the one who will finally release my love from her slumber.' He smiled. 'I have been waiting an age for our reunion.'

'Hear, hear,' added the captain.

'Which can't happen soon enough,' Albray finished, not liking the way the two men were doting on me.

Not that I was complaining; I had never had the pleasure of being in the company of so many good-looking males at once. And I had been jealous so many times of Albray's close relationship with and attraction to Ashlee Granville that it was nice to see my husband being the jealous one for a change.

Taejax joined us in the corridor. 'But the most important thing of all,' he said, looking from me to Albray, 'is that you are the parents of the woman who will wake the consciousness of every being evolving in this world.'

The fact was sobering, although Taejax had not meant it to be so. 'No pressure, of course,' I said, and forced a smile of pride that probably looked more like bewilderment.

'Never fear,' the captain said, 'Tamar will have the greatest army of guardians ever assembled on the Earth to protect her.'

'That *is* reassuring,' I admitted.

'Well then, let us get on with the task of waking them, shall we?' Sinclair motioned us to the exit hatch. 'I hope you don't mind a wee climb.'

The wee climb required us to scale the huge metal panels that constituted the *Kleio's* sails in order to reach the earthen bridge that spanned the width of the immense cavern. As Albray and I climbed — Sinclair simply levitated to the bridge — I thought how it was no wonder Ashlee had been so in awe of the *Kleio*, for even to my eyes she was a vessel from the future, though she was the product of the ancient past. Her sails were not of cloth, but magnetic panels designed to absorb the different free energy sources available on Earth, including blue flame energy.

'Sorry we have to position *Kleio* beneath the bridge, but it's a bit of a tight squeeze parking her in here,' Sinclair explained as we finally reached the top of the mast and, with his aid, stepped onto the bridge.

As I gazed around the giant underground chasm, lit in part by the exterior lights of the *Kleio*, I recalled Ashlee's tale of Taylor boldly challenging a winged Dracon here in order to save the woman he secretly loved.

'Do the Dracon still have access to this place?' I asked as the captain got us moving again — this time towards a small antechamber with three portholes, one of which I knew led to the subterranean complex hidden beneath the Giza plateau.

'Of course. The underground world has always been their domain,' he advised. 'But they cannot follow us through the portholes; their genetic structure is not developed enough to endure the passage.'

426

'They didn't have any trouble gaining access to Giza when we pursued Levi there,' Albray said warily.

'That is because our presence in the Amenti antechamber lowered the frequency enough to allow the Dracon the opportunity to penetrate its defences,' Sinclair explained. 'Had we stayed away, they could not have breached the security shields.'

'But we are supposedly more spiritually mature now, is that it?' Albray queried.

'Your association with your twin flame,' the captain motioned to me, 'has heightened both your personal frequencies more than you know. Otherwise you could never have conceived the living key to Amenti.'

Albray was still not entirely convinced. 'But surely there are certain activations one needs to perform before attempting such a passage?'

'You have performed those activations in past lives,' Sinclair explained, showing great patience in my opinion.

'But what of the astral seal that gave Ashlee so much trouble in her lifetime?'

'Mia and yourself are the exceptions to the rule, as you were born too early to be affected by the seal and Mia was born too late.' The captain looked at Albray quizzically. 'Can we not go into the reasons why — the full explanation is rather lengthy. Can't you just trust me?'

I was more than convinced, but Albray still had a chip on his shoulder. 'You never trusted me, so why should I return the favour?'

'Because we're on the same team!' Sinclair said, exasperated. 'And I am eager to see your wife and pending child on the far side of this porthole, where they will be beyond Dracon reach.'

'A valid point,' Albray conceded. Turning my way, he kissed me. 'I shall go first.'

'I'll be right behind you,' I assured him.

Albray gave Sinclair a warning look, then strode into the central porthole and vanished.

'It is a delight to see him jealous,' the captain commented. 'Do you think me mean to enjoy the frustration of another?'

I had to laugh as I could empathise completely. 'In the case of Albray and yourself, I'd say a little delight may be justified. Still, Ashlee never loved Albray romantically, you realise that?'

'I do,' Sinclair admitted. 'Still, he did not make my life as Earnest Devere any easier.'

'From what I have gathered from Ashlee's tales and my own research,' I said, 'it will be the soul-mate of Lillet du Lac who will have a bone to pick with Albray.' I felt a little uneasy about Albray being reacquainted with the woman he'd endured a seven-hundred-year curse for.

'And Taylor has a bone to pick with Lillet's soul-mate, and so on and so forth,' the captain emphasised. 'What we have done through the ages to help each other cannot be held against us now that the bigger picture has been made clear, for we were only acting upon what we knew at the time. We are all bound to be attracted to other staff holders, for we share a group goal and see a little of ourselves in one another.'

I smiled, feeling a little more comfortable with our destiny. 'And what part of yourself do you see in Albray, captain?'

'The part of me that will fight to the death to defend those I love,' he replied. 'He is a good man, and as soon as I have finished equalising the annoyance karma between us, I am sure we will be fast friends.'

I found this amusing. 'Now that you have walked the Halls of Amenti, aren't you supposed to be beyond revenge?'

'Polaris, my higher self, is beyond redress, but I am not,' Sinclair advised. 'So long as we entertain a human form, we retain our human nature. And how boring would we be if we did not?'

'Indeed,' I agreed, comforted by the fact. 'So I am not going to emerge from Amenti with a great saintly consciousness?'

'Heavens, no.' Sinclair looked amused. 'The saints and saviours of humanity were exactly that: human. However, we Ceres, the Staff of Amenti, were never part of the human consciousness of this planet. We were not condemned to this physical existence; we chose it — which makes us more insane than your average human.'

I laughed. 'That explains a lot,' I said, considering Albray and his heroic tendencies. 'So Jesus Christ was not one of us?'

Sinclair shook his head. 'But the Magdalene certainly was ... guess which one?' His grin was discomfiting.

'Me?' I squeaked, most unconfidently.

'You carried the key to human salvation once before,' he said, 'and you are carrying her again.'

I wanted to ask whether the Black Madonna was a key incarnation of mine that I would revisit in one of the Halls of Amenti, but as I doubted the captain could answer, I'd just have to wait and see.

'So angelic consciousness and saintly consciousness are very different?' I asked.

Sinclair nodded. 'For angels will venture where saints dare not and cannot tread. Now . . .' He motioned me to the porthole.

I hesitated, feeling apprehensive. 'I've never done anything like this in a conscious state,' I said.

'Time to live a little then,' he encouraged playfully, 'for behind each fear lies a secret wish.'

He was right, for my true desire was to not fear such opportunities, but embrace them, as Ashlee had done.

'Here goes,' I said, and wrapped both my arms around my belly in an attempt to suppress the rising butterflies of excitement in my gut. Then I moved into the central waterfall of liquid-light.

DRAGON QUEENS AWAKE

The passage was instantaneous, just as Ashlee had described. I was momentarily filled with light and felt a wall of suction pulling me forth into the huge altar room that was the antechamber of Amenti. Large stone stairs ascended in long, curved levels to a platform and altar block. The light emanating from the portholes behind us illuminated the entire chamber.

'There you are!' Clearly Albray had begun to wonder what was taking us so long. I apologised, realising I had, inadvertently, aided Captain Sinclair to annoy Albray yet again.

'The captain was just explaining the difference between saintly and angelic consciousness,' I said.

'What would he know about either?' scoffed Albray.

'Now you're just being arrogant.' I grew tired of his petty dislike of Sinclair. 'Once you have walked the Halls of Amenti, you'll be in a better position to judge him.'

'I do not have to walk Amenti to know he is trying to cause trouble between us.'

I could hardly deny this as Sinclair had admitted as much himself. 'Then don't let him bait you,' I advised quickly, as the captain emerged through the porthole behind me.

'Well, kiddies, this is the end of the line for me,' he said.

'I don't understand,' I said, wary of being left to our own devices.

An Anu warrior emerged from one of the outer portholes to join us. He was even taller and fairer in looks than Taejax, and his entire being gave off a slight illumination that was not human. Still, his appearance was very well defined and his physical presence was only slightly less dense than our own.

'Lugh Lamhfada.' The captain greeted the new arrival with a slight bow, as if he were royalty. 'Your timing is impeccable, as always.'

'Operating beyond time as I do, I have no excuse to be tardy,' the Anu granted.

The captain introduced us to Lugh, telling us that he was a brilliant carpenter, mason, harpist, poet, storyteller, physician, goldsmith, leader and warrior among the Anu — and that he would be our guide to our respective resting places beneath the blue flame inside the Hall of Life.

'I shall see you both in one hundred years,' Sinclair said, then waved and departed back through the central porthole.

Albray wasn't sad to see him go. 'That sounds a long time,' he said, 'but I doubt it will be long enough.'

I hated to be negative, but I had to agree. 'Why should one hundred years make any difference, when two hundred has made none?'

Our new guide ascended the stairs to the altar stone and, standing before it, produced an ankh tool. He held it out before himself and focused his will through it; a beam of blue flame energy shot from the ancient tool into the altar stone and the stone wall behind the altar began to ripple like water. The stone vanished in a blaze of light, exposing the tunnel beyond.

'Shall we?' Lugh invited us to follow him into the Amenti complex.

This was where Albray and I committed ourselves to the Amenti scheme that we could no longer recall having partially masterminded. The next time we returned to this chamber we would be fully fledged members of Amenti's staff, and considering the situation brewing in our original time–space reality there was nothing I wanted more.

I shall skip the details of my own experience of Amenti for that is another book entirely. Suffice to say, my journey was unique to me. As Sinclair had met Ashlee and guided her through her negotiation of Amenti's halls, so too did Albray's enlightened being meet me in

Amenti's outer chambers and see me through my own trials and revelations. When I asked how it was possible for him to be here with me when he was currently journeying Amenti himself, he said that time was meaningless here and that I had done him the same service.

The lifetimes I perceived in Amenti's halls were also unique to me, as was the knowledge I gained and the skills I remembered. Much of my experience in Amenti will be brought to light as this story unfolds, and so I proceed with the telling.

Albray awoke in the Chamber of Life and was greeted by Lugh Lamhfada.

'I suppose you expected Princess Charming to awaken you?' the Anu warrior teased. 'But never fear, I did not kiss you.'

'That is just as well,' Albray laughed; he may have been stiff and groggy after his long slumber, but his sense of humour was still intact. 'For it was not you I imagined spending happily-ever-after with ... No offence.'

'None taken,' Lugh said and passed him his clothes. 'You might want to put these on before the Dragon Queens awake.'

'What?' Albray groaned and managed to pull his naked body upright to look out from the newly opened pod that had been his home for one hundred years.

In the tranquil blue glow cast by the large light tube that extended from floor to ceiling in the centre of the chamber, Albray could clearly see the twelve pods evenly spaced around the blue flame emitter in a flower-like formation. He could tell that all the pods on his side of the chamber were open and deactivated, as there was no ultraviolet light emanating from the seal around the rim of the pods. The six pods on the opposite side of the flower were all still closed, however, and their seals glowed intensely.

'You are the last of the Princes to awake,' Lugh advised, as Albray pulled on the jeans, shirt and boots that he had worn into Amenti.

'Will all the Dragon Queens awake at once?' Albray asked, and jumped out of his pod. Instantly the ultraviolet strip around the lid and the base of the rim switched off.

'That has always been the plan,' replied Lugh. He seemed most inspired by the pending event.

'Oh dear.' But Albray barely had time to consider how uncomfortable that situation could be for him when Lugh went down on one knee in reverence, his eyes fixed on something behind Albray.

Albray turned to see that the spirit of a very beautiful female being had entered the chamber. She appeared half-human and half-Anu, and was composed only of astral matter. 'Who is she?' he asked Lugh quietly as he bowed down beside the Fey warrior, who regarded the beautiful spirit as a mortal might revere a goddess. Indeed, she was more beautiful and goddess-like than any human woman Albray had ever seen. She was extremely tall, dark-skinned, violet-eyed, and had a body that was slender and perfectly proportioned to her height.

'She is the Great Mother architect of the evolution of my people,' said Lugh. 'She is Kali. She is —'

'My daughter-to-be!' Albray was overwhelmed at the prospect of protecting such a beauty. 'Heaven help me,' he muttered as he watched the spirit move towards the tube of blue flame energy in the centre of the Chamber of Life, oblivious to their presence. 'What is she doing?'

'Awakening her guard.' Lugh's tone suggested that he felt he was stating the obvious.

The spirit stepped into the blue flame and immediately a flame of violet ignited within it, which consumed her completely.

'Tamar!' Albray was alarmed by her disappearance.

'Do not fear,' Lugh advised, as they watched the light of the blue flame pillar die out altogether, leaving only the ultraviolet seals of the remaining pods to light the room. 'Your daughter is alive and well in the belly of your woman.'

The sound of all six seals opening at once startled Albray, and he looked on in anticipation as the pods opened to expose the Dragon Queens slumbering within. Each wore only a glistening white strip of fabric around their chest and thighs, and their skin glistened with ORME oil to protect against and absorb the light of the blue flame.

'The six most perfect females in history and it has been my privilege to know most of them,' Albray said reverentially. 'I feel I am the most blessed and cursed man on Earth!'

Lugh gave a hearty laugh. 'You are a flame-bearer, therefore you are!'

Albray approached the pod closest to him, where I lay.

My consciousness was drawn back to Earth by the kiss of my lover, which, when I realised what was happening, I found very romantic. 'Hello, my prince,' I smiled, delighted to see him as always.

'Hello, my goddesses.' He smiled down at me. 'I have just seen a vision of our daughter and she is the most beautiful being this world will ever behold.'

'You wouldn't be biased now, would you?'

'Well, she has the most beautiful mother on Earth, so it is to be expected.' He kissed me again.

A buxom brunette sat up in the pod alongside mine. 'Where is my prince?' she demanded teasingly.

Albray backed off a little when he realised all the Dragon Queens were stirring.

A redhead slid out of the pod next to the brunette. 'Oh my ancestors!' she cried. 'Can it be you, Albray?' She choked on emotion at the sound of his name. 'Are you ...?' She neared to touch him and burst into tears when she felt a solid body. 'You are alive!' She flung her arms around my husband's neck and he responded with great affection.

'Yes, Ashlee, I am, thanks to all your efforts,' he told her, then suddenly remembered my existence and set her near-naked form at a distance in order to introduce me. 'This is the woman responsible for my release from the curse,' he said. 'Mia Montrose, meet Ashlee Granville-Devere.'

'Actually, it's Mia Devere these days,' I reminded my husband, which flustered him as he had been very quick to remind Captain Sinclair of the same fact.

'Yes, of course,' he said, looking embarrassed.

Ashlee's face reflected both her delight and her apprehension at

434

meeting me. 'It is an honour, Mia, for you have done what I could not,' she said.

'The pleasure was really all mine,' I replied, and slid out of my pod to confront the woman I had envied and admired for so long. 'We bested Molier for you while we were at it.'

Ashlee, although I was sure she sensed my animosity, could not help but be pleased by the news.

'Then I am the one who needs to thank you, Mia,' said another voice from one of the furthest pods.

Albray was stunned breathless by the sound of her voice. 'Lillet?' he said, and moved off towards the source of his fascination.

'In one of my lifetimes I was the Lillet du Lac who knew you in your darkest hour,' she confirmed as he stepped into the light shed by her pod. She melted into a smile, which she had rarely done during the lifetime in which he'd known and loved her. 'Hello, brave knight.'

'Hello, princess,' he replied with a smile, as he had referred to her thus when he meant to tease her.

She was no longer vexed by him, however, for she launched herself out of her pod and into his waiting arms. 'I am so sorry, Albray,' she said, hugging him tight as their tears of joy and sorrow began to flow freely. 'I never wanted to be your curse.'

'You never were.' My husband near choked on his sincerity and, despite my jealousy, I was touched to see their reconciliation.

'Your man certainly gets around,' commented the sultry brunette beside me, who, by a simple process of elimination, I figured to be the original Dragon Queen herself, the mighty Lilith.

Once Albray and Lillet had regained control of their emotions, Albray looked up to see the two women he'd once known as Lady Susan and Ajalae Koriche. Both were waving hello and motioning him towards me. I stood with my arms crossed, feeling as dejected and insecure as any newly-wed pregnant woman would when seeing her husband expend so much affection on other women.

'Oh, honey …' Albray approached to reassure me, but I backed away to indicate that I didn't need his attention.

'I am fine with this,' I said.

Lillet moved past Albray to approach me. 'You did everything you promised me you would,' she said, and her goodwill and sincerity were so genuine that I found myself embracing her. Lillet had been a spirit guide to me during my encounter with Molier, advising me through her journals and in my dreams.

'I said I'd make the world a better place,' I recalled, 'but I have not.'

'You made *my* world a better place,' Albray ventured, and all the women present sighed, thinking him very sweet.

'Give yourself some time,' Lillet encouraged me and we embraced again.

'Dragon hug,' Lilith decided, and like the Great Mother she was, she motioned all her girls together into a tearful, swaying mass of bodies. Now all the pods had shut down, the crystal ceiling in the chamber began to give off a subtle, soothing light.

'Isn't this wonderful?' Lugh said to Albray as both men gazed at the huddle of near-naked female warriors.

'Heaven and hell all at once,' my husband replied, making Lugh laugh.

Our Anu host set about handing out robes, explaining that there was more suitable attire awaiting the Dragon Queens on board the *Kleio*. But there was no robe for me — I was handed the clothes I had worn into Amenti. Once we were both dressed, Lugh escorted us down a long corridor to the Amenti antechamber containing the three liquid-light portholes, one of which led to the Cave of Mamer and another to Lugh's realm.

'You and your partner have a different path to walk for a time,' Lugh advised.

'Starting with the opening of the Hall of Records,' I said, recalling our task.

Lugh nodded and led us all down the stairs in front of the altar towards the portholes, after which the stone wall behind the altar reconstituted to conceal the passage beyond.

'The rest of you ladies will be collected by Captain Sinclair presently,' he said.

The women all appeared keen on the idea, especially Ashlee, but I was a little disappointed to have to part from my sisters before

I had been given the chance to really know them. My feelings must have been reflected on my face.

'When will we see our sister again?' Ashlee asked Lugh.

'Not until Kali has come of age,' Lugh replied, and all my sisters sighed in disappointment with me.

'But that will be over thirteen years from now!' Lilith protested.

'Only for Mia,' Lugh pointed out. 'The rest of you are operating outside of time, and Captain Sinclair will be taking you all off to the future, after he returns Mia and Albray to their present.'

'But Mia will miss bonding with us,' Ashlee said sadly.

Perhaps she was keen that I should get to know her so I no longer saw her as a threat to my relationship with Albray. In truth, I *did* know her, and deep down I knew also that there was only one man for her — the captain of the *Kleio*.

'The plan was not of my design,' Lugh said, waving aside our objections. 'It was you of the Amenti Council who drew up the schedule; I am just following your orders.'

'Would you like me to chronicle all that unfolds with us until next we meet?' Ashlee stunned me with the very thoughtful offer, but I felt too overwhelmed to accept.

'I am sure you will be busy; I wouldn't want to impose,' I said.

'Mia, you will publish the story of your bloodline,' Lugh piped up. 'Thus you might want to consider that you will be missing part of the tale later if you do not continue to collaborate with your sisters now.'

In truth, the thought of publishing what I knew in a fictional tale had occurred to me already. I had begun sorting through the notes of my discoveries in the Sinai with Albray, and of his adventures with both Ashlee Granville in the nineteenth century and Lillet du Lac in the twelfth. I turned to my sisters and addressed them by the names I was most familiar with, even though clearly most of these women were not the incarnations I had read about.

'Ashlee, Lillet, Ajalae, Susan, Lilith,' I said, 'your stories have been completely life-altering for me. I would never have been able to free Albray or defeat Molier without your inspiration. So yes, I will be as honoured to read your future journals as I have been to read those you have penned for my benefit in the past.'

'No need for journals,' Lugh advised, 'for now that you have walked the Halls of Amenti, your full psychic potential has been realised and you are all telepathically linked on a subconscious level. Therefore, your experiences can be conveyed to Mia in her sleep, and when it comes time to write her tale, the stored information will surface for her reference. So you see, she will miss nothing!'

The Fey warrior received a round of cheers and blown kisses from all the female company, which he lapped up. 'How I wish I had a physical form so that I could hug you all,' he said. 'I could use my provisional physical coating, but alas I would feel nothing and probably crush you all.'

'That is exactly *why* you do not have a physical form,' Albray pointed out.

Before Lugh had the chance to retort, Captain Sinclair emerged through the central porthole. His eyes immediately came to rest upon Ashlee, as though he sensed her presence before his physical senses could confirm his instinct.

'Ladies . . . thou art a sight for sore eyes,' he said with great charm.

I had imagined this moment might be awkward for these two souls, for they wore different incarnations to those in which they had loved during their final lifetimes. Yet from the second they sighted each other, it was clear this did not matter.

Ashlee approached the captain and took hold of both his hands. The pair spoke in whispers for a moment and then merged into a kiss. It was not the kiss of desperate passion that one might expect of long-lost lovers, not heated, or lustful, or in any way rushed. Instead, it was as if their bodies had melded into a beautiful sculpture depicting the kiss that had all the time in creation to unfold.

Ashlee's sisters were far more respectful of Ashlee and Sinclair's reunion than they had been about mine and Albray's, but when the pair finally came back to Earth Lugh could not resist. 'I miss having a body,' he said. The comment was amusing and dispersed any awkwardness that might have ensued from the very touching moment.

'Well, ladies, we should depart,' the captain said. 'I'm sorry to rush you, but I've been unexpectedly entrusted with an additional mission.'

He looked to Ashlee as if she were responsible, and at once she knew what that mission was, for she had borne witness to it in a past life. 'The Signet Map?' she queried and the captain nodded. 'Lilitu is on board the *Kleio* at present?'

Captain Sinclair nodded gravely. 'You must not meet.'

'We do meet,' Ashlee said confidently.

'Shh!' the captain insisted, turning a small circle to contain his frustration and alarm. 'The first rule of time travel is that you do not disclose information pertaining to the events of your past that pertain to my future, or else we may alter our present, which is very favourable at this time. Any disasters or successes we have endured were all worth this moment.' His eyes swept over her physical form, clearly relishing the sight.

'Agreed,' Ashlee confirmed, but seemed a little confused about how best to proceed.

'Just allow events to unfold as they did,' he advised, and Ashlee smiled and winced at once. 'What is the matter?'

'I cannot say.' Ashlee looked regretful but determined.

'That is just as well,' the captain replied, pleased that Ashlee understood his position, but her adverse reaction had him worried now. 'Does something happen to Lilitu?'

Ashlee opened her mouth to respond.

'*Ashlee!*' Lillet warned, for she also knew the outcome of the mission as Lilitu had been her sister in that lifetime.

'As I was going to say, I cannot say,' Ashlee replied, looking to Lillet to reassure her.

Albray spoke up. 'Be that as it may, it might be best if you two were not left alone together until after Lilitu has disembarked from your ship, captain.'

The Dragon Queens chorused their agreement. Ashlee and Sinclair were both clearly dismayed by the ruling, and Sinclair gave Albray the evil eye.

Albray merely shrugged. 'It is in the best interest of the plan,' he said.

'We won't discuss the mission,' Ashlee said, offering a compromise to her sisters, but all shook their heads.

'Sorry, angel,' Lilith laid down the law. 'This mission is vital in many ways, to the both of you and the plan. So until Lilitu is safely delivered back to the thirteenth century where she belongs, the two of you shall have the pleasure of my company at all times.'

Both Ashlee and Captain Sinclair gave a resigned smile.

My sisters kissed me farewell, but Albray waved to the departing women from afar, to avoid getting into more trouble. 'It has been a pleasure catching up, ladies. Have fun, captain.'

The look of vengeful challenge on Sinclair's face said it all.

'The pleasure was ours, Albray,' Lilith said on behalf of all the sisters, then turned her attention to me. 'You take good care of our little goddess-to-be,' she instructed like a proud grandmother, which was all it took to send the sisters and myself into an emotional huddle again.

Albray and Captain Sinclair were frustrated by the delay — how were they ever going to separate us?

Albray spoke up first. 'Ladies, as delightful as your affection for each other is to watch, I need my wife back as we have a rather pressing prior engagement.'

'You do remember how to unlock the Hall of Records?' Lilith asked us.

In the sixth hall of Amenti I had been reconnected to my silent watcher, my dweller on the threshold, Meridon, who along with her partner, Arcturus, had been recruited onto the Amenti Project because of their skill for etheric architecture. I knew exactly how to gain access to the ancient time capsule for I had designed it, and Arcturus had incorporated the flame-bearer lock mechanism, to which our combined personal sonic was the key, along with the sonic frequency of the Anunnaki Queen, Kali. The inclusion of Kali's sonic in the lock mechanism meant that the Hall of Records could not be opened until she had been conceived by us, her final set of Earthly parents.

'You will all have access to our equipment within the hour,' I assured my sisters, and Albray nodded to second my claim. The sooner the task force that was to protect our child gained access to their stash of elite weaponry and technology, the easier Albray and I would feel about the arrival of our extraordinary baby girl.

Once Lugh had wished us all well and departed through the porthole that led him home, Captain Sinclair and my sisters left together, leaving Albray and myself in the Amenti antechamber.

'So,' he looked to me, 'what is the plan?'

'You do not recall how to find the Hall of Records?' I thought this odd as he had nodded so confidently when I had assured my sisters that we would have it opened in no time.

'Do you recall how the lock mechanism works?' he challenged and I had to admit that I did not. 'You have your job and I have mine. So,' he said again in an alluring, cheeky fashion, 'are you going to tell me what we have to do, or shall I be forced to take persuasive measures?'

He pulled me close, but as I was not in the mood for games at present, I gave him his answer in full.

'Once inside the Hall of Records, we flame-bearers are going to draw down the blue flame frequencies from the Sphere of Amenti, which have not flowed through the Earth grid since the demise of Atlantis. With the combined bio-energetic field of the orange, blue and violet flames, we will infuse the Earth grid with an energetic upgrade, which will trigger a spontaneous expansion of multidimensional awareness, memory and identity in those human beings on Earth not yet under the control of the Nefilim's frequency fence. But it won't be until the violet flame-holder comes into her power at the age of thirteen that the grids of Tara and Earth will begin to merge, whereupon the Halls of Amenti and the Sphere of Amenti will begin to open for mass ascension back to Tara.'

'Yes, I realise that.' Albray rolled his eyes at my little spiel. 'My real question was *where* do we gain entry?'

'Right here.' I smiled.

'But what about the Fibonacci spiral?'

'We'll use it as a meditation to separate our subtle bodies from our physical forms,' I explained.

Albray frowned and shook his head. 'No, I meant that I understood we needed to be at the spot designated by the centre of the spiral on the Giza plateau in order to gain access to the Hall of Records?'

'We are in the centre of the spiral,' I said, and pointed upward. 'That spot on surface Earth is directly above us; I know because I saw this place during my astral descent into the Earth when I visited the Akashic library in search of Jamila. The entrance to the Hall of Records is located in the same space we are frequenting, but on an astral level. There are three channels that lead from that room,' I motioned to the portholes. 'Sound similar to what Jamila described?'

'Whoa.' Albray was impressed that we were further advanced in our mission than expected. 'So what are we waiting for?' He sat himself down to begin the meditation for astral separation. 'Let's spiral.'

REVELATION 29

THE HALL OF RECORDS

We both lay down to perform the spiralling technique, which would liberate our subtle bodies from the physical. Jamila had foretold that we would find ourselves in a room of red granite, which was hardly surprising as that was what this chamber was made of too. But the building blocks of this chamber on the astral level of awareness were made of a mineral I had never seen before: it was iridescent and glowed with a pretty pearly colour. The three portholes that looked like blue liquid-light waterfalls on Earth were now swirling vortexes of purple. In the corner of the room was the pot that was the key for negotiating the way safely through to the Hall of Records. Jamila had said that the right person would know how to read what was written on the pot and would choose the right path.

I moved to the pot, which appeared brand new, as did the entire chamber, and crouched down to read it. In my nightmares I had not been able to decipher the message, but that was before Amenti, before I came to know Meridon.

'What does it say?' Albray asked anxiously. My confused expression wasn't encouraging. 'Can't you read it?'

I could read it all right, but what it said wasn't very helpful. 'It advises that the blue flame is the fastest route to Amenti.'

Albray looked at the three spiralling vortexes with bewilderment, as did I. 'That doesn't make sense, as Amenti is the fastest route to the blue flame, not the other way around. Are you sure that's all it says?'

443

I nodded and stood to recall what Jamila had told us about this stage of the journey. 'In two of the channels lies death, and the third channel will suck us in and never let us go.'

'Only if we're not the flame-bearers,' Albray added.

I shushed him and turned to face the three channels. 'The right person will make it to the door beyond the guarded channels and, upon arrival, will produce a particular sound and this sonic will open the door,' I quoted. Then I turned to face the altar stone, where I knew a concealed doorway lay in the physical world, a doorway that was opened by blue flame energy. 'We've skipped a step in the journey,' I concluded. 'We don't have to pick a channel because we are already in the room beyond them! Only the true flame-bearers could make it here, as we and our fellow Council members are the only humans who have knowledge of or access to the Hall of Life. Only we and the Anu know there is a doorway in the wall behind that altar stone.'

'Honey,' Albray said affectionately, 'you're good.'

'It was nothing.' I waved off the praise and I prepared for my next trick. 'Watch this.'

I positioned myself in front of the altar and, holding my hands palms out before me, I willed my dormant blue flame energy into the ancient stone.

'Holy cow!' Albray backed up a few paces as a stream of blue energy shot from my palms and into the stone altar. The wall beyond dissolved into nothingness and the secret passage revealed itself. 'No wonder only the true flame-bearers could make it past this point,' he commented. 'How fortunate for us that you are the only human channel for the blue flame.'

'Indeed,' I said as we proceeded into the long hall beyond. It was entirely different from the hall that was its counterpart in the physical world: its walls, floor and ceiling emitted their own light and even the air was illuminated.

'I've been here before,' Albray said.

I recognised the place too. 'En route to Amenti,' I said, and he nodded.

Along one wall were etched in light the images of the forty-eight chromosomes of Christ consciousness, and on the opposing side the hall branched into many other halls and rooms. I knew what was in them all: the technologically advanced equipment that had been stored here for the benefit of the Staff of Amenti and their plan. At present these rooms were locked and would remain so until the Hall of Records had been opened.

'Well done,' Albray told me. 'This is exactly where we need to be.'

'I know,' I said. 'Although I'm a little hazy on what happens from here.'

Albray smiled. 'My turn to impress you then.'

'By all means ...' I motioned him to take the lead and he did so with confidence. 'Jamila said that among these rooms there is a golden stairway —'

'There is indeed.' Albray proceeded to the end of the corridor and turned right towards the entrance to the Amenti chamber.

'The lock to the Hall of Records is in the Amenti chamber?' I queried.

'Of course,' he replied as we approached the great cavern that hosted the island on which the golden stairwell to Amenti was located. 'Both the Arc Porthole passage, which is hosting the Sphere of Amenti at present, and the Hall of Amorea are to be found there. They are the means by which we will channel the data from the Sphere into the epicentre of the grid located at the Earth's core.'

'What?' I was perplexed. 'There are only the six portholes of Amenti's halls in the Amenti chamber.' I had been there; I had seen the set-up.

'Trust me, they're there,' Albray assured me.

We approached the entrance to the cavern and the limestone bridge appeared before us, granting us passage to the central island.

'Isn't there supposed to be a holograph above the stairway that names the three persons who are appointed to enter?' I asked.

High above us, the ceiling of the chamber was composed of huge glowing crystal clusters; water ran down the inner walls into the darkened void below. Once we'd reached the central island and the bridge had vanished, Albray urged me to look up: there in the large crystal above us was reflected a holographic image of three symbols. One was a picture of a vial, much like those once hidden in the Star-

Fire Temple at Mt Serabit in the Sinai — which, incidentally, was also designed by Meridon and Arcturus. Another was a symbol that looked like the ringstone to which my husband's spirit had been attached for many centuries. And beneath an image of our daughter was a symbol of the Grail, for she was the last of the line.

As we gazed in amazement at the symbols, the golden plate beneath our feet vanished and Albray and I plunged into the depths of Amenti. As we descended, the velocity of the fall decreased until we were merely drifting down, then floating and alighting in the great central chamber.

I was disappointed to find nothing had changed here — there were still only six portholes and no other passages or rooms to speak of. 'Are you sure about this?' I asked Albray.

'Sure, I'm sure,' he said, and walked over to the pool in the centre of the chamber. 'Do you want to see a neat trick?' He grinned as he jumped up onto the rim of the pool, then stepped onto the liquid surface and proceeded to walk on water.

I squealed and approached the pool in wonder.

'I present to you the Hall of Amorea.' He motioned to the pool beneath him, then levitated into the air and waved to me before disappearing into a light-emitting funnel in the centre of the ceiling directly above the pool.

'Albray?' I called, a little wary of stepping onto the porthole, as it was not a time passage as Amenti's halls were, but a stargate. Its surface glistened the most striking shade of indigo; when I dared to run my hands over the glistening watery surface it felt a little like very fluid jelly. *Spectacular.* It amused me that during all our comings and goings through the Halls of Amenti, none of us ever thought to look up at this chamber's ceiling. At its highest point, it disappeared into a huge funnel, which shed light upon the central pool, although one had to actually stand in the pool of water to view the light source.

'Come on, Mia,' Albray encouraged. 'It's perfectly safe.'

I stepped up onto the rim of the pool and glided out over the surface. 'I'm doing it!' I squealed again as I reached the rim of the spotlight that the funnel shed on the pool and my feet lifted off the ground.

I looked up at my husband, levitating not far above me in the huge tube, and then high beyond him to the extreme end of the perpendicular funnel; there, glistening silver like moonlight on the ocean, was the entrance to the Arc Porthole passage. This portal connected Earth to the central sun of the Pleiades system where the Sphere of Amenti had been hidden since before the demise of Atlantis.

The passage was an emergency security measure that had been incorporated into the Amenti system for activation in the event that anyone ever tried to exploit the Sphere of Amenti for unsafe energy practices — thus the Amenti Council had the means to prevent the same disaster that had occurred on Tara from repeating itself on Earth. Originally the Sphere of Amenti had been hosted on this planet. But when Hermes foresaw the demise of Atlantis, he contacted the silent watchers overseeing the Amenti scheme and requested that the Amenti Council withdraw the Sphere down the Arc Porthole passage, lock the porthole and shut down the Signet Grid.

These opposing portholes were larger, more imposing versions of Amenti's halls and perfectly round. The Arc Porthole was rimmed with silver, the primary surface colour of its liquid-light shield. Beyond this shield the Sphere of Amenti was currently making its return voyage to Earth in order to be here by the time of the interdimensional planetary alignment of 2012. This alignment would span a five-year period, and if Amenti's doors were not opened by the end of 2017, humanity would be trapped in this lower harmonic universe for 25,000 years until the next interdimensional planetary alignment. And as the Earth was fast being raped of its resources, it was unlikely it would survive long enough to see the next alignment — especially if the Nefilim and Dracon had anything to do with it, and they had *everything* to do with it.

I floated to a stop near my husband and he reached out and took hold of my hands. Touching his subtle form was more intense: the contact was more lucid, like holding someone in a dream, but his personal energy was far more potent than it was when we made physical contact.

'So, here we are, at the crossroads of time, space and dimensions — the Grand Central Station of Earth evolution!' he said.

'Here we are,' I echoed, overwhelmed as I gazed down upon the indigo liquid-light porthole below us, our suspended forms reflected in its surface. 'So what happens now?'

Albray let go of my hands to pull me close with one arm. He held out his free hand, palm down, over the Hall of Amorea, and advised me to do the same thing, but with my palm facing up.

'Now what?' I asked, leaning away from him a little as I was still somewhat perturbed by all his flirting this day, and he was suddenly very amorous.

'You are going to draw down the blue flame energy from the Sphere of Amenti, whilst I use the orange flame to direct the data into the Earth's core where it will be distributed through the Earth's natural grid. This will boost the consciousness levels of humanity on Earth as the borders between physical and astral worlds begin to merge in preparation for this planet to again host the Sphere.'

'Okay.' I was following him so far.

'However, you and I, as the conduits of this energy, have to form a connection for the blue flame energy to pass through us into the Earth's core.' He grinned mischievously.

'Are you saying we have to have sex?' The idea was rather appealing, yet I did not wish to forgive his earlier insensitivity so easily.

'That would be nice,' he said, 'but a kiss would suffice.'

'I don't believe you.'

'It's true,' he insisted. 'I wrote a kiss into the lock's programming code. And not just any kiss: it must be one of unconditional love and understanding.' He batted his eyelids sweetly.

'So I'm supposed to just forgive your flirtatious ways, am I?'

'And I shall forgive yours,' he replied.

I gasped, feeling that I had been wrongly accused.

'Pause for a moment and think back over your past lives on this Earth,' he urged before I could begin to argue.

As I did, I realised I'd had just as many varied indiscretions with our other Council members as he had. 'I knew no better,' I said, defending my past actions.

'Nor did I.' He drove home his point with a smile that I found myself returning. 'Forgive me,' he asked, and I could tell from his tone that it was desperately important to him. 'I know better now, Meridon.'

His use of my true name opened the floodgates of my heart and out poured all the warmth and compassion I possessed. 'I love you, Arcturus, and I forgive you. But I feel I should mention that the captain told Ashlee that they could not kiss here in Amenti.'

Albray's seductive smile broadened as he closed the distance between his lips and mine. 'That is because a kiss in this chamber can be a very explosive event.'

As I immersed myself in the kiss, the darkness behind my closed eyes erupted into the colour of orange, then blue, and then a long intense shade of violet that set our entwined bodies spinning. We clung to each other to prevent being washed away by the light-streams of energy that rushed down the long funnel above us and into the opened portal to the Earth's core below. Our kiss, which at first felt surreal, gradually became more tangible as the great rush of energy died away. When we stopped spinning, we touched down to Earth in physical form.

The sound of applause drew our consciousness back to reality. We were back in the altar room outside the Amenti complex, where we had left our physical bodies, and around us stood the female contingent of the Amenti Council and Captain Sinclair.

'Figures you'd work a little romance into the schedule,' commented the captain.

'There's always time for a little romance, captain,' responded Ashlee seductively as she moved off after the rest of the ladies.

'Well done,' Lilith called to us as she brought up the rear, disappearing along the corridor and into the complex.

'Did we succeed?' I asked, slipping away from my husband.

'I do believe so,' Captain Sinclair said cheerfully.

'How do you know?' I asked, and he directed my attention back to the corridor my sisters were traversing.

Susan, who had gone ahead of the others, rushed back to spur her sisters forth. 'Everything is here,' she cried, 'our weapons, tools, systems! The Hall of Records is open for reference — come and see!' She squealed with delight and disappeared down the tunnel once more, my sisters making haste after her.

Albray and I were keen to follow, but the captain moved into our path. 'I'm sorry, but both of you still have time to serve within the Earth scheme, therefore you are not permitted entry past this point at this time.'

'What!' Albray protested, even though he accepted that to permit us to see what lay beyond would cause a breach in security. 'We opened the damn thing!'

'It is in the best interest of the plan.' The captain taunted Albray, just as my husband had taunted him earlier. The look on Albray's face made me fear a punch-up was imminent, but, to my great relief, Albray saw the humour and both men began to laugh.

'You have not seen the last of me, captain,' Albray warned.

'I have for at least a decade, my friend,' replied Sinclair. 'It is time to get you both home, but before you go take this.'

He handed me what appeared to be nothing and at first I thought he was being funny, but as I closed my hand I felt something enclosed there . . . a ring.

'It has been retuned to a frequency beyond the band widths accessible by the Dracon,' the captain explained, 'and so its signal is untraceable. Wear it until your daughter comes of age, and then pass it to her. If either of you are ever in trouble, I will learn of it.'

I took his gift with gratitude, as any additional safeguard for my daughter was welcome by me. That was the last time I laid eyes on Captain Sinclair or the Dragon Queens.

Below this finishing line was a freshly scribbled note: *Until today.*

FROM THE JOURNAL OF TAMAR DEVERE

My heart jumped into my throat as I read these words; in my gut I knew my mother had penned it today. All the events that had taken place at the mall this morning suddenly made sense. It wasn't mall security who had arrived to deal with our two mysterious stalkers; it was the Dragon Queens protecting me!

'My own personal, really hot, kick-arse security team — all right!' I punched the air, at once inspired and terrified by the notion. That was why my mother could be so sure that the stalkers had been adequately dealt with. And this invisible ring was how the Dragon Queens found us.

I felt safer knowing the ring's true function, and realised Mum had known this when she gave me the ring and her journal to read. Then I burst into tears, overwhelmed by what lay ahead.

THE HALL OF TIME CODES

Destiny will come for me this evening, when the last of the time codes is integrated into my being. This isn't a fantasy! The tales of the Dragon Queens I've so wanted to contribute to have really been about me all along. For I am the reason wars are fought, religions are created, secret societies are formed, conspiracies are executed and plagues are released upon the Earth.

The globe inside my reading light unexpectedly popped as I was writing my journal; it scared me witless as I was left in darkness. I glanced at my clock to realise that it was past 7 p.m. and rather later than I'd expected. I rose and flicked the switch for the overhead light, whereby the bulb in it promptly popped and darkness prevailed.

'Just great.' I decided it was time to have a good heart-to-heart with my parents anyway.

When I exited my room, however, I heard my mother speaking with someone in the lounge room. I froze still to listen. It was my father; he must have come home whilst I was absorbed in my reading. I hesitated to go in and greet him, as he and Mum were speaking in hushed voices — which would seem to indicate they were talking about me.

'How much danger is she in?' Mum was saying. 'Should we relocate her before tonight?'

'Nobody wants to relocate her before Kali finishes her work with *The Book of Codes*,' Dad replied.

'I think we should just ask Tamar what she knows, and see how best we can be of aid,' Mum suggested. It sounded as if Dad was agreeing

452

with her, so I backed into my room to avoid being caught eavesdropping.

As I waited in the darkness for my parents, wondering if I should just walk out and confront them, a bright ball of light came shooting through my window and stopped dead in the centre of my room. As I looked on, amazed, a feeling of time slowing crept over me. Then I was suddenly aware of being constrained for I could no longer move.

I awoke naked on a cold, flat metal surface in an entirely white room that was awash with light. My being was panicked to the core at being so exposed and vulnerable in an unfamiliar place. Strange grey beings with large black eyes peered down at me — they reminded me of descriptions of aliens in accounts of human abduction. Was that what had happened to me?

'Hello, sweetheart,' a voice said.

My instinct told me this was a malign presence. I looked around but could see no one beyond the grey beings, who by now had backed away from the table. Then I glimpsed an undulating shadow moving about amid the glare of the white room.

'It seems I found you just in the nick of time, princess. One more day and you would have been a force to be reckoned with.'

It was Pintar, I knew it in my gut — a hell of a time to finally learn the difference between a psychic premonition and my imagination.

'You do remember . . . I'm touched.'

'Where is Mathu?' If my enemy was going to read my mind, better that the subject was of my choosing.

'Dead!' Pintar barked, annoyed by my concern. 'I chewed up his soul and spat it out.'

I didn't believe a word he was telling me; I didn't want to believe it. 'Then why aren't you wearing Mathu's form?'

'It caved under the pressure of our struggle.' Pintar clearly enjoyed breaking the news. 'And so his soul has been cast adrift of the plan, just like mine and many others.'

Sorrow filled me against my will, for I did not want my enemy revelling in my pain.

'So you see, there is no point in you seeking Amenti, your Majesty, for your prince will not be awaiting your arrival,' the horrid entity gloated. 'Hence you, the last of the Dragon Queens, are now the underworld's most eligible widow.'

I was filled with so much hatred that all I could do to release it was to cry, like the useless weak-willed girl I was.

'Two things,' Pintar continued. 'Firstly, to prevent you from ever completely joining with that Anunnaki witch, my little grey friends here are going to microchip you and bring you under our frequency fence, along with fifty-five per cent of the Earth's population.'

He was trying to imply the bad guys were winning the war for human consciousness. I assumed that the frequency fence he spoke of worked in the same manner as other artificial seals that had been placed within the frequency bands of mankind's subtle bodies by both sides in the inter-time war. The frequency seal would act as a barrier to prevent a soul-mind ever progressing beyond a certain frequency, thereby stunting the evolution of the species until the seal was lifted.

'Secondly, as you may note, I still have no body.' Pintar's tone was more malign now. 'And in order to regain the body to which I am accustomed, I need a Dragon Queen to mate with one of my Dracon warriors. Guess who that lucky lady is?'

I didn't hear what Pintar said beyond that, for I began to scream. Beneath my panic, however, my mind was still working. If only Kali were here, I thought, she would equalise this situation. *Oh, why isn't she here?* Then it struck me: all I had to do was fall asleep before I was sedated and Kali *would* be here.

I ceased screaming and fell quiet and still. My focus moved inward to block out the evil distractions around me and I focused on sleep as if my life depended on it. Which it clearly did. As panicked as I was by my predicament, I was also exhausted and my body didn't require more than one invitation to shut down.

FROM THE DIARY OF MIA DEVERE

Albray had come home early to calm my fears about Tamar's safety, but somewhere during that conversation we realised that over five hours had elapsed that we could not account for. Upon noting the time irregularity, our first concern was for Tamar. She was not in her room as expected, nor anywhere in the house — she had simply vanished!

Panic gripped my heart, for I knew that this time in her life was critical to Tamar's development; I could not have picked a worse time in all her thirteen years to drop the ball.

Calling in the police was not an option for us, for we had done our best to keep Tamar hidden and an extensive search would expose her to those we wanted to protect her from. The task force we needed to call was no longer available to us, for I had forsaken my main connection with the Dragon Queens when I gave Tamar the ring. My only hope was that the ring would help our allies track her down and keep her from harm. Of course, there was also the option of connecting to my sisters in my sleep, but in my current state of panic I had precious little chance of dropping off.

I stood forlornly in my daughter's bedroom after checking it for the third time, when I spied her diary sitting by her bed. It was begging me to break its lock to reveal my daughter's experiences of the week just past. I reached for the item, then placed it back down again.

'What's wrong?' Albray asked. 'Just force the lock.'

'I promised her I'd never read it,' I explained.

'I feel this situation overrules your promise,' Albray appealed. When I shook my head, he lost his patience. 'Well, I never made such a promise.'

He reached for the journal, but was distracted by a noise coming from within the house.

We both slipped into the hallway, straining our ears to pinpoint the location of the disturbance; it seemed to be coming from the library, which we had only just searched, twice! Albray retrieved a large broadsword from one of the many on display on the walls in our hallway. I grabbed up a couple of daggers, just in case.

Towards the library we crept, then put our ears to the door to get some idea of the identity of the intruder before entering. A guttural snarl sounded behind us and we turned to confront several reptilian warriors closing in on us from both ends of the hallway. Albray guided me around into the library doorway behind him, to protect me while he engaged the reptilians. The library door opened behind me and I

455

was pulled into the room. The door slammed shut, trapping Albray in the hallway.

My aggressor held me under the arms and was restraining my head with both his hands, but my arms were still free.

'Sedate her!' my captor ordered his companion.

I could not hope to kill a Dracon with a blade, unless I had the opportunity to stab where I could sever the spinal cord. However, Dracon, like humans, had to breathe to function properly, and as they relied on their rib muscles to draw breath in and out of their lungs I aimed for the reptilian's ribcage. My aim with a knife was lethal since I had journeyed the Halls of Amenti, for there I had remembered my skills as a *ventilatore* priestess in Ancient Egypt, where I juggled knives to predict the future and cast them with deadly accuracy to protect the greater interests of my homeland and our Pharaoh.

My blade took the reptilian warrior down, but not before he got his shot away. The dart hit me in the leg and my body went to jelly.

'Next time you'll be quicker off the mark,' my captor jeered to his fellow warrior, who was clearly in agony and, so I thought, incapacitated for a while. 'Shoot yourself, will you, and then get up here and give me a hand.'

To my dismay, the wounded reptilian removed my knife, extended a metal spike from his wristband and gave himself a mini injection — of ORME, I assumed, for the wound healed straightaway.

My captor thrust me roughly into his companion's grip. 'Hold her,' he ordered.

The angry Dracon squeezed one of my breasts and stuck his long pointy tongue in my ear. 'I'll finish her off,' he growled.

I spotted a nice heavy vase sitting on one of the library shelves and willed it to collide with my attacker's head. 'Argh!' He dropped me to nurse his wound, now oozing green fluid.

'You're not going to have any juice left to kill her if you can't avoid getting wounded for five seconds!' the warrior in charge said, and reached for the picture that concealed my wall safe.

They were after *The Book of Codes*! I knew Tamar had yet to complete the activations that her alter ego, Kali, was running her through in her sleep. If the activations that would draw her higher self into her human form were not completed, she would never realise her full potential as Kali and would be unable to unlock Amenti — which was precisely why the Dracon were seeking the book.

'Bring her here,' the leader commanded. When his colleague hesitated, he gathered me up himself and, clutching my hand, sank my fingertips into the keypad. The safe lock deactivated, the door flipped open and I was dropped to the floor.

I willed anything in the room that was not pinned down towards the thief; I simply could not allow them to steal this precious family heirloom that was an esoteric treasure of vital import to the world. But the Dracon ducked and fended off the various flying objects that hurled themselves towards him, and tucked *The Book of Codes* under his arm. Then he activated the metal spike in his wristband and bent down towards me.

'She's mine!' his colleague objected, and dragged my attacker backwards to battle it out.

Albray burst through the door, a reptilian head in each hand. 'She's mine actually,' he said, and tossed a head at each of the reptilians. 'Give me the book, or you shall force me to take it.'

But the Dracon vanished from our midst. I would have cried had I had any control over my bodily functions. Albray came to check on me, but I was unable even to blink my eyes to assure him that I was okay; I looked like a complete zombie, I was sure.

'What in God's name have they done to you?' my husband asked.

There was a knock on the front door. Albray was hesitant to leave me, but when it was repeated with more urgency, he relented. 'I'll be right back,' he said.

I heard the door open and Albray greet our guest with astonishment. 'Captain Sinclair!'

'I'm here for *The Book of Codes*,' the captain said, and I heard the door slam and both men move rapidly up the hallway.

'You're too late,' Albray said as they entered the library. 'And where is our daughter?'

'We have her,' Sinclair said, crouching down next to me to see how I fared. 'We recovered her before Pintar's little grey men could bring her under the control of the frequency fence.'

'Is she all right?' Albray demanded.

'She's fine,' the captain assured us both, 'but she is vulnerable until she integrates those last codes.'

Albray placed a hand on Sinclair's shoulder so that he might understand his sincerity. 'Thank you, captain.'

'No, thank you.' The captain surprised Albray with his response. 'Pintar had taken most of us out with these darts when your daughter showed up and saved all our arses. These bullets don't affect her, so long as Tamar is asleep and Kali is in control. Once the last codes are integrated, Kali and Tamar will permanently be as one and she will be unstoppable.' The captain's tone was a little uncertain.

'You sound somewhat worried about that,' Albray said.

'Well ... Kali seems a little overzealous about her duties.' Sinclair was clearly choosing his words carefully so as not to offend Tamar's parents. 'She asked every one of those reptilians today whether they chose to join her in life or in death, and when all chose death she killed them precisely and mercilessly. When I asked her how she felt in the wake of taking so many lives, she said that only when every reptilian form is destroyed will the evolution of the lost Anunnaki be assured.'

'A fair reason,' Albray, the warrior, agreed. 'Now, what's wrong with Mia?'

'The effects of the dart will wear off presently,' the captain said, and lifted me in his arms.

'Do you mind?' Albray objected.

'So sorry ... you were always taking off with my wife, so I just figured it was kosher.' The captain bundled me into my husband's arms. 'You want to see Tamar, I take it?'

'Of course,' Albray said.

'Then follow me.'

The captain led us out of the library and towards the front door. I had to wonder where he'd managed to park his transport in the middle of Sydney.

'Ta-da!' Sinclair motioned to the park across the road from our house, which was devoid of people at this late hour. 'Our entry lies right over there by the bins. Follow me.'

Albray carried me into the empty park, but there was no sign of the *Kleio*. 'Well, I hope you're going to tell us your ship is cloaked, or else — ouch!' Albray's head collided with something hard and metal.

'I said to follow me,' Sinclair said, pointing out that Albray was making his own way to our destination. 'And yes, *Kleio* is cloaked.'

'You are so like Devere,' Albray observed.

'Funny about that,' Sinclair grinned and, passing by the bins, he vanished.

On board the *Kleio*, I was laid in a cabin on a very comfortable bed beside my daughter, who appeared to be unconscious.

Albray sat down beside Tamar and stroked her hair, thankful beyond belief to see her. 'Is she asleep?'

'I believe she is in a deep meditative state,' the captain advised.

Albray refrained from disturbing her further. 'So what is the plan, captain?'

'Well, if the mountain cannot come to Mohammed, we will just have to take Mohammed to the mountain.'

'The Hall of Time Codes,' Albray said, instantly understanding what the captain had in mind.

'It is a trap,' Tamar said without disturbing her relaxed state of being. Her voice was somewhat more sultry and mature than that of our teenage daughter.

'I am aware of that,' Sinclair assured her. 'And now that we know of our enemy's incapacitating darts, we will take steps to combat the threat.'

I knew that the Staff of Amenti, despite our exposure to the blue flame, were not truly immortal. For in truth, no one could be immortal on the physical Earth plane, or any of Earth's planes, for time here had a beginning and an end. Amenti's staff were a thousand times more resilient than the average human being — they healed faster and had limitless stamina — but we were still affected by any drug, weapon or illness that was damaging to man. We felt the same pain as any human did when wounded; we just had a far better chance of surviving an attack.

'We need only hold off the Dracon long enough for you to integrate the last codes,' the captain concluded.

'Indeed.' Tamar smiled, her eyes still closed. 'Provide me with that window of opportunity, Polaris, and I will turn the tide of this war.'

I AM

By the time *Kleio* was parked inside the Cave of Mamer once more, outside the labyrinth that led to the Hall of Time Codes, I was starting to regain control of my fingers and my head, but the rest of my body was useless. 'Please do not leave me here,' I begged my husband.

Albray frowned apologetically. 'It's too dangerous to take you in this state,' he reasoned and I knew he was right.

It was heartbreaking — I'd given my all to raising Tamar and now I couldn't be present for what would be one of the most significant and perilous moments of her life. I wanted to protect her just one last time, before she became the ultimate being in self-sufficiency. As it was, I couldn't lift my arm, let alone wield a weapon.

Tamar rose from her meditation and came to stand over me, her face devoid of expression. 'We would like our mother with us,' she said and touched my forehead. Instantly, the debilitating serum oozed out of the tiny hole in my leg where the dart had embedded itself and full control of my form was returned to me. I floated to standing, no will required, as though a great weight of gravity had been lifted from me.

'Sweet goddess,' I said and hugged my daughter tight to me. 'Tamar.'

But Tamar did not hug me back, nor did she protest my affection — she was completely impartial. 'We should go,' she informed me and exited, leaving Albray and myself bemused by the transformation in our daughter.

'We must remember that this is Kali in control. She has not fully integrated with our sweet daughter yet,' Albray said hopefully.

He was right: there didn't seem to be any trace of our daughter in the goddess's demeanour at present. Still, Tamar must have had some influence subconsciously or Kali would not have bothered to heal me.

'Then let us ensure she gets that equalising opportunity,' I said.

Albray's work clothes transformed into a black rubber all-body suit that had the resilience of steel. Its collar sat high around his neck, forming a protective barrier against the Dracon's fatal ORME spikes. I willed my clothes to assume the same form. My shoes stretched up to my knees and the heels flattened out into rugged black boots. Albray handed me my knife belt and I strapped it on, then we pursued our daughter into the cavern beyond the ship.

The captain had gone on ahead to check in with our staff-mates, who were scattered throughout the labyrinth that led to the hall of codes. We followed our daughter up the cavern stairs to where Ashlee stood guard, her labrys in hand.

'Kali,' she said, and nodded to acknowledge the Anunnaki Queen as she passed into the tunnel system.

'Solarian.' Tamar returned the gesture.

'Arcturus.' Ashlee greeted Albray with a smile, which became wary as she looked to me. 'Meridon. No sign of reptiles.' She backed up to follow us through the labyrinth.

The next vital turn was guarded by Levi and Lillet. The pair acknowledged our daughter in the same manner Ashlee had.

'Thana,' Tamar replied with a nod of respect to Lillet, then her partner. 'Levi.'

Levi's celestial name was the same as that of his incarnation as Ashlee Granville-Devere's son, which was why as a child he had insisted on changing it from Thomas, even though he did not consciously know why until he'd walked the Halls of Amenti.

Once our party had passed, Levi and Lillet fell in behind us, to aid Ashlee to cover our rear.

At the spot where the labyrinth stretched into a long tunnel, the original Dragon Queen, Lilith, awaited, broadsword in hand; although she had designed the original labrys, the sword had always served her well. On guard with her was her partner, Akbar.

'Denera, Zalman.' Tamar greeted them as she passed.

At the entrance to the hall was Lady Susan and the key incarnation of her husband, James Devere, who went by the name Arthur.

'Talori, Castor,' Tamar greeted them.

'Welcome, Kali,' said Lady Susan excitedly as Tamar moved past her and into the hall. 'We cleaned up a bit.'

The Hall of Time Codes had been completely restored to mint condition. Only the ceiling of the structure differed from Ashlee's description of the hall as it had existed upon Tara: the glass windows that had once flooded the hall with sunlight had been replaced by great glowing slabs of crystal that cast a lovely subtle light over the chamber.

'You no longer need ankhs,' Tamar gathered as she gazed at the ceiling.

Once upon a time, only ankhs could manipulate physical matter so perfectly. But after our time beneath the blue flame, the Staff of Amenti no longer needed these tools to manipulate physical matter; we were all now personal channels for fifth-dimensional energy.

'Magnificent,' Tamar said, nodding to Susan and her twin flame. Then she strode into the centre of the gallery, where Ajalae Koriche stood waiting. 'Vespera, your work has never looked better.' Tamar turned circles to view all the vibrant time codes imprinted on the walls, her face full of admiration.

Once Ajalae had made her journey through the Halls of Amenti, she realised that *The Emerald Book of Thoth* had done nothing but awaken her own memory. She knew how photosonics worked because, as Vespera of Tara, she had developed the technique with her partner, Dexter.

Tamar looked to the entry at the far end of the hall, which Polaris, Taejax and Taylor were guarding. In the void that was the entrance, a solid barrier of stone manifested. Once all Amenti's staff were assembled in the hall of codes, the entrance to the labyrinth was also sealed by stone. Satisfied that all was as secure as it could be, Tamar approached the second last of the time codes that she had to integrate. Then she hesitated and looked back to us. 'There is one of us missing. Where is Mathu?'

'No one is sure.' Levi volunteered the sad news.

'The elders?' Tamar asked.

'They say he has not returned to Sirius B,' Levi informed her, 'but that is not to say that his soul-mind has perished. I summoned him back from the ethers over a hundred years ago and allowed him to use my body to destroy his Emerald Book.'

'And where did his soul proceed to from there?'

Levi shrugged. 'The scribe told me that he needed to make amends for his past mistakes in order that he might again be permitted to incarnate into human form, but whether he did or not, I cannot say.'

'Did any of you phone me recently and warn me of danger?' Tamar queried of all the staff members, and when each assured her we had not, she smiled in knowing.

'He has not perished,' she assured us all, for without Mathu none of us would return home. 'My prince will find us in time for Amenti's opening.'

My fellow Dragon Queens and I formed a circle of protection around Tamar, and the men positioned themselves near the entrances, keeping watchful and alert.

I had to admire my daughter as she turned to her code work. Our tall, slender girl was fast transforming into an image of a living goddess — her olive skin had darkened many shades, her already dark hair was now jet black, and her ebony eyes had turned a haunting shade of violet, a trait indicative of the Anu. She had grown into the most perfectly beautiful creature I had ever seen, but my little girl was gone forever. I had known this would happen, but I was going to miss being needed by her.

Tamar had moved to the final activation when I sensed a disturbing presence — a sensation I had felt before, in Giza. I knew it was not Molier, as Albray and I had disposed of him before Tamar was born.

'Pintar!' all the Dragon Queens concluded at once, and the force swirled around us, stirring up the atmosphere.

'Use your third eye, people,' Ashlee advised, 'and he's perfectly visible.'

Just as I caught sight of the seething thought-form of dark grey energy that was Pintar, it darted out through the stone wall entrance guarded by Sinclair and company. Moments later the stone barrier began rippling from the centre like fluid and from beyond the thinning void a screeching noise echoed. A large winged Dracon came swooping through the breach and into the hall and grabbed Captain Sinclair's dart gun from his holster on its way past.

'Watch out, it has my gun!' the captain cried in warning.

Taylor remained focused on the doorway, straining to will the stone to harden once more. 'They must have stolen some ankhs,' he suggested, for it was the only possible explanation for their breach of the barrier.

Zalman and Levi raced to aid Taylor, while Taejax, able to move faster than any human, wasted no time in racing the winged Dracon to its target. Before we even realised what was happening, Taejax had launched himself into the path of the liquid nitrogen dart that was headed straight for Tamar. The reptilian took the dart in the chest, froze, and then splintered into a thousand pieces as he hit the floor.

'I can keep this up all day, I have plenty of ammunition,' Pintar gloated. He had inhabited the Dracon's body in order to launch his assault.

Many more winged Dracon soared into the chamber and we were suddenly busy deflecting the predators away from my daughter. Each of us had our own unique way of disposing of the reptilians, using fighting and psychic skills developed during various incarnations in past and future time.

Lillet launched an arrow spiked with a dose of the same liquid nitrogen serum from her crossbow and brought Taejax's killer to the ground in a shattering mess. However, I could see with my third eye that Pintar had not been destroyed. The dark mist of his thought-form merely leapt to another Dracon.

Lady Susan had a very neat trick that nearly got her killed by one of my blades. Her key incarnation was a shape-shifting princess, Mèlusine, and unbeknownst to me she used this skill to transform into a Dracon to confuse the enemy. Thankfully she transformed back into her human form a heartbeat before I cast my knife at her.

'An honest mistake,' she called to me as she unleashed her whip and latched it around the waist of a flying Dracon. A strong jerk brought the creature crashing to the floor, giving me the opportunity to stab my knife deep into the spine at the base of its neck. Susan cheered our teamwork.

Captain Sinclair had raced to reclaim his dart gun after Pintar dropped it, but another winged demon got there before him. 'Still here?' it taunted in a voice that was all too familiar and aimed the dart gun at the captain.

An axe-blade severed the creature's head from its shoulders. Its body fell to the ground, revealing Ashlee behind the strike. She reclaimed the captain's gun and tossed it to him with a grin. 'Pintar is jumping from drone to drone,' she informed him. 'We'll have to destroy every reptile in the hall to be rid of him.'

Taylor, Zalman and Levi were unable to hold the stone entranceway intact and Dracon foot soldiers began slipping through. It was only a matter of moments before we would be overrun by our enemy; all our superhuman strength and psychic ability could not hold the swarm of creatures back. Our greatest fear was that one of them would reach Tamar and grant Pintar his chance to prevent her transformation.

Tamar, who had been quietly chanting her activations, suddenly raised her voice. The sound was so stirring that it brought tears to my eyes and to the eyes of my allies — and to my surprise I saw there were more of those in the room than I could have imagined. The angelic song sent half the Dracon present into a fitful frenzy, particularly the winged beasts. However, many of the foot soldiers assumed semi-Anu forms at the sound and turned to attack their former brothers. It seemed Taejax had left a powerful legacy. Pintar may have discovered and destroyed our double agent, but it seemed there were plenty more to step into his place. If these creatures could see their way to bettering themselves for the greater good, then perhaps this planet stood a fighting chance of survival after all.

In that moment of commotion, one of the winged Dracon slipped through our defences and landed next to Tamar. It activated the ORME spike on its wrist, pushed Tamar's head forward and placed the spike at her neck. 'My only regret is that Mathu is not here to see this,' the creature yelled.

I slit the throat of the reptilian detaining me and raced towards my daughter, only to be knocked to the ground by one of the winged beasts and then engaged in battle with several foot soldiers, who intended to rip me apart with the etheric blades that extended from their knuckles.

Tamar sang louder, which aggravated the beasts all the more, including the creature Pintar inhabited; it seemed the frequency was too high, too pure, for them to tolerate. Then I realised that something more than Tamar's song was delaying Pintar's strike against my daughter; he seemed to be embroiled in a mental debate with himself.

'Did you really think you could be rid of your light?' said a voice, and I recognised it as Mathu's. It seemed Pintar had not completely shaken his good side as he'd boasted. 'I accept you, Pintar, as the part of myself that needs to be loved, embraced and understood,' Mathu continued.

'No!' Pintar cried out in panic, and dug the claws of the creature he was inhabiting into its own flesh, attempting to gouge out the positive spirit that shared this body with him. In doing so, he was ripping the beast apart, mortally wounding it.

As Tamar's chant became even more loving, the Dracon began to flee on foot and wing, the developing Anu recruits hot on their heels. Mathu kept Pintar pinned inside the one remaining bloodied creature.

'I revoke my wish to be rid of you,' he said, countering the creature's violent attack on itself by hugging his arms around his body. 'It is only through my pain, my bad experiences and mistakes, that I can truly learn how to care for another.' The creature raised his eyes to look upon my daughter. 'Before us stands my queen in all her glory; she is my strength, my hope, my rapture.'

'Stop!' But Pintar's appeal for mercy was weak; he tried to wriggle free of Mathu's embrace but was fading rapidly.

Tamar finally spoke. 'I know you have been through great trial and torment, but no matter how heinous your crimes, it is never too late to repent.'

Mathu was reduced to tears. 'I forgive myself. I have learned better and have no need to fear my past self any longer.' The green blood of the winged Dracon ran red, and this time there was no protest from Pintar.

'I love you, Mathu.' Tamar ran to embrace the dying creature as it collapsed to its knees. 'And I miss you.'

'I failed you so many times ...' Mathu could barely breathe due to remorse and his injuries. 'I hurt you so badly ...' He gasped as he relived Pintar's memory of raping Charlotte.

'But you loved me deeply too,' Tamar emphasised, before the creature breathed its last.

She did not wish to call her prince back to the battered beastly form he'd just relinquished and so she lowered the corpse to the floor. 'That is the last we shall see of Pintar,' she said. 'Now we only have the Nefilim to contend with.'

'And what of Mathu?' Captain Sinclair queried. For without Mathu's physical presence, how would we continue with the opening of Amenti?

'Our priority is to activate the rest of the Signet stations,' Tamar decreed. She looked at the captain. 'Mathu will find us before the matrix is operational.'

'I trust you are right,' Sinclair said and bowed his head respectfully.

Susan looked about at the oozing green remains of the battle. 'What will become of the Dracon with no one to lead them?'

'Some will no doubt seek service with the Nefilim,' Lilith suggested.

Levi was more positive. 'Those who have awoken their spiritual side will join our cause.'

'And the remainder will probably go back to hunting in packs in third-world countries,' Taylor offered, being more of a realist. 'Where no one will miss their victims.'

My daughter looked to the greenish splinters of melting matter that had once been Taejax. 'This one is bound for Sirius B, where he will join the ranks of his Anu ancestors and eventually evolve up to the next harmonic universe.'

I approached my daughter, so wanting to hold her, and yet I felt awkward. She turned and embraced me. 'Mum, you were *totally* sick today, and so was Dad!'

'Well, thank you, sweetheart.' It seemed the integration was complete. I breathed in her scent and kissed her cheek; I could no longer reach her forehead, she was too tall. Tamar even towered over her father now.

'I am so proud of you, princess.' Albray joined our hug.

'The only way to best a demon is with love,' Tamar said, letting Albray know that he had been her inspiration. He was astounded by her comprehension skills and restraint.

'I fear had I been closer to Pintar, I would not have been so quick to adhere to my own advice,' he confessed. 'It's a good thing you took charge.'

Tamar had not changed so much; she still seemed pleased to receive her parents' attention and praise.

'Are you all right?' I pulled back to look her over. She was more vibrant than I had ever seen her.

'I'm fine,' she assured me. 'Kali and I are one now, and we have the staff to resurrect the Signet Grid and bring down the Nefilim and their frequency fence!'

The rest of the team cheered. I had never seen Tamar so euphoric, and indeed I shared her sense of excitement regarding the mission ahead.

'What a totally awesome ending for your second book,' she said, and squeezed my shoulders, thrilled for me.

It was at that.

I AM Tamar.
I AM human.
I AM love, fear and compassion.
I AM hope.
I AM dreams.
I AM a sculptor of reality.
I AM Kali.
I AM Anunnaki.
I AM a planetary leader
and the conscience of my people.
I remember my mission here, and all I sacrificed to be here.

Mathu, my dearest companion, was the ultimate price I paid to have my Hall of Amorea built. In order to meet with the Amenti Council, I first had to address the Elohim's Interdimensional Association of Free Worlds. To atone for the failures of our kin on Earth and on Tara, my Prince and I were ordered to relinquish our greatest treasure: our constant association. In all of the time that my Prince and I would spend re-evolving on the Earth planes, we would only be permitted to incarnate in a physical form, at the same time, twice. In our first Anunnaki incarnation, we would inspire each other to the human cause. In our final human incarnation we would form the key to open Amenti's halls for all humanity. This was how the balance between the human and Anunnaki races would be restored: the race responsible for humanity's de-evolution would also be responsible for humanity's ascension — our selfless sacrifice would atone for our kindred's all-consuming selfishness.

The Staff of Amenti know nothing of my agreement with the Elohim Council, and I believe they would have despised the Anunnaki involvement in the Amenti scheme if the Ceres were able to fathom such an emotion.

Before our descent into the Earth scheme, we Anunnaki did not love as humans know love, we did not desire the emotion of another — we were attracted to a like-minded intellect. Mathu was my perfect intellectual match: he challenged and inspired me, amused and advised me. Now that I remember all he truly was to me, I crave his company tenfold and I grieve the eternity we have spent alone on Earth. My sorrow is human, but my determination to find my Prince is divine.

I know now what love is — the love of family, friendship and the sacred human feelings reserved for the object of your desire. My Prince is out there somewhere, in human form, and quite likely unaware of his destiny, just as I was.

I shall find my sleeping Prince and wake him with my kiss. And he shall remember all he has forgotten.

Come, demons, deceivers of cosmic law, bear witness to our love and see in it your redemption and demise.

For I AM your judge and liberator.
I AM your Queen and saviour.
I AM the cosmic karma
of your unrealised nightmares.

470

Demons, heed my promise,
your world domination is at an end.
Your souls are due to me
and I AM coming
to collect . . .
I AM.

GLOSSARY

Ankh — an object or image resembling a cross but with a loop instead of the top arm; used in Ancient Egypt as a symbol of life.

Blue Flame of Amenti — (keylonic dictionary) constitutes Earth's portion of Tara's morphogenetic field stored in the Sphere of Amenti. Visually, this standing wave pattern looks like an electric blue flame with a pale shade of green, about 10 centimetres in height. The souls on Earth can ascend out of this universe through the fifth dimension — blue flame — and continue their evolution through Tara.

Cathars — a religious order that was declared heretical by the Roman Catholic Church, which began the Albigensian Crusade to wipe the Cathars out. The name Cathari means 'pure' in Greek, and it was rumoured that the Cathars were hiding many of the secret treasures pertaining to the Grail legend.

Density — (esoteric) the eighth sphere — the lowest rate of vibration of atoms. Inhabited by souls too new in the evolutionary scale to understand physical life whilst in a physical body; they desire to take an unrighteous path and create their own hell plane to inhabit.

Dragon Queens — the daughers of Lilith, who descended via the line of Cain. The spiritual daughters of Enki — the Lord Sama-el — who carry the Gene of Isis and the mitochondrial DNA of the Grail bloodline.

Etheric Double — (esoteric) an invisible electromagnetic field that interpenetrates everything in the universe, from the atom to the great central sun. This field absorbs emanations from everything, forming a pattern for its future existence.

Etheric World — (esoteric) the overall picture of invisible space. The atmosphere that contains all seven levels of energies (seven planes) with their functions and life forms. Also known as the Otherworld.

Fire-Stone — (Grail lore) the organic equivalent of ORME, given to select kings prior to general human use of ORME; essentially, the menstrual blood of the goddesses of the Anunnaki.

Grail (Messianic) bloodline — (Grail lore) in medieval times, this was the line of Messianic descent that was defined by the French word Sangreal, meaning 'royal blood'. This was the bloodline of Judah — the kingly line of David, which progressed through Jesus and his heirs.

Halls of Amenti — (keylonic dictionary) the dimensional passageways one must pass through in order to ascend out of Earth's time matrix, through the blue flame held within the Sphere of Amenti, and home to Tara.

Light-body — (esoteric) an invisible, electromagnetic energy field completely surrounding an entity, which acts as a blueprint for that entity, adjusting the vibrational frequency of the atomic structure in accord to that entity's level of awareness. Also known as Aura.

Light centres — (esoteric) an invisible, interdimensional system comprising seven concentrated centres of energy located in the light-body between the base of the spine and the tip of the head. Also known as the Chakra system. These concentrated energy centres are called the root, spleen, solar plexus, heart, throat, third eye and crown chakras, and each is perceived clairvoyantly as a colourful wheel or flower. Light centres convert cosmic energy into body energy and vice versa.

Mitochondrial DNA (mtDNA) — DNA that is not located in the nucleus of the cell but in the mitochondria. mtDNA is typically passed on only from the mother during sexual reproduction, and there is little change in mtDNA from generation to generation, making it a powerful tool for tracking family lineage.

Morphogenetic field — (keylonic dictionary) all matter and forms of consciousness, including planetary bodies and human bodies, are manifested through a morphogenetic (form-holding) imprint, which is composed of specific patterns of frequency. The morphogenetic imprint holds the instructions and design for form-building. The Earth's morphogenetic imprint is held within the blue flame of Amenti. Forms manifest and evolve as patterns of frequency are drawn from a unified field of energey within which the morphogenetic field is placed. This drawing-in to the morphogenetic field of frequency patterns progressively expands and creates an evolution of form through the fifteen-dimensional universe.

Nature elemental — (esoteric/fairy lore) etheric world beings akin to the four elements of nature: Earth, Air, Fire and Water. Ranging from a very high to a low level of intelligence, they keep themselves occupied with the development of the natural world and are, understandably, wary of human beings. Also known as Nature spirits.

ORME — (alchemy) also known as Ormus, the Philosopher's Stone, the Elixir of Life, the White Powder of Gold, Ma-na or Manna. Is also an acronym for 'Orbitally Rearranged Monatomic Elements' — see David Hudson's research (internet). In Grail lore, ORME is the Highward Fire-Stone, which is also related to Star-Fire, or the Fire-Stone — see Laurence Gardner's books (Bibliography, p. 477).

PGMs — Platinum Group Metals. These eight metals are: ruthenium, rhodium, palladium, silver (light platinum group); osmium, iridium, platinum, gold (heavy platinum group). In a monatomic high-spin state, these precious metals can lose their chemical reactivity and metallic nature, resulting in a state of superconductivity — a resonant condition complete with Meissner magnetic fields, Cooper pairs, and electrons that have literally changed into light (photons). These precious metals have the unique ability to remain stable in an ORME form, resulting in levitation (weight losses), fundamental biological and human physiological effects, and beyond to applications in Zero-Point Energy exploration.

Priory of Sion — (Grail lore) an order said to have had its earliest roots in Hermetic and Gnostic thought. In 1070, a group of Crusading knights formed the basis for the Order de Sion, which was formalised in 1099 by Godefroi de Bouillon. For a century, the Knights Templar and Sion were unified under one leadership, though they publicly separated at the 'cutting of the elm' at Gisors in 1188. The Templar order was eventually destroyed by King Phillipe Le Bel of France in 1307. The Priory of Sion is also linked to numerous other underground schools of thought, such as Rosicrucians, Freemasonry, Arthurian and Grail legends, and Catharism.

Sangreal — (Grail lore) the Holy Grail. In English translation, the definition Sangreal became 'San Graal', then 'Saint Grail'. The word 'saint' related to 'holy', and so developed the now-familiar term, 'Holy Grail'. See Laurence Gardner's books (Bibliography, p. 477).

Sangreal Knighthood — (Grail lore) the Sovereign Order of the Sangreal, or the Knights of the Holy Grail, was a dynastic Order of Scotland's Royal House of Stuart.

Seven Bodies of Man — (esoteric) the Physical body, Astral body, Mental body, Causal body, the Spirit, Monadic essence and God consciousness.

Seven (higher) Planes of Existence — (esoteric) Physical, Astral, Mental, Causal, Spiritual, Monadic and God consciousness.

Signet Grid — (keylonic dictionary) the organic interdimensional core energy systems of a planet, along with the inherent portals, vortexes, ley lines and stargates by which a planet is connected to many other interstellar, interdimensional, space–time systems.

Sphere of Amenti — (keylonic dictionary) morphogenetic field of the human race, created to give the souls fragmented from Tara and lost in the Earth's dimensional fields the pattern of the twelve-strand DNA imprint necessary to re-evolve into their original Turaneusiam form. The Sphere of Amenti serves as a host matrix (surrogate morphogenetic field) through which the lost souls of Tara can evolve and return home.

Star-Fire — Ancient name for ORME.

Tara — (keylonic dictionary) planet counterpart of Earth located in the harmonic universe above our own.

Time codes — (keylonic dictionary) also known as 'Veca codes', these are the mathematical programs of manifestation that clear all unnatural seals from the bodies of humans.

Ventilatores — (knife throwers) Priests and Priestesses of Ancient Egypt (1994–1781 B.C.) who juggled knives to predict the future and draw aside danger — juggling was prominent in religious and mythological rituals. Contrary to popular belief, women were the first to be described as jugglers.

BIBLIOGRAPHY

Baigent, Michael; Leigh, Richard & Lincoln, Henry, *The Holy Blood and the Holy Grail*, Arrow Books, UK, 1996.

Boylan, Patrick, *Thoth or the Hermes of Egypt*, Kessinger Publishing, USA, 1922.

Deane, Ashayana, *Voyagers — the Secrets of Amenti*, Wildflower Press, USA, 2002.

Doreal (trans. and interpretation), *The Emerald Tablets of Thoth-the-Atlantean*, Source Books Inc., Nashville, 2002.

Gardner, Laurence, *Lost Secrets of the Sacred Ark*, HarperCollins, London, 2003.

—— *Bloodline of the Holy Grail*, MultimediaQuest International, UK, 2001.

—— *Realm of the Ring Lords*, MultimediaQuest International, UK, 2000.

—— *Genesis of the Grail Kings*, Bantam Press, UK, 1999.

Pool, Daniel, *What Jane Austen Ate and Charles Dickens Knew*, Simon & Schuster, New York, 1993.

Powell, Arthur E., *The Solar System*, Theosophical Publishing House, London, 1985.

Stephens, John Lloyd, *Incidents of Travel in Egypt, Arabia, Peatrea and the Holy Land*, Dover Publications, New York, 1970.